Can't Buy Me Love

Can't Buy Me Love

CHRIS KENRY

KENSINGTON BOOKS
http://www.kensingtonbooks.com

KENSINGTON BOOKS are published by

Kensington Publishing Corp.
850 Third Avenue
New York, NY 10022

All Kensington titles, imprints and distributed lines are available at special quantity discounts for bulk purchases for sales promotion, premiums, fund raising, educational or institutional use.

Special book excerpts or customized printings can also be created to fit specific needs. For details, write or phone the office of the Kensington Special Sales Manager: Kensington Publishing Corp., 850 Third Avenue, New York, NY 10022, Attn. Special Sales Department. Phone: 1-800-221-2647.

Library of Congress Card Catalogue Number: 00-108709
ISBN 1-57566-845-9

First Printing: May, 2001
10 9 8 7 6 5 4 3 2 1

Printed in the United States of America

For my two wives, Jim and Jeff

ACKNOWLEDGMENTS

Thanks to Pete Lindstrom, Jim Holik, and the Duchess, for helpful readings; to Quin Wright and Tracy Weil, for technical assistance; to Kevin Dougherty, for having such a perverse library; to my family and to Bill Weller, for being there; to David Maddy (and the group of bored US West trainees), for the penis paintings, and for more filthy epigrams than I could ever have possibly imagined.

Thanks especially to Alison Picard and to John Scognamiglio, with whom it has been a pleasure to work these past few months.

"Immaturity" is one more word that requires definition. To men it means the inability to stand on one's own two feet. A woman flings it at anyone who doesn't want to marry her. Here I find myself for once inclined toward the masculine view. I feel that, though no one must ever deny his dependence on others, development of character consists solely in moving toward self-sufficiency.

—Quentin Crisp, *The Naked Civil Servant*

Part One

The End of
La Vie En Rose

TRAIN WRECK

Even now, almost five years later, I still wonder what Paul was thinking. I guess only God knows, and He is being decidedly silent on the subject. Paul was my lover. I say *was* because he no longer is. He stepped off the curb one bright April afternoon and was struck, dragged sixty-eight feet, and killed by the light-rail train, and thus, to establish a metaphor, derailed my life from the effortless track on which I had been traveling.

The controversial light-rail system had been in place for nearly a year when it happened, and people were only just beginning to get used to it. In its first few months of operation, several cars and a few pedestrians had been struck, so the city's transportation authority mounted a vigorous ad campaign warning people to pay attention to the trains and not, as many people did, try to race them. It was an annoyingly thorough campaign, with billboards and bench ads everywhere, and one that Paul was surely aware of, so ignorance can't have been the reason. Nor can it be entirely explained by the fact that he was an Englishman, and as such was used to looking to the right instead of to the left, and had possibly looked the wrong way before he started crossing. The transportation people, for obvious litigious reasons, liked this theory, as did the newspapers, since it gave the story an interesting twist, but Paul had been living here for over twelve years by then, in which time he had crossed many a street safely, so that probably wasn't very likely either.

I myself theorized that it happened because he was an architect. In fact, that was what had first attracted us to each other. He was an architect and I was an art history major. We shared a love of architecture and were both distressed by the impending destruction of a building designed by I. M. Pei, a swooping parabaloid structure that had been part

of a failed department store and was soon to be torn down. This in-
censed Paul, who loved both Pei's work and the city of Denver (in which
he, Paul, had made his fortune), so he quickly organized a grassroots
committee to have the parabaloid designated a historic landmark, and
thus thwart the destructive plans of the developer. But, alas, in vain, as
the politicians in our fair state of Colorado, most of whom still think the
sun circles the earth, could not see something built in the late 1950s as
having any historical significance whatsoever. Now, if it had been a
sports stadium he was trying to preserve . . . But I digress. The reason I
think the I. M. Pei parabaloid was responsible for his errant step into
mortality is this: presumably he was walking back to his office from
lunch that afternoon and had just strolled past the building a few blocks
before he reached the tracks. Having seen it, he was probably preoccupied with its imminent destruction, and was surely thinking of ways to
prevent it when he should have been looking where he was going.

It was a neat and tidy explanation, and one I eagerly fed to friends
and family for months afterward. It seemed plausible and palatable
enough, but unfortunately that doesn't make it true. I could point to
several different possibilities for Paul's lapse of attention, but as wise
Gandhi once told his whining grandson, "Every time you point the finger of blame somewhere else there are three fingers pointing back at
you."

So with that in mind I have to admit that I suspected that Paul's mind
was preoccupied with nothing other than yours truly. The three fingers
were undeniably pointing to me as the probable cause of his demise, and
I knew it.

If my suspicions were in fact correct, and I was clouding his thoughts,
I hoped at least that he was thinking of me fondly and remembering all
the happy times we spent together—the many trips we'd taken, the sex-
filled afternoons, the look and feel of my chiseled body, the beautiful
garden I'd painstakingly landscaped, the Christmas dinners and the
birthday parties I'd planned and executed. In short, how deliriously
happy I made him.

But who was I kidding. Earlier, on the very same day he was killed,
we had what my parents like to euphemistically call "a discussion."
And, in truth, it was a very parental discussion: he was the parent; I was
the child. In it he told me, in no uncertain terms, that although he loved
me and had never minded supporting me "in quite high style" while I
decided what I was going to do with my life, I was now twenty-five, had

been out of college and jobless for nearly three years, and really needed to do something other than work out, tan, read magazines, and plan entertaining and expensive dinner parties. And of course he was right. Looking back, I see that my lifestyle then was hedonistic in the worst sense, but I honestly didn't see it that way, and thought he was being unnecessarily petty. Didn't he see that I worked very hard? That in my own way I was highly disciplined? I worked out five times a week, sometimes twice a day, I spent months landscaping the side yard and redecorating the house, and when I wasn't doing that I was busy improving my mind and making myself a more informed member of society by reading *Time* and *Architectural Digest* and *The Economist* (in addition to *People, Us, Vanity Fair, Details, Men's Health, W., Spin,* and *The National Enquirer*).

And yet somewhere in the deepest darkest recesses of my mind I knew he was right. I had gotten lazy, and all of the "work" I was doing was just an excuse, although an excuse for what I had no idea at the time.

Because he loved me, Paul had allowed me to lead a very cushy existence, and I suppose it was inevitable that the spoiled child had begun to take for granted the one doing the spoiling. All the more so because I knew that despite our argument he would never take action on his frustration. He would never make me get a job, would never cut off my pipeline supply of money. Paul was whipped, and all I had to do to smother his misgivings was have raucous sex with him and afterward tell him how much I loved him, would always love him, and on and on and on. . . . So when he blew up at me that morning as I headed out to my lawn chair by the pool with the new issue of *Entertainment Weekly* and a bottle of Pellegrino, I barely lifted the earphone of my Walkman to listen, but made a mental note that I'd have to put on quite a show in the sack later that night. He yelled and pleaded with me there in the kitchen that morning, and I'm sure that my eyes, safely hidden behind my sunglasses, were rolling in their sockets at the silliness, the pettiness of it all.

By now you are probably wondering who I am. Call me manipulative, or selfish, or lazy, or even Ishmael, if you like, but my real name is Jack. Jack Thompson. My mother is a devout Democrat and a big fan of the Kennedys, so I was named after President Kennedy, which is fine by me, because I was actually born under Nixon's reign, and I'd hate to be called Richard, although Dick might have been a more appropriate name, considering. My upbringing was what you could call upper middle class, and I have spent my whole life right here in Denver, Colorado. Oh, I went away to college and have traveled, but for some reason I've always returned. I used to wonder why I came back. Denver is not an especially cosmopolitan city, and I've often thought myself more suited to New York or Boston or San Francisco, but for me Denver always seemed safe, and I suppose that is why I never left for long. I don't mean safe in terms of the crime rate or the climate. There are plenty of drive-by shootings and paralyzing blizzards to make one feel insecure, but Denver felt safe because I knew it was a place where I would always be taken care of. Trouble might arise but someone, usually my parents or Paul, was sure to squash it back down for me.

Even right after Paul's death, when I really should have been afraid, I still felt fairly safe. I went to the morgue to identify him, which was a grisly task as half of his face had been scraped off, and fretted only about what to do with the body. No worries about the loneliness ahead of me or the whereabouts of a last will and testament. No, just a small worry about what should be done with the corpse. My best friend Andre, who is not squeamish about death, having nursed one dying lover himself, went with me.

"Girl," he said as we left the morgue (on Planet Andre, everyone is a "girl"), "I suggest cremation, but if that's not an option then definitely a closed casket."

But as it happened, even that decision was not one that I had to make. In fact, shortly after his death, every decision regarding Paul and his estate was made for me, even when I decided that I did want to have a say in the matter.

Enter Wendy.

Paul's only living relative was an elder sister, Wendy, who was named sole executor of her brother's estate. Wendy and Paul were not close. In fact, in the three years I'd been with Paul there had never been, to my knowledge, a phone call or letter between them. She had never approved of her brother's "lifestyle choice," and had, for all intents and purposes, lobotomized him from her memory. However, upon her hearing of his death and discovering that he had become a fairly wealthy architect, her memory suddenly returned, although it certainly did not soften, and, like some atomically mutated monster, she emerged from her lair, wreaked havoc, and then retreated again to where she'd come from.

She arrived at DIA less than two days after being notified of the accident, took a suite at the Brown Palace, and set to work finding a lawyer. When she hired one, she made it his first priority to have me forcibly removed from the house by some very large men with very legal eviction papers, who started changing the locks before I'd even left.

I met her only once, with her lawyer, when I was allowed back into the house late one afternoon to collect some of my belongings, but it was a meeting that had lasting effects on the rest of my life. She was what Andre would call an "old Irish potato," meaning she was best described by adjectives like "tweedy" and "ruddy." She smoked endlessly and had, I noticed, developed deep wrinkles around her mouth from the decades of repeatedly forming it into an O around her cigarettes. As the day went on, her crimson lipstick would work its way into these rivulets, making her mouth look all bloody, as though she'd just finished devouring her young. I remember thinking as I watched her that if Paul had aged as gracelessly as she, maybe it was better that he had died relatively young.

Knowing little about Wendy, and naively figuring I'd give her the benefit of the doubt despite the fact that she'd had me evicted, I tried to reason with her as we—she, the lawyer, and I—sat in the living room of the house Paul and I had shared, cardboard boxes littering the floor. They were seated on the bank-green Chesterfield sofa that I'd always loved, and I sat opposite them on one of the cardboard boxes, the rest of the furniture having been packed away or sold.

I have a tendency to gush when I am nervous, filling up awkward silences with a flood of words, and so it was then as she and the lawyer sat stonily observing me, saying nothing. I told her that I completely understood her having me removed from the premises when she did not know me from Adam, seeing as she and Paul had been out of touch for so long. I told her how much I'd loved Paul, and how an hour didn't pass that I didn't think of him. I told her all about the memorial service and the flowers I'd ordered and the poetry I'd recited. I then went on to say that I hoped she and I could share our grief, maybe console each other, give each other a shoulder to cry on, and I'm afraid I even shed a few tears.

Christ, why didn't somebody stop me? If Andre had been there he certainly would have. He'd have yanked me out into the hallway and hissed, "Girl, why don't you shut the fuck up! That bitch doesn't care!

She thinks you two were Sodom and Gomorrah living here. She doesn't want to share any of your damn grief!"

And it was true; she had no interest in hearing any of the lurid details of her brother's seedy life, let alone commiserating his loss with me. In fact, my attempts at commiseration probably had the reverse effect and turned her against me more than she already was. But in the absence of levelheaded Andre, on I gushed. Finally it was Wendy herself who intervened.

"Mr. Thompson," she said, crushing her cigarette into a piece of venetian glass, which, in retrospect, I should probably have restrained myself from telling her was "never meant as an ashtray."

"It's nice to know that my brother was so, uh, loved in his lifetime . . ."

Here she paused and took one of my hands between her dry, scaly fingers, her voice annoyingly condescending. ". . . and I can tell you're upset. It's all been quite a shock. Nevertheless, we have to pick up the pieces and carry on, so I think we'd really better get down to the details, as I haven't much time left, and Mr. Branson"—she gestured with her pointy beak of a nose to the attorney—"is on a tight schedule as well."

I nodded, wiped my eyes with the tissue she'd pulled from her sleeve, and took a deep breath. She patted my hand, released it, and leaned back into the sofa.

"I don't know what financial arrangement you had with my brother, for, how shall we say . . . services rendered. . . ." She paused here, and I looked at her for a few moments honestly bewildered, like a foreigner being given complicated directions. A deer in the headlights. Blink. Blink.

"Well," I muttered, "nothing was ever really spelled out, but we were essentially married and managed things the way most married couples do."

She winced visibly when I said the word *married,* and took another cigarette from her maroon box of Dunhills, lighting it with a cheap plastic lighter she took from the pocket of her sweater. I went on. "Paul was carrying most of the financial load, until I, uh, got settled into a career."

"Yes, I see," she said, inhaling deeply. "And what line of work are you in now?"

I hesitated, but continued, flattered that she seemed to be taking an interest in me. "Well, I studied art history and classics in college, so ideally I'd like to do something in one of those veins. Paul really encouraged that. He was always trying to get me an internship at the Art

Museum, or a job in a gallery, but, well, I guess I just never found my niche, so to speak."

"And what do you do now?" she repeated, her voice tinged with impatience.

"Uh, now? Well, let's see, mostly I've been working as a sort of weight trainer at a gym and teaching some swimming lessons. It pays a little, but I usually take it out in trade." I smiled shyly. "For workout privileges and supplements," I added.

"Yes, I see," she said, arching an eyebrow and examining the end of her cigarette. "In trade."

After a long, agonizing pause in which she sized me up with her reptilian eyes, she nodded slightly to the lawyer, who then pulled a file from his briefcase, opened it, and took over the conversation.

"Mr. Thompson," he said, giving me a plastic smile, "whatever the nature of your relationship with the deceased and whatever financial arrangement you may have had with him in the past, he made no provision for you in his will, nor in his life insurance policy."

At this point he removed a copy of the will, dated 1988, from a manila folder and gave it to me. I had never really given much thought to wills or estates, and certainly never to something as abstract as life insurance! I naturally assumed it would be several years before we needed to consider anything so adult as a will. My family was well off and I had never really known want or need. Every possible form of calamity had been covered by my father or my father's policy, just like the umbrella in the commercial. If I needed a doctor, I went to one. If I wrecked the car, it went in to be fixed and I drove a rental. When I took a lacrosse stick in the mouth and lost a tooth, I went to the dentist and he made a new one.

With Paul, my life went on as usual; I just had a different provider. His insurance covered domestic partners, so we took advantage of it. I expected it. Took it for granted. When I moved in, he took over my father's role (as icky as that sounds), and I assumed that if there was something important like a will or life insurance Paul would certainly have seen to it, just as he had seen to my car and medical insurance. But, as I stared down at the paper before me, dated April 11, 1988, long before we had even met, I saw that he had not. His death was sudden and unexpected and had not been prepared for. Certainly it should at least have been discussed, seeing as we were both gay men living in the nineties, and had, between us, attended more funerals than we cared to count.

But we had not discussed it, and the potential consequences of that failure to communicate presented themselves to me then. The sun peeked over the horizon in my infantile brain and I began to comprehend the situation. I finished looking over the will, which was all legalese, and looked up. They were both eyeing me with vaguely bored expressions.

"What does this mean?" I asked, my hands suddenly very cold. The lawyer shifted his weight on the sofa and coughed unnecessarily into his hand.

"Essentially what this means," he said, "is that there was no legal tie between you and the deceased. And my client"—he gestured and smiled at Wendy—"being the next of kin, is entitled to the entire estate."

He paused and the sun inched a little higher.

"Again, what does this mean?" I asked more urgently, thinking of all my things: the artwork, the venetian glass, the bank-green Chesterfield on which they sat, the pewter gardening tools, the small German kitchen appliances, the copper cookware, the coffee-table books, the little Phillipe Stark lamps, and everything else that I now saw sprouting wings and flying away. It was like an inverse episode of *The Price is Right:* the show was going backward and all the gifts from the Showcase Showdown were going back behind the curtains. I spun the wheel backward, losing my winnings, and eventually was told by that booming voice of Johnny to go take my seat in the audience with the rest of the nobodies.

The lawyer gave his little cough again, pulling me out of my reverie.

"What this means, Mr. Thompson, is that in the eyes of the law you are entitled to nothing."

I gasped.

"However," he went on, "my client, sympathetic to your plight, has graciously selected a few things that you may have."

"And those are?" I asked hopefully.

He pointed to two boxes, one of which I was sitting on, and a suitcase, positioned conveniently close to the front door.

"We determined which personal effects belonged to you and which belonged to the deceased. Since you were essentially a lodger here, you were given all of the clothing that was determined to be your size and one bike and one pair of Rollerblades, as there were two sets of each in the garage. I think you'll find that my client has been more than fair."

The sun was searing me now. I was getting screwed and I really didn't want to listen to someone tell me that I was getting a good deal. I stood up but was so angry and shocked that it took a while for anything to come out of my mouth. I felt the helplessness of the wrongly accused, the shock of the innocent victim, the stupidity of the cuckold, and when the words finally did come, they were not witty.

"Rollerblades? I don't want fucking Rollerblades! I get *Rollerblades?*"

"And a bike," Wendy added cheerfully.

"Mr. Thompson, please!" the lawyer protested. "You're getting more than you're entit—"

"Please yourself!" I shouted. "These aren't just things; these are my things."

I tried to cry, thinking that might help my case, but the tears wouldn't come so I just stood there looking constipated. Again there was a long silence in which the lawyer and I exchanged nasty glances, our jaws clenched, while Wendy sat, calmly sucking on her cigarette. She exhaled noisily, as if thoroughly bored and annoyed, and then rose from the sofa and walked to the stairs. When she was halfway up she turned, as if she'd just remembered something.

"Oh, Mr. Thompson," she said. "There is one more thing you'll be getting."

"And what's that?" I asked, my tone sarcastic, wondering what she could possibly concede. Again she formed her lips into a bloody O and said quite simply, "Out."

She then turned and skipped like a schoolgirl up the remaining stairs, flicking her ashes on the carpet as she went.

The lawyer escorted me out with my boxes and the Rollerblades, which I violently hurled into the bed of the truck I'd borrowed. I'd anticipated making several trips, but that was it—two boxes, a suitcase, a pair of Rollerblades, and a bike. Obviously she had not given me all of my clothes, since my socks alone would have filled the suitcase, but at that point it felt useless to argue, and I was feeling a little ashamed that I had shown myself to be more upset about losing the twelve-speed Waring blender than about losing Paul. I drove slowly down the driveway, past the rows of lilac bushes I'd planted last fall, now in full bloom. When I was far down the driveway, out of sight of the house, I reached out and ripped a large branch from one of the bushes. It was an unsatisfying gesture.

I drove around aimlessly for a while, not knowing where to go or what to do. I felt I'd come unexpectedly to the end of a book. I turned the page eagerly to see what would happen next but there was no more type, only blank sheets of paper. Paul was gone, and for the first time since his death I felt a tinge of worry as I realized that he would not be coming back. Until then, I'd sort of believed that he was just away on a business trip and would be back soon to sort out all the lunacy that had transpired in his absence. I had watched much too much daytime TV as a child and far too many episodes of *The X-Files* as an adult, so as I drove I indulged myself in the imagining of several different conspiracy theories:

I believed that he would somehow come back from the accident, and it would all have been a bad dream. It hadn't really been his body in the morgue, but that of another dressed like him. An impostor! The real Paul had been kidnapped and was being held in some underground hovel by strangely silent criminals who were not asking for ransom.

Or he really had been injured and, suffering from amnesia, was being nursed back to health in a mountain convent by kindly nuns who would patiently help him regain his memory and take back his life.

Or the whole accident had been staged as part of the Witness Protection Program and Paul would return with a new face and identity, like when an actor got fired or quit a soap opera and a new one was hired to take his place. I would accept this new Paul without question.

Whatever the scenario, I thought, he *would* return. He'd come and get the house and belongings back from his evil, withered sister in a big dramatic showdown worthy of a nighttime soap opera like *Dynasty* or *Falcon Crest,* and we'd live happily ever after.

Of course I knew that this was ridiculous and absurd. No one in a soap opera ever lives happily ever after, and I had, without a doubt, identified his all too real dead body in the morgue. But maybe my theories were not all that ridiculous. His whole death had been absurd, and when a death occurs suddenly, like Paul's, it is incomprehensible in its simplicity and the shock does take some time to wear off. As I drove around that day it was definitely wearing off. I felt sad, yes, but more than that I was disappointed. Like at the end of a good night at a dance bar when they suddenly turn up the lights and start herding everyone toward the exit.

ITALIAN NOSTALGIA

In my life I have found nostalgia to be a very dangerous thing. Unlike hindsight, which shows you your folly in a painful, morning-after clarity, nostalgia is a pretty store window into the past, smeared with Vaseline, all dreamy-looking. If hindsight is 20/20, then nostalgia is a look back through rose-colored glasses. Rose colored glasses that filter out all those pesky rays of truth, showing you happy times, usually much happier than they actually were, that are gone forever. Sure, you'll be happy again in the future; you may even be happy in the present, but nostalgia takes you by the hand, leads you into the past, and shows you a happiness you'll never quite have again—because you never really had it in the first place. To most people nostalgia is sweet. To me it is bitter and masochistic, but most of all, completely useless. Nevertheless, here's a hefty dose of it:

Paul and I met, as most gay men meet, at a bar. We didn't really meet there, but it was the first time we noticed each other. I was still in college, home for the summer, working for a landscaping company during the day and going out nearly every night with Andre. We had the bars on a tight schedule back then, according to which one was likely to be the most crowded on a given night. Mondays we went to the Compound, Tuesdays to Charlie's, Wednesdays and Saturdays to the Metro, etc. . . . On Sunday afternoons there was always a crowd at a bar called Soc's and, like faithful little lemmings, we were there every Sunday. Its unabbreviated name was Club Socrates, as in a place to corrupt the youth of Denver. Get it? If not, don't worry, neither did anyone else, which is why they shortened it to Soc's and made it into a sports bar. The bar itself was small but it had a huge patio and dance floor outside, so most of their business came during the summer. In fact, I don't know of anyone who went there in the winter, but everyone who was anyone in the gay community went there on Sunday afternoons in the summer.

On this particular Sunday in August, Andre and I were there, of course, drinking and dancing and being our fabulous selves, boldly eyeing guys we thought were good-looking. Paul was one of these guys. He was funny to look at because he was so short and was with a group of friends who were all very tall, and I remember that I kept losing sight of him when his friends would crowd around.

"Who's the midget?" I asked Andre. He spun around excitedly, clearly hoping to see an actual midget, and followed my gaze over to Paul.

"Oh, that one," he said, his voice revealing his disappointment. "Girl, that's Paul Oswald. English, I think. He's some big-deal architect, or as big a deal as an architect can be in this town. Big fish in a little pond. He did that new building for Channel Eight—that one with all the columns that looks like it was left over from the *Ben Hur* set."

"He's not bad-looking," I said, staring at him. Andre winced and gave an expression most people reserve for entering Porta Pottis on a hot day.

"That little limey?" he cried. "You don't want him! He's one of those weird fags who didn't come out of the closet until he was, like, thirty-five, and from the look of him, that was not yesterday."

I watched Paul as he gazed up at his tall friends like a child who'd wandered into his parents' cocktail party, and then, finally, he caught me looking. We held eye contact for a moment and smiled at each other, but then his view was blocked by a wall of bodies, and Andre, hearing the opening bars of a Madonna song, impatiently dragged me through the crowd and onto the dance floor.

That was it. We didn't see each other again that night, nor even that summer. It wasn't until late autumn that we actually met. I had returned to school in Boulder, and was taking a class on classical Roman architecture. It was an interesting class made boring by an uninspired professor who hated the subject he was teaching, so I strolled into the classroom one Wednesday afternoon expecting the monotonous worst, as usual, only to find Paul sitting at the front of the class waiting to give a guest lecture on the Pantheon. He looked familiar but I couldn't really place him until he took his place behind the podium and nearly disappeared behind it. Aside from being short, he was handsome. He had a beautiful mop of dirty blond hair that was always attractively unkempt, and a long, elegant nose. His chin was pronounced, and he wore round tortoiseshell-framed glasses. He looked classically beautiful in a studied, Ralph Lauren way. Or, if I am less nostalgic and charitable, in a false, pretentious way. He gave a wonderful lecture in his crisp, concise English accent, growing more and more animated with each slide he clicked onto the screen. He really was brilliant when talking about architecture, and it was clear from his enthusiasm that he had found a career he really loved. I think that was partly what I found so intriguing about him.

After the lecture, as I was waiting in line in the cafeteria of the student union, I noticed him sitting at one of the tables wearily listening to the drone of the usual architecture professor. I watched them shake hands as the professor pointed to his watch and got up, leaving Paul sitting alone. I quickly paid for my coffee and wound my way to his table before one of the other students had the chance to jump in.

"Was he boring you as much as he bores us?" I asked, gesturing at the departing professor.

"I suppose he is a bit dry," he said shyly.

"You're too kind," I said, and moved into the seat recently vacated by the professor. "He's the only one who could take something Italian and make it as exciting as oatmeal." He laughed and I flashed him a smile.

"I've, uh, seen you before, I think," I said.

"Oh?"

"Yes, last summer," I said, and hesitated, remembering his latent sexuality. "We never really met, but I think it was at a bar called Socrates."

He smiled. "Yes, of course," he said, snapping his fingers. "I remember. You're Andre's friend, and no, you're right, we never did meet. Let's rectify that." He extended his hand and I took it in mine.

And so it began. We talked for hours that day about the Pantheon and Rome, and before we parted he invited me to go to dinner the next night. The next night led to the next weekend, which we spent together, going through the Art Museum, and eating out, and having sex a ridiculous number of times a day. That weekend led to the other evenings together and then to the following weekend and then the following Monday and Tuesday night, and before long I was coming down to Denver or he came up to Boulder nearly every night. I spent so much time with him or traveling to him that I'm afraid I didn't do very well in school, but it was my last year, and my class load was light, so I didn't really worry. Neither did my parents, who were so enamored with Paul when they met him, and what they saw as his positive influence on me, that they overlooked my mediocre final grades. In fact, I'm afraid they liked him more than they liked me, but then that was probably because of his accent and his small stature. It sounds stupid, but the two combined were a very charismatic mix.

For graduation, Paul took me to Italy for three weeks, and the nostalgia I have about that trip is the most bittersweet and persists even to this day. We flew to Milan in the first week of June, and from the moment we touched the ground it was as if everything—the weather, the scenery, the architecture, the food, our accommodations, the little navy blue convertible we drove—had all conspired together to make the trip magic. Or maybe it was just that we were so in love. Or so I thought. Madly, blindly, wildly in love. The kind of love eighty percent of all pop lyrics are about. The kind of love movies and fiction teach us to expect. The kind of love that burns brightly for a few months, a year or two at most, and then fizzles out like some grand firework, leaving only memories.

In the mornings we'd have breakfast and then go quickly to see the architecture in whatever city we happened to be in. It's difficult to convey the significance of this, but it was something we had both studied and were both passionate about. Seeing together the structures and artwork that we loved and respected cemented another bond between us. Paul was far more knowledgeable than I, so I learned something everyplace we went. His specialty was Italian Gothic, but he was knowledgeable about any movement or time period and was as comfortable talking about painting and sculpture as he was about architecture. I remember, in Florence, walking through the Uffizi Gallery together looking at all the Botticellis and Raphaels and Titians, and being amazed by all Paul knew about them, about the techniques used, and the histories of their subject matter, little anecdotes about the artists. Each day was filled with revelation, and my respect for him was raised to nearly impossible heights. He, I think, was thrilled to have found in me a receptive companion, someone who would listen to all he said and ask relatively intelligent questions.

Every afternoon we spent making love in our hotel room, the sun casting slanted rays on our naked bodies through the shutters. We would rise just as it was setting. Then we'd shower and dress and go out and join the evening crowds of well-dressed people strolling the streets.

We'd stop and have a leisurely drink or two and a few cigarettes on some piazza or *gran via,* watching the people as they passed by, and then wander some more until we found a place to eat. And eat we did! Food and wine and desserts, the memory of which I still cherish (nostalgically, of course). We'd stuff ourselves and drink far too much, and then after dinner we'd walk some more, aimlessly, leaning into each other and slowly losing ourselves in the labyrinth of streets, becoming so lost that we'd have to hail a taxi to take us back to our hotel. Once there, we would make love again, or try to anyway, usually falling asleep in some degree of undress, clinging to each other like two spent swimmers. . . .

One day, toward the end of the trip, we were relaxing in the evening sun in a café on the Piazza del Campo in Siena, drinking our second or third Campari and soda, having just agreed that we'd found the ideal spot in all the world.

Siena is a medieval city that has wisely banished the automobile from most of its narrow streets. At its center is an expansive, orange-brick piazza, surrounded by tall brick buildings and a soaring clock tower. In July and August, this is the sight of a rather barbarous horse race, but it was quiet then; the flap of pigeons' wings as they ascended to the clock tower and the low murmur of the other patrons in the café the only disturbances of the tranquil sight.

I was talking lazily, commenting on the cathedral we'd visited that morning, and about a German couple I'd met, but I soon realized that Paul wasn't listening. He was looking very solemn and seemed nervous about something.

"You all right?" I asked. He nodded and smiled but it was clear that something was bothering him. He shifted his weight in his chair and then reached in the pocket of his jacket and removed a small, purple-velvet box, which he set down on the table and nudged toward me. I was surprised, because the one thing we had really not done the entire trip was shop, and I wondered when he'd sneaked away to purchase something. He smiled but said nothing. He put on his sunglasses and gazed absently at the clock tower.

I said nothing and quickly flipped open the box. Inside was a key, not an elaborate brass number, or a tiny diary key, but a plain old ordinary suburban house key.

"I don't get it," I said, and looked at him, confused.

He continued staring out at the plaza. Several times he started to say something but then hesitated. Finally he turned to me, clearly wanting to touch me, but the café was crowded, and he was always shy about such public displays.

"I . . . I don't want to scare you," he said, his voice soft and low. "So this can mean something or it can mean nothing, or you can use it whenever you'd like, but I don't want you to take it the wrong way. What I mean is, I don't want to scare you."

I looked down at the key, suddenly understanding its meaning, and I felt happy.

"It's a key to my house and I'd . . . What I mean to say is, if you'd like to, I'd like you to move in with me."

"And where will you live?" I asked, and grinned over at him.

"Well, right," he said, relaxing a bit. "I'll live in the garage out back, I guess. Look, can't we be . . . I'm serious about this. Nothing would make me happier than if you were to move in with me. I know you've just finished university and aren't quite sure what you're going to do, but I'd like to be a part of that, and I don't mind carrying you until you find something."

I smiled and pressed his hand in mine, the key between our palms.

"I will," I said, and gazed reverently into his green eyes. . . .

Okay, put on the brakes here. Pull the needle off the record. Push the pause button on the remote control, and wipe that Vaseline off the lens! Let's analyze this situation more closely in the clinical light of hindsight. Clearly, *clearly*, I can see that our troubles began there in tranquil Siena. The barbarous horse race may as well have commenced right then. The charm was wound up. The die was cast. The seeds of destruction were planted in all too fertile soil. It sounds like I'm being overdramatic, and maybe I am a bit, but the transfer of that key was what started the demise of my integrity and, consequently, the demise of any respect we had for each other. I was just out of college and truly had no idea of what I was going to do with my life. I had never been on my own as an independent entity, and was of such a nature, and at such an age, that I knew nothing other than relying on the support, financial and emotional, of others. Paul's offer to "carry" me was the equivalent of pouring a big glass of whiskey in front of an impressionable and inexperienced youth and saying, "Umm, yummy!"

He paid all of my bills and kept an elegant roof over my head, rent free. He spoiled me like a child and I reacted by behaving like one, accepting his largesse, and continuing to accept it, for years until I was little more than a swollen sponge. I took it initially thinking it would last only a short time until I started a career and made my own money, but, over time, it dulled me, made me lazy. I became dependent on him, and this gave rise to resentments on both sides.

Yet, if the truth is told, it was probably more my fault. Paul gave me tremendous opportunities, but I lacked the character to recognize them as such. The problem was, I didn't need assistance, or generosity, or opportunity handed to me on a silver platter. I needed to struggle. I was fresh from college but I needed to learn. I needed to take the knocks the real world offered and fight to forge myself into an independent being. The arrangement we agreed to that evening in Siena numbed that fighting spirit, lulled it into a drowsy complacency, from which it did not stir for the next three years.

BURL

When I had calmed down, about an hour after leaving Wendy and the lawyer, a thought occurred to me, and I drove as quickly as I could to a 7-Eleven. Inside, I put my card in the ATM, entered the access code for the joint checking account Paul and I had opened two years ago, and did a balance inquiry. It spit out a receipt, like a mocking tongue, that showed a balance of $2.90, indicating that Wendy, the crafty bitch, had gotten to it before me and had withdrawn all but the minimum needed to keep the account open. She couldn't close it out completely without my consent.

Feeling discouraged, I stepped outside and lit a cigarette. I usually don't smoke, but every now and then, especially in moments of high drama like the one I envisioned myself in then, it seems the only thing to do. I sat down on the curb in the parking lot and pouted. Again I tried to cry, but I couldn't, as the situation was more pathetic than tragic despite my dramatic attempts to perceive it otherwise. I sniffled self-pityingly for a while, thinking, *Oh, God, what am I going to do? How could this happen to me? Where am I going to go?* But I came to no great conclusions.

Since my eviction I had been staying at my parents' house, but I clearly couldn't stay there forever. *What was I thinking?* I wondered to myself. *That I'd be in the will? That Wendy would be kind and give me some money and a place to live?* I should have seen that coming way back when the lawyers came and changed the locks. I guess I just assumed that I'd be taken care of as I always had. Like a tightrope walker in the circus I had the air of confidence that comes with the knowledge that there is a net below. Someone had always been my net, there to catch me, or protect me, or make sure I was protected. I had no reason to think differently. Now everything was changing fast, and I was beginning to suspect that the net beneath me was probably moth-eaten or maybe was not there at all.

I chain-smoked three cigarettes, gazing blankly at the sun as it disappeared behind the mountains. I glanced across the parking lot at the pay phone and an idea struck me. I got up, walked over to it, and dialed directory assistance. When I got the number I'd requested, I hung up and waited a few minutes, mentally rehearsing what I would say. Finally I dialed. It rang several times before being picked up. The sound of loud disco music playing in the background assured me I'd dialed correctly.

"Hello, Burl?" I yelled.

"Hello? Whosere?" he slurred. Evidently the phone had woken him up.

"Burl, it's Jack."

"Whosat? Jus' a minute." From the sound of the phone bouncing on the floor I gathered he'd either passed out or gone to turn the music down. I'd begun to give up hope when the music stopped and I heard his feet shuffling back. He cleared his throat and said, in his best professional voice, "Burl Crawford here."

"Hey, Burl, it's Jack." There was silence for a moment, followed by a poorly feigned recognition.

"Oh, yeah! . . . Jack! How ya doin'? You musta left without sayin' good-bye this mornin', son. Hell, you 'bout wore me out last night, I tell you!"

"Burl, this is Jack Thompson. I was Paul Oswald's boyfriend. . . ."

I envisioned his thoughts then as a train chugging along through the alcoholic fog. Finally it reached the station.

"Oh, now a'course it's you!" he boomed. "I have to admit, though, I had you pegged as my boy from last night, and I can't tell you how glad I am you're not him! I'm gettin' old, Jack!" he whined. "I can't keep up the pace with you kids anymore." Then, lowering his tone to a whisper, he added, "But damn if I sure don't like to try!"

"Burl."

"This one last night, ooowee!"

"Burl."

"The cutest little behind, why I coulda—"

"Burl!" I shouted, not wanting to hear the particulars of his trick's ass. "I think I'm in trouble!"

"Okay, okay."

"I'm sorry," I said, and took a deep breath. "I'm . . . It's just that . . . I guess I'm a little bit scared."

"Well, hell, if you think you're in trouble you've probably called the right person, because I'm always in trouble." He laughed heartily at his own joke.

"I need to talk to you tonight if I could," I said.

"Yeah, sure, a'course. But what do you mean you *think* you're in trouble? You're not sure?" he asked, slipping into his gentle lawyer voice.

"No. Listen, we'll talk about it when I get there. I can be there in about fifteen minutes; is that okay?"

"I'll leave the light on for ya."

On the drive across town I thought maybe I'd made a mistake turning to Burl. He was the type of fag who saw any verbal exchange with a male under the age of thirty as a veiled invitation to bed. This, combined with his affinity for the bottle, made him invariably annoying.

Burl Crawford had once been a highly successful prosecuting attorney in his native Oklahoma, but his penchant for young boys had gotten the best of him, and he had been jailed briefly and disbarred when an amateur video of his came to light showing him in several compromising positions with two young men just under the age of eighteen. Needless to say, he lost his job but avoided a heavy sentence because neither of the two would press charges. He was a pervert, yes, but he was an amusing and generous one. His job gone, he had no choice but to leave and try to start over somewhere else, which he had done quite successfully in Denver, opening his own consulting firm. He was lucky, in that a person with a less-developed sense of humor might have caved in at the shame of being caught in such a situation and having his career ruined, but not Burl. He was like a lovable, mischievous cartoon character; a giant anvil might fall on him, but he'd just pop back up, dust himself off, and go on to find more trouble. He was never repentant for his actions because he never saw any of them as really wrong.

Most men, or, for that matter, most people, want to be wanted. We all want someone who is attracted to us and excited by us, someone who yearns for us (as long as this yearning is not psychotic in nature), or at least someone who can fake it. Burl was seemingly an exception to this. He did not seem to care one way or another if his partner had a genuine attraction to him. In fact, I think he liked it better when they were reluctant, because then, when they did give in, he had the added satisfaction of having persuaded them with his charm. It was flattering to his ego in an unusual way. Watching him in action, at a bar as he plied his victim with liquor, or at a dinner party, as he casually placed the hand of the boy seated next to him on his crotch, I was always reminded of a rather grotesque poem I'd read in school. In it, the narrator tries to entice a woman into the sack with the dubious argument that they've essentially already done the deed, since they were both bitten by the same flea, and in that flea their blood commingles. Burl's strategies usually worked, but if not, he could always bring out the added enticement of money.

Burl was nothing if not colorful. He had shown up at Paul's memorial service late, his trick from the night before in tow. He wore a yellow satin shirt, a gaudy pair of Versace sunglasses, and reeked of cologne, which only slightly overpowered the reek of alcohol. He carried with him a half-empty Bloody Mary.

"In case they don't have communion," he had said with a wink.

Later, in the receiving line outside the church, he hugged me tightly, for a very long time, and caressed and patted my ass while whispering in my ear how sorry he was. He said to be sure and call if I needed anything, and because "Well, hey, you're single again." Bad taste? Definitely, but with Burl it would have been more of a shock if he had offered weepy sentiment. Sentiment was one of the few things Burl chose not to wear on his sleeve. He kept his private side just that—private. He and Paul had been good friends, but on what exactly they based their friendship, I never knew. They were both heavy drinkers, frequented the same bars, and were always having boy troubles: Paul with me, and Burl with whichever little trick was trying to weasel money out of him in any given week. I knew he'd liked and respected Paul, so that's part of the reason I called him. My own brother is a lawyer, too, and I could have gone to him, but I thought Burl would be more receptive to my role as victim. More malleable.

He wasn't as stupid as I thought.

It was after nine when I arrived at Burl's house, and true to his word he had left a light on for me. *Probably the bedroom light,* I thought as I rang the bell. A moment later he whipped open the door. He was wearing a burgundy and gold silk bathrobe and heavy, black-framed glasses with very thick lenses. A lit cigarette dangled from his lips, and he raised a nearly empty highball glass and shook it coyly.

"Drink?" he asked.

"I think I could use one." I sighed, and walked through the dark foyer into the living room. I heard more disco music playing on the stereo, and noticed, with a sad feeling of jealousy, that he had the same Bang & Olufsen stereo I'd hoped to collect from Paul's house earlier that afternoon.

Burl's living room was dramatic in its severity. No earth tones here, unless you considered black and white earthy. It was a large room that seemed all the larger because of the whiteness: white walls, white trim, white carpeting. There were two overstuffed black leather couches each facing an enormous glass coffee table, the legs of which were in the shape of male caryatids. On that table, among the ornamental marble obelisks, the silver candlesticks, and the sticky coasters, there was a selection of the soft-porn-passing-as-art-books that are so popular with gay men, and which I hate so much. One corner of the room was dominated by a big-screen TV, in front of which sat, like a sacrificial altar, an overstuffed black leather La-Z-Boy. On one side of this was an overflowing pedestal ashtray and on the other was a similar caryatid-supported end table with the heavy burden of four remote controls. A bachelor's paradise. Burl stood in the far corner facing the wet bar, which was all black granite and chrome, above which were several glass shelves displaying row after row of liquor bottles.

"I hope you like Manhattans," he called, " 'cause I've had a hankerin' for 'em all day." He turned down the stereo and brought me a drink, the size of which was worthy of the name Manhattan. We clinked glasses.

"To us," he said, and gave me a sly wink. I rolled my eyes, took a sip of my drink, and wondered, as it burned its way down my throat, where this was leading. I tried to compose my thoughts and to remember the details of my meeting with Wendy. I took another, larger sip and sat down. Burl sat very close and threw one arm over the back of the sofa behind me. This action revealed more of his expansive thigh than I cared to see, so I looked up, only to be confronted with his face, less than a hand's distance away from me.

"So," I said, leaning forward, and purposely setting my wet glass on one of the photo books, "have you met Paul's sister?"

"No, I don't believe I've had the pleasure, but the word on the street is that she's a pruney bitch."

I smiled, remembering her leathery face. "Oh, no, not at all," I said. "She's a peach."

Burl raised an eyebrow.

"Yes, ever so nice," I said, affecting an English accent, my voice sharply sarcastic. "She invited me back to *my* house today, and we spent all afternoon together reminiscing about Paul, sharing our private memories, poring over the family albums, comforting each other in this time of loss. She's really quite lovely, and we've become very close. She's even invited me to come visit her at her place in the country—Bitchstead or Monstershire, or wherever the hell she's from."

I downed the rest of my drink and coughed.

"Yes, 'pruney bitch' describes her well," I said. "Unfortunately, she's a pruney bitch who is now in possession of all my stuff." I fell back into the couch and leaned into his shoulder. "Please tell me she's not legally entitled to it," I whined petulantly. He got up, grabbed my glass, and walked toward the bar. I sat up again, confused, and decided that maybe I'd better treat this more as a professional consultation.

"Like I said on the phone," I continued, trying to shake off the effects of the drink, "I need some legal advice. Can she really do this?"

Burl said nothing. I could hear him mixing and pouring more drinks. When he finished, he brought them over and set them both on coasters. He then walked over and plucked a remote and a pack of cigarettes off the end table. He turned off the music completely and offered me a cigarette. I declined, so he lit one for himself and sat, this time on the sofa opposite me.

"She can't, can she?" I asked again. Still he said nothing but smoked pensively, his eyes roaming the ceiling.

"Well?" I asked, taking a drink.

"Well," he said. "She can and she has."

I picked up my large glass by its elegant stem and took an inelegant chug, realizing that this meeting was probably not going to be any more pleasurable than my meeting with Wendy that morning.

"Maybe I will have that cigarette," I slurred. He tossed one over to me.

"Well, damn it, Jack, what do you want me to say? I hate to say I told you so, but I did try to get you two to draw up wills ages ago, but you didn't, so it all goes to the next of kin."

"Which is me!" I cried, blowing out a big cloud of smoke. "Isn't there any way we can contest it?" I asked, rising and pacing the room, cocktail in one hand, cigarette in the other, realizing how much I sounded like a character from *Melrose Place,* and how this severe black-and-white room fit that role perfectly.

"I mean the will is old. . . ." I continued.

"It's less than ten years old," he said, laughing, "which to your puppy-dog eyes seems like a long time, but in the legal scheme of things it's not unreasonable." He downed his own drink.

"Now, son, I know you're thinking, and rightly so, that you are the next of kin, but this here's the Hate State, remember? Some people here aren't real fond of homos. If they had their way we'd all be living in Sin Francisco or locked away in some mental hospital." He poured us both the last of the Manhattan from the shaker.

"It's not pretty, but what it comes down to is this: she has very strong legal legs to stand on and you have puny little toothpicks."

"Sshiit," I slurred.

"Son, you know if there was any way I could help you I would, but you have to believe me when I tell you that you're just bangin' your head against a wall. I wouldn't take this case if someone paid me in full up front, because it would be a big ol' waste of time."

As he spoke I thought of all the credit-card debt I'd amassed in the past year, largely in secret from Paul. It was well over thirty thousand by now, and thinking of it, I dragged deeply on the cigarette.

"Another drink?"

"No," I said, my tongue feeling heavy. "Any more and I won't be able to walk, let alone drive."

"Well, then by all means have one."

"No, I really need to go," I said, but made no move to get up.

Even now it's not clear what happened later that night, but I know I stayed and that we drank at least one more shaker of Manhattans. I vaguely remember dancing on the sofa with Burl while we both sang along to Cher's "Gypsies, Tramps and Thieves," but not much after that. I awoke the next morning, my twenty-sixth birthday, alone in Burl's four-poster bed, feeling like I had a mouth full of sand. I was naked save for my underwear, which was keeping my ankles quite warm.

The fact of my sleeping with someone when my lover was barely a month in the grave was bad. The fact that the someone was his drunken, overweight, hillbilly friend was worse. But the real sting came when, struggling to get dressed and out of there, I reached into my pants pocket for the car keys and pulled out three crisp hundred-dollar bills. My head throbbed, and it took me a moment to realize what it implied, but as I looked more closely at the bills I noticed that it was all spelled out for me quite literally. Burl had taken a blue ballpoint pen and drawn little conversation balloons coming out of Ben Franklin's mouth. *Thanks again for last night,* read the first caption. The next said, *For services rendered,* and the last, *Cum again soon!* with one of Franklin's eyes penned into a crude wink. I was furious, and my head pounded as I struggled to remember what had happened.

Later Burl said it was probably nothing, but that he couldn't remember either, and he gave me the money "just in case." He said that toward the end of the evening I started crying, and it was then that he put me to bed. He has never answered to my satisfaction how my underwear came to be around my ankles.

"Hell, I probably dumped you at the bottom of the bed and then pulled you up to the headboard by your arms. Your underwear must have slid down then."

Yeah, right.

I rubbed my eyes, set the money on his desk, and grabbed some paper and a pencil from one of the desk drawers, intending to sit down to write him a caustic note saying that I was sorry he had misinterpreted a drunken roll in the hay as sex for hire. I say I *intended* to write it because I no sooner sat down than nausea raised me up again and I ran to the bathroom.

FAMILY VALUES

As exiles go, my parents' house is not a bad one. It is a large structure, vaguely Tudor, made of gray stone, with three large gables and a turret in front. As a child I had always wanted my bedroom to be in the turret, envisioning the many nights I would secretly climb down the ivy-covered stones into the arms of my waiting lover. Instead my father used it as his study, and it was the place my siblings and I came to associate with punishment or "talking-tos," as my father called them. It is where we sat as my father silently perused our report cards and asked, "Do you really think you did your best?" the place we went to get our allowances, or ask for a permission slip to jump on the neighbor's trampoline, or to sign birthday and Mother's Day cards. I always thought of it as the brains of the house—an image now reinforced by the presence of a giant telephone antennae shooting out of the top.

Returning to the nest at the age of twenty-five is not usually heralded, but my father was easier on me than he might have been because Paul was so freshly dead. Nevertheless I did not want to seem presumptuous, and had thus been reluctant to unpack much of anything, out of fear that to do so would imply in my father's mind (and my own, for that matter) that my stay was somewhat permanent.

My mother would have loved that. In the three weeks I'd been home, she and I had shopped extensively, filled all the pots and planters around the house with annuals, made mango sorbet, selected new upholstery for the dining room chairs, taken a class on ikebana, and had gone to three baseball games. Day after day we went along, as blissfully happy as Oedipus and Jocasta, until my father returned home in the evenings and spoiled everything by making us both feel guilty: me for not working, and my mother for indulging me.

My father has always been rather stoic and severe, but he used to be a much better sport. He used to see my mother and me, and my twin sister, Carey, more as his court jesters than his relations, always there to entertain him and make him laugh with our stories of the interesting things we did and people we came in contact with. But those were the days before he, like so many people in the country, came under the moral spell of an aged black nun called Sister Melanie, and lost his sense of humor.

Sister Melanie is a retired inner-city school principal from Atlanta who has somehow morphed herself into a ridiculously popular talk-radio personality. This she has done largely by emphasizing personal responsibility above all else and by taking all the problems of her callers and placing them squarely back in their own lap. She is so effective, in part, because she is a very small, blind woman and appears, on the surface, to be all Southern gentility. Then she bares her teeth, and this dichotomy is somehow appealing to certain masochistic segments of our society. Lately she has become the darling of the Republican party because she routinely bashes the welfare system and because of her tough moral code: no sex before marriage, no abortion, and no using addiction as an excuse for anything. She is ruthless when people make mistakes and argues against giving second chances ". . . because that makes it seem like actions have no consequences."

What she is most famous for, however, are her slogans: little phrases and sayings that she incorporates from time to time into her broadcast. Sometimes they rhyme, other times they don't, but they all serve as a simple reminder of her philosophy. She reads through them in the voice and diction of a beat poet or a Baptist minister, and many times she can throw them out at callers as one-sentence answers to their problems:

AGONIZED MOTHER: "Sister Melanie, my son got kicked out of school for having marijuana in his locker. He has a bad drug problem and we really want to help him. What can we do?"

SISTER MELANIE: "Listen, honey, it's nice that you want to help him, but you know what I say: Abuse is no excuse! You need to stand back and let him face the music. The school administrators were right to kick him out. I'm surprised they didn't turn him in to the police. I can tell you that's what I would have done if he was at my school. He needs to make the decision to fix himself. Remember, addiction is a fiction!"

My father became acquainted with her quite by accident when he discovered one of her books in the seat pocket of the plane in which he was traveling. He read it, liked it, and that was it. He was a convert, and from then on he never stopped trying to convert the rest of us. Worse than that, he sought out any and every opportunity to use her philosophy to point out the shortcomings of his family, most often mine.

On the flip side, my mother is fun and light and airy. She is a favorite of all of my friends because she has a thick Southern drawl, and a sort of ditzy naivete characteristic of women who grew up sheltered in the 1950s. She is one of the last living remnants of the white-gloved Dallas society that has now all but vanished. She met my father, who was much less dogmatic then, at a sorority tea dance her sophomore year at SMU. They dated all through college and married a week after their graduation, much to the dismay of her parents, because my father, while good-looking and highly ambitious, didn't have a penny, and his family was borderline white trash. Her family, on the other hand, was rolling in it, and had been for generations.

Aware of his in-laws' reservations about him, my father, always a proud man, refused to accept, and refused to allow my mother to accept, any money whatsoever from her parents. So for the first few years of their married life, until my father got established, they endured what my mother likes to call "the hard time." This meant they lived in an apartment instead of a house and had a dishwasher that was a machine as opposed to a woman who washed dishes. I've seen pictures and home movies from this period and I can assure you it was hardly as bad as she led us to believe. My father used to laugh at her descriptions and stories of "the hard time" because for him it was a huge step up from his lean bachelor days.

Reluctantly, my grandparents respected his wish that he and my mother accept no money from them. But they managed to sidestep this rule by taking my mother on shopping trips every time they blew into town, which was about once every three months. Whole wardrobes were updated on these trips, and the young couple's small apartment was, piece by piece, lavishly furnished. In addition, my mother made two trips to Europe in these years of poverty, ostensibly as her younger sister's chaperone—trips bankrolled by her parents that left my father grumbling over his TV dinners while she was gone.

As for my father's side of the family, its history is clouded by myth and hyperbole. Dad never grew tired of telling my brother and sister and me how lucky we were to be living in a plush house in a beautiful neighborhood, because he had not been so lucky growing up in rural Minnesota. His father had been a farm laborer, and his mother had manned the counter at the local Woolworth's cafeteria. They both worked hard but still never had enough money, so my father had to take a part-time job cleaning cattle stalls just to keep the family's collective head above water. To hear him tell it, he had to work from sunup to sundown and had grown up with nothing but old corncobs to play with, which is probably true, but I'll never know because he is an only child and both of his parents died long before I was born. Conveniently, this allows him to embellish his stories in any way he wants without fear of contradiction. I should be so lucky.

My father is an admirable man, despite his gruff exterior and current lack of humor, and I know he has worked very hard to attain everything he has. But more important than grit and ambition, Dad has been blessed with tremendous foresight, which has enabled him to see upcoming trends before they are up-and-coming. He jumps in, makes lots of money, and pulls out before the market dries up, or becomes saturated, or whatever dry or soggy business analogy you want to use. He started out in the oil industry, made heaps of money in the sixties and seventies, and then quit just before the Arabs flooded the market. He then took the money he'd saved and opened a store selling computer products, which he quickly expanded into a chain of stores. He fortified that business, sold it for a staggering profit, and moved on to cellular phones in the late eighties. Back then, the phones seemed like nothing more than an elitist novelty, and therein lies my father's wisdom: somehow he foresaw the trend, and knew that soon *everyone* would be carrying little phones.

Oil executive, software pioneer, CEO of a communications company. All of his titles. I wonder what he'll do next.

I never gave much thought to the idea of titles (until recently, when I was branded with one), but when you think about it, we live in a society where people are largely defined by the work they do. Don't believe me? Take a look at the obituary section of the newspaper. At the end of life everyone is defined by their work: Wanda the systems analyst, Theodore the hairdresser. Bob the doctor. Simone the bus driver. I should have realized this early on, since my father was constantly asking my brother and sister and me what we wanted to be when we grew up. My sister and brother always had quick answers. "I want to be a fireman!" or "I want to be a doctor!" But I'd just shrug my shoulders or say something disturbing, like "I want to be Mommy!" The truth is, I never gave it much thought at all. Not even in college, which is the time most people formulate at least a rough outline for their life's work. I had selected art history as my major before I'd even started my freshman year, and was met with an avalanche of condescending smiles and comments: "What are you going to do with that? Open a museum?" or "You'll be flipping burgers with that degree." All implying that I was being terribly frivolous and decadent and was wasting my parents' hard-earned money. I heard these comments so many times that eventually I began to believe them, and became embarrassed by what I was studying, like I'd been caught taking nothing but gym classes.

Then I met Paul. And there, finally, was someone who thought I'd been wise in my choice of study. He showed me just a few of the countless avenues I could travel down with my education, and actually encouraged me to explore them, but by that time it was almost too late. I had been indoctrinated well and believed that while those avenues might have been open to someone as wise and brilliant as he, they would not be open to me with my useless B.A. Then Paul and I moved in together, and that effortless living situation did nothing to spur me on to look for a job. For me, work was always a vague cloud just over the horizon. I knew it would blow in and block the sun someday, but to my mind there was no reason to hurry it along.

I thought about all that as I drove away from Burl's that morning. I had almost reached my parents' subdivision when I made a U-turn and decided to avoid going home for a while. I was afraid my father might be there, and I didn't want to walk in wearing the same clothes I'd had on last night, making it more obvious than it probably already was that I hadn't slept there. Instead I went to the gym. I wasn't scheduled to work, and it wasn't the time for my usual workout, but I felt I should punish myself for my drunken, slutty behavior the night before. What better way to do that than with a grueling workout? I changed my clothes, said a few casual "hellos" to some of the lunch crowd, and got on the StairMaster. I set the resistance fairly high, hoping to burn away the Manhattan cloud from my brain. It was tough going at first, but once I got the rhythm down and started sweating, I felt better.

While climbing the staircase to nowhere, I thought again about the night before and the money that was tucked away in the pocket of my jeans in the locker room. The meaning was clear enough: it was a payment, but what did my taking it mean? What did that make me? I told myself it was a joke and that I'd have the last laugh by keeping it. I told myself it was his way of helping me out, and that I should be thankful. I told myself I'd take it, use it to silence my most annoying creditors, and then pay it back to him when I could. I was a pro at rationalizing. My brain, just like my body, initially protested what I was doing to it, but eventually it quieted down and I adopted one of those scenarios, I don't remember which, as the party line.

And yet, somewhere in the back of my mind, I knew that the money was just what it had said—money paid "for services rendered." In a subliminal way that's probably why I had gone to Burl's. I hadn't gone for legal advice; I knew Wendy was legally justified. I hadn't gone for commiseration or remembrance. I had gone for monetary help. I desperately needed money and didn't want to hit up my parents—again—and I knew that Burl had more money than he could count. I also probably knew, again in the back of my mind, what I'd have to do to get it, and I did it. I had to have a few drinks under my belt first, but it really wasn't a laborious task. I like sex, and even bad sex can be kind of good. As unattractive as Burl is, I did find it kind of thrilling to be doing something so . . . taboo.

I finished the StairMaster, did a back-and-biceps weight circuit, and then stuffed all of my clothes from the night before into my gym bag. I figured I wouldn't bother showering, as I would just have to put the dirty clothes back on. On my way out I stopped at the desk to look at my schedule for the coming week. I was working only two evenings. *That will have to change,* I thought as I walked out to my car. I made a mental note to ask my boss, Fred, if I could pick up more shifts and start getting paid in money instead of trade.

I pulled into the driveway and was relieved to see that my father's car was not there. I sat for a while, not wanting to go in and have to dig through my sloppy pyramid of boxes to find something to change into, but I did need to get showered and changed, as the rest of the clan was coming to dinner to celebrate our birthday. I say "our" because my sister and I are twins, and have always celebrated our birthdays together.

One cake, matching presents, questions about who was born first and whether or not we can read each other's thoughts and feel each other's pain. That is a birthday for twins. Although we shared the womb for nine months, my sister Carey and I have surprisingly little in common—least of all our appearance: I am tall and slender while she is shorter and tends to be "chunky," as our mother would say. One can't help but wonder if the wires didn't get crossed somewhere along the line, because she has always been more boyish: playing with trucks, excelling at sports, helping our dad with the yardwork, whereas I was perfectly content to stay indoors perfecting recipes for my Easy-Bake oven.

As I went into the kitchen and mixed myself a protein shake I saw my mother in the backyard, trying to position, with the help of her aged gardener, Mr. Matsumoto, what appeared to be a heavy stone lantern on a large stone pedestal. The two of them made quite a pair: a small, hunched man with graying black hair and a weatherworn face, and a six-foot, unnaturally blond woman with a slash of red lipstick and huge, white sunglasses.

She had hired Mr. Matsumoto at the beginning of the summer to help her transform the backyard into a traditional Japanese garden, an interest she'd developed after taking a landscape architecture class focusing on Japan at the botanic gardens. Landscape architecture was a subject she'd developed an interest in on a three-week trip she'd taken to Japan—the same three-week trip to Japan she'd taken to study Japanese pottery. When she returned, her potter's wheel and kiln were quickly moved from the garage to an obscure corner of the basement, and the garage was filled with sacks of ornamental stones, and the ripe stench of manure and mulch. From a new Peg-Board rack on the wall hung all manner of strange trimming tools arranged with the meticulous intensity characteristic of her new Asian friends.

This garden was the latest in a series of what my siblings and I called "Mom's campaigns." These were interests that she would discover, usually by chance, embrace like a new lover, investigate and probe, and then abandon completely when a new, more interesting one came along. My father said it all started when they took possession of the house and she undertook her first—and longest—campaign: to renovate and redecorate. I was too young to remember this, but my father relishes telling the story of how she knocked out walls and erected new ones, ripped up eighty percent of the flooring and replaced it with wood or tile, painted and repainted, upholstered and reupholstered, bought and returned draperies, fought with contractors and tradesmen, and somehow found time to give birth to three children before she had finished.

From there she went on to orchid growing, and from there to cake decorating; then Spanish lessons became her passion, then marathon running, photography, the climbing of all of Colorado's mountains above fourteen thousand feet, oil painting, furniture refinishing, bird husbandry, macrobiotic cooking (through which we all suffered the most miserable stomach cramps), pottery, etc . . . Each campaign lasted from six months to a year, maybe two, and was then quickly discarded and forgotten about when the next interest hooked her.

Marathon running is the perfect example. Her passion for it started when Jim Fixx died and she became interested in his life while reading his obituary in *Newsweek*. She then read *The Complete Book of Running,* quit smoking, outfitted herself with all sorts of shoes and sports bras and nylon shorts, and threw herself into it completely. She got up every morning at five A.M., ran for nearly an hour, came home, stretched, bathed, and read *Runner's World* over her morning coffee. Every weekend she was off doing another race and had elaborate charts detailing her splits and finish times. She developed new training friends and running partners, and a new vocabulary in which she spoke of shin splints, carbo loading, and runner's high. She loved it so much that she, like my father, sought to convert us all. She failed, most notably with my sister, Carey, who was then interested in another form of high that had nothing to do with running, and refused to participate in the family relay in which my mother had entered us.

Japanese gardening was the latest campaign, and as I watched her and Mr. Matsumoto straining to lift the stone into place, I thought I'd better offer assistance.

"Need some help?" I called, stepping out onto the back porch.

"Oh, honey, goodness, yes, this is so damn heavy and I'm afraid Mr. Matsumoto has a hernia, although I can't find the dictionary to find out for sure. He keeps lifting up his shirt and showing me some scars."

Together we positioned the stone into place on its pedestal, and they both gave a sigh of relief.

"Oh, sank you, sir," said Mr. Matsumoto, shaking my hand enthusiastically and nodding rapidly. "You vely stlong." He then took off his gloves, picked up a burlap sack of pellets, and hobbled over to feed the fish in what had, just a week earlier, been a kidney-shaped swimming pool. Now it was officially "the koi pond," and was slowly being surrounded by meticulously trimmed shrubs and dwarf trees. Where the diving board had been, a waterfall now trickled down a small mountain made of large, carefully placed stones.

"What time did you leave this morning?" my mother asked, brushing the sweat from her forehead with a grimy glove. "I didn't even get to wish you a happy birthday!" She hugged me tightly and kissed me on the cheek.

"Uh, I left pretty early," I lied, and stared intently at Mr. Matsumoto. "I had to open the gym."

I could feel her eyes regarding me suspiciously from behind her sunglasses. She was about to question me, but I sidetracked her.

"Hey, what is this anyway?" I asked, gesturing toward the stone.

"Oh, isn't it fabulous!" she cried, clapping her hands together, her suspicion dispelled. "It's a lantern, of course. Mr. Matsumoto had one of his cousins ship it over from Kobe. The temple it was in was destroyed in the earthquake, and they got it for a bargain-basement price."

"It's beautiful," I said. "The whole garden is looking great."

"Thank you, honey, do you really think so? Mr. Matsumoto has been helping me so much with the more traditional aspects. We're thinking of putting either a teahouse or a Zen rock garden over under the maple in the corner, but he hasn't decided if the balance is right yet."

"A teahouse!" I exclaimed. "What will that be for?"

"Well, for having tea ceremonies, of course. It's all very ritualized stuff. Mr. Matsumoto was trying to explain it to me this morning but his English isn't very good and I couldn't really understand it. But whatever—it sounds like a fun idea, doesn't it?" she said, gesturing vaguely to the maple. "A little teahouse over there under the tree . . ." I nodded.

"You look tired, honey," she said, putting her arm around my shoulder and leading me toward the house. "Why don't you lie down before dinner. Your sister and brother won't be here until seven, and God only knows when we'll see your father." I nodded, and was actually glad that I'd be seeing my sister and brother, as I hadn't seen either of them since Paul's funeral.

"Maybe I will lie down. Will you wake me in a little while so I can shower?" I asked, heading toward the stairs. She nodded.

"Oh, I almost forgot," she called. "How did the meeting with Paul's sister go?"

I hesitated for a moment, remembering Wendy as she flicked her ashes and skipped up the stairs.

"I'll tell you about it later," I said, and went up to my room.

My old bedroom was dark and cool, and lying down on the soft bed felt wonderful. I had been staying in the same room I'd had as a child, but there was not a single vestige of me there anymore. When I moved away to college my mother had taken all of my things to the basement and "redid" the room. Gone were my giant posters of David Bowie and Nirvana, my black light and my large water bed, having been replaced by a more conservative decor: two mahogany twin beds with a small table between them, white carpeting, white lace curtains, and a long, low dresser, also of dark mahogany. The walls were sparsely adorned with framed pictures of dead relatives and scenes from an English fox-hunt. I was glad my decor was gone, as I found the white room relaxing, and I fell asleep easily, feeling the last waves of my hangover lap gently on my brain.

And then I was fishing, by myself, in a small rowboat on a lake high in the mountains. The evening sky was overcast and the air was very still. There was not even a breeze, so the lake was as smooth as a sheet of glass. I was fishing, casting out my line in a graceful arc and then slowly reeling it back in. I cast once, twice, a third time, and then suddenly felt a strike. I reeled in quickly, only to find a pair of eyeglasses at the end of the line. I unhooked them, examined them closely, and realized they were Paul's. I cast again and a moment later I felt another strike, this one so strong that it nearly pulled the rod from my hands. I pulled back sharply to set the hook and the tugging subsided a little. I reeled furiously for what seemed like a very long time, and eventually I saw a large object rising slowly from the depths. As it neared the boat, I saw that it was Paul, and that I'd hooked him in the mouth. I reached over and pulled him into the boat, noticing how light he felt. He smiled and seemed fine, but was unable to speak because of the hook. I rummaged clumsily in the tackle box and eventually found a pair of pliers, which I quickly used to remove the hook. I expected a lot of blood, but instead I heard a hissing noise and felt air coming out of the hole where the hook had been. The hissing got louder and I watched, horrified, as Paul deflated and rose up, in a spiral motion, out of the boat and into the sky. When he was empty, his sac of a body arced and fell downward, hitting the water with a weak smack.

Suddenly, I heard voices behind me. I looked over at the shore and saw Wendy and the lawyer, nearly doubled over with laughter, pointing at me and clutching their stomachs, she almost unable to hold her cigarette. I stood up, shaking with anger, and as I did so, both of the wooden oars fell from the sides and sank rapidly. The two laughed even harder, if possible, and then reached down and picked up some rocks and started hurling them at me. It was only after they'd landed in the boat (and they *all* landed in the boat) that I realized they were not rocks at all, but were the heavy pieces of venetian glass from Paul's house. *Thud! Thud! Thud!* They clanked as they landed in the bottom of the metal boat, perfect hits every time. *Thud! Thud! Thud!* And slowly the boat began to take on water and to sink. *Thud! Thud! Thud!*

I sat up in bed, and it took a moment to realize that what I'd been hearing was not venetian glass paperweights, but knocks on my bedroom door.

"Jaaack." It was the nasally twang of my mother.

"Are you awake, little birthday man?" The door creaked open and I could see her severe silhouette. She was wearing a black tunic, her hair pulled back in a long ponytail and held in place by what were evidently some very long chopsticks. She looked like a blond ninja as she came over and sat next to me on the bed.

"Yeah, I'm awake," I mumbled. "Sort of."

She smoothed my sweaty hair back from my forehead.

"You all right?" she asked.

"Yeah, fine," I said. "Just a bad dream."

"Oh, baby, do you want to talk about it? You know I took that dream class at the Free University last year."

"No, Ma, really." I sighed, falling back on the bed. "I think I understand this one."

"Well, you just rest some more. There's no real rush. Carey's going to be late, and your dad and Jay and Susan are making drinks in the kitchen. Just take your time. We can eat anytime; almost everything is cold."

As I came down the stairs I heard laughter coming from the kitchen. I listened for my sister's voice, but knew that if she were there, hers would most likely be the only voice I'd hear. It's not that she was loud, necessarily, but her stories did tend to fill up the room and push everyone else to the fringes. In that respect she and my mother are more alike than either one likes to admit. No, the voice I heard then was that of my father, and the subject was, as always, business.

"So I told him, 'Tommy, we've got to keep offering the stock option to new hires; it keeps 'em interested in the company. Keeps 'em honest if they feel like they're a part of it.'"

"Oh, I couldn't agree more, Mr. Thompson," said Susan, my brother's fiancée, who owns her own temporary agency. "The worst problem I have is with people who are apathetic about their work."

"Please, call me Dad."

"Hey, hey, little brother," said my brother Jay, jumping up from his stool when he saw me in the doorway. He grabbed me in a headlock and nooggied my scalp as I stood, crouched over, looking at the floor, waiting patiently for him to finish. Ironically, I was hardly the "little" brother. I was taller and weighed at least a third more than he did, his growth stunted from too many hours behind a desk staring at a computer monitor. If I'd chosen to, I could, in one swift movement, have had him flat on his skinny little back. But I humored him, gritting my teeth, and eventually he released my head, and we all laughed as I straightened my hair.

"Here's one half of the party," my dad said jovially, patting me on the head and again messing up my hair.

"Funny that you're here before your sister, since it was the other way around twenty-six years ago. We just about had to bribe you out of there with candy, ha ha ha. Would you like a drink, son?"

My stomach turned.

"Just a soda, thanks," I said.

I didn't drink partly because of the amount I'd drunk last night, but mostly because I've always felt a bit awkward drinking around my parents, especially my father. Like it's something I'll never be quite old enough to do.

"Happy birthday, Jack," said Susan, smiling broadly and giving me a little wave, the light glinting off her new engagement ring.

"Thanks." I smiled shyly. I was slightly angry at myself for feeling suddenly shy and intimidated by this crowd, but to me, they were somewhat intimidating, all still dressed in their suits from work, my mother and sister nowhere to be seen.

"So what have you been up to today, Jack?" my father asked, and I could hear in his tone the expectation of my lame response. I did not disappoint.

"Um, I, um, worked at the gym for a while, went and got some of my stuff from Paul's—"

"Yes," my dad interrupted, "I saw the boxes. Looks like you're going to be staying a while?"

"No," I said, making an effort to stifle the sarcastic response that wanted to come out. "I'm going to be your guest for a while, just until I can find a place."

"I see," said my father, making no effort to stifle his own sarcasm. "My guest. Kind of like that tapeworm I picked up in Indonesia in seventy-four." We all laughed, but seeing the direction the evening was headed, I thought maybe I'd need more than a soda to get me through it. Through the sliding glass door, I spied my mother, once again on the back lawn, cutting some flowers from the garden next to the pool/pond. She looked up, saw me watching, and smiled. I wished she would hurry; my father's mood usually softened in her presence. Mercifully, I heard the front door slam then, and in trod my twin, looking frazzled and plump in her pale pink nurse's scrubs. Her hair was a rat's nest of blond, and her face was attractively offset by a pair of smudged John Denver glasses. She was then employed as an emergency room nurse and had evidently come straight from work. She dropped her sizable hemp purse on the floor with a thud.

"God, what a day!" she said, pushing my brother off his stool and occupying it herself.

"If they made me do one more catheter, damn! I've never been so close to throwing in the towel. 'I'll lose fifty pounds,' I thought, 'and start that modeling career Mom always wanted for me.'"

My mother entered, flowers in her arms, having caught the tail end of Carey's proclamation.

"That is not true," she protested. "I've always been very proud of your career. I knew you'd go into something medical ever since the day old Mrs. Spellman phoned to tell me that my darling twins had set up a little Barbie hospital out on the front sidewalk using a box of my maxi-pads as the stretchers and ketchup for blood."

Carey laughed and got up and gave her a hug. She spied my father mixing drinks and went over to the improvised bar.

"Drinks!" she said. "Yes, please."

"What would you like, Caroline?"

"What would I like?" she thought, drumming her fingers thoughtfully on her chin. "Something cold and clear . . . and not at all yellow." We all laughed.

"How about a Manhattan?" he asked. I winced.

"Hi, little buddy," said Carey, giving me a big hug and a kiss. In the month since Paul's death, she had been very . . . sisterly, I guess, and made a point of phoning me every day, which was nice because she had never liked Paul. For the most part, my family had loved Paul, and spoke in reverent tones about how impressive his work was, how smart he was, what a charming accent he had. Carey was the notable exception. She usually maintained a facade of politeness when they were together, but in private that fell away and I would hear things like, "That boyfriend of yours needs to take the stick out of his ass."

From Paul it was much the same: we would get in the car from a dinner with Carey, and before he'd even start the engine he'd say, "Now I know you two are twins, but I can honestly say that I'm glad you're nothing like your sister. Obnoxious!"

It was difficult for me being in the middle, trying to gently defend one to the other, explaining that he was just English, or she was just very outspoken, so whenever possible I had kept them apart.

Over the years Carey and I certainly had our differences, but she'd always been accepting of me and my lifestyle. When I was fourteen and my mom discovered the stash of male underwear ads I had painstakingly collected and organized from a variety of catalogs and kept hidden between the mattress and the box springs of my bed, Carey was the only one who didn't freak out about it, and was a great help in bringing my parents and older brother around to accept the fact that I was gay. For reasons like that, I suppose I was subconsciously dubious about Paul. Although I was happy that the rest of the family adored and accepted him, that happiness was overshadowed by the fact that Carey did not.

After dinner that night, as we all sat around the table drinking coffee and picking at the remains of the seven-layer birthday torte my mother had made according to the rigid guidelines in the May issue of *Martha Stewart Living,* the conversation, as usual, turned to business and moneymaking. Business is my father's hobby, in the same way my mother has her hobbies, but with the obvious difference that he has kept the same one seemingly since birth, and she changes hers with dizzying frequency.

"I've always been at the right place at the right time," my father was saying. "Most people think that's lucky, but really there's little, if any, luck involved in it. I've always positioned myself to be there."

We had all heard this before, with the exception of Susan, who now sat entranced by his business lore.

"I was in the oil business in the fifties and sixties," he said. "But I could see the money leaving there, so I got into computers. Now it's cell phones. Keep one step ahead of trends, that's what I always say; that way, when everyone else catches up, I'm ready with something to sell them."

Susan nodded reverently, stirring her coffee.

"Now you must have had some foresight to have jumped on the temp bandwagon," he said.

"Well, yes," she said proudly, "I suppose I did. I worked for an insurance company while I was completing my M.B.A. and I remember wishing I had a less demanding job since my studies were taking up so much of my time. I kept thinking, 'I know all of these computer languages, I'm a great manager, surely I could find something less taxing.' I noticed we were using a lot of temporary employees to do some of our more menial data entry and clerical stuff, and that the agency employing them was doing a really sloppy job with their billing and scheduling, and I realized I could do it better. It was that simple."

"The best ideas usually are," said my father.

"Isn't she great!" said Jay, squeezing Susan's hand and giving her an admiring gaze.

"Yes, she is," said my father. "She'll make a lovely addition to the family. But what does she think about marrying a lawyer?"

"I think it will be wonderful," she said, and smiled shyly.

"Jay had a future in software design," Dad said. "I don't know why he decided to change direction midstream. Law seems a little unstable."

"Come on, Dad," Jay protested. "You know how much I hated it. I'm like you—I don't like working for other people. Especially other people who are dumber than me and expect me to sink to their level."

"But law?" said Dad, a sour look on his face. "You'll always be working for someone else. Usually some criminal thug."

Jay laughed. "At least that will make it interesting! But seriously, Dad, that's the way it is with any job. You work for your customers, Susan works for her clients, Carey works for the hospital and her patients. Jack . . ."

He paused awkwardly.

"Well, Jack will be doing the same thing."

I suppose I should have felt flattered that I got a mention, since my mother, absently sipping her coffee like an autistic child, her mind off on her koi pond or her teahouse, was overlooked completely.

"My point is," Jay continued, "we all work for someone else. At least as a lawyer I'll be more puppetmaster than puppet."

"And what," said my father, shifting his weight and his gaze toward me, "is to become of my other son?" Suddenly all was quiet, and all eyes, even my mother's, turned to me. There was an expectant silence. It was like I'd just mentioned E. F. Hutton and everyone was waiting to hear my investment tips. I shrugged and tried to look nonchalant, but my intestines felt like they were digesting broken glass.

"Are you still working at the gym?" Jay asked, breaking the silence, knowing full well that I was.

"Oh, yeah," I said cheerfully, "but only part-time."

"Can they make you full-time," he asked, "or would you even want to do that?"

"Funny you should mention that," I lied. "Because I actually talked to them today about going full-time, which I'd like to do and they would too, but right now they can't afford it."

"*They* can't afford it," my father said derisively. "Hell, *you* can't afford it. You need something that will pay the bills. What do they pay you there anyway? Six, seven bucks an hour?"

"What about going back to school?" Susan chimed in.

"Yes," said Jay, enthusiastically. "I've always thought you should take the LSAT."

"Christ." Carey groaned. "You think everyone should take the LSAT. You just want to have a higher score than all of us."

"That's only partially true," Jay said, smiling slyly. "I also think Jack would do well in law school. It gives life some structure."

"I don't know," I said hesitantly, wishing we could get off this topic.

"You'd make a great lawyer," said Susan. "You're good-looking, you're articulate, you have a strong voice—"

"Good God, Susan," Jay protested. "There's a little more to it than that! You make it sound like being a newscaster."

"Sorry, darling," she said, laughing slightly.

"Well, if not law," Jay said, "maybe you should go back for something else, like an M.B.A., or even an M.F.A."

"I have thought about it," I said, and my mind recalled the many discussions I'd had with Paul on the very same subject, Paul dealing out the possibilities like cards and me unable to make sense of my hand, totally uninterested in the game.

"I don't know that going back to school is really the answer," I said. "I mean, there are lots of things I'd like to study, but nothing that will help me find work. As much as I hate to admit it, Dad is right: I need to make money."

"What?" my dad said, cupping his hand around his ear theatrically. "Did everyone hear that? Did someone just say they think Dad's advice is wise? I don't believe my ears, but I'll throw in my two cents and agree: the last thing you need is another useless degree."

It always went this way: my father making me look stupid and me not knowing what to say.

"Now, Steen, stop," Mom interrupted. "His degree is not useless! I've learned a lot about arrangement, color, and anesthetics from Jack."

Carey and Jay snickered; Susan bit her lip. "Mom," said Carey, "I think you mean aesthetics, not anesthetics."

"Whatever," she said, dismissing the correction with a wave of her hand and turning to me.

"You were an enormous help when it came to positioning the artwork the last time we redecorated, and the cushions we're all sitting on now—I never could have found them without your help. So don't you listen to your father and his talk about a useless degree." She leaned closer to me, shielded her mouth from my father's view with a cupped hand, and whispered, "His little phones are not the most useful things in the world."

"Barbara!" he roared. "I can hear you quite clearly, and let me remind you that those useless little phones are what enable you to have any goddamned chairs at all." His voice was stern but he was smiling, as was she.

"My point," she continued, speaking to me but looking at my father, "is that maybe you need to try to make money doing something that you love instead of trying to fit yourself into the business mold. I mean, you're very good at ast . . . asmat . . ."

"Aesthetics," I said.

"Yes. And I think maybe you should do interiors, or some sort of design work."

A collective groan.

"Thanks, Mom." I sighed. "I appreciate the compliments, but I think the last thing the world—or the market—needs is another gay decorator."

"Another wise thing coming from my son's mouth," said Dad. "That makes two tonight. I think you should go for the hat trick." He chuckled a moment, but then became serious again, gesturing at me with his coffee spoon.

"Look, son," he said. "When your mother and I started out it wasn't easy. We lived in a tiny one-bedroom apartment and certainly didn't have meals like we had tonight."

My siblings and I exchanged expressions of *Oh, no, not again,* and settled back for what we knew was coming.

"I wanted to be with my new bride more than anything," he said, smug and self-righteous. "But I knew that sacrifices had to be made. I had to travel and work all the time to get myself established. The answers weren't just going to pop out at me. And that's what you need to realize: work is just that—work. Regardless of what you do. You have to work at it to make it succeed."

It was alarming how similar he and Paul sounded. I had heard this same speech countless times during the last year we were together.

"Look at your sister," he said. "She's not completely sure which direction she's headed, but she's working hard. She hates her job, but then so do most people. Most of the time I'm not wild about mine—"

This was a bold-faced lie.

"—but I have to do it, and usually the payoff outweighs the tedium."

I was thankful my sister interjected here, holding up her black-nailed hand in protest.

"If I can interrupt the prophet of doom for a minute. First of all, I do not hate my job. I hate the ass-wiping and mopping up puke, but for the most part, I love it, which is why I went into the field I'm in and not something like accounting. Not because it pays well, because God knows it doesn't pay enough, but because I like it. Mom is right," she said, looking at our father, but speaking to me, "you'd better do what you like, or at least something you can stand, or you'll never be successful. I mean, look at Dad. He complains and whines, like most men his age, but he's doing something he loves. He loves it so much it's hard to keep him off the subject. And Jay, look at Jay, who loves law so much he thinks everyone should be a lawyer. Why did he quit computers? Because he hated it. It sucked. It was the wrong thing. And when you realize that, it takes a lot of courage to change your course, but it beats the shit out of the alternative."

Jay nodded his agreement, seemingly amazed at Carey's uncharacteristic burst of eloquence. I too was surprised, and regarded her with a warm feeling in my heart. It did not last.

"You're smart, Jack, you have an amazing body, and you're good with people. I think you're a natural for physical therapy."

"Physical therapy!" I cried, somewhat disgusted, as I pictured myself in a tepid whirlpool surrounded by harnessed old women in skirted, one-piece bathing suits.

"Now don't knock it," she said, becoming very animated. "CU has this really awesome program that only takes three years, and I have this friend, a guy whose sister used to work with me in the head shop, and he's just like you. He's not a fag or anything, at least I don't think he is, but who knows. Anyway, he's totally into working out, just like you, and you're both also really patient with people. You're totally alike. You'd be perfect. This guy has almost a year left until he graduates and he's already getting job offers. It would be so cool if you got in, because then we could both go to—" She stopped abruptly and looked around coyly, and then back at me.

"Well, that's just what I think you should do," she concluded.

I eyed her quizzically, wondering what she hadn't said, but she was looking down at her lap.

"Back to your point about doing what you love," said Dad, and went off into a long-winded oratory on how if everyone did only what they loved the world would be full of candy makers, etc. . . . I tuned him out almost completely and thought instead of what my next boyfriend would be like. The one who would come and rescue me from the ivy-covered turret late some night. I was almost to the point where we sped away in his big Jaguar, or maybe it would be a Range Rover, up into the hills, when I was rudely awakened from my reverie by a smack in the side of the head with a flying piece of frosting that had been catapulted from my sister's fork across the table. Without missing a beat I quickly grabbed at the remnants of my torte and flung them at her as she attempted to duck beneath the table.

"Oh, for Christ's sake!" said Dad, throwing his napkin down on the table in disgust.

"Children!" my mother shrieked. "The wallpaper!"

We stopped almost as suddenly as we'd started, my sister, brother, mother, and I all laughing uncontrollably. My father looked annoyed, and Susan, the newcomer, not knowing how to react, looked down at her plate trying to control her giggles.

"Honestly, Caroline!" My mother laughed. "You're twenty-six going on thirteen."

"Well, my God," Carey said, "Dad's lecture was getting so damn boring I had to do something."

"You had to bring the attention back to you," Dad said angrily. "If there's one thing I hope you twins can learn as you creep ever so slowly toward adulthood it's that there are more diplomatic ways of changing the subject than by making a scene."

"Oh, screw diplomacy." Carey laughed. "It's my birthday." Then looking at me she added, "It's our birthday. And besides, have I ever got a subject changer!"

She got up and ran out of the room, returning with her hefty purse, which she set on the table and rummaged through until she found the envelope she was looking for. Waving it significantly in front of us she asked, "Are you ready for this?" We all nodded and she removed the letter and read the following:

Dear Ms. Thompson:
After stringent revue of your test scores, recommendations, and work history, it is with great pleasure that we offer you a place in the University of Colorado School of Medicine. . . .

We all listened attentively, too shocked to say anything. My mother was the first to speak.

"Oh, my God, Carey!" she cried, amazed. "A doctor! This calls for champagne!" And like a black-and-blond lightning bolt she ran through the swinging door to the kitchen, thrilled to have another occasion to furnish.

My father had tears running down his cheeks, which was almost frightening because he never cries.

"I'm so proud of you, honey," he said, smiling at Carey and getting up to give her a hug.

"We all are," said Jay, taking Susan's hand in his and presenting a united front of happiness.

"A doctor. Wow!" said Susan.

"Way to go, little sister!" said Jay, and he put up his hand for a high five.

"Jack," said Carey, noticing my lack of enthusiasm. "What's the matter? You're white as a sheet."

And I don't doubt I was.

"What? Oh . . . I'm just . . . so proud of you," I stammered, my voice more bewildered than congratulatory.

She wasn't buying it, and eyed me angrily from across the table, clearly disappointed that I wasn't happy. Then her expression softened somewhat and I saw that she understood, even before I did, and was sympathetic. She understood that I was happy for her but that in contrast to her I now looked even more pathetic than I had earlier that evening. It was our twenty-sixth birthday, and her stock was soaring through the roof while mine was about to crash through the floor. She was going to medical school and was going to be a doctor. My stoner twin sister, who had been virtually written off as a lost cause years ago, had just announced that she'd been accepted into medical school! I was unemployed and living with my parents. I had never in my life held a job that paid more than six dollars an hour, but had, nevertheless, amassed debts equivalent to the GNP of some third-world countries. If that wasn't bad enough I had a brother who had just gotten engaged and had just graduated with honors from law school. There I sat, numb, frosting dripping off my ear, trying desperately not to cry.

Through the swinging door separating the dining room from the kitchen I caught glimpses of my mother arranging the champagne flutes on a silver tray and folding a crisp linen napkin around the bottle. She looked over her arrangement critically and smiled, satisfied. Then, from one of the folds of her tunic, she pulled out what looked like a small compact and held it at a distance, evidently checking her hair and makeup in its small mirror. Again satisfied, she returned it to her pocket.

As I watched her, I thought about insurance, of all things, and wondered what would happen to her if my father suddenly died and left her no money, no insurance. How would she survive? I thought how the two of us were alike: excelling at esoteric hobbies, but when it came down to putting a roof over our heads or food on the table, what did we know? Oh, we knew all about organic herb gardening, and Georgian furniture, and innovative ways to make centerpieces. We knew the correct way to set a formal table for a variety of occasions, and what to look for when buying an artichoke, but what skills did we have that could be considered marketable? This was not so important for my mother, as she has an arrangement with my father—he is the provider and she is the homemaker.

That is what they'll put in her obituary, I thought. *Barbara Thomp-*

son, homemaker. And it's right that they should. She was remarkable as a mother, and had excelled at patiently nurturing and raising her children, excelled at taking care of her husband, at maintaining an elegant home, so who could begrudge her a few frivolous, expensive hobbies? She and my father are from a different era, and their marriage is different from the equal and independent marriages of today. She was a prize for him and he kept her like something to be treasured. In exchange, she bore him children, kept a beautiful home, entertained his associates, and kept him entertained. It was a good model for them, and one that had worked for thirty-five years. Unfortunately, I was realizing then, I had adopted their model in my relationship with Paul and it clearly hadn't worked. Paul had never wanted a dependent "wife" to support, but he did want me, so he put up with my expensive hobbies and my laziness. But instead of being grateful for his indulgence, I regarded him as stupid, gullible, and weak. A pushover. A patsy.

My parents' relationship was symbiotic, like the bird that rides on the rhino's back, picking off bugs. The rhino gets relief from the bugs and the bird gets food and protection—both the rhino and the bird benefit. My relationship with Paul was more parasitic: I was, as my father said, the tapeworm, happily feeding off of Paul while he stoically endured the considerable discomfort.

It would have been different if I'd been living off of him while I went to school or worked on writing a book, or tried to start a business, but the sad, pathetic truth is that I lived my spongy existence with him for no reason other than that it was easy. I did it so that I could work on building the body of Adonis, so that I could lounge around reading magazine articles about the British royal family, so that I could dabble in the art of French cooking. I did it so that I could exist as a noun and not a verb. I was a beautiful body, a warehouse of trivial information, a hothouse flower.

After toasting Carey's bright future, it was time for the two of us to open our gifts, which lacked an element of surprise, as we both knew they'd be nearly identical to the gifts we'd received on our previous birthday. From our father, we each got ten shares of stock in his company, and an inspirational book. The year before it had been Dale Carnegie's *How to Enjoy Your Life and Your Job.* This year it was *Grow Up! . . . Before It's Too Late* by Sister Melanie. As twins, we usually got something matching, and that year was no exception. Jay and Susan gave us each striped cotton sweaters that were supposed to look nautical but, in truth, looked more like prison garb. Twins were still a novelty to Susan, and she hadn't realized how stupid it is to give them the same clothes, especially since we only vaguely resemble each other. Nevertheless, the sweaters were an improvement over Jay's gift last year, which was nothing.

From my mother we each received a card that she'd made herself using coarse, fibrous paper and pressed wildflowers, containing a little coupon, which she'd also made herself, entitling the bearer to *One free afternoon of shopping with Mom*. In addition to this we each got a small box, which we opened to reveal an odd little video game.

"They are just the cutest little things," she cried, pulling one of her own (what I'd earlier thought was her compact) from the folds of her clothing.

"Mr. Matsumoto got one for me from his cousin in Japan and I sent away for two more. They just arrived today. Don't you just love when things work out like that?" She beamed, and then began explaining how they worked.

"It's just like having a baby in your pocket. Once you activate it, you start the incubation process, and that lasts for about two days. While that's going on you have to keep it with you all the time to keep it warm."

"It measures your body temperature?" Carey asked.

"Well, no, but a little beep goes off and if you don't respond, it lowers the temperature. If the temperature gets too low, it won't hatch."

"How interesting," said Susan, moving in for a closer look.

"Now did you say you ordered this from Japan?" my father asked, his brain analyzing the market potential.

"Yes, from Mr. Matsumoto's cousin. They're flying off the shelves over there. He really had to pull some strings to get even one, let alone two," she said proudly.

"Hmm," said Carey, returning it to its box. "I don't know that I'll have time for this, but what about next Thursday for shopping?"

"Now, careful . . ." my mother said, looking nervously at Carey's toy. "I just thought they might be like a pet for you two, since neither of you has one."

"Yeah"—Carey snorted—"a crying, beeping, baby pet that never gives you a minute's rest! If I'm going to invest that much time I think I'll wait for the real thing."

I myself was intrigued with the gift, but more by my mother's intentions in giving it to me. I had never really had a pet, or anything to take care of.

"What happens when it hatches?" I asked.

"Well, then you have a little creature."

She came over next to me and flipped hers open. She pushed a tiny button and a "little creature" materialized on the small screen. It was sort of a hybrid fowl-mammal and, like most things designed to appeal to Japanese girls, it was ridiculously cute, with large eyes and a small mouth that emitted a series of electronic chirps.

"That means it's hungry," she said. The whole family was hovering around us now, intent on the toy. She pressed a button, which quieted it, and a small bowl of food appeared on the screen. We watched it eat.

"There's another beep when it needs water and a different one when it needs its little poopies cleaned up, and even one when it just wants some attention," she said.

"What happens if you don't take care of it?" Jay asked.

"Well, I know you lose points, but I don't know what else. I couldn't really understand what Mr. Matsumoto was saying, what with his English and all."

I regarded the little thing thoughtfully.

"This might be good for me to have," I said, and felt my father's large hand pat me gently on the back.

WORK ETHICS

In three months a lot can and does happen. Three months is the duration of an entire season, it is the gestation period of the Chinese pug, and the amount of time necessary to navigate the Amazon River from beginning to end in a kayak. And yet, in the three months following my twenty-sixth birthday not much progress was made. Three months passed and I was still living with my parents, and not making enough money to change that fact. My creditors had quickly discovered my new address and felt free to call at any hour of the day or night with filthy threats and dire warnings of the harm that would come to my credit record if I failed to pay. My parents were annoyed by all the phone calls, and their suspicions were inevitably aroused. Suspicions that were confirmed one day when my father perused several of the monthly statements that I'd carelessly left lying on the kitchen counter. His reaction was a mixture of rage and disappointment, and for several days following the discovery he rarely spoke, just looked at me and shook his head.

It used to be that people feared sinning against God. Today we fear sinning against TRW or Equifax. The credit report has become the earthly book of Saint Peter, where a meticulous record of all past sins is collected. People still fear Judgment Day, but now it comes far more often than the biblical one, such as when you're at a restaurant and your card comes back declined, or when you try to get a loan and they pull up a long sheet listing how you made a late payment on your Visa back in 1981.

You may be asking yourself why, if I came from such a well-off family, and had such a wealthy lover, did I even think of gambling with credit cards. I'll try to explain, but like most stupid things, it doesn't make sense.

In college I'd had one credit card. "Only for emergencies," my father had said when he cosigned the form, and with that in mind I had rarely used it, charging a few nights out here, a few tanks of gas there, but not much else. The funny thing about credit cards is that they breed like rabbits, and soon I found I had a wallet full of little Visas and MasterCards and Discovers, and scarcely knew how they'd gotten there. I'd get such genial letters from the companies telling me, that because of my "sterling credit rating" I was now eligible for the gold card with a spending limit of five thousand dollars.

After college, when I lived with Paul, I rarely used my cards. At least in the beginning. We had a joint checking account, which he had packed with money, and I withdrew from that as I needed it. Paul was unaware that the job at the gym paid me no money—a fact that probably would have killed him faster than the light-rail, and one I hid by charging some things on my own. I withdrew about three hundred dollars a week from the joint account to cover living expenses. These "expenses" did not, of course, include rent, utilities, phone bills, car payments, insurance payments, or other mundane bills, which were all taken care of by Paul. No, the three hundred dollars was for shopping and movies and lunches with Andre—the real essentials.

This highly agreeable arrangement went on unquestioned for two years, but then for some reason Paul began to wonder why I never deposited a paycheck into the joint account. Usually I could pooh-pooh his suspicions away with a grin and some nocturnal gymnastics, but later, when he grew more insistent, I explained, with a straight face, that Fred at the gym was paying me cash under the table and so I didn't want to deposit it and leave a paper trail for the IRS to follow. Paul would believe this, I thought, since he, like all rich people, was always seeking new ways to keep his money out of the hands of the tax collector. He gazed at me doubtfully through narrow slits of eyes and said in an icy voice that if that was the case then surely I could cut back on the amount I had been withdrawing, and make do with an allowance, (he actually used the word *allowance*) of one hundred dollars a week. It was then that I really started to get into trouble. Rather than go out and get a better job, one that actually paid, I kept the one I had and started paying for things with credit. I bought groceries, meals out, books, magazines, CDs, clothing, sent flowers, etc., etc., and the more I charged the more inclined the kind people at Citibank and American Express were to raise my limit, or to send me more cards. When one card would reach its limit, I would transfer the balance to a new card with a slightly lower interest rate and start charging again on the freshly vacated card. I had colossal minimum payments each month, but in a vivid example of the snake feeding on its own tail, I paid these minimum payments with cash advances from the cards themselves!

But why did I do it, you are probably still asking yourself. Greed? Compulsion? Of course they both come into it, but they were fueled more by a skewed desire to fit in. To keep up with the Joneses. I felt different from the people who surrounded me: my superachieving family, my successful lover, our wealthy circle of friends. My charging was an ill-thought-out attempt at legitimacy, an attempt to make myself appear to be an independent person, one who could not only take care of himself but one who could do it with style. I was an impostor! I surrounded myself with all the perks of success: the latest mountain bike, the best ski equipment, the multi-CD car stereo, and oh so many clothes, ignoring the little fact that I had no income.

Honestly, I thought of the whole thing as a small loan that I would surely be able to pay off as soon as I got the vague job (with the high salary) that was surely waiting somewhere off in the gray future. But, as I've said, my life with Paul was comfortable and safe and there was little to spur me on to find this job. I was tired of trying to decide what I'd do, so I gave up and decided not to decide, telling myself that the best decision would come to me once I stopped trying to force it.

Shortly after my birthday dinner, my brother's fiancée offered to find me a temporary position through her firm. Not having any other immediate prospects I went down to her office bright and early one Monday morning, filled out the necessary paperwork, and took a typing and computer test. I then watched as the bemused test-giver looked over my results and my resume. I had neither work experience nor skills, and it was evident I'd be difficult to place. She repeatedly went into Susan's office and closed the door, returning with a knit brow to dig up some more possibilities on the computer. Finally her face relaxed into a smile.

"I think we've got something."

What we'd got was a job, ironically enough, for a credit card company, doing telephone authorizations. They had recently expanded their operations into Canada, and I got the job because I could speak French (although this was the kind of work they could have hired a French poodle to do). The work involved sitting at a cubicle desk wearing a telephone headset that would answer automatically whenever a call came in from a store or restaurant for an approval code. They have machines to do this now, but then it was still a job for human resources, of which I was one. When the line connected, I'd ask for a four-digit merchant number, which the other party would recite. I'd punch this into the computer and then ask for the card number and the amount of purchase, and then dutifully type them in. The computer would then make a decision (I imagined a tiny bespectacled woman, like Miss Jane from *The Beverly Hillbillies,* inside the computer poring over credit reports) either to grant an approval number, in which case I recited it to the merchant, or it would tell me in block capitals that the transaction was declined, and would sometimes even ask the merchant to confiscate the card. I felt terrible when either of these last two occurred, having been on the other end so often in the past three months. I envisioned the poor person waiting at the register, or sitting at the dining table, and the embarrassment they were about to be confronted with. But after typing in and spitting out numbers for eight hours, I became less sentimental and found that I barely noticed my responses. Approved, declined, whatever. It was monotonous, boring, mind-numbing work.

As for my coworkers, whom I'd see on breaks, or when they poked their heads around the cubicles during downtime, they were, for the most part, unskilled, uneducated women, late-middle-aged, most of whose husbands had either died or skipped town. There was a despair and a hopelessness about these women. None had ambition, none expected to improve their lot in life with their meager wages, so they pissed away the majority of it on the Home Shopping Network, or on the collector's plates and dolls advertised in the Sunday supplements. It was my fate to be stuck in a cubicle between two such women.

On my right, I had the craft-obsessed Doris. Her husband had died of cirrhosis of the liver, but before that he managed to gamble away everything they had, which was why she now found herself, at the age of fifty-five, in the basement of an office building doing temp work. She was a large bleached blonde (that particularly false color of blond that is a silvery white) who teased her hair mercilessly into a cap of cotton candy and then attached a girlish bow to the back of it. Her eyebrows were of her own creation and resembled nothing so much as the antennae of a large butterfly. Her upper body, which I could see whenever we leaned back to speak to one another, was very petite, but the first time she got up to go on her break I was shocked to see that her hips ballooned out and her legs had the circumference and solidity of an elephant's. I say she was craft obsessed because she was forever knitting, with various skeins of pastel yarn, little toilet tank cozies, and Kleenex box covers with dolls' heads, or attaching rhinestones in an elaborate pattern to some new piece of denim.

On my left was Rhonda, the chronic liar and conspiracy theorist, always certain that someone was out to get her fired or to steal her boyfriend, Rudy, whom none of us had ever met because he probably didn't exist, but who was, nevertheless, always buying her expensive jewelry or flying her off to Vegas for the weekend. She was sinewy and birdlike, with the gravelly voice of a smoker, and a penchant for vengeance. She loved to take the side of the woman scorned, and for that reason she talked incessantly about the scandals involving wronged celebrities: Princess Diana, Mia Farrow, Hillary Clinton, Whitney Houston, Lorena Bobbitt. All the famous women whose man troubles were regularly paraded across the weekly tabloids. She always sympathized with their plight and loved to comment on how their husbands should "fry" or "have their nuts cut off!" Then, rid of these cads, the women could find some Prince Charming who really loved them. I remember one time she was getting very heated about the plight of poor Sue Ellen she'd seen on a rerun of *Dallas* and I had to gently remind her, in reassuring terms, that Sue Ellen was a fictional character and surely wasn't really suffering all the indignities heaped on her by that scoundrel J.R.

At first I enjoyed their banter back and forth, and more often than not I would join in, as I too had been a longtime subscriber to *The National Enquirer*, and was familiar with the cast of characters. But in time I grew tired of hearing about the latest trailer-park catharsis that had been played out on *The Jerry Springer Show* (they both taped it), and found it difficult to feign enthusiasm for the new Erica Kane doll. It made me tired and a bit sad because I saw how these women adopted the troubles and triumphs of the stars as a way to fill the emptiness of their personal lives and the tedious monotony of their "professional" lives: heads trapped in cubicle desks, the phones automatically answering in the headsets, the impatient people on the other end spitting out numbers—all for six dollars and ten cents an hour.

Here was Thoreau's "quiet desperation" in all its pathetic detail, and

I was a part of it. I was miserable, and I was not even making enough to send the minimum payment on my credit cards, let alone enough to get out of my parents' house. My supervisor, a woman of twenty-five with four kids and a GED, assured me that if I stuck it out for ten months, I'd go far. They'd hire me on as a real employee, with health benefits and a higher hourly wage. Oh, boy.

In fact, the only thing that didn't actively depress me about the authorizations department was the one other man working there, Marvin, whom I immediately recognized as a fellow member of the homosexual tribe when I saw the walls of his small cubicle desk, which were plastered over with clippings of dead movie stars. Typical of most everyone working there, Marvin was overweight, and his huge expanse of ass barely fit on the chairs we were given. Although he was large and very masculine-looking, with his bull neck, Roman nose, and his perpetual five o'clock shadow, his feminine nature was betrayed by the nasally lisp of his speech and hands that he never seemed to know what to do with. We would meet on our breaks or lunch and found that we shared the common bond of widowhood, his lover having died the previous year from AIDS.

"That's terrible!" he said when I told him about Paul's unfortunate demise. "But you're lucky it was quick. Roger lingered on for two long years. Of course there was nothing left after that, no money, I mean. So here I am working in hag hovel."

We became allies in our miserable situation, talking endlessly about old movies and the eccentricities of our coworkers, usually in the privacy of the men's bathroom. In time, because of our association and our homosexuality, we became known as "the girls" by all the women we worked with.

I kept the job for nearly a month, which would try the sanity of any rational being, but then I could take no more. I arrived one Monday morning, slightly hungover from a night of drinking margaritas with Andre, and, after saying some hellos, took my seat at my cubicle. I looked at the screen and my headset, and realized I was going to have to sit there for the next eight hours. I shuddered and felt nauseous. I turned to go to the bathroom, and I truly intended to go and splash some water on my face and then return, but when I reached the bathroom I didn't stop. I continued on down the hall, then went up the stairs to the lobby, past the guard station, out the front door, and across the huge expanse of parking lot to my car. I knew my leaving like that was terribly irresponsible and would disappoint both Susan and my father, but so be it. I would call Susan and apologize, I thought as I started the ignition, and would find another job before I told my father. It would be that simple. I drove straight to my parents' house and left Susan a message on her home phone, thanking her for her help and apologizing for my hasty departure. She called back later that day and was nice, in a weary way.

"It happens all the time," she said, meaning people quitting. "Don't worry about it. The only problem is, we don't really have any other unskilled jobs right now."

I thanked her, said I understood, and hung up, the word *unskilled* still ringing in my ears.

I had lunch with Andre the next day, since, once again, I had time on my hands. I told him my troubles and asked him what he thought I should do.

"What should you do?" he asked in a tone that implied the answer was obvious. "You get back out there and find another job!"

"It's not that simple," I whined. "I can't do anything."

"Oh, girl, stop it! You are better than that. Look, I'm not one to blow sunshine up anyone's ass, but didn't you give me the same talk once yourself? Remember? There I was toiling away in housewares at Foleys, my many talents going unappreciated, and you said, 'Look, you're better than that; there's an opening at Louis Vuitton. You'd do so much better working there.' Remember? Well, I followed your advice and look what happened! I wasn't working there a month when I met Menachem, and where would I be today without him? Oh, I'd probably have made out fine, but life would certainly have been different."

Menachem was Andre's now deceased "boyfriend," whom he had met while working at the aforementioned baggage store. Menachem, an old Jewish widower who had endured two years in Dachau, a forty-year loveless marriage, and a life of hard work spent running a furniture empire and raising two daughters, tottered into Louis Vuitton one morning to find a gift for his granddaughter's bat mitzvah. He left four hours later with a small clutch purse, a wallet, a key holder, and a date with Andre for the following evening. Menachem was old, but he was at an age when he valued a sense of humor more than physical beauty, which is very rare, especially among gay men, although none of us, Andre included, was ever sure that Menachem was gay. Not that it mattered, as he was surely free from the grasp of sexual desire by then, and so cared little what Andre did with other men, as long as the majority of his time was given to him. They were an odd pair: a small, elderly Jew and a tall, flamboyant young black man, but anyone who spent time around them could tell they loved each other. Somehow they each satisfied the other's need for attention. They lived together for two years, and in the end, Menachem showed his appreciation by leaving Andre a sizable chunk of his fortune. Andre never revealed the amount, but it was enough to enable him to purchase a loft downtown, drive a nice car, and have a closet full to bursting with clothes.

It was difficult then for me to take advice from Andre because our lives, up until recently, had run on parallel tracks: neither one of us had worked much, both had acquired rich boyfriends early on, and both had been widowed. But there the parallels ceased. Andre had been widowed, but his lover had lavishly provided for him, whereas mine had left me with nothing. Ironically, Andre, who now had no need to work and could thus justify filling his days with shopping and museum visits and long lunches, worked longer and more diligently than he ever had before. I, on the other hand, pouted and bemoaned my misfortune and generally railed at the gods who were punishing me with this unlucky fate. I realized this then, as I sat poking at my food, and decided that maybe I should listen.

"What do you think I should do?" I asked humbly. He thought for a moment.

"Well, there's always waitressing."

"But I don't have any experience."

"Oh, please, it's not rocket science. You ever eat in a restaurant?"

"Yes, of course," I said, my humility ebbing away in response to his patronizing tone.

"Well, then you're qualified. You just take their order and you bring 'em food. Most of it's a beauty contest, anyway. If you're pretty to look at the customers will forgive almost anything. You'd be perfect."

"Have you ever done it?" I asked.

"Hello," he said sarcastically. "Like, I still do it. What do you think being a stewardess is? Nothing but high-altitude waitressing."

"I guess it's worth a shot."

"Sure it is! The money's usually not great at first, because they give all the good shifts and tables to the people who have been there longest, but if you can get in somewhere that's just opening up, the money can roll on in. Do you want me to help you?"

I thought about it and then nodded slightly.

We finished lunch and then went back to Andre's loft. He made a few "social" phone calls and found out that a new restaurant was opening next to the capitol building the following week. He then made a few more calls and got me an interview the next day.

"What should I say?" I asked.

"Girl, just go in there wearing some fierce outfit and smile a lot and be Mr. Friendly."

"But what should I say?"

"Whatever they want to hear, girl. Lie, lie, lie." And he shook his head from side to side as he said this. "They can't nail you for perjury. Tell them you're from Texas or somewhere stupid and obscure like that, so they won't call to check references. Then tell them the names of some of the restaurants you've worked at. Just make them up, something French maybe, or Italian, you know those names better than most people—just make it sound authentic. Also, tell them they've all closed—the restaurants, I mean. They're not in business anymore."

"This isn't going to work," I said, shaking my head.

"Girl! Don't be all meek! You need this job. You've got to make it work! It's all theater to get your foot in the door."

Reluctantly I went to the interview, which was with a wizened woman of indeterminate age called Madge, and her partner, Cecil, who had drooping shoulders and an equally drooping mustache. The restaurant was to be called Palladio's and would serve "upscale Italian food with an emphasis on impeccable service." I smiled and nodded as Madge spoke, trying to formulate a strategy. Earlier that day I had gone to a tanning booth and done a grueling chest workout, which I showcased by wearing a tight white turtleneck. I smiled unrelentingly.

"Tell us a little about your work history," Madge said, as she looked over my application.

Having rehearsed a few simple scenarios, I felt fairly confident, but nevertheless, nerves took over once I started talking, and I told a long rambling yarn about my most recent restaurant job. I told all about the happy days I'd spent working at La Maison de Poisson in Dallas, and about the owners, Marcel and his wife Michelle, and how they had sold the restaurant and moved back to Provence to while away their golden years. I should have stopped then but I didn't, and before I knew it I was out of control, telling stories of my last visit to France and how I'd stayed and worked on their vineyard and how they love me like a son because their own son, Jacques, was killed in a rodeo accident back in Dallas.

"Can you be here tomorrow at nine for training?" Madge interrupted.

"Uh, sure! You bet!" I said, and heaved a sigh.

"Good, we'll see you then."

I started training that Wednesday, and the restaurant opened on Friday of that same week. Predictably, it did not go well, and my service was anything but impeccable. Madge had done lots of advance advertising, so the first night we opened was a madhouse. I had seven tables in my section and, in some way, managed to screw up every order. I served dessert to a bewildered table of ladies who had yet to order dinner, and served dinner again to people who had already eaten. I stabbed myself with a corkscrew and bled all over another table, and I sloshed a drink in the lap of an unamused businessman. But that was just what happened to the tables I served. There were several in my section that I managed to overlook completely, and then grew paranoid thinking they were staring at me because I was doing such a bad job instead of just trying to catch my attention. I remember at one point droopy Cecil leaned over the bar conspiratorially and whispered, "You been smokin' weed?"

Had I smoked all the weed in Humboldt County I could not have done worse. We all did poorly that night, but I was by far the worst, and in our meeting at the end of the shift I was held up more than once as a scandalous example. And yet I found that Andre was right: I was good-looking, and that fact made people much more indulgent and forgiving. I just sat there in the break room, exhausted, grinning penitently when another example of my poor service was given, and everyone smiled over at me tenderly, as if I were a naughty puppy they didn't have the heart to spank with the paper. Further proof of Andre's theory was that in spite of my lousy service, my tips were quite good, out of pity, I'm sure, but also because I took the time to stop and speak to people and tell them some anecdote about Marcel and Michelle (who had now become quite real in my mind).

As cute as I was, or imagined myself to be, and as nice as Madge was, I was not cute enough nor was she foolish enough to allow me a repeat performance of my opening night, and the next week I discovered that I was scheduled only lunches. This was unfortunate, because few people bothered to trek up the hill from the offices downtown, and those thrifty

Scots who did enjoyed a ridiculously cheap lunch menu. My tips grew smaller and smaller, which did not help my finances. Everything I made at that point went to Citibank or Discover or Wells Fargo or American Express. I was assured, however, that the tips would improve when I got back on the dinner shift, which meant I had to prove myself worthy of being scheduled for the dinner shift. That wasn't likely to happen anytime soon, as my serving skills seemed to get worse instead of better over time. Each day was nothing more than another opportunity to accidentally smack someone in the head with the water pitcher as I pulled it back from refilling their glass, or to forget to give my orders to the kitchen, forcing a red-faced Madge to comp at least one meal every shift I worked. I was a mess, and I cursed Andre hourly for leading me to believe that it would all be so easy.

After the third week of this bedlam, Madge asked to speak with me after my shift. She waited until everyone had left and then sneaked behind the bar and pulled out a bottle of Beaujolais Nouveau and two glasses.

"They have this wine in Provence?" she asked, pouring me a large glassful.

I nodded, and launched into another tale. "It was the favorite wine of Marcel's first wife, Margot. She was in the resistance movement during the war, but was killed when she was caught trying to smuggle some files stolen from the Vichy government." (I'd stayed up late the night before watching the History Channel). "She was Marcel's first love, and the mother of his eldest daughter, Maria."

"Of course she was." Madge sighed, and took a big gulp of her wine. "Jack, Jack, Jack. Such a cutie."

I gave her my best *Aw, shucks* grin.

"I hate to have to do this," she said, "but I won't beat around the bush. We're going to have to let you go."

I panicked, thinking of my conversation earlier that day with Dwayne from Wells Fargo Bank, who suggested I get the money I owed on my Wells Fargo MasterCard by selling my plasma.

"If this is about Senator Paine's wife," I said, reassuringly, "my mother has a dry cleaner who can work miracles and I'm sure he can get—"

"Jack."

"—the stain out."

"Jack, it's not that. Actually I hadn't heard about that until right now." She groaned, closing her eyes and massaging them with her fingers.

"Look," she continued, "let's put the cards on the table. You're smart, you're good-looking, and God knows you can tell a good story, but in the twenty-five years I've been in this business I've never come across a crappier waiter. Cecil and I both knew you'd never done this before when we hired you, but we took a gamble anyway. No offense, but it hasn't worked out."

"Look." I was frantic. "I know I can learn. I'm getting better ev—"

"Jack!" she interrupted, sternly this time. "You are not cut out to wait tables. It's not the end of the world. You should almost take it as a compliment. You don't want to end up a bitter old crabby alcoholic like me, do you? You're young; move on. You'll find something else."

We finished the bottle of wine and talked for an hour, watching the tepid November sun pass over the dome of the capitol building. The evening waiters started coming in to prepare for the dinner shift, and I said good-bye to Madge, promising to come back and visit, but vowing privately that I never would. I stepped out into the cold evening, depressed by the thought of having to start all over again. December loomed on the horizon, which meant Christmas, and I had no money. Now I had no job. What would I tell my dad? What would I tell Dwayne?

6

S.I.L.V.E.R.

Job hunting, for the unskilled and uninitiated, can be a dismal, disconcerting task. I had been pampered and coddled for so long that actually having to go out and look for work, let alone do it, was like returning to Earth and trying to walk after I'd spent years floating weightless in outer space. I knew I had to do it, knew I could do it, but part of me kept fighting it. Not knowing how to start, I first drove around looking for help wanted signs in store windows. While that might work for high school students, it didn't take me long to figure out it was not an effective plan of action for me unless I wanted a retail or food job paying six dollars an hour, with no insurance. Insurance was the latest thing, my father had been harping on the importance of: "What happens if you break a leg or get multiple sclerosis? Who's gonna pay for that?" Next I started looking in the newspapers, scanning the Sunday employment section, circling all the jobs that looked promising enough to pursue on Monday morning. While that kept me busy on Monday, and sometimes on Tuesday, by Wednesday everything had dried up and I found myself again with time on my hands. Time on my hands and no money.

It's odd, but when you're qualified for nothing, you can imagine yourself doing just about anything. I would read job titles and descriptions in the paper and romantically slip myself into some interesting and colorful occupation like milkman, or a chimney sweep. I guess it's a sign of my lack of confidence that I never even thought seriously of doing anything with my degree. Granted, art history is not the most useful degree to have when looking for work (ranking right up there with Latin and philosophy), but I never even entertained the possibility of getting a job at a museum or a gallery, which is surprising, because I certainly spent enough time in them then.

When most people are between jobs, either they put all of their energy into looking for a new one, writing and rewriting résumés, networking, interviewing, etc., or they spend a lot of time on the sofa in the living room with the drapes drawn, eating cartons of snack cakes and watching reruns of *The Andy Griffith Show*. I would surely have headed down this latter path into the land of afternoon-TV zombies, except for the fact that my father was then doing most of his work from home and he never would have tolerated it. That being the case, I did two things: I worked out and I went to museums.

I worked out because, well, that's just what fags do. We are beauty and body obsessed, and hell, I'm no exception. I figured if the rest of my life was sliding downhill I might as well look good going down. So to speak. My attraction to museums was more individual. I loved museums because they appeared to me then like well-lit oases of order and organization, in which everyone spoke in hushed, reverent tones. So different from the mess that was my life.

After I got fired from the restaurant, I spent most of my days at one or both of these two places. Neither of my parents knew of my dismissal, so I had to get out and make it appear that I was doing something. My dad was furious when he discovered I'd quit the temporary job, so I knew he'd be less than thrilled to discover I'd now been fired. To avoid his wrath I decided not to mention it until I'd found another job. Then I'd probably tell him I'd quit because something better had come along.

Until then, I got up each morning and got ready for work, as usual. I ironed my work shirt in the kitchen while my father ate his breakfast and read *The Wall Street Journal*. I gulped down my own breakfast, making it seem I was full of purpose and in a hurry, and out the door I went. The problem was that I would get to my car and have no idea where to go.

That particular December day I worked out at the gym first and then went to the art museum. Before its last remodeling, the Denver Art Museum was especially well suited to hiding out. Each floor had a series of independent halls and rooms in which there were countless little niches and partitioned areas containing books and videos on different subjects. I could go into one of these niches and go undetected by the other museum patrons. There I could delve into a book on da Vinci, watch videos on the lost wax method of bronze casting or Amish quilting techniques, and be completely transported away. I could read up on Chinese-export porcelain and Peruvian inlaid furniture, or the history of artistic representation of the Virgin Mary. Some days I just sat for hours watching Andy Warhol movies. The time-wasting possibilities were varied and seemingly infinite, and, since I was expanding my trove of esoteric knowledge, it was hardly a waste of time!

I showed Paul's pass at the entrance that day and took the elevator to the fourth floor. I took a place in one of the burgundy niches in the Spanish Colonial section and began idly flipping through the pages of a book on Frida Kahlo. A few moments later I detected something bright out of the corner of my eye and caught a faint smell of marijuana. My head bobbed up but I was too late to see anything. I sat up to see more, but my view into the larger hall was narrow, and was further blocked by some large glass display cases.

The glass cases were full of silver trinkets from South America and were arranged in a large square, leaving a small room in the center. In that room, I knew, there was a chair and a small desk, and I gathered that whoever had passed by was now sitting at the desk probably reading the small book that rested there. It was a blank book with a pen tethered to it by a string, in which museum visitors were invited to add their thoughts and recollections about silver—a gimmicky thing, probably designed to silence claims that the museum is elitist by adding something interactive. It is not a very interesting book, but can be funny to look at, as it is full of misspelled vignettes about Aunt Mable and how she always served the holiday turkey on a big silver platter that she had painstakingly polished, or some dumb little Girl Scout song comparing friendship to precious metals. As I said, it is a silly book—a judgment I feel highly qualified to make, having spent the better part of an afternoon reading it in its entirety.

I heard low chuckling and strained to see through one of the glass cases. My view was obstructed by the silver pieces, but I made out the legs of the chuckling person, who was seated at the desk. At first the legs appeared to be those of a Catholic schoolgirl, since all I could make out were dark stockings and a short plaid dress. Then the body shifted a bit and I noticed that the legs were not stockinged at all, but hairy, and sheathed to midcalf in a pair of heavy black combat boots. One of the legs appeared to be tattooed with a representation of dinosaur vertebrae, which circled all the way up the thigh to the hem of what was, on second glance, a kilt.

I was staring intently at this when suddenly I heard the book slam and saw the body rise. I was startled and my book slipped to the floor with a bang. I recovered it quickly, opened it, and stared at it intently, not wanting to be caught. I was too late. The kilted one came out from behind the cases and stood staring at me, saying nothing. In the awkward moment that followed, in which he obstinately stared at me and I obstinately stared at my book, I grew suddenly conscious of the whir of the building's ventilation system and the loud ticking of my watch. I felt my face redden as I stared blankly at the wild pictures in the book, hoping he would move on. Finally he did, turning and walking with heavy footsteps toward the elevator. I waited until I heard the ping announcing the elevator's arrival before looking up. He was still staring right at me, and I noticed that his short hair was an inky shade of black, much darker than his goatee, and that on his hands he wore white cotton gloves. Our eyes met for an instant; then he stepped onto the elevator and was gone.

A few minutes passed, during which time I stayed seated until I was sure he wouldn't be returning. Then I got up, calmly returned my book to the shelf, and walked as casually as I could into the silver room. I sat down in the chair, looked around to see if anyone was watching, and opened the book.

On the last page were some small, haikulike poems, written in lush cursive by a Mrs. John Trumbull, all using the letters from the word *silver.*

> *Spring*
> *Is*
> *Lovely.*
> *Violets*
> *Everywhere*
> *Round.*

Went the first.

> *Some*
> *Icebergs*
> *Leave*

Vessels
Evidently
Ruptured.

Went the next, and the rest got progressively sappier as one's eyes moved down the page. Until the end, that is, where another one had been scrawled in crude, block capitals, evidently by the kilted visitor.

Shitting
In
Lunch boxes
Violates
Every
Rule.

I laughed out loud and then quickly looked around to see if anyone had heard me. I tried to think of my own haiku, and I studied the silver goblets and crowns and ornate platters surrounding me, hoping to draw some inspiration from them, but alas, the muse wasn't with me. Or rather, she was being held hostage by my creditors, because the only words that came to mind were financial and terribly prosaic:

Surcharge
Insurance
Loans
Visa
Employment
Repossession.

STUFFED ANIMALS

In retrospect, I should not have gone shopping. (How many times have we all said that?) It gave me the worst case of buyer's remorse, and, had I not gone, the whole mess later that night could have been avoided. Hindsight again. If only I had ignored my mother's invitation and gone on with my day as usual—working out, driving around aimlessly, hiding in museums, movie theaters, or malls, I never would have been exposed.

Or would I? I suppose exposure was inevitable. No lie, no matter how elaborate, could hide the truth forever. The calls from collection agencies were becoming more frequent and more insistent, and they had no sympathy for my lack of employment. No, the truth was bound to come out, and yet, given time, I could certainly have orchestrated its debut a little better. Could have dressed it up and put a more favorable spin on it. But I was still young and naive and careless then. Hardly the spin doctor I am today.

If I'd known then what I know now, I would certainly have handled things differently. When my mother stepped into my room, tiptoed over to the bed, and whispered in my ear, "They're having a huge sale at Nieman's today!" I'd have been much more firm and resolute in my resistance. I would have lied and said, "Ah, Mom, I'd like to, but I have to work," or I would even have told the truth and said, "Ah, Mom, I don't have any money and my Nieman's card is maxed out." But as I was ignorant of the consequences my actions would have, I opened one eye and said, without a moment's hesitation, "South entrance, say, two o'clock?"

"By the men's shoes?"

"Exactly."

"I'll be waiting." And she rose and tiptoed from the room as stealthily as she'd entered.

As much as I yearned to get to Nieman's early, before everything had been picked over, I decided that since my mother was still ignorant of my unemployment, it would be prudent to put her off until afternoon, when I could pretend to be coming off the lunch shift.

I looked at the clock. Eight-thirty. Time to start the day's performance. I got up, yawned, stretched, and looked longingly back at the rumpled bed. *Must be disciplined,* I thought, and tried to shake the sleep from my head. I threw on some clothes and a ball cap, ironed my work shirt in the kitchen—in full view of my father—and then stuffed it in my bag and went to the gym. There, I ran for half an hour on the treadmill, did a grueling leg workout, and then loitered in the empty locker room, shaving in the steam room, trimming my nails, styling my pubic hair, anything to pass the time until two o'clock. Finally I got dressed and went and ate a huge breakfast at a café nearby, lingering over my coffee and the new edition of *Colorado Homes and Lifestyles.* When I'd exhausted that I still had three hours to kill, so I drove east across town to the Natural History Museum.

I love the Natural History Museum and greatly prefer it to the neighboring zoo because, well, because it is a place to view nature at its most obedient. There is no smell, and the animals are never hiding away in corners of their cages or sleeping in their little dens, but are always perfectly visible in their quaintly "natural" settings, usually displayed in a scene of high drama from their abbreviated lives. Gazelles leap away from some unseen predator, and monstrous grizzly bears stand on hind legs, teeth bared and claws ready to strike. Mountain goats teeter precariously on a tiny cliff, and a rhino, kicking up dust with its front hoof, seems poised to charge.

When I entered the museum that day, I instinctively avoided all of the dinosaur bones and gemstones and the IMAX movies, all so popular with the screaming kiddies, and took the long escalator to the darker upper floors, where the peaceful dioramas of the Canadian Rockies and the African plains, the South American rain forests and chilly Antarctic, never failed to transport me, momentarily at least, far, far away.

I went to the third floor that day, to the African section, because it was somewhat pathetic and small, and, consequently, one of the most infrequently visited. It was also one of the dustiest, which could be excused, I suppose, if one were to imagine Mt. Kilimanjaro, painted in the pastel shades of morning on the back wall, having recently erupted.

I walked around briefly, enjoying the feeling of soreness in my legs from my workout, and then, as was my custom, I went and sat on the bench next to the entrance. From that spot, if I remained very still, almost as still as the animals, my presence went undetected by other visitors and left me free to watch the peculiar activities engaged in by the other museum patrons.

This was more entertaining than it sounds, because when people think they are alone they become very uninhibited and interesting to observe; they scratch indiscriminately at their crotches or carry on little conversations with themselves. Children invariably go under the velvet ropes designed to keep them out of certain sections and, since the dioramas were not then covered by glass (a fact that has recently changed), some people, quite a few people actually throw coins into them, as if they were some sort of idolatrous wishing well.

On this particular day, I seated myself opposite an exhibit of lions, which is a favorite of mine, largely because it is such a mess. Oh, the arrangement is noble and lovely (a mother lion lies surrounded by playful cubs, while the father lion stands on an anthill looking off across the plains), and the animals are beautifully stuffed, with no visible signs of mange or bullet holes. But then there are the eyes—large, soft, almost dewy eyes that one would never associate with any lions outside the studios of Walt Disney. My theory is that the taxidermist must have run out of lion eyes when he was stuffing them, or maybe he just didn't know what a lion's eyes looked like, because the ones he used were surely meant for a kinder, gentler animal such as a deer or a cow. This ocular mishap, combined with the lions' majestic poses, makes an amusing contrast and causes nearly all passersby to look twice, and sometimes to comment out loud, which is what I was hoping for that afternoon.

I had been sitting silently for about half an hour opposite this friendly pride, listening to the people's reactions as they stood before it, absently picking their noses, or removing stale gum from their mouths and depositing it on the wall. In that time I had counted three "Will you look at thats," and two comments about the dust, and then the hall was empty again, and remained so for what seemed a very long time. I was getting bored, and had just gotten up to move to another section when I heard footsteps approaching. I hunched down again. A moment later, a figure dressed all in black entered the room. At first, because of the darkness and because of his white hair, I thought it must be an elderly man, but this was soon disproved by the quickness and agility he displayed as he strode quickly and purposefully up to the lions. Unlike the previous patrons, he said nothing, but stood very still, and seemed to be studying them closely and writing some notes down in a notebook he was holding. He wrote furiously for about five minutes, looking from his page into the diorama and back again, and sometimes he seemed to be sketching. When he had finished he shut the notebook and tucked it under his arm. He glanced around slowly in all directions, and then, seeing no one, he placed both hands on the railing and hopped into the diorama. He stepped carefully, so as not to upset any of the savanna grasses, and made his way up the small incline to the group of lions. When he reached them, he examined the adults briefly, but seemed especially interested in the cubs, poking and prodding them and examining their stitched-up stomachs and stiff paws. He smacked the back of the female lion, raising a cloud of dust, and gave a slight sniffle, of contempt or allergies I wasn't sure, and then scribbled some more notes in the notebook. When he'd finished, he closed it again, put the pen behind his ear, and walked down to the railing. He peered over the edge cautiously, looking to the left and to the right, and then placed the notebook under his arm once again and vaulted out. He landed squarely on both feet, the sound of his heavy boots on the floor echoing loudly through the hall.

He looked around nervously. Seeing no one, he made his way quickly over to the hyenas, a pack of which was staring hungrily at a herd of water buffalo painted on the far wall. I couldn't actually see into this exhibit from my vantage point, but because I was a frequent visitor, I knew what he was looking at. His procedure at this diorama was the same: some quick notes and sketches in the notebook, a quick look around to see that the coast was clear, and then a hop over the bar.

Gone to the dogs, I thought, as I watched him disappear. I heard some rustling and a thump now and then, and at one point he poked his head out to see if anyone was coming, but then he disappeared and didn't vault back over. I was curious, and my curiosity won out over my patience, so I left my bench and walked over to the hyena display. I approached stealthily and stopped just outside the circle of light coming from the diorama. In the shadows I knew I was quite invisible to him, but I nearly betrayed myself with a gasp when I realized that he was the same guy I had seen last month in the silver room. His hair and his gloves were a different color, but the dark goatee and the thick brows were unmistakable. He looked up when he heard me, but after a moment, hearing nothing more, he resumed stuffing one of the hyena pups into a small duffel bag and then zipped it shut. He set the bag on a small termite mound and started rearranging the diorama to conceal his theft when suddenly the bag started rolling. His eyes grew wide as he watched it tumble out of the diorama. He dove to grab it but missed, and fell facedown with a thud. I leaned forward, into the circle of light, and slowly picked up the bag. His jaw dropped as his eyes followed the line of my arm up to my face, and for a moment we regarded each other wordlessly. Before either of us could say anything, a stern voice rang out.

"Sir," it said, and I quickly turned to look. I saw a figure approaching through the darkness but couldn't make it out from my position in the light. I moved outside the circle and saw that it was the obese museum security guard, slowly wobbling toward me from the entrance, her long braid swinging from side to side. She almost never came up to this floor, but probably wanted a break from all the baby-sitting she surely did downstairs. I thought of running, but then regained my composure and casually flung the duffel bag over my shoulder and gave her an open, questioning look. Out of the corner of my eye I could see and hear the hyena-napper scurrying around trying to conceal himself, and I feared he might panic and make a run for it. The guard was almost to the point where she could see into the diorama, and I could only surmise what would happen if she caught him in it and me holding a bag. I cleared my throat noisily and took several steps toward her.

"It's the bag," she said tersely, pointing to the duffel bag. A shiver went through me, and I started sweating.

"The bag?" I asked, looking at the strap on my shoulder.

"You can't carry that around," she said. "You'll have to put it in one of the lockers downstairs."

"Oh, yes." I sighed, relieved. "Yes, of course, and, uh . . . where . . . are the lockers . . . ?" I asked, trying to sound ignorant.

"Downstairs," she said impatiently. "By the gift shop."

We stood facing each other, she waiting for me to move on, and I waiting for some idea to roost in my brain. I realized that if I was going to be any help at all to my endangered friend I needed to get her out of there, but I could think of nothing and didn't want to get in trouble myself, so I thanked her and walked briskly toward the escalators, leaving him to fend for himself.

I wondered about him as I went out to my car and drove the short distance to the mall, but after five minutes in Nieman's, dazzled by the smell of new leather shoes, he and the bag in my trunk were all but forgotten.

Later that evening things got ugly. I'd gone straight from the museum to Neiman's and shopped with my mother as planned. Our spirits were high as we pulled up in the driveway and began unloading all the purchases, with the exception of the hyena pup. As I lumbered toward the house with my bags of new clothes I saw the drapes move in the upstairs office and knew my father was watching. He'd picked up some clients at the airport that afternoon and was not supposed to be back until late that evening, but evidently there had been a change of plans. I knew it was bad to have him see me with all of the booty, as he had undoubtedly been fielding calls all afternoon from my creditors. I looked at my mother and could tell by her sick expression that she had seen the drapes flutter, too. We both knew we were in trouble, so without a word we hurried inside and hid the bags in the utility room closet.

At the dinner table that evening my father sat silently while my mother and I chattered on and on about the teahouse and how pretty it was, and the greens she'd used in the salad and how delicious they were, and the weather and how nice it was, and anything else we could think of to keep the conversation light and fluffy and away from the subject of shopping. Then, as I did every night at dinner, I threw in some fictional tales about the restaurant. Mundane things really, like how many tables I'd had, or how one of the customers had been rude—stories that usually merited nothing more than a polite nod or an "Oh, really?" from my father. This time, however, he paused in his eating and set down his knife and fork. He shifted in his chair, wiped his mouth with his napkin, and leaned toward me.

"So how is the job, Jack?" he asked, and something about his sardonic tone tipped me off that there was more behind this question than what he was asking.

"Uh, fine, I guess. Tips could have been better, but you know how it goes," I said carefully.

"It gets pretty busy at lunchtime, doesn't it?" he said. I nodded, took a sip of my water, swallowing it with difficulty, and set the glass down slowly. I had a pretty good idea where this was going and I didn't like it. I avoided making eye contact with him but could feel his gaze boring into me as I poked at my chicken breast.

"Boy, I'd sure say they're busy!" he said heartily. "Line almost around the block. I wish I'd made a reservation, because I took some clients there today and we had to wait almost twenty minutes for a table. I tried to catch you this morning before you left to see if you could make one for me, but you were in an awful hurry. Didn't want to be late for your shift, I suppose."

I said nothing but looked straight at him, defiantly, my jaw set. Why didn't he just come out with it? Why did he have to string me along? He looked down at his plate and pushed the vegetables around with his fork.

"I spoke to your manager," he said. "Madge, is it? Nice woman. Straight shooter, like myself, doesn't bullshit. I liked her."

He paused, took a bite of his food, and chewed slowly. When he swallowed, he calmly took a sip of water and continued.

"I told her I was your father and she really lit up. Evidently she's very fond of you, which was good, because like I said I was with some important clients and she ushered us right in past the crowds and gave us a great table by the window. Beautiful views of the capitol building, don't you think?"

I said nothing. I looked to my mother, who was chewing contentedly, clearly at ease now that the conversation was in what she perceived to be less treacherous waters.

"Then, Jack, I'll admit," he said, giving a sarcastic laugh, "I got a little confused. Madge gave us our menus and asked me 'How is Jack, where's he working these days?'" He took another bite of food and poked around on his plate. My mother looked up, perplexed.

"Maybe you'd like to explain," he said calmly. The long silence that followed clearly indicated that I did not wish to explain, so he went on.

"Madge told me you'd been gone almost a month, which I don't mind saying surprised me more than a little, because I've been sitting in that kitchen every morning watching you put on one hell of a show!"

I looked down at my plate, trying to decide if the truth was worse than any fiction I might create. The silence went from being tense to just annoying.

"I got fired," I said softly.

"Wanna tell me why?" he asked, knife and fork poised for the kill.

"Because I'm a shitty waiter, all right?" And I threw my napkin on my plate. I took a deep breath and tried to remain calm. My heart was pounding and I was shaking. They regarded me silently, clearly expecting more.

"Look," I said, trying not to sound whiny and not really succeeding. "I've been trying really hard to find something else. I've been going through the paper and going out and looking every day. I'm sure something will come along," I said as lightheartedly as I could, "but I just haven't had any luck yet." Even before that last sentence was out of my mouth I realized that I'd said the wrong thing. I hoped he hadn't caught it, but his reddening face confirmed my fears. My father is a great believer in self-determination and the belief that we can all rise above the myth of fate to shape our own destinies. For that reason, when I casually mentioned "luck" and things "coming along" he saw me handing responsibility for my life over to some nonexistent deity, and that was very bad.

"It's not about luck!" he shouted, slamming his silverware down on the table. "It's also not about spending the whole day shopping with your mother spending money you don't have!"

"Steen, please."

"No, Barbara, this has gone on too long!" He stood up and threw down his napkin. "He's twenty-six, for Christ's sake, and he's been spoiled rotten his whole life. First by us, then by Paul, and now by us again! This is not doing him any good. If he's ever going to learn to fly on his own we've got to stop spoon-feeding him and take off the training wheels!"

I looked back down at my plate and bit my lip hard. To laugh then, or even to crack a smile, would have been fatal. It was not unusual for my father to get this angry, but his ire was more often directed at the IRS or a rival sports team than at me. This time I knew it was bad, as it had been smoldering in him since his lunch at Palladio's. Seeing my mother and me pull up and unload a large portion of the Neiman Marcus men's department only added fuel to the fire. I had read enough of the Sister Melanie book he'd given me for my birthday (which I kept, appropriately, in the rack next to the toilet) to recognize, in spite of his mixed metaphors, that he was giving me her tough-love platform. I thought of pulling a teenage move and rolling my eyes, or fleeing from the room in tears, but something kept me rooted. Maybe some masochistic desire to be ridiculed, maybe embarrassment, definitely fear.

"I've been thinking about this all afternoon," he continued to my mother, "and I hope you'll back me up on what I'm about to say."

I could feel his gaze on me, so I continued to look down at my plate, realizing there was no escape. I'd have to sit there and take it.

"Son, we both love you very much," he said, "but you have abused your privileges, and I'm afraid you must suffer some consequences."

"But, Stee—" my mother started.

"Let me finish!" he cut her off, sharply banging his fist on the table. He took a breath and continued looking at me. He smoothed his hair back with his hand, trying to regain his calm.

"We agreed, after Paul died, that you could live here until you found a job and got back on your feet. Well, you've found three, and quit or gotten yourself fired from all of them, knowing all the while that you had a safe place to hide away at the end of the day. Worst of all, you lied to us about it," he said, his voice choked with that horrible tone of disappointment that is far worse than any anger he could possibly have vented.

I nodded meekly and tried to explain, "But Dad, come on, I have tried, it's just taking a little—"

"No 'buts,' Jack," he said sadly, and fell back onto his chair. "By this time next week you need to find a place of your own."

A shudder ran through me.

"But I don't have any money," I whined, regretting my *but*.

"I know that," he said, becoming very matter-of-fact. "I am aware of that and I have a plan."

I was not eager to hear it.

"Your mother and I will give you—do you hear me, *give*, not loan— the first month's rent and the deposit on a new place. In addition, we will give you one hundred dollars, but that is it!" he said firmly. "You are on your own after that. We have given you our home for the last I don't know how many months and you've done nothing. You've lied to us. It breaks my heart to do this, but that's the way it's got to be; you have abused your privileges and you cannot go through your whole life without paying the price."

My mother ran from the table in tears. My father watched her leave, shook his head, clearly trying to formulate something more to tell her later, and then gave me a withering look and walked out himself, leaving me alone. I closed my eyes and tried hard to imagine Sister Melanie tied to a stake and surrounded by burning copies of her books.

JACK HITS THE ROAD

And so I left my parents' house. My mother and father fought about it, but in the end she could not wear down the zeal of Sister Melanie's convert, and after a while even she began to believe that it might be for the best. Nevertheless she stuffed a check for two hundred dollars in my pocket as I was leaving and said it was payment for all of the work I'd done on the garden and the teahouse. She also took me shopping again, much the way her parents had taken her shopping, for the things needed to furnish an ugly apartment comfortably. I'm afraid I also charged a bit more on my own credit cards for some vertical blinds and bath linens, which I justified by the fact that I had finally found a job working in an espresso bar downtown. Unfortunately, I was fired the following day because I had forgotten to set my new alarm clock and overslept on the first morning I was to open.

The apartment I found was near a park in a turn-of-the-century building. My father said he would pay no more than four hundred dollars, which limited things considerably, but since I wasn't working I had no shortage of time to spend looking at places. The building was not bad, but my limited budget forced me to take a ground-level unit with a lovely view of the garages and dumpsters in the alley. It was quite a step down from my parents', and quite a leap down from Paul's, but it was something I'd never had before: a place of my own.

Until college I'd lived in my parents' house, and then at college I'd lived with roommates. Then came Paul's house, which was just that: Paul's. But this little room, with the layers of paint over layers of wallpaper, and the square-plate light fixtures, and the weak shower, was all mine. Granted I was not the one paying the bills, but I was going to be, and that meant I could do whatever I wanted. I could come and go as I wanted, could eat when and what I wanted, could hang whatever pictures I wanted, and could even hang those pictures in the nude. It was fabulous! And fabulously, depressingly lonely, as are most first nights in a new apartment, which is why I quickly invited Andre over.

He arrived at seven-thirty and brought a case of red wine as a house-warming gift and a Pet Shop Boys disc that he had borrowed from me some months ago. He was clad in black pants and a black turtleneck, and over this he wore a smartly tailored houndstooth jacket. His hair was neatly styled in silky waves and he wore large tortoiseshell sunglasses, which he lifted to his forehead as he assessed the space from the doorway, reluctant to enter. I could see him scanning the defects: the hideous, worn linoleum in the kitchen, the poorly mounted ceiling fan that shook and whirred threateningly, the prehistoric appliances.

"I know it's not great," I said, "but I suppose I'll have to get used to it. I'm poor now, remember?"

"Now, girl, I didn't say a thing." He stepped lightly into the kitchen and looked around cautiously, as if he'd just entered a construction zone without a hard hat.

"It's . . . cute," he said. "In a bohemian way. It suits you. I love the sofa and the lamps." And he moved over to where they sat in the middle of the room and examined them closely.

"You're not that poor," he said, "if you can afford these."

"I am," I protested. "I have Mom to thank for those."

He nodded and laughed.

"Barbara always comes through."

And indeed she had. I started out with just a bed and a TV and a desk from their basement, but when she was done shopping I had a new sofa and end tables, two leather club chairs and a coffee table, and two table lamps and a floor lamp. There were new dishes and kitchen items, a cedar-lined chest full of sheets and blankets, and a potted fig tree (which soon died from light deprivation). All of these things had either been dropped off when I was gone or had been delivered, with little notes saying that she was thinking about me, or that she hoped my job hunt was going well. I gathered that my father had told her not to see me or speak to me until I'd been on my own for two months, since that is what Sister Melanie recommends in her second book, *Making Adults out of Unruly Children,* in order to foster the idea of independence. That was fine, except for the hurdle of Christmas, which, much to my father's chagrin, presented itself during my two-month banishment—a hurdle he cleared by taking my mother on a vacation to Barbados for the holidays, leaving us kids to celebrate on our own.

Christmas that year was dismal. No fancy gifts from Paul, no gourmet meal painstakingly prepared by my mother. Instead I got a crappy CD from Carey, and ate take-out Chinese with my brother and his Jewish fiancée.

Andre and I decided on a pizza, and I went across the hall to phone in the order. When I came back I found him standing in the middle of the room nervously eyeing the ceiling fan. I shut it off.

"This isn't so bad," he said, stepping out of a pair of black suede shoes and stretching out his lanky frame on the sofa. "It's dark, but it'll be fine until you get on your feet. I bet the rent's cheap anyway."

"Mmm," I said vaguely, uncorking one of the bottles of wine and pouring out two glasses.

"What do you mean, 'Mmm'? What are you paying for this?" he asked with a grand sweep of his arm.

"Four hundred plus utilities," I muttered quickly, taking a huge drink from my glass, pretending to study the back of the disc.

"Hmm, four hundred plus utilities, let's do the math," he said, counting on his fingers. "You have rent, you have utilities, you also have the cost of a new phone hookup, car insurance, gas, food, miscellaneous spending money, and of course all of those little credit card payments. . . ." He stopped counting and looked at me. "Now, sugar. Sweetie. Don't take offense at what I'm about to say, but are you going to be able to afford all this on your coffee-shop wages?"

"I'll be fine," I said, still staring at the disc. My eyes stuck on the song title "How Can You Expect to Be Taken Seriously."

"Giiirrrlll . . ." he purred, meaning *Cut the bullshit.*

"No!" I snapped, slamming the disc down on the table. "I probably would not be able to afford it on my coffee-shop wages, but that's sort of a moot point now because I don't have any coffee-shop wages anymore."

"What?" He swung his feet back to the floor and sat up.

"I got the ax again."

He covered his eyes with his hands and slumped back down into the couch. "Oh, no, girl, no," he groaned.

"Oh, yes, girl, yes," I said. "How do you think I feel? I can't even hold down a six-dollar-an-hour job."

We both emptied our glasses and filled them up again. I took another sip and then calmly confessed all the horrible details of my situation. I told him I'd been using my credit cards to pay my bills but that almost all of my cards were now maxed out and I had exactly seventy dollars in cash, twenty of which was going to pay for the pizza we'd just ordered. I said I was relieved the phone hadn't been hooked up yet because if it had, it would surely be ringing night and day with inquiring calls from my friends at Citibank.

He listened to my sob story attentively and reacted with all the melodramatic gasps and hand gestures I'd come to expect from him, but when I'd finished, and we were digging into the newly arrived pizza, he was surprisingly matter-of-fact.

"Well," he said, wiping his mouth on one of the new linen napkins, "desperate times call for desperate measures, that's my motto."

"What?" I asked, confused. He chewed slowly, pouring us both more wine.

"Girl, did I ever tell you about my uncle?"

"I think maybe a little," I said, remembering only that Andre's mother had died when he was very young and that after that he'd been bounced back and forth between foster families and his only living relative, Uncle Billy, A.K.A. Miss Shanda Lear—transvestite and heroin addict. I'd known Andre since high school, where we had the academic misfortune of being lab partners in a physics class, but in all those years he had rarely spoken of his past. I recognized his question as a rare opportunity to discover something about it, but wondered, nevertheless, what it had to do with me.

"You know my past is not my favorite topic of conversation, so I'll make this as short as possible. As much as I hate to say it, you and old Miss Mess have quite a bit in common." (Miss Mess being Andre's term of endearment for Billy/Shanda.)

"How's that?" I asked, somewhat offended but still intrigued.

"Well, you both have tastes that run well beyond your means to afford them, and you always neglect the everyday things like food and keeping a roof over your head."

"I don't see how—"

"I don't think I'd finished speaking," he said in a curt manner that reminded me unpleasantly of my father.

"Now Miss Mess was just that—an irresponsible, drug-addicted mess—but it's a funny thing about addicts; they're not stupid, and before those kind people from social services carted me away I was able to learn a few things, which I'll now gladly pass on to you, if you'll take them."

I nodded, albeit tentatively.

"First," he said, "you need to learn how to work the system. If you've been fired from a job, which happened to Miss Mess on a regular basis before she gave up working entirely, and which has even happened to me a time or two, then you are eligible for unemployment. Unfortunately, the law has changed now and you have to be employed for a minimum of six months to collect, so that might not work for you. Darn. Next time try to stick it out a little longer, if at all possible. It can be very profitable."

"Thanks," I said sarcastically. "I'll keep that in mind."

"Well, okay, you can't collect unemployment. There are other programs you can take advantage of."

"I don't think I need—"

"Girl, don't interrupt," he said sternly. "I'm trying to help."

"But I'm not—"

He held up a hand to silence me.

"The food stamp program was another one that Miss Mess used with great success."

"Food stamps!" I cried indignantly, and was again silenced by the hand, accompanied this time by lowered eyelids and a disapproving shake of the head. Only when I had been silent several seconds did he resume speaking.

"Now Miss Mess rarely used her stamps for food; in fact she was shooting so much smack at the time and eating so little that she got down to a size six, which helped her do a wicked Diana Ross, if nothing else."

"So what did she do with the stamps?" I asked.

He smiled and leaned forward till he was perched on the very edge of the sofa. "Aha," he said, "that's the crafty part. She sold them. On the street. Fifty cents on the dollar."

"And used the money for drugs," I said gravely.

"Hell, no!" He laughed. "She had a budget. She used the disability check for drugs. The food stamp money was reserved for new wigs and shoes and an occasional Donna Summer album. Now I don't think you could pull off a disability," he said, running his eyes over my body looking for possible handicaps, "so we'll probably have to throw that on the heap of useless options, right next to the unemployment. Anyway, girl, my point is that there are ways to work the system until you get back on your feet. I'm not necessarily saying you should take it as far as Miss Mess, but I do think it's worth considering. Middle-class pride will get you nowhere."

"Thanks, but no thanks. I'm sure something will come along and it will all work out," I said with a confident tone that was fooling no one, least of all me. I wanted to dismiss Andre's suggestions as ridiculous. *Things aren't* that *bad,* I thought. But in that moment I saw how they could be. I saw how quickly my precarious financial situation could break loose and tumble downhill, and that scared me. I quickly changed the subject.

"This wine's delicious," I said, uncorking the second bottle and scrutinizing the label. "Where did you find it?"

A few days later I met Andre for lunch at a restaurant in Cherry Creek. It was notorious for its expensive decor and its bad food, but in spite of that, it was currently *the* place to be seen, and being seen was always high on Andre's agenda. It was a turn on the old "If a tree falls in the forest . . ." idea, but in this case, to paraphrase Andre, "If you go out to lunch and no one sees you, for all intents and purposes you don't exist and might as well have stayed home alone and eaten a sandwich." I had come at Andre's invitation, which implied, I hoped, that he intended to pay. However, if this was not the case, I was fully prepared to write a hot check to cover my share.

Having arrived at twelve-fifteen, the time appointed for our meeting, I sat waiting for nearly twenty minutes until Andre finally strode in, looking tall and striking in an olive green sweater and black sunglasses. It was in this public environment that Andre thrived, going from table to table making small talk, exchanging bits of gossip, doling out compliments. He didn't remove the glasses when he came in but raised and lowered them as an accessory of expression while working the crowd, elevating them only when someone said something intensely interesting. It was a good way to gauge the juiciness of the gossip: if it was a boring table the glasses never went up, whereas if the speakers had tales to tell, they went up and down like a seesaw. He was twenty minutes late when he entered the restaurant, but this rounded out to a full half hour by the time he finally reached our table.

"You're worse than a politician," I said in mock disgust as he approached.

He smiled proudly, sat down, and flattered me by removing the glasses altogether and placing them in a shapely leather box. He snapped it shut and set it on the table between the salt and pepper shakers and a small vase of daisies.

"You know you're going to forget them," I said, "and what will that make, four pairs this year?"

"Girl, don't I know it, but don't you worry." He gently patted my hand. "I won't forget this pair—they're Mizrahi, and I'm quite attached to them. Not to be mean or anything," he added, leaning forward and scrutinizing my face, "but you might think about getting a pair yourself."

"Me?" I asked. "Why?"

"Because you look like a basset hound with those circles under your eyes."

"I haven't been sleeping very well," I said, and wasn't it the truth! If I wasn't taking calls from creditors I was lying awake all night worrying about them.

"Obviously," he said, "that I can see. I can also see by the way you're popping out of your shirt that you are evidently spending all of your waking hours at the gym."

"It's the only thing that relaxes me." I shrugged.

Our waiter arrived.

"Can I bring you guys something to drink?" he asked.

"Yes, please, Tom, you look fabulous today," Andre schmoozed. "Are you still sculpting?"

"Yeah, I am." He smiled, surprised that someone remembered he was something other than a waiter. "I'm actually gonna have a show in July at Southend."

"That's great, great," said Andre. "I'm on their mailing list, so I'm sure I'll hear about it, sugar. Say, what was that new white that I had last time? It was sort of *je ne sais quoi....*"

"I think you mean the fume blanc."

"Yes, that was it. I'll have a glass of that."

"Okay, and for you, Jack?"

I considered my empty wallet, and the grim prospect that I might have to pay.

"Nothing, thanks, just water."

"He'll have the same," Andre said suddenly. Tom looked at me. I looked at Andre, who lowered his eyelids and reached across the table and patted my hand. "Trust me, girl, you'll probably need a drink when you hear what I've got for you. He'll have one of the same, Tom."

I nodded my assent, figuring that if I was writing a hot check anyway there was no real reason to be frugal, and Tom walked away to fill our order.

"That Tom has the most beautiful hands." Andre sighed. "It's too bad he makes such god-awful sculpture with them."

"So what's this news?" I asked, hoping it did not in any way concern me. I was not eager to listen to another one of his brilliant schemes to find me a job, or to milk the system.

"Is this something we're going to celebrate, or is it news that will merit something stronger than wine?"

Andre puzzled for a moment, twisting a large silver ring around on his finger.

"Hmmmm," he mused. "It's really nothing—remember that; it's really nothing. It's just an opportunity that presented itself, and I thought you might want to take advantage of it."

"What is it?" I asked, unable to hide the dread in my voice.

"Now, I don't want you to be offended by any of this. You know I adore you and I just want what's best for you. In a way I'm just the messenger, so remember, don't kill the messenger. I promised I'd ask you."

"Ask me what?" I was trying to remain patient but knew that he was going to drag this out.

"Like I said, it's an opportunity. Remember that. I know you've been looking to, how shall we say, improve your lot in life, so when this came up I thought of you."

"So this is an opportunity?" I asked skeptically, visions of Amway and Mary Kay popping up in my mind.

"Yes," he said. "And you know I thought of you first."

"Uh-huh. Why me?"

"That's a good question," he said, "and I know I have a good answer to it somewhere. I thought of you because I . . . well, because I know you've been going through a rough time lately with Paul's death, and the jobs, or lack thereof, and I think this might help you out."

"I don't think I like this . . ." I said, crossing my arms on my chest, my suspicions mounting. "You're sounding tricky. You'd better just spit it out."

He leaned back and looked at me, offended, almost wounded. I didn't buy it and shook my head.

"Oh, all right," he said, giving in. "Just don't get mad, okay? It's just that someone I sort of know has expressed an interest in you, and, well, I think enough time has passed. I think . . . well, maybe you should think about dating again."

"Dating!" I shouted. "And maybe you should think about minding your own business. That's the 'opportunity'? A date! Christ, the last thing I need—or want—is a date!"

I was lying, of course, and I'm sure that fact was glaringly transparent to him.

"Girl!" Andre hissed, looking around nervously at the other tables.

"And why would I need you to find me one? Like I couldn't find my own date. Is that what you think?"

I realized people were staring, so I lowered my voice and leaned forward.

"I have not ever, nor do I now, need any assistance in finding a date."

"Well," he said, unsnapping his case and putting his sunglasses on again. "Smell her. Nothing like making a scene, is there? Forget I mentioned a thing."

"I'll try."

"Good."

"Fine."

We studied our menus in hostile silence. Tom returned with our wine.

"Did you open a new bottle?" I asked, looking at my small, half-empty glass.

"Yeah, of course."

"Good. Then let's not let it go to waste. Bring us the rest."

"You want the bottle?" he asked, excited at the prospect of a bigger tip.

"Yes."

"We do?" asked Andre, surprised.

"We do," I said, scowling at him across the table.

"Well, all right then. Whatever will make princess happy. Let's hope they take Visa, or if that doesn't work, Discover, or Amex. . . ."

Tom disappeared again with our new order, and we glared at each other from time to time over our menus until Tom came back with the wine.

"I gather you have someone in mind," I said, still looking down at my menu, a tinge of bitterness in my voice.

"We're not talking about it, remember?"

"You might as well tell me who it is," I said.

"Why? So you can throw another tantrum?"

"Look, I'm sorry," I said softly, pouring him some more wine. "I'm just a little touchy about some things lately. I haven't been sleeping well."

"Oh, I know," he said, his voice softening, "and I didn't mean to piss you off. I was trying to explain, before you flew off the handle, that it's not really a date."

"I'm sorry," I said. "I won't do it again. Who is it?"

"Do you really want to know?" he asked coyly. I nodded. Tom returned.

"Ready to order?"

I did so quickly, but Andre, as usual, lingered annoyingly over the menu.

"Is that made with field greens or Bibb lettuce? Hmmmm, salmon does sound good, but is that fresh or frozen? Grilled or blackened? Can I get the haricot vert instead of the potatoes? Oh and some water, please, Tom."

Finally Tom went away and I looked at Andre, exasperated.

"Who is it?" I asked.

"What? Oh, that." He sighed, feigning disinterest. "Well, he happens to be very wealthy."

"Okay. Good. So what's wrong with him?"

Andre raised his brow and considered the question.

"That's a toughie," he said. "It's hard to know where to begin."

"Is he married?" I asked.

"Oh, God, no. I think he may have been, once upon a time, but probably not."

"Uh-huh, how bad is he?"

"Let's just say he's not very pretty."

"Who is he?"

"I don't think you know him. I barely know him. His name is Frank Glory. Affectionately known to his small circle of friends as 'Hole.'"

"Hole?"

"Hole."

"You're right; I don't know him. Who is he?"

"Well," said Andre, leaning closer to the table, warming to the subject. "He happens to be one of the hundred richest men in Colorado, according to *Mile Hi* magazine, although I'm sure they were a little reluctant to publish that fact."

"And just what business is 'Hole' in?" I asked. Again Andre raised an eyebrow and looked around. Then he leaned forward and whispered.

"Here's where we get into murky waters. He owns a sort of chain, you know, retail stores."

"Retail stores?"

"Yes, out of which he sells a variety of merchandise: magazines, books, clothing, and accessories, all, uh, sort of pertaining to sex."

"Oh, no!" I groaned. "You mean he owns porn shops!"

"Twenty-seven of them, to be exact, spread over nine states."

I rolled my eyes. "And just why, exactly, did you think I'd be interested in him?"

"Now, girl, let's keep a tight rein on that temper. I never would have thought of you except that, like I said, he's been watching you for a while. He thinks you're pretty and he wants to get to know you, but he doesn't really want you for your body."

"Oh, he doesn't? Well, that's flattering, I guess. A wealthy, ugly man who works in the sex trade has admired me from a distance but doesn't want me for my body. This opportunity is sounding better all the time. What *does* he want? Someone to clean his house? Someone to man the cash register at one of the twenty-seven stores, or maybe I'd be a regional manager."

"All right," said Andre, fed up. "I think that's enough. You're getting offended, and there is no real reason to. Sometimes you are so suburban. Can't you step out of that middle-class mentality for just a minute? I've tried to be diplomatic in my presentation, but get a little wine in her and she turns into a spitting cobra. To be as clear as I can be," he said, taking a deep breath and placing both hands palm down on the table, "he does not want you for sex. He does not want you to do retail. He does not want you to work for him at all, really. He wants you for . . . well, I'm not really sure, but I don't think you have anything to worry about."

"Oh, you don't?" I cried. "And why's that?"

"Oh, lord, I'm not setting you up with Jeffrey Dahmer, for Christ's sake. Look, Hole has heaps of money but he's not pretty, and he doesn't have many friends."

"So that's where I come in? Friend of the friendless?" I asked. "I fail to see the opportunity here."

"Of course you do, girl," he said, patting my hand condescendingly. "Doesn't surprise me. Middle-class mentality. If the opportunity isn't dressed in clothes from Target and driving a taupe minivan you wouldn't recognize it. The opportunity is that he's willing to pay you to be his companion, and girl, if anyone needs money right now, it's you."

I mulled this over in my mind. Andre sipped his wine. Neither of us spoke for several minutes.

"How would it work?" I asked.

"Good question. Like a tulip in the springtime, her mind has finally opened. All the details haven't been worked out, but I was thinking he would of course pay for the cost of whatever we did that evening, maybe give you a clothing allowance, and then some sort of monetary compensation for your time. Not an hourly rate or anything, kind of leave it up to his discretion."

I was amazed that he had thought it out so thoroughly.

"What do you mean, 'we'?" I asked.

"I mean I'll help, of course, and will take him out on some of the evenings, but you can keep all of the money."

I smiled and looked up at Andre, who had put his sunglasses back on.

"If I didn't know better, I'd say that was something like a nice gesture on your part." And I tried to catch his eye.

"Girl, of course it is," he said, waving his hands in the air flamboyantly and then flipping me off. "I'm full of nice gestures."

"How did you meet him?" I asked.

"Another good question! I guess I'll have to tell you the truth, because I can't think of a good lie on such short notice. I know him from one of his shops, which I used to frequent when I was dating Menachem, who was not, bless his old weak heart, a dynamo in bed. I needed some things to, how do you say, stimulate my imagination, and Hole's little stores cater to people with needs like that. Now, in one of those cruel twists of fate, the little smut peddler lives in my very building, and I guess he's seen you come and go, or seen us out together, whatever. He pitched the idea to me one day at the mailbox. It's not a big deal, really.

I know it has the faint whiff of prostitution, but it's not really; he just wants company."

"And you're sure I won't have to bend over in order to help him?"

"Yes. He made it very clear that no sex need be involved unless you wanted it to be, and believe me, girl: you wouldn't want it. He's seventy if he's a day, and like I said, he is *not* pretty. But I was thinking, maybe we could help him with that, too. Sort of make him over. Help him get some better outfits going, get rid of that frumpy hairdo."

"A makeover?"

"Exactly."

GAME PLAN REVISIONS

Shortly after my dismissal from the coffee shop and my lunch with Andre, I decided to forget about welfare and the idea of becoming Hole's companion. Instead, I set my sights firmly on acquiring Burl as my next boyfriend. Not as a life mate, mind you, but as a transition—a stepping stone on to someone better. That sounds calculated and cold, I know, and it was, but I didn't see it that way at the time. I was frantic and frightened and was not thinking of anything but how I could save myself. Burl would be the branch I'd grab to pull myself out of the whirlpool of debt I was being sucked into. He was hardly an ideal savior, but I decided I might as well put all my faith in him because at that point (as I sat in the cruel light of a Saturday morning, the Visa, Discover, and Nordstrom's bills in my lap, all screaming for attention, and Andre's frightening suggestions swimming in my head) Burl seemed the most accessible person with money. And money was what I needed above all else. With that in mind I came up with hundreds of reasons why he'd be the perfect boyfriend: he was rich, he had a nice house with lovely appliances, he was smart and could be quick-witted, and in dim light he was not all that bad-looking. Never mind about his acute alcoholism, his obnoxiousness (both public and private), and the fact that he is more lust-driven than a fourteen-year-old boy. I would be a settling influence on him, and his money would enable me to settle and stop feeling panicked all the time. I could buy some time to figure out what I was going to do. No more whiling away the carefree days as I'd done with Paul. No, I'd taken a sip from the bitter well of poverty and it was enough to know that I wanted no more. This time around I'd be good. I'd be grateful. I'd get a job and start thinking seriously about school or a career.

My strategy for conquest was two-pronged: First, I made myself available socially, which was hardly difficult, for who could possibly have had more free time than I. Burl was never one to dine at home, and for that reason he was always on the lookout for a dinner companion. I slipped easily into this role, ready at a moment's notice and in need of meals wherever and whenever I could get them.

Second, I submitted to everything he wanted to do. Of course this included sex, although it's probably unfair to say I submitted to it, for that implies it was against my will, and that was hardly the case. Burl was by no means my type, but what with Paul's death, and living at my parents' place, opportunities for sex had been few, and consequently I was much less discriminating than I'd been in the past. Nor was Burl a demanding lover. In fact, I was the one who usually initiated sex when we'd return to his house, but my efforts were rarely rewarded with anything more than a sloppy kiss before he'd roll over and pass out.

The sex was actually the easy part; it was trying to keep up with his social life that nearly killed me: the drinking in dive bars, the rounds of parties, the tedious business dinners—at which I played the role of "nephew," the golf games and tractor pulls and drag races—all of which I endured, an enthusiastic smile plastered on my face. Burl loved the cigar and martini revival that was then in full swing, and we spent hours in bars catering to those fetishes, talking politics or watching televised sports, which would have been fine if the night had ended after that. It rarely did. The martinis and cigars were just appetizers for the rest of the evening, which usually led to a wine-soaked dinner and then dancing shirtless to incredibly loud music in an after-hours bar with a bunch of club kids. The kind of evening I enjoyed when I was a kid. The kind of evening I even enjoy now, from time to time, but when it was a nightly ritual, as it was with Burl, it did tend to get stale. Stale or not, I needed the money, and that was the one thing about which he was not remiss. It was never really mentioned between us, but in the morning when I got up and got dressed I always found that sometime the night before he had stuffed at least fifty dollars—usually a hundred—in my pants pocket. I wanted to feel bad about it. Felt I *should* feel bad about it, but honestly I didn't. The nights out on the town were work, so I felt I was justified in seeking compensation. Yet at the same time I realized that if I wanted to stick to my plan and convince him I was serious about becoming his boyfriend (which would of course lead to moving in together and opening another joint checking account), I'd have to start declining his money.

The idea was that this noble gesture on my part would convince him of the purity of my intentions, would show how I loved him for himself and not for his money. It was a risky gamble, especially considering my financial state, but one I was convinced would result in high profit, so, the next morning as I put on my pants, I removed the money from my pocket and placed it in plain sight on his bedside table. For the rest of the week I followed this same procedure. After the first few days, once he realized I hadn't dropped it and he stopped restuffing it in my pocket, my plan seemed to be working, and I thought I detected in his eye a tenderness and an affection that had not been there before.

This all changed rather abruptly when I came over to collect him one Sunday morning for a brunch date. I had not seen him the previous night, as I'd gone skiing the day before with my brother (his treat, of course) and was so exhausted after driving home that the prospect of drinking and dancing into the wee hours seemed unbearable. I begged off, made some excuse, and told Burl I would see him the next morning a little before eleven.

It was all blue skies and sunshine when I came to pick him up, and I pulled up in front of his house between his big silver Mercedes, which looked like Helen Keller had parked it, and an enormous red station wagon. I rang the doorbell several times and was not surprised when there was no answer. I was sure he had not spent the previous night at home with a good book, or made it a Blockbuster night, simply because I had stood him up, so I fully expected to have to rouse him. I tried the door. It wasn't locked, so without hesitation I went in. After all, we were practically boyfriends, and it would only be a matter of time before he gave me my own key. Disco music was playing faintly in the background, and I was pleasantly surprised to hear the sound of the shower coming from the master bathroom. I followed the trail of clothing, which was laid out night after night, since Burl usually started undressing as soon as he got out of the car or the cab. It was not unusual to find shoes and the odd sock on the walkway leading up to the house. The trail took me to the bedroom. I pushed open the door gently, and peeked in. All the blinds were open and the sun was streaming in.

Maybe he had made it an early night, I thought tenderly. I knocked on the bathroom door and pushed it open a crack. A cloud of fragrant steam wafted out.

"Morning, Burl," I called sweetly. "It's me. I'm a little early so don't rush. We're supposed to be there at eleven, which means if we make it by eleven-thirty we'll be fine."

I went back in the bedroom and sat on the edge of the bed to wait for him to emerge from the shower. I thought briefly about joining him, as a sort of surprise, but I was already dressed and ready, and as I looked at my watch I saw that if he hurried we might actually make it by eleven-thirty. The shower stopped and I heard the glass door snap open and then shut again.

"I apologize about last night," I called, "but we skied really hard, and traffic was terrible on the way down, so I really would have been a wet blanket. Where did you go?" I asked, examining a matchbook from Palladio's on the bedside table.

He mumbled some response, made unintelligible by the towel, and I realized he must be hungover. I'd never known him to rise this early on a weekend.

"How 'bout a drink before we go?" I called. "A little hair of the dog to get you going? I can make a great screwdriver if you've got any orange juice."

Not waiting for a response, I got up and went to the kitchen, grabbing a bottle of Stolichnaya from the living room bar on my way.

Burl's kitchen was an epicure's dream: an enormous, eight-burner Viking stove, granite countertops, German appliances, and glass-front maple cabinets—all of which went unused since he never ate at home. *That will all change,* I thought as I stood examining the meager contents of the refrigerator. There was a big jar of maraschino cherries, a smaller one of cocktail onions, some rotting containers of Chinese food, and a bottle of Coke that was surely flat because the lid was missing. I closed the fridge and looked in the cabinets. Eventually I found an ancient jar of Tang and improvised a screwdriver from that, making Burl's mostly vodka and mine mostly Tang. I went back to the bedroom, drinks in hand, and came face-to-face with a towel-clad man, smiling slyly, who was clearly not Burl.

"Who are you?" I asked, frightened, the drinks sloshing onto the carpet.

"Relax." He laughed, pointing to the dripping glasses. I hastily set them on the dresser and looked around for something to wipe my hands with.

"I was on the swing shift," said the toweled one, and he gave me a wink. "Burl said you'd be coming by for him today, but I don't think he's going anywhere for a while." He nodded toward the bed. I looked at him and at the bed and then charged over to it and whipped back the down comforter. There was Burl, flat on his back, right next to where I had been sitting. His walrus body, clad in nothing but a very unflattering floral thong, was sprawled, spread-eagle, on the mattress. He flinched only slightly from the light, rolled onto his side, and emitted a long, rattling fart. I threw the comforter back over him and looked accusingly at the stranger.

"Who are you, and what are you doing here?" I demanded, although this last part was a wee bit redundant.

"Dude, relax." He laughed. "It's okay."

He turned around, dropped the towel completely, and slipped on a pair of boxers he had picked up from the floor. His body was lean and smooth, except for his legs, which were quite hairy and up one of which crept a tattoo of a dinosaur skeleton. I didn't make the connection immediately, because the hair on his head was now a peculiar shade of ruby instead of black or white, and of course because I was more than a little distracted by his nakedness.

He turned around again and introduced himself, clearly not remembering me from either one of our previous encounters, although that really wasn't surprising, since he had hardly gotten a good look at me on either occasion.

"I'm Ray," he said. "You've gotta be Jack. Burl said you'd be here this morning and for me to wake him up about ten-thirty, and dude, I did try, but he's out for the day, I think. We didn't even get back here till almost seven and—shit!" he cried, grabbing my arm and twisting it to look at my watch. His hand looked surprisingly dirty for someone who had just emerged from the shower. "I have to meet my next guy in half an hour."

He followed the clothing trail into the living room, picking up select items and putting them on as he went. I followed and watched, dumbfounded, as he got dressed. I wanted to say something but couldn't, and was alarmed to notice that I was becoming aroused.

"You look familiar," he said, dropping his pile of clothes on one of the white sofas and picking out a shirt and a pair of socks. "You been working Denver long?"

"What?" I said vaguely. I was confused by his question, yes, but also by the mere fact of his being there, and the gold rings that sparkled from his right eyebrow and his navel were mesmerizing.

"Denver," he repeated, hopping into a pair of black jeans. "You been workin' here long?"

"I don't . . ." I started to reply but then hesitated, still unsure what he was asking. Anger and curiosity and an odd desire competed for dominance in my head . . . and below my belt.

"That Burl"—he chuckled, pulling a tight, green velvet T-shirt over his head—"sure can put it away. He dragged me all over town last night. We ended up at Amsterdam dancing with all the pretty boys. Not really my crowd, but the music's good and it made Burl happy."

He picked up his own watch and looked at it.

"Shit!" he said, and ran back to the bedroom. I followed, feeling angry and wanting to say something but not knowing what exactly.

"So how long you say you been here?" he asked, eyeing me curiously. "I know I've seen you around. Do you have an ad running?"

"Look," I said, collecting my wits and rolling them up into a hard ball to throw at him. "I don't know what you think, but—"

He pulled back the covers of the bed and shook Burl. I paused, intent on what he was doing. Burl's body jiggled on the bed but he didn't wake. He shook him again.

"Burl!" he yelled, very close to his ear. Burl's eyes opened momentarily, rolled in their sockets, and closed again.

"He's out," said Ray with a shrug. "Guess there's only one thing to do."

He propped Burl up slightly in bed and pulled the comforter up, securing it under one of his chins, and kissed him on the forehead. He then picked up Burl's pants from the floor, pulled the wallet from the back pocket, and started removing cash.

"You can't do that!" I cried, and moved to grab the wallet away from him. He turned away quickly.

"Sure I can," he said. "I'm taking two hundred, which I think is fair, since I got him home safely and stayed all night. Now, he was too drunk to really do anything and he won't remember much of it later, but that's not my fault, and I did stay all night."

He stuffed the money in his front pocket and handed the wallet to me.

"You might as well take yours now, too, unless you wanna sit around all afternoon until he wakes up."

"Look!" I hissed, snatching the wallet away. "I'm his friend, not some . . . some rough trade he picked up for a wild night. I think you'd better get out of here. I'm just his friend, okay? I don't take money for being someone's friend."

He gazed at me, his amusement evident in his green eyes. He pulled on a suede jacket, removed a pack of cigarettes from an inside pocket, and lit one. He was suppressing a laugh, but one snorted out as he exhaled. He headed for the front door. I was enraged to the point of speechlessness now but I followed him nonetheless. When he was halfway down the front walk, he turned and gave a wave with his blackened hand and another condescending wink. I shot him a nasty scowl and slammed the door.

I stood for a moment, fuming, but then leaned forward to the peephole and watched his distorted body as he made his way down the walk and got into the red station wagon. When he'd gone, I stood for a minute in the foyer and then wandered back to the bedroom. I looked at the cigarettes and ashtray on the bedside table, at the wet towel on the floor, at Burl's snoring head poking out from under the covers. I stood in the same spot for at least five minutes, considering. I was astonished, insulted, embarrassed, intrigued, and more than a little confused.

Eventually I walked over to the dresser and set down the wallet. I picked up one of the drinks and took a sip. Mostly Tang. I set it down and picked up the other. Mostly vodka. I took three or four giant gulps, enjoying the burning sensation as the alcohol rolled down my throat and into my stomach. Three more gulps and the glass was empty. I picked up the other glass and then walked calmly over to the bedside table, where I picked up the dirty ashtray. I then looked around the room for any other dishes and, seeing none, I went to the kitchen. There I emptied the ashtray in the trash and the glasses in the sink, and then put them all in the dishwasher. I then walked back to the bedroom, picking up Burl's clothes as I went, and laid them all out neatly on the chair by the window. I picked up the wet towel from the floor, used it to wipe up the ashes on the table and the drink rings on the dresser, and then carried it to the bathroom and put it in the hamper. Returning to the bedroom, I fluffed Burl's pillow and propped him up somewhat so that he wouldn't choke on his vomit if it came to that, and straightened the comforter so that it covered his feet. I was going to leave, but I hesitated, and stood staring out the window for a good five minutes. I walked over to the dresser and picked up the wallet. Then, as nonchalantly as I could, I went over to the window. With one hand I twisted the blinds shut, while with the other I deftly removed two fifties from Burl's wallet.

After all, I thought, *we did have a date.*

I slipped the wallet back in the pocket of his pants and took a quick look around. Satisfied, I left the bedroom and went out the front door to my car.

DESPERATE MEASURES

The day after the ill-fated brunch I got up early, resolved that my life would be different. I went and worked out and then actually went to a job interview at one of the newspapers for a data-entry position. The only requirements were fair typing skills and some knowledge of computers. Since I had neither, I lied on the application, thinking I'd charm my way through the interview and be able to learn what I didn't know once I got the job. I hadn't anticipated the skills test that they use to weed out the people like me who lie on their application, and for which they handed me a number as soon as I entered, telling me to wait in line with the other applicants, of which there were many, all looking more competent and skilled than myself. I didn't waste their time. Instead, I left the building and walked toward Andre's loft in lower downtown.

Andre had left the day before on a weeklong trip to Australia and we had arranged beforehand for me to bring in his mail (a staggering amount of magazines and catalogs) and water the plants. In return, I could use his phone and voice-messaging service until mine was hooked up, which, at the rate the phone company was moving, would be sometime in the next millennium.

I took the elevator to the fourth floor of the loft, went in, and promptly helped myself to what was left in the kitchen. After much hunting, I found a dry bagel and a small can of orange juice, which I took over to the sofa and ate while I checked messages. I dialed the access number.

You have three new messages. To listen to your messages, press one.

First message, sent Sunday at three-twenty-two P.M.

"Hi, Andre, It's—"

Message skipped. Next message, left Sunday at six-nineteen P.M.

"Jack-o! I hope this is the right number to reach you. I thought we were goin' to brunch, son. Hee hee hee. Hope I didn't spoil your plans none. But hey, if you're interested in dinner, in say, about an hour, get back to me. It's about six-fifteen now. You need to get yourself a pager or somethin'. Maybe a cell phone. Toodaloo."

Message erased. Next message, sent Monday at eight-oh-nine A.M.

"Hello? Hayley Mills calling Hayley Mills. This message is for Jack. Just checking to see how my evil twin is doing. Call me. Love ya. Oh, I almost forgot; you might wanna call Mom. I guess her little Nintendo bit some virtual dust. She's a wreck—more so than usual, I mean. Call me."

Message erased. End of new messages. To listen to your messages press one. To send a message press two. To disconnect, press the star key.

I should have hung up. Hindsight again. I should not have been nosy and listened to Andre's message, so I'll admit I have only myself to blame for the torment it caused me, but who, put in a similar situation, would not do the same thing? It was like reading postcards; you didn't want to be seen reading someone else's, but if no one was around it was completely acceptable. I pressed one.

First skipped message, sent Sunday at three-twenty-two P.M.

"Hi, Andre, it's Michael. I know you're out of town because I just came from brunch with Jack and he told me you're in Australia. Say hi to Olivia for me. Ha, ha. Anyway, I just wanted to call and say hi, and give you the latest on your friend Miss Thompson. Well, a bunch of us met for brunch at the Dome and he shows up at like one o'clock, looking all moody and tough in his sunglasses, and chain-smoking. I mean, when did that start? Anyway, Christian, the little bitch, asked him why he didn't bring Burl. As if we didn't *know* why! That lush hasn't seen a Sunday morning since he turned twenty-one, and he was seen by just everyone the night before making quite the spectacle of himself on the dance floor of Amsterdam with a guy who looked like Satan. Anyway, Jack just blew up, girl. I wish you could have seen it. Said he wasn't 'that drunk pig's keeper' and went on and on about fags and how catty and slutty we are. Uh, hello! I felt like saying, 'Look in the mirror, Becky, we're not the ones who have been screwing the drunk pig. We are not the shameless gold-diggers who drove our boyfriend to jump in front of a train!' I'm guessing he and Burlina had a fight, which is good, because I'll be the first to agree that Burl Crawford is one disgusting unit. Jack could do much better. God knows somebody's got to take care of him. Poor thing, just doesn't know what to do without Paul. Anyway, he settled down after a few mimosas, but he didn't eat a thing, and kept getting up to go out and smoke. It was too weird. Then he just left without saying good-bye, leaving a fifty on the table—which was a relief because we were all dreading another awkward moment with the credit car—"

Message skipped. End of messages. To listen to your messages press one. . . .

A cold, sick feeling settled in my stomach and I sat there stupidly holding the phone. Numb.

To change your personal options, press four. To disconnect, press the star key.

I leaned back on the couch and stared up at the billowing clouds as they rolled past the skylight. The loud squawking of the phone startled me and pulled me back down to earth. I hung up the receiver absently and sat very still on the couch, too embarrassed to move. I knew I was alone but I felt I was being watched, and if I didn't move maybe I'd become invisible. Maybe I could just squeeze myself down into the cushions of the couch and hide with all the lint and small change.

I'm not sure how much time passed. I remember sitting up and pounding the cushions with my fists, then getting up and pacing the room, alternately fuming and crying. In retrospect I think I was having a kind of breakdown, because I remember finding myself seated on the floor, staring at the wall and just groaning. I lit a cigarette and looked out the window at the trains coming and going from the station across the street.

To change your personal options, press four.

If only it was that easy, I thought, and wished I was a passenger on one of those trains, heading off into the mountains. Off to start my new life in a place where no one knew any of my dirty secrets, my failings, my flaws. A place where I could start over with a clean slate. Get my life in order. Get a career going. Get a decent place to live. Not be such a mess.

Of course I had no idea where this friendly Nirvana of high-paying, fulfilling work and beautiful apartments lay. Nor did I have any money to pay for the ticket to get there. And who'd want to take trashy Amtrak anyway? No, if I went, I'd be romantic about it and stow away. Boxcar

Jack, ridin' the rails. Boxcar Jack, the spoiled hobo, the lazy bum. *Bum.*
I considered the word. The politically incorrect name for the homeless
alcoholic. It had a quaint, almost folksy sound to it. It was a word my
grandparents used when talking about politicians and deadbeat dads,
and I realized, with horror, that it now applied to me. My parents
weren't talking to me because I was such a bum. My friends were talking about me for the same reason, and I was wooing a fat, middle-aged
alcoholic who was more of a bum than me but who was, nevertheless,
not interested in me. I lit another cigarette, inhaled deeply, and exhaled
with a despairing sigh worthy of the best tragedian actress. I got up and
headed for the refrigerator, where I'd seen an open bottle of wine. I was
starting to cry and could feel myself sliding down the slippery tube of
self-pity. I gave in to it and took the bottle over to the couch, not bothering with a glass, in accordance with my bum status. I turned on the
TV, figuring I felt pathetic already, so why not make it worse?

Jeannie was locked in her bottle by Major Nelson. Click. Samantha
was serving martinis to Larry and Louise, while Darrin argued with Dr.
Bombay in the kitchen. Click. Aunt Bea was fixing lunch for Opie.
Click. A soap opera. Click. Pine-scented cleaner. Click. Truck-driving
school. Click. The Home Shopping Network (where the tables have
been turned and the commercial has become the entertainment). Click.
A talk show. I paused in order to discern the topic of discussion or the
identity of the celebrity guest, but before I could do that there were
more commercials. Laundry detergent with special whiteners, low-cal
frozen entrees, tampons, soft drinks, an advertisement for the programs
on TV that evening, and finally back to the talk show.

This particular hostess, a former news anchor deemed too old for
prime time, presided over one of the milder talk shows, which meant
there were no flying chairs or bleeped-out cuss words. Of course it had
its share of white trash and white-trash topics, but generally she tried to
take the high road, usually at the expense of entertainment and, consequently, ratings. This was the dry toast of TV talk-show entertainment,
for people who couldn't stomach the naughty antics on the other shows,
and was very popular among retirees.

"We're back," purred the blond, tight-eyed hostess to a din of applause, giving a smile that was about as genuine as a bowl of wax fruit.
The applause subsided. "We're back, and my guest today is nothing if
not controversial. She's a teeny, tiny little woman, but one who is, despite her stature, having an enormous impact on the moral direction of

our country. She has been a nun, a teacher, a civil rights worker, an author, and most recently a syndicated radio talk-show host. This woman has dedicated her life to helping others help themselves, and I'm personally thrilled to have her here today. She has a new book out, called *Sister Melanie's Guide for the Single Mother.* Love her or loathe her, please welcome Sister Melanie!"

"Oh, Christ!" I moaned. "This bitch is the last one I want to hear from now."

I picked up the remote and pointed it like a gun at the screen. I made a shooting noise but didn't change the channel. Something, my self-pity probably, made me hesitate. I'd never actually seen Sister Melanie, and my curiosity overrode my desire to see if Jeannie had escaped from her bottle. I took a swig of wine and sat up on the edge of the couch, staring intently at the screen. She emerged slowly, a small black woman in dark glasses and a modern version of a nun's habit: black scarf on her head, black cardigan sweater over a white shirt buttoned to the top, gray below-the-knee skirt, black stockings, and small black flats on her feet. A large silver crucifix swung pendulously from her neck. She looked like Ray Charles in drag. The hostess approached and hugged her, and then took her by the arm and guided her down to the conversation pit. She was old, that was certain; her face was like wet leather and her hair, wisps of which were visible at the sides of her habit, was white. The applause subsided as the two sat down.

"Welcome," said the hostess. "I'm honored to have you here today."

"Why, thank you," she said, her voice as smooth and authoritative as it was on the radio. "It's a pleasure to be here."

"Before we talk about your new book, let's give the people some background on you. Tell us where you came from."

She then went on to relate the familiar tale of her being raised as an orphan in a convent, her blindness occurring at an early age after an outbreak of scarlet fever. She talked about her work in the civil rights movement in the sixties, and her work in the inner-city schools of Atlanta, which led to her subsequent disillusionment with liberal politics, and led her to condemn the welfare state as the true opiate of the masses.

"Your new book," the hostess said, holding up a copy, "*Sister Melanie's Guide for the Single Mother.* I have to ask you about it."

"I hoped you would," Sister Melanie said slowly, patiently.

"First of all, I have to ask how can you, a nun, possibly write a guide for single mothers? I mean, obviously you've never been a mother your-self."

The audience laughed nervously.

"No"—she smiled—"that's true, I've not, and the book is not a par-enting guide. I'm no Dr. Spock—one of him was more than enough—but I have dealt with many children in my time, and what I do know, and what I've noticed firsthand, is the effect of poor parenting on chil-dren. How the lack of attention or the wrong kind of attention can make life much harder for them. In this book I try to help people avoid the mistakes so many parents make."

"But why direct it at single mothers?" the hostess asked, a look of in-tense interest on her face.

"Statistics," she replied. "Statistics, confirmed by my own experience and observations, clearly show that there is an alarming number of sin-gle mothers, who need help the most. I figured I'd direct it at them as a sort of wake-up call. I wanted to help women who are obviously on the wrong track already, having children out of wedlock, usually when they're not much more than children themselves, get back on track and fix their own lives. Only then can they make a stable environment for their own children."

Loud applause. The hostess joined in.

"That brings up my next point. You've been accused of being overly harsh and rigid in your philosophy, of expecting too much, of setting impossibly high standards for those who are the least likely to be able to reach them. I mean, let's face it, single mothers have a tough time al-ready, what with finding a job and finding an apartment and finding day care. They can use all the breaks they can get, and yet in your book you chastise them for accepting many forms of help. How do you respond to that?"

Sister Melanie smiled and gave a condescending little laugh.

"You ever do the high jump?" she asked. The hostess giggled.

"Not recently, no."

"Well, if you do the high jump and they only set the bar, say, six inches off the ground, how do you feel when you clear it?"

"Not very excited, I guess."

"Exactly!" She nodded. "When the bar is too low there is no sense of accomplishment when you clear it. I very much believe that people will rise to the level of the bar—will rise to the level of expectations. To the level of the challenge placed before them. Especially children. None of us is as weak as we seem. And honestly, are there any goals in this book that are impossible to achieve? I don't think so."

Applause.

"Okay," the hostess continued, "you deal at length with the issue of welfare in your book in a chapter entitled 'The Dole Is for Bananas,' and somehow I think your views here manage to offend liberals, conservatives, just about everybody. Are you coming out in favor of the system or against it?"

"Both!" she said and smiled a broad, tight-lipped, enigmatic grin. "I am glad the system is in place, but I think the way it's used is a problem. It's used as a drug when it should be used as a Band-Aid. I have no problem with people using welfare to get them through a tough spot in life, but, like I say in my book, 'Use it, then lose it, but never, never abuse it.' "

Applause and several cheers of "You go, girl!" came from the audience in response to one of her trademark slogans. As the applause quieted down she continued.

"The only problem I have with welfare is that it takes responsibility away from able-bodied people, and to me that's just like giving them a handful of drugs. It makes them lazy. It makes them dependent instead of independent. It stunts their growth."

"Interesting."

"Let me tell you a story. May I?"

"Please, by all means."

"It's something that happened in the sixties, during the civil rights movement. I was doing some educational work in Watts and there had been some trouble the night before, some fights between whites and blacks, and it turned into a nasty riot, with tear gas, police, burning buildings. It was truly a nightmare. One of my worst memories. Well, the next day some of us nuns organized a peace march, a call to end the violence. We got community leaders and police and people from the neighborhood and together we marched up and down the streets singing. Now what I remember most was not the smell of burning tires or the eerie silence as we walked and sang, but some graffiti that was described to me by one of the children we were marching with. It had been spray-painted on a bridge that was in the process of being torn down. On one side, someone had spray-painted the word 'decay,' and under that was a picture of a skeleton. On the other side was a picture of a bird flying up to the sky, and underneath that was written the word 'evolve.' That image kept running through my head all the rest of the day, and I realized that was what it was all about—we individuals make the choice every day: evolve or decay. We could fight amongst ourselves and riot and loot and destroy our world, or we could work together to make it a better place. Decay or evolve.

"And so it goes when an individual is on welfare; that person makes a choice every day: either they use it to help themselves evolve into something better, or they abuse it and go nowhere—they decay."

"More talk with Sister Melanie when we return."

I muted the set and made the choice to go to the kitchen and get a wineglass. A sure sign of evolution, I thought.

Andre's refrigerator door was covered in postcards, mostly from friends or boyfriends he'd met in exotic locales. I stood looking at them while imagining myself on some sandy beach somewhere or staying at a ritzy hotel, when my eyes fell on a card I'd sent Andre years ago. It was a postcard of a movie poster for the film *Cat on a Hot Tin Roof*. I took my cigarette from my mouth and examined it more closely: a young Paul Newman on crutches, whiskey bottle in hand, and behind him an equally juvenile Elizabeth Taylor with a pleading, exasperated expression on her face. It was a look I'd seen often on the faces of Paul and my father. I turned it over so that the picture faced the refrigerator. Then I took my wineglass and bottle and returned to the sofa. They were already talking again, so I hit the volume button.

"—feel hemmed-in or trapped by circumstances or situations, what I want to show single mothers, and anybody else, for that matter, is that it is possible to change your life. Evolve or decay, *you* make the choice every day." Applause.

"One of the chapters I liked the most in your book," said the hostess, "was the one entitled 'Self-Delusion Is Self-Pollution.' Can you tell us a little bit about that?"

"Well, yes, of course. This chapter really is the most important in the book because it deals with being truthful to oneself, and to my mind that's the most important thing. No progress of any sort can be made until one is honest with oneself. In the book I make it vital that these girls start with honesty. They weren't raped, they weren't seduced—they made bad choices. First in sleeping with the boy before marriage, and second by not using condoms. I tell them 'Don't dirty yourself by claiming you're a victim.'"

"Yes, but don't you think that these girls are sometimes acting out of ignorance?"

"No, I honestly don't." Sister Melanie laughed derisively. Then her tone changed to one of impatience.

"Look here, I may be a teeny, tiny, blind nun, but I've seen more than most. I haven't been teaching all these years at some Waspy East Coast finishing school. I've been in the 'hood. Down in the trenches. These girls aren't stupid, they know about sex and condoms, they watch TV. They made the choice. They made the mistake. Often it's the same mistake their mothers made: they got pregnant thinking it would give them a way out, a new life, when in fact it does give them a new life—a baby! And then their new life needs to be given over completely to motherhood, to raising and nurturing that child, and if they can't do that, if they can't give one hundred percent, then they need to give that baby up for adoption to a family who can. They need to stop with the self-delusion and admit the truth! The truth that maybe they can't take care of the child. The book is for those women, too—the ones who do choose adoption, but mostly it's for the ones who decide to keep the children. I give them lots of practical information, a guide to resources and really, a guide for living. . . ."

They droned on, but I wasn't paying attention. The wine had made me drowsy, and I stared vacantly up at the swirling clouds, a mantra running through my head. *Self-delusion is self-pollution. Self-delusion is self-pollution. Mendacity, mendacity, mendacity. To change your personal options, press four. To change your personal options. Change your personal options. Change your personal options. Evolve. Decay. Evolve. Decay. Evolve . . .*

I got up and walked over to the window once more. I stood there drumming absently on the glass with my fingers like a bored animal in a cage. I then walked over to the desk and pulled a phone book and a pad of paper from one of the drawers and sat looking at them for a very long time. I flipped to the government pages and stared down at the list of numbers for social services. I picked up the phone and dialed one of the numbers.

I made a few inquiring calls and found out what I needed to do to qualify for public assistance, wrote down the information and the addresses I needed, and then folded up the paper and put it in my shirt pocket. On a fresh sheet I wrote the following:

Mr. Glory,
Our mutual friend Andre has spoken to me about how we may be of use to each other. If you are still interested please leave a mes-

sage on Andre's phone, as I am taking all of my calls there until my own phone is connected.

Sincerely,
Jack Thompson

I folded the letter and sealed it in an envelope. I then dialed Burl's number and left the following message:

"Burl, you big lug, or should I say big lush! It's me, Jack. You missed a great brunch and I shouldn't forgive you, but I'll give you the chance to make it up to me tonight. Leave me a message at Andre's and let me know when I can reach you. Ciao."

I hung up the phone, turned off the TV, put my glass and ashtray in the dishwasher, and went out the door and down the elevator. When I got to the front door I looked at the directory next to the buzzers and saw that Mr. F. Glory was in unit 1C. I walked quietly back down the hallway and slid the note under his door. As I walked out of the building and back to the shuttle it was not Sister Melanie's words that echoed in my head but Andre's: *Desperate times call for desperate measures. Desperate times call for desperate measures. Desperate measures.*

SOCIAL SERVICES

As soon as I walked into the west office of the Denver Department of Social Services, I realized I'd made a mistake. In my zealousness I had forgotten that I was still wearing the suit I'd chosen for my job interview that morning and was by far the best-dressed destitute person in the building. I was even better dressed than the man working behind the counter, who eyed me skeptically as he handed me a number and the application to fill out, and told me to wait until I was called. And wait I did. For nearly three hours. The application itself was fairly simple, asking for information about job status, married or single, children or no, if I'd been fired or had quit my last job, my income status, any disabilities, how much rent I paid, and the total of all bills (which in my case was extremely high). It didn't take me long to fill it out, but by the time I finished they were only up to number seventeen, and I was number forty-three. There were no magazines to read, no TV to watch, just a mess of kids running around, and the prevailing smell of urine. I went back out to my car and drove to a Denny's, where I got lunch and read the entire newspaper before driving back. When I returned, almost two hours later, they were up to number forty, so I sat down and waited as patiently as I could.

Finally forty-three was called and I was ushered by a small Hispanic woman, with half glasses on a chain around her neck, into a small, windowless office with a picture of a cat hanging by its front paws onto the limb of a tree over the words, *Hang in there, Friday's comin.'*

She sat on one side of the desk and I on the other as she looked over my paperwork and asked a few questions.

"You got fired from your last job two weeks ago?"

"Yes."

"An' then before that you got fired from another job?"

"Yes."

"What you do for money since then?"

"Well, nothing, really. I've had some help from friends and, well, that's all, really."

"How much you got in your bank account?"

"Two dollars and ninety-seven cents."

"That's the only account?"

"Yes."

"No wife. No chil'ren?"

"No."

She scrutinized my form in silence a moment and then set it on the desk and turned it around so that I could read it.

"What's this you have here on line thirteen, stocks and bonds?" she asked, pointing to the form, eyeing me warily over her glasses.

"That's something my father gives us every year on our birthdays. It's stock in his company," I said innocently, but sensed trouble.

"And how much is that worth?" she asked.

"I really have no idea." I shrugged.

"Guess," she said somewhat impatiently.

"Maybe a thousand dollars, maybe two."

She let out a disgusted hiss, pushed her glasses up on her nose, and leaned back in her chair.

"Sir, I don't know why you're here but we're very busy. Public assistance is meant for people who need help, people who have hit the bottom and don't have anything. I don't think that's you," she said, gesturing toward my suit. "You can still sell this . . . stock; you can still get by till you find a job."

I smiled, realizing it was pointless to explain about the impossibility of selling the stocks without infuriating my father, who insisted they were never meant to be sold but were to be kept as a nest egg. I was free to spend the quarterly dividend checks, but these were for small amounts—not even enough to cover a month's rent—so I usually used them to buy a nice pair of shoes. Nor could I explain about the dark cloud of credit card debt I had looming overhead, and the car insurance and the phone bill. I had hit bottom, but it was evidently a false bottom, under which there were deeper and darker spaces.

I smiled uneasily.

"I'm sorry to take up your time," I said, and got up and left.

Now, one would think that after a humiliation like that I'd have given up on the welfare idea and gone home. Well, I did go home, but it was only to shed my suit and change into a pair of ragged jeans, a sweatshirt (which I turned inside out to conceal the Tommy Hilfiger logo) a pair of ancient high-top sneakers, and a sweaty ball cap. I may have bombed out getting welfare, but I was determined to succeed at the food stamp office.

Before I left, I surveyed myself in the cracked mirror on the back of the bathroom door, hoping I looked dejected and down on my luck, like something out of the Great Depression. I didn't really look poor but I looked poorer than I had before. "Desperate times call for desperate measures," I muttered. "Work the system. Jack the bum. Act the part."

I drove to the address I'd been given over the phone, a nondescript single-story office building, and went in and got similar forms from a frizzy-haired woman in a headset who didn't look at me skeptically as she gave them to me. In fact she didn't look at me at all, but merely handed up the paperwork and pointed to the machine that dispensed the paper numbers. I took one and went and sat down in a group of fold-up chairs arranged in chaotic rows.

The first thing I noticed was that there were, ironically, a lot of fat people waiting to get food stamps. I suppose I noticed this because it was so contrary to my preconceived idea of them as Dickensian characters, with large, sunken eyes and tattered clothing. For the most part these were large people whose fat stretched the seams of their polyester outfits. I realized that staying thin was now a distinction of the upper, moneyed classes. Too much Hamburger Helper and too many loaves of Wonder bread had made these bodies what they were.

Here too was the melting pot I'd heard so much about in elementary school history classes. Every possible ethnic group and nationality seemed to be represented, and English was heard only rarely. Even the signs on the walls were translated into Spanish and Chinese and Arabic.

Like a bad day at the U.N., I thought as I took my seat with the other "delegates."

The food stamp paperwork was almost equivalent to the welfare paperwork: same status questions, same questions about bills, same questions about bank accounts, and same questions about stocks and assets, which I left blank this time. I was lying, yes, but I didn't care.

Use it, then lose it, but never abuse it, did come repeatedly to my mind, but I dismissed it as nothing more than an annoying song stuck in my head.

Screw her! I thought. *I'm sure I'm not the first one to abuse the system.* A fact that was confirmed by a conversation I heard behind me between a man and a woman.

"They tried to Jew me the last time," he said, "by givin' me less stamps because of my unemployment checks, but I marched right in there and told that bitch she'd better not cut me down or there'll be hell to pay."

"Yeah, I hear that!" the woman replied. "I slipped up once and told 'em about some money I was making under the table and they tried to nail me on it. 'Fuck, no!' I said. 'You can't prove it!' And they couldn't. You can't let 'em step on you."

"That's for fuckin' sure!"

I finished the paperwork and took it back up to the blond woman at the desk, who set up an appointment for me at eight A.M. the next morning and gave me a sheet telling me all the things to bring with me: a picture ID, Social Security card, all my bills for one month (I wasn't sure I could carry them all), a rent receipt, and a letter from my last employer stating that I had indeed been fired.

I returned the next morning, took a number, and waited. Shortly the number was called, along with eleven others, and we all herded into a back room. A woman then came around and collected all of our bills and receipts in order to make copies of them. Again we waited. Then, one by one, we were called into a cubicle by the caseworker.

Again I eavesdropped on the conversation behind me between a young man and an older Vietnamese woman.

"I gotta get these stamps today," he said. "I been livin' in my van for a couple months now, but it's winter and I'd like to find a place. The cops always harass me 'cause I ain't livin' nowhere and I got thrown in jail once 'cause I got caught smoking pot at a rest stop. What I'd like to do is drive on down to Mexico. I heard the winters are nice, and maybe I could find me a wife."

His tale was punctuated by the shocked oohs and ahhs of the Vietnamese woman.

"I don't know how you can live like that," she said.

"It used to be even harder," he said. "I used to have my two dogs living in the van too, and then one of 'em went and had pups. Seven pups! And all of us just livin' in the van. It was nice havin' 'em there 'cause they'd nuzzle up to you at night and they were awful cute. Awful fuckin' messy, too! So I had to get rid of 'em."

How he did this was not something he related.

"I'm on disability too, on account 'a I got my leg cut off by a chain saw."

At which point his number was mercifully called, and he hobbled off into the cubicle.

What the hell am I doing here? I thought. *What am I trying to prove? This has got to be one of the most asinine things I've ever done.*

I was just about to get up and leave, forget the whole thing, when my number was called. I hesitated a moment, but then rose and walked into the cubicle. I was met by a cheerful, chubby woman who was surveying my paperwork.

"Wow!" she said, an amazed expression on her round face, "you've sure got some bills."

I shrugged my shoulders sheepishly.

She punched some numbers into the computer and said, "Well, Jack, it looks like you qualify for seventy-four dollars in stamps, which you can pick up this afternoon."

"Thanks," I said, not meeting her gaze and getting up to leave.

"Wait a sec," she said, grabbing my sleeve. "You need to report to Job Search tomorrow at nine A.M.; let me give you the address." She continued talking while she wrote. "They'll oversee your job search, help you make a resume, stuff like that."

Great, I thought. *Let's hope they're magicians.*

"They can even help you start your own business if you're interested in that," she said.

"That sounds interesting," I said, wishing she'd hurry with the address.

"Really?" She stopped writing and looked up. "I mean, if you're really interested it's a great program."

"I don't see how I'd have time to start a business if I'm out looking for a job," I said.

"That's the beauty of it," she said. "If you participate in the micro-business classes, you don't have to report to Job Search."

I thought about it for about a nanosecond.

"Sign me up!"

TURNING TIDE

When I returned to Andre's later that evening, I had several new messages. The first was from Burl saying we were on for dinner. *Good,* I thought to myself, and calculated that the evening would net me at least a hundred dollars, maybe two hundred dollars if I actually stayed the night. That would cover the minimum payment on the Discover bill and would, if I got two hundred dollars, also enable me to toss something over the fence to American Express.

Next there was another message from my sister imploring me to call our mother, as she was now very upset at not hearing from me. I knew I should have called earlier, but something, maybe a kind of shame that my situation had not improved any in two months, prevented me. I would have liked to have called and left a message, but the phones in our house were so technologically advanced—what with caller ID and call forwarding and last-call return, and the fact that there were just so damned many of them—that it was nearly impossible for me to call and just leave a message. So I called my sister's apartment instead and asked her to tell them that I was fine but just really busy. Carey would hate that vague answer, and I knew that would tip her off more than anything that I was not fine, that all was not well, but so be it. I had to admit, I was beginning to see some of the wisdom in Sister Melanie's tough love/separation policy. If I had seen my parents then it would have done none of us any good—they'd have worried and I'd have felt embarrassed. Yes, it was better that we not see each other for a while.

The next message was high-pitched and whiny, like an out-of-tune violin being played by a less than talented third grader.

"Jack, Frank Glory here. Received your note this morning. Thank you. I mentioned you in passing to Andre; I'm glad he told you. Why don't we have dinner some night this week, and maybe go listen to the piano and have some drinks. Give me a call."

I had to think about that one for a minute. My decision to send the note had been so impulsive that I didn't really know what to do now that he'd actually responded. I'd been counting on Andre to coach me through it, maybe even go with me, but he would not be back for almost a week and I didn't see any reason to wait that long, especially since Frank was now awaiting a response. I dialed his number and was thankful when I got the answering machine. I left a message saying I'd pick him up the following night at seven. If that wasn't okay, he should give me a call at Andre's. If it was okay, he need not respond.

I hung up the phone and went to the window again. Outside it was dark and the streets were crowded with rush-hour traffic. Over at the station the trains were still coming and going. I looked down at my watch. Five-thirty. So much had happened since this morning, my head was spinning and my thoughts were not clear.

Thank God! I thought. *My father doesn't know what I've done today.*

The date with Burl was predictably long, but I drank less than usual, which made the evening—and the following morning—much easier to manage. We had a great dinner and talked and laughed, and I wasn't offended when he flirted with our busboy, or when he wanted to go to a strip bar after dinner. In fact I actually had fun because I felt like all the pressure was off and I was just out with a friend. Granted, if I'd been out with Andre I would not have gone home and slept with him, but with Burl that's just what I did.

The sex itself, when Burl was sober enough to go through with it, was actually rather flattering. He took great pleasure in undressing me slowly and then watching me jack off. Usually we'd start out in the living room on the couch. He'd sit down and I'd straddle him, and slowly he'd undo the buttons of my shirt, or, if I was wearing a T-shirt, he'd run his hands under it, gently squeezing my pecs and my shoulders. It was great because, as anyone who lifts weights as much as I do knows, it's wonderful to be worshiped. To have someone run their hands over your body and really appreciate all the work you've put into it. Oh, I'm sure there are some people out there who'll say that they lift purely for themselves, for their physical well-being, but if that was the case then we'd all stick to cardiovascular workouts, and the weight gain–supplement industry would not do millions of dollars in business each year.

Once Burl had my shirt off, I'd get up and just stand in front of him. Again, more buttons or zippers would be undone, and slowly he'd lower my pants and move his hands languidly along my calves, up my thighs, and up under the fabric of my underwear, gently squeezing my ass, moaning appreciatively. He'd lean forward and push his face into my crotch, inhaling deeply and feeling my hardness, all the while stroking my ass with his fingers. Then, slowly, he'd pull down my underwear and release my cock. He'd stare at it for a few moments before eagerly taking it in his mouth.

The dialogue that goes along with this is almost inevitable, and usually comes in urgent whispers.

> Him: *God, you have a great body. Damn!*
> Me, flexing: *You like that? Yeah, your hands feel great.*
> Him, undoing my zipper: *Mmmmmm.*
> Me: *Yeahhh, I'm so fucking horny.*
> Him: *Oh, yeah!*

The actual sucking usually lasted less than three minutes, and then he'd suggest we go into the bedroom. I'd step out of my pants, pull off my socks, and walk ahead of him, thus enabling him to admire my ass. In the bedroom I'd lie on my back on the bed and run my hands over my chest and cock while he undressed and watched me. Once undressed, he'd jump onto the bed like a Labrador puppy and we'd roll around and kiss for a while, during which he might suck my cock again or lick my ass. Eventually he'd get up, kneel at the foot of the bed, and watch me jack off. Some theatrics were involved in this and I, of course, did more than I would have if I were say, jacking off in the shower before going to work in the morning (if I'd had a job to go to, that is). I'd moan and caress my chest, run my fingers over my asshole, my eyes closed all the while in apparent ecstasy. I've heard some guys say they have to think of something else or someone else, or have some pornographic image in their head, but usually the whole idea of someone getting so excited over me, in turn, makes me excited.

Like the Bard says, drinking ". . . provokes the desire but it takes away the performance," and because Burl drank so much, he almost never came, and rarely even got hard, so his pleasure was secondary to mine. So after about five or ten minutes I would say, in a voice hoarse with lust, "Dude, I can't wait much longer. I'm gonna hafta come."

To which he'd respond, "Yeah, fuck, yeah, I wanna see you shoot! Shoot it, baby, come on!" And I would. Then, ironically, he would be the one to fall down on the bed, exhausted. Usually he fell asleep almost immediately. Then I would get up, towel off or take a shower, and then either crawl back into bed next to him or quietly dress and leave. Regardless of whether I stayed or went, the second I got back from the bathroom I'd go straight for Burl's pants on the floor and take the amount of cash I deemed my services to be worth from his wallet—if he had not already placed it in my pocket. On the night I've just described, the first where I'd had sex with Burl and had no delusions of its going anywhere romantically, I decided not to stay the night. It had been a tiring day and I could easily have gone to sleep, but we were on a different footing: he was the client and I was the service provider, and I wanted to show him, and myself, that this was the case. So instead of two hundreds, I took just one, a hundred and a ten to be exact, because I knew I needed to get gas, and placed the bills in my wallet next to my newly acquired, brightly colored food stamps. As I walked out to the car my mind was empty but there was a spring in my step.

The following night I arrived on the doorstep of Frank Glory at precisely seven o'clock. I did not knock at first but stood there thinking, afraid of what I was doing but knowing that my financial circumstances demanded that I do it. I didn't know what he expected, or what I expected, but I was fairly certain that some money would change hands, and that was what I needed above all else. I knocked and waited nervously. I waited a long time and knocked again. Finally I heard dragging footsteps approach the door and stop. I knew I was being examined through the peephole. The knob then turned slowly, back and forth, but the door didn't move. I could hear someone breathing heavily on the other side and some nasal cursing.

"Push on the door!" the voice yelled.

I reached down, grabbed the handle, and easily pushed open the door, revealing a tiny, exhausted-looking old man who appeared even tinier framed as he was in the giant doorway of the high-ceilinged loft. He was clad in a red-and-black-checked bathrobe, and had oxygen tubes coming out of each nostril but connected to no visible canister. I didn't know what to say, and just stood there with my mouth open, staring.

"Come in, come in," he said somewhat impatiently. "I don't pay to heat the whole hallway."

I shut the giant door reluctantly and stood there while he appraised me.

"You're even better now that I get to take a good look at you," he said, removing, with difficulty, a pair of huge, black-rimmed glasses from his bathrobe pocket and adjusting them on his face. "Splendid. Very nice." He shuffled his way around me, and I felt awkward and embarrassed, like I was meeting an old relative that I'd not seen since before puberty and they were now commenting, a little too vocally, about "what a fine-looking young man I was becoming." To break the spell, I introduced myself. He shook my hand in both of his.

"Yes, I know who you are, such nice hands. Come in, come in. You can see I'm not dressed. I usually have a nurse but I knew you were coming so I let him go early."

I did not like the way this was shaping up.

The loft was nearly identical to Andre's—one giant room with tall windows, a kitchen off to one side, and evidently a bedroom and bathroom behind two other large doors, which were now shut.

"I tried to get dressed myself," he said, "but the bedroom door shut behind me and now I can't get the damn thing open again. All my clothes and the damned oxygen are in there, so if you could open the door now . . ." he said, panting, his breath becoming more labored. I opened the bedroom door as easily as I'd opened the front and realized he must be very weak. Then, as if reading my thoughts, he rubbed his hands together and looked up at me.

"Arthritis," he said.

He hobbled past me into the room, which was dominated by a large hospital bed, and quickly hooked his dangling tubes up to the oxygen bottle, which had, I noticed with some alarm, been running the whole time he'd been locked out of the room. I went over and discreetly opened one of the windows. He stood there breathing deeply for a while.

"So where do you wanna eat?" he asked, but didn't wait for an answer. "I was thinking we could try that new place that opened across from the capitol—what's it called, Pinocchio's or somethin'?"

"Uh, no! I don't think that's a good idea," I said. "It gets, um, really smoky in there and I'm sure you don't want that."

"Don't want that! Hell, I'm a smoker myself," he said, pointing to an overflowing ashtray next to the bed. "The smokier the better."

I tried another approach.

"I don't think we could get in without a reservation," I said, my voice tinged with disappointment.

"On a Tuesday? Well, maybe you're right, new place and all."

"What about the Forum?" I said brightly, naming what is possibly the oldest, stodgiest Italian restaurant in the city. The lasagna was thick, the drinks were stiff, and the clientele was ancient. I'd probably be regarded as nothing more than a good grandson taking out his old grandpa. Best of all, it was all but unknown to the gay community, so I figured it highly unlikely that I'd run into anyone I knew.

"The Forum, the Forum . . ." he mused, trying to recollect it. When he did, his face lit up. "That's the place up north, right? Why, I haven't been there in years. Yes, let's go there! Come on, help me get dressed."

He was so small and bony that dressing him was like dressing a small child. It was a bit of an ego boost to lift him so easily and to hear him comment on and appreciate my strength. It was a boost, but it was also disturbing and a bit sad as I reflected that I, too, would be old and withered one day, and I wondered what he'd looked like at my age. I scanned the room for some photographs but the walls and the surfaces of the furniture were bare, with the exception of a small desk in the corner by the door, which was covered in neat stacks of paper and three bound ledgers.

Once he was free of his pajamas, he put his robe back on and led me to the closet. It was high-ceilinged like the rest of the loft, and was filled with row after row of brightly colored suits, shirts, and shoes. Scarves hung like vines from an impossibly high bar to the right, and the back wall was devoted solely to hats and belts.

He walked through the closet muttering softly and pensively, "The Forum, the Forum," examining his suits. Finally he decided on a navy one with enormously large lapels and flared legs. To go with it, he chose a burgundy silk shirt and a patterned silk ascot with a matching pocket hankie. While I was dressing him it became apparent that he had not worn any of the clothes he had selected in quite some time, as they now hung on him like a child playing dress-up with his father's clothes. He confirmed this by telling me that it had taken him so long to decide on something because he was trying to remember exactly what he had worn the last time he had gone to the Forum. He had been successful in his search and did not try to conceal his pride.

"The body may be going to shit, but the mind," he said, thumping his temple with his index finger, "is still sharp as a tack."

The shirt and jacket cuffs rolled up nicely but the pants hung a good two inches too long and looked ridiculous rolled up on account of the flared legs. I tried pulling them up higher and cinching them with a belt around his torso, but the waistband reached his chest before the hems came off the floor, and he thought that might be uncomfortable after a while.

"And besides," he said peevishly, "it will make the shirt look ridiculous."

It was all becoming so comic and sad at the same time that I didn't know what to do as I stood back and looked at him standing there, sucking on his oxygen, like a pile of Halston's laundry.

"Pins," he wheezed between breaths. "We need some pins and I don't think I have any."

"Andre probably has some upstairs," I said. "I'll run and get some."

I sprinted from the apartment and took the back stairs to Andre's apartment, relieved to get away for a moment, but not knowing if I should laugh or cry. I stopped on the landing, leaned over, and banged my head repeatedly on the rail. *How did I get into this?* I thought, and into it I surely was. I thought of not returning. I'd call and apologize, make up some excuse, say something came up. Then I remembered the doors, and the oxygen, and the fact that he'd let the nurse go for the night and I realized I couldn't just abandon him. He'd surely do himself in somehow. I had to stay, and I tried to convince myself to make the best of it. I banged my head once more on the railing and then ran the rest of the way to Andre's, where I stole some pins from a sewing kit I found in the bathroom. I looked at myself in the mirror, half expecting to see some careworn, pinched mess, but I was smiling, and soon that gave way to laughter as I considered the absurdity of it all. I went back downstairs.

"I'm curious," I said as he stood on a footstool and I knelt before him, pinning up his pants. "How did you get into your line of work?"

He laughed so convulsively at this that he fell into a coughing fit and had to suck on the oxygen a good thirty seconds before he could respond. When he did, his tone was serious.

"Kiddo, when I was your age, about a fucking century ago, I wasn't pretty. Safe to say I was ugly. And that's probably why old age hasn't been that hard for me to take. I was ugly young, and got used to it. I'm ugly now and nothing's changed—except the lungs crappin' out on me, and the arthritis—oh, Christ, the arthritis!" He moaned and massaged his hands. "But all in all, I'd say I'm happier now. Most fags can't deal with getting old. Hell, most people—men, women, gay, straight—can't deal with it, but I like it. People expect you to get ugly as you get older, and finally people treat me like I should be treated. See, I never fit in as a kid. Not in the gay or the straight world. The gay world was more underground then, but it was no less shallow than it is today. Fags loved the little popsies, and the musclemen, just like they do now. Nothing's changed. Nothing will ever change." He paused here and seemed lost in his last thought. I was nearly done with the pinning but pretended to be making some adjustments so as not to disturb his narrative.

"I was the ugly duckling that never grew into a swan. I knew I liked men and I knew most of them didn't like me. It was hard enough for me to get sex when I was young, but as I got older, it was almost impossible."

He paused now and his breathing became heavy. I thought maybe he'd fallen asleep, but he went on.

"I was very unhappy when I was your age, and you may not have noticed when you were rolling up my sleeves, but I made a sloppy attempt to kill myself and spent two years locked away in the state hospital in Pueblo."

I lifted him up onto the edge of the bed and I pulled the desk chair over and sat before him. He crossed his legs and continued.

"After I got out, I was pissed off at the world. I was mad that the stupid, small-minded pricks that populate the earth had almost made me kill myself, so I decided if they weren't going to accept me, then fine.

Fuck them. If I couldn't be beautiful or loved, or even liked, I decided I'd be rich, and I have never regretted that to this day. With money you can tell just about everyone to go to hell." He paused and asked me to retrieve his cigarettes from the table. I did so, lit one, and handed it to him.

"So I started opening my little stores," he continued. "All my little boutiques catering to man's baser desires. And you know what?" he asked, pausing dramatically. "Man bought! Man bought super-eight films and dirty magazines. He bought filthy novels and lubricants and rubber toys. Truckload after truckload of the stuff. But where I really made my fortune was in the arcades. Who would have thought that all those quarters would someday pay for all this?" he said, and gestured grandly at the loft and all that was in it, which was not much other than a hospital bed and a dresser and a desk, but I got the point.

"Now get me to a mirror," he barked. "Of course its on the back of that damned lead door."

I stood, helped him down off the bed, and guided him over to the door and swung it closed. He adjusted his large glasses and examined his reflection.

"I can't go out like this," he cried. "I look ridiculous!" I was about to protest, or to suggest another outfit, when he said, "Where's my hat? This looks like shit without a hat."

I brought him his hat, a burgundy-banded, wide-brimmed cream fedora, and he made a great show of positioning it on his head, with the overall effect being that of a large, polyester toadstool. As I watched him adjust his ascot l realized that no one at the restaurant was going to think I was taking Grandpa out to dinner.

"Okay," he said, satisfied with his appearance. "Let's get the hell out of here."

At his insistence I drove us to the Forum in his lemon yellow Coupe Deville. The car had not been driven in months, so the tires were very low, which made it feel even softer and more insular—like we were traveling in a giant yellow marshmallow. I had the valet park the car and led Hole slowly up the front steps and into the dark restaurant, Predictably, and luckily, it was not crowded, and he kept me entertained, over a bottle of Chianti and a huge meal, with bawdy stories from Denver's past.

After dinner, as I was driving to our next destination, he started waving his hands excitedly.

"Pull over here," he cried, pointing to the right. I obeyed, slowly maneuvering the car into a space along the curb. We had stopped in front of a grimy storefront, a dirty neon sign proclaiming it to be Adam's Garden. I shut off the motor. We sat in silence for a moment as he stared reverently out the window.

"This is the first store I opened back in fifty-six."

I nodded and tried to imagine what it had originally looked like, but then thought it must have been pretty much the same.

"New politicians are always coming in trying to clean up this street," he wheezed. "Most of them are gone now, but the old Garden is still growing like a weed. We'll open our thirtieth store this coming year, and you know what? I still do all the bookkeeping."

"Would you like to go in?" I asked. He thought for a minute.

"No," he said airily. "I've spent enough time there, and time isn't something I have much of. Maybe we'd better get to Monroe's."

I pulled back onto the street and drove the several blocks to the bar.

Monroe's, as it was called, was a relatively new piano bar that had opened on Capitol Hill. It was a small place with only five stools at the bar and maybe fifteen tables. In one corner there was a massive, white grand piano. It was so big that I thought it must have been assembled in the bar because it seemed physically impossible that it could have fit through the door. The walls were all mirrored, their reflective surfaces broken at regular intervals by framed posters of scenes from the life of Miss Monroe: her skirt flying up as she stood over the subway vent, top-less calendar poses, singing "Happy Birthday" to President Kennedy. . . .

Despite all the mirrors, it was a dark place, and the upholstery and carpeting, both a deep shade of purple, did not help. Nor did the smoke, which, as soon as we sat down, Hole took great pleasure in contributing to. Our waiter came by and Hole ordered us both gin martinis. When our drinks arrived we sipped them in silence. The martini tasted good, but I was hesitant to drink it. I was feeling strange, like I didn't want to get drunk. Like I needed to stay sober in case something should happen.

"Why, there's Ray," Hole said, his face breaking into a smile. I fol-lowed his gaze to the bar and there stood the young man I'd seen at Burl's house and at the museums. My jaw dropped, but somehow, after all of our bizarre encounters, I was not surprised to see him. He was now conservatively attired in black jeans and a black sweater, and his hair was, once again, jet black. His eyebrows were dark and thick, and the same small gold hoop glinted from the edge of one of them. Hole waved to him and he made his way toward our table. He leaned over, encircling Hole from behind, and gave him a kiss on the cheek. He looked across the table and winked at me.

"Are you here all by yourself?" Hole asked hopefully.

"Nah," he said, and nodded back beyond the bar. "My guy's on the phone. Okay if I sit down?"

"Of course, of course. This is Jack, my escort for the evening. Jack, this is Ray."

We stared at each other awkwardly and remained silent as we each considered what to say. He smiled and extended a gloved hand for me to shake. I did so and was about to say something typical like "Pleased to meet you," or "Hello," but when I tried I found I couldn't speak. I was thinking of the hyena pup, still in the trunk of my car, of the dinosaur tattoo, and of the absolute fool I'd made of myself the other morning at Burl's. All of these images whirled in my mind like so many beanbags being juggled, and I sat holding his hand, not wanting to let go until I knew more. I snapped out of it, released his hand, and he sat down in a chair next to me. Hole looked from one of us to the other, an amused expression on his face.

They spoke briefly, although I was lost in my own thoughts, trying to slow them down and give them some order. After a while, Hole asked if I would walk him up to the piano.

"I know the player and I'd like to sit with him awhile. You don't mind, do you?"

I shook my head, escorted him up, and then went back and sat down opposite Ray. I was nervous and didn't know where to look. He stared at me, grinning, then slowly slid my drink toward me. I gave a nervous laugh, muttered "Thanks," and then took a large sip.

"I'm sorry about the other morning," he said.

"Don't worry about it," I said. "I'm the one who should be sorry. I kind of lost it."

"Yeah, you look familiar, though. Guess I was wrong."

"Only partly," I said, lighting a cigarette. "What do you think about people crapping in lunch boxes?"

He cocked his head, confused, but then it registered and he snapped his fingers. "Dude, that is so funny; I knew I recognized you. You go to the Art Museum much?" he asked.

I gave a vague nod. "I also go to the Natural History Museum . . ." I said, trailing off. His head jerked and his gaze riveted on me. I studied my drink.

"The last time I was there," I said, raising an eyebrow and moving my finger slowly around the wide rim of my martini glass, "I stumbled upon something quite interesting. Or should I say, it stumbled upon me."

Now he was the speechless one, and looked around nervously.

"Don't worry," I said reassuringly. "He's quite safe. Is it a he? So hard to tell when they're that young. Anyway, he's been no trouble, quiet, doesn't eat much, hardly laughs at all. Sometimes I even forget he's there."

His face relaxed into a smile, but then fell as he looked over my shoulder to the bar. I turned around and saw a man in his forties, good-looking but a little thick around the middle, emerge from the shadows and lower the antennae of a small cellular phone.

"Duty calls," he said, and in his voice I detected a faint tone of disappointment. "But hey," he added, removing a card from his wallet, "maybe we should go for coffee sometime, Jack. Seems like we have lots to talk about."

I took the card and quickly put it in my shirt pocket. "Yes," I said. "I'd like that."

He got up, patted me on the back with one gloved hand while waving at Hole with the other, and then walked back to the bar. I watched his reflection in the mirrors and watched as he spoke briefly to the man with the phone. The man then paid their tab and they left together.

A few minutes later Hole came tottering back on the arm of the piano player.

"That Ray!" he said. "I didn't even get to say good-bye."

"No," I said.

"Did you like him?" he asked.

"He's . . . different," I said.

"I'll say. That boy's a treasure. My absolute favorite."

In the car on the way home I asked some questions about Ray and was given, not surprisingly, some lengthy answers. I learned that he had moved here the year before from Los Angeles because of his drug problem. Allegedly he was in recovery ". . . although he still smokes pot like there's no tomorrow." His only income, as far as Frank knew, was from hustling ". . . but he uses most of his money to pay for his little art hobby."

Back at the loft, I undressed Hole and put him in a fresh pair of pajamas. While he was in the bathroom, I hung up his clothes, straightened up his bed, changed his oxygen bottle, and fashioned a doorstop out of several bar coasters I'd had the foresight to pocket from Monroe's. He waddled out of the bathroom, his wheezing worse than it had been all evening. I led him over to the oxygen and connected the tubes, and he sat breathing deeply until he could speak again.

"I'm fucking exhausted," he said as I removed his robe and lifted him into bed. He lay on his side and I tucked him in all around. I then went to the doorway, switched off the light, and hesitated for a moment, not knowing what to do next. I walked slowly back to the bed and lay down next to him, our bodies spooned together, my arm around him. I could feel his thin shoulder blades as they rose and fell with his labored breathing, and felt the faint touch of his fingers caressing my forearm as he gradually fell into sleep. I stayed for maybe an hour, thinking about the evening—about Hole's stories and about Ray, and then I got up, as gently as I could, and went back upstairs to Andre's.

MICROBUSINESS

The next morning I didn't get up until after eight because I had mistakenly set Andre's alarm for P.M. instead of A.M. This was unfortunate because I had to report to my first day of microbusiness classes at nine and would have to wear my same smoky clothes from the night before, since I didn't have time to go home and change. I tried on some of Andre's clothes, but after ripping the seam trying to squeeze into one of his shirts I gave it up and decided I'd better wear my own.

The microbusiness office was at the upper end of downtown, which is a short shuttle bus ride away from Andre's. I figured I might as well take the shuttle and leave my car parked in his garage rather than attempt to find parking on a weekday morning. The office building was nice on the outside, all streamlined Bauhaus steel and glass, but on the inside it was typical government-issue: dirty, neglected, and devoid of any decorative touches. No office art or reception desk. No furniture. Just an empty lobby with elevators on either side and a podiumlike structure on which rested a black tablet indicating which offices were on which floors. I examined it briefly, found what I was looking for, and took the elevator to the third floor. From there I followed some handwritten signs indicating that room 300 was for beginning GED classes, 301 was for teen mothering classes, and 303 was for microbusiness classes. I made my way to the correct classroom and opened the door. It was a large room with a whiteboard on one wall and tables arranged in a C-shape facing it. I took a seat to the left, between a woman who looked to be in her fifties, and seemed grandmotherly and gentle as she sat quietly doing a cross-stitch, and a stout man of indeterminate age in a black suit. He wore thick glasses that magnified his eyes several times and emphasized that one of them was lazy. On the other side of the table were two young Latino men, one stocky, the other skinny, both clad in oversize clothing and dark sunglasses. They sat, arms crossed, and looked very bored. Next to them was a short, thin African-American woman, her hair pulled tightly back in a ponytail, and next to her, coloring quietly with crayons, was her young daughter.

We all sat silently, staring into space or doodling on notepads, for what seemed like a very long time. Finally a small woman shuffled in, her head and torso completely obscured by stacks of files and notebooks that she carried. Blindly she made her way to the desk and managed to set everything down in a tottering heap without any of it falling to the floor. She then looked around the room, smiling at us all, and repositioned a stray piece of hair that had fallen into her face. Although her beauty was a bit dated, most would agree that she was very good-looking. She was in her mid-thirties, heavily but not unattractively made up, with artificially blue eyes and a black mane of hair, elaborately feathered. She was obviously short, but just how short could not be determined because she wore heels that added several inches to her height. Unlike many women, she was adept at wearing heels and strutted back and forth in front of the whiteboard as easily as if she had been wearing cross-trainers. She went back out of the room, and returned a moment later with her coffee mug, from which she took a long, slow drink, examining us over the rim. She set down the cup, pulled a marker from her heap, and wrote her name on the whiteboard.

"Good morning," she said. "My name is Tina DeHerrera, and I'll be your main instructor for the next ten months of the microbusiness program." She picked up her mug again and took another long sip.

"You are all here because you expressed an interest in starting your own business." She looked each of us in the eye as we nodded. "Unfortunately, the statistics for new-business success aren't very good. Seven out of ten new businesses will fail in the first three years," she said, pausing for effect. "Not very encouraging, is it?" Another pause as we all shook our heads.

"What those statistics don't tell you," she continued, pacing back and forth in front of the whiteboard, "is that most of those businesses fail because of poor planning and management, not because the concept or the product was bad. Always remember, someone made money from the Pet Rock. You understand?"

We nodded; the older woman chuckled.

"What this program will do, over the next six months, is give you the knowledge to make your idea succeed, okay? We will teach you how to market your business, how to open a bank account, keep books, and pay taxes. You will learn how to hire employees and do payroll, and finally, before we've finished you will submit a written business plan—a road map—to tell yourself and the rest of us where you're going and how you're going to get there. I can't stress the importance of this enough. Not having that road map at the beginning is the reason most businesses fail."

She looked around the room, again pausing to make eye contact with each of us.

"At the end of the six months," she continued, "you can submit your business plan to the rest of the class, and to the advisory board. Then, regardless of your credit history, you can apply for a five-hundred-dollar loan."

My heart sank as I calculated that five hundred dollars would pay roughly one-eighth of my MasterCard bill.

"Some background on me," she said, and came around in front of the desk, leaning her ass on it and crossing her legs.

"I have a B.A. in business, which I have to say didn't really teach me much. I have run two small businesses of my own, and that taught me plenty!"

"What kind of businesses, ma'am?" asked Slow Eye.

"I ran a small advertising firm for four years, which I sold for a small profit, and now I run a small trucking company with my husband. It's just getting off the ground, but last year we saw a profit for the first time since we started it two years ago. Okay, why don't we go around the room and you can each introduce yourself, and tell us your idea for a business."

She pointed to the African-American woman, who stood up confidently.

"My name is Sharise, and this is my daughter, Brandy. Um, my idea for a business is to help people make their own Web pages for the Internet. I learned how to do it really well at my last job, but my boss was stealing money and the company went broke, so that's why I'm here, um, because I think I could do it better than he did."

She sat down quickly.

"Thank you," Tina said. "That's a good point. Many businesses are started by people who watched someone fail and have learned from watching others' mistakes." Her gaze moved on to the next table, where the two Latino guys stood up in tandem. The larger of the two spoke.

"My name's Antonio and this is my homie, Victor, and we're sick of working for other people and getting paid shit and treated like shit, see, and we want to start our own construction company. We got our own tools and Victor's got a pretty good truck, and what I don't know, he knows, and what he don't know, I do." They looked at each other and nodded and then looked around at all of us and we nodded and they sat down.

"Okay, great, thank you. You brought up an excellent point: how many of you are sick of working for other people?"

Hands shot up all around, no hesitation.

"Excellent," she said. "That's one of the biggest reasons for wanting to start your own business. I'm glad to see you all have that spark inside you."

Next was the old woman sitting next to me. She set her cross-stitch on the seat next to her and stood up shyly, pulling her cardigan closed and adjusting her glasses.

"My name's Millie," she whispered, "and—"

"Millie," Tina interrupted, "we can't hear you, sweetie."

Millie blushed, cleared her throat, and started again, louder and much more rapidly.

"My name's Millie and I like to sew, and my idea for a business is to make children's clothing."

She then sat down hurriedly and stared down at her lap.

"Okay. Great," said Tina. "And Millie, do you have anything that you've made that you could bring to the next class?"

Millie looked up, startled, but then smiled. "Oh, yes!" she said.

"Okay, good, we'd like to see it." Tina's gaze fell on me, and I realized that I was totally unprepared. In an instant I saw that all of these people had some idea, some plan, whereas I was here only to avoid being forced to look for a job. I stood up and looked around, feeling as shy and awkward as poor Millie.

"Uh, well," I stammered, "I've sort of been doing some fitness training and teaching some aerobics classes at a gym I go to, and, um, I'd like to expand on that, I guess."

"Okay, good, and what did you say your name is?"

"Oh, sorry, I didn't. It's Jack. Jack Thompson."

"Okay, Jack Thompson, and who do you want to target with your business—what kind of clients do you want to attract?"

"Um, I guess clients with money."

Everyone laughed.

"Yes," Tina laughed. "That always helps. Thank you."

I sat down feeling foolish, but was curious about the slow-eyed man next to me, so the feeling didn't last. I could see that his black suit was old and in dire need of dry cleaning, and yet there was a quiet elegance about him as he rose and buttoned his jacket, folded his hands in front of him, and in a deep, soothing voice, scarcely louder than Millie's, said, "Good morning, my name is Salvatore Varga. The business I'm interested in starting is one in which I would videotape weddings and other happy occasions." He looked around the room somberly, unbuttoned his jacket, and sat down.

"Okay, great, and what kind of work did you do before, Salvatore?" Tina asked.

"I was a mortician, ma'am."

"Sounds like you *are* looking for a change." She chuckled.

"Yes, ma'am, that is quite true," he said softly.

"Okay," she continued, moving back around behind the desk, "you all have some interesting ideas. I think this is going to be a good class."

The rest of the time was used in explaining the mandatory attendance policy (no more than one unexcused absence or we were out of the program and would lose our stamps), handing out reading materials, which she deftly extracted from her pile of props, and watching a segment of *60 Minutes* in which Mike Wallace interviewed the Bangladeshi originator of the microbusiness idea.

The program was initially created to help third-world women who had business ideas, but no money to realize them, and who would have been laughed out of a bank had they gone to apply for a loan.

Great, I thought as I sat there in the dark. *I'm on par with a third-world woman.*

In the shuttle on the way back to Andre's, my thick packet of materials under my arm, I thought back to the other students in the class and how they all had at least a sketchy road map of where they wanted to go. Then I compared their ideas to the one I'd thoughtlessly given as my own and I felt humbled. Gone was the feeling of snide superiority I'd felt when I'd first gone in. It would be possible, I thought, to expand the personal training, but somehow my heart wasn't in it. I thought of the five-hundred-dollar loan and how I had somehow managed to get almost thirty thousand dollars in what were essentially loans through credit-card companies, and again I shuddered to think how I'd ever pay it back.

When I got back to Andre's there was a pink envelope on the floor that had been pushed under the door. Inside there was a blank thank-you card containing three one-hundred-dollar bills.

SATAN CLAUS

The next day I woke up at seven-thirty feeling rested and refreshed, as I had stayed home the night before, attempting to be domestic and settled. I had cleaned my apartment and made dinner, resolving to be more frugal with money. In this vein I made the decision to stop using my credit cards for anything other than the most pressing emergencies. I should have cut them and burned the pieces, but my plan was much less final and, if I do say so myself, quite clever, like something Martha herself might have thought up if she had credit problems. What I did was this: I took all of my credit cards and put each one in its own Ziploc bag. These I filled with roughly eight ounces of water, sealed them up, wrapped them in craft paper, labeled them with permanent marker, and placed them in neat rows in the freezer. The idea was that if I wanted to use one of the cards I'd have to wait at least long enough for the ice to thaw, during which time I could weigh the importance of the emergency or the necessity of the purchase.

With that in mind, I got out of bed, pulled on a pair of boxers, and immediately went to the freezer to examine my handiwork. Such a simple solution, I thought, and I almost believed that freezing the cards had effectively frozen the debt, too. Feeling lighthearted and proud of myself, I skipped over to the window and looked out. The weather was hardly reflective of my spirits. It was cloudy and cold and rain splashed off the lid of the Dumpster. I returned to the kitchen, made some oatmeal and a protein shake, and sat down to write out long-overdue payments to Chase Visa and Allstate. It was a relief to finally be able to send them some money, and I found I didn't dwell on how it had been earned. I felt no shame. On the contrary, I felt the saucy little thrill that goes along with having pulled something off that is slightly naughty. I'd made more in those two dates than I would have in two weeks of working at the coffee shop. I thought back to the guy from the museums, and wondered how much he made. I took my wallet from the pocket of the pants I'd worn yesterday and removed his card. *Ray* was all it said, and listed a phone, pager, and cell phone number, all of which indicated to me that he was fairly successful at what he was doing. I tapped the card on the table, considering. Maybe he could help me out, I thought, although in what way I really wasn't sure. I picked up the phone and was pleasantly surprised to hear a dial tone. Finally US West had flipped the switch. I dialed the first number on his card and it rang once before I remembered it wasn't even eight o'clock. I hung up quickly. I felt antsy and wanted to talk to someone, but the only ones I knew who were up this early were my parents. I thought of my sister's message and decided to venture a call to my mother. My dad had probably already gone to work or was in his study, where he received only business calls, so maybe he wouldn't answer. Just to be safe, before I dialed their number, I dialed *67 to block the call, so that my name would not show up on their caller ID. That way I could hang up if my father answered, and he couldn't trace the call. I had nothing new to tell him about my employment status and was not in the mood to be grilled about it. It rang twice.

"Hello." It was my father's deep baritone. I hesitated, but didn't hang up.

"Dad?"

"Jack?" He sounded surprised. "That you?"

"Yeah."

"Where are you calling from? It says your number's blocked."

"Uh, I'm calling from Andre's. He must have that permanent-block thing. My phone's not hooked up yet."

"Tell me about it." He groaned. "US West gives me nothing but headaches. How are you, son?" He sounded concerned.

"Uh, yeah, I'm fine. I got another job," I lied. "This one almost pays the bills."

"You doing okay?"

"Oh, yeah," I said, wanting to reassure him. "I'm even taking this sort of business class."

"Really?"

"Yeah, it's offered through the state. It just started yesterday, so I'm not sure what it'll be like."

"Good to hear," he said in a backslapping voice. "Good to hear."

"Is Mom there?" I asked, wanting to change the subject.

"Actually, she's not," he said. "She just left. She had an early appointment at the vet."

"The veterinarian?" I asked, confused, since they didn't have any pets.

"Yes." He sighed. "Your mother's off on another one. She went and got herself two dogs yesterday."

"No way! What kind?"

"Oh, hell, I don't know. Little things, huge paws. I guess they'll get pretty big. They've been running 'round the house smashing into everything." He laughed. "It's probably my fault. She was a little upset when the batteries died in that thing the gardener gave her so I said, sorta offhand, you know, 'Why don't you go out and get some sort of real pet?' Well, I was thinking a bird maybe, or a gerbil or something, but I come home last night and step right in a pile of crap. You'll have to come by and see them. They're real pieces of work."

I paused, surprised by the invitation.

"Yeah, I will. Well, I'd better get going," I said, feeling suddenly awkward.

"Holy cow, it's after eight. I better get moving too or I'll spend all morning sitting in traffic. Son, listen, it's been good talking to you. Your mother will be sorry she missed you."

"I'll call her later."

"Or stop by."

"Uh, yeah, okay."

"All right, I love you, Jack."

"Uh, thanks, me too. I mean, I do too. 'Bye, Dad." And I quickly pushed the hang-up button. I sat on the edge of my bed, staring at the wall, astonished. His invitation and "love you" comment were completely unexpected and out of character. My dad and I had never been what you could call close. Carey and Jay were much more the sporty/academic sons he'd wanted, whereas I was the slightly embarrassing anomaly that he didn't quite know what to do with. Ball sports are a perfect example of this: while Jay and Carey were off hitting home runs and scoring touchdowns, I was the one who struck out at T-ball, the one who scored a goal for the opposing team, the one who was too busy arranging weed bouquets in the outfield to notice the ball as it bounced a foot away from me. From an early age I knew I was somewhat of a disappointment to him, so I naturally gravitated into the more accepting realm of my mother. My father and I kept our proverbial distance. Ironically, now that some real distance had been put between us it felt like we were somehow closer. I couldn't understand it.

I'll have to go back to Sister Melanie's book, I thought, returning the phone to its cradle, *and try to see where all this is coming from.*

I paced around the apartment, feeling claustrophobic, so I put on my gym clothes, a baseball cap, and a windbreaker, threw some clean clothes in my gym bag, and started out. I got to the mailboxes in the hallway, paused, and then returned to my apartment. My eyes went straight to the card I'd left on the dresser. I went over, picked it up, and grabbed the phone again. I dialed my voice-mail number and recorded a message.

"Spring is lovely, violets everywhere 'round. Actually it's pretty gray outside, but hey, it's Thursday morning, early. I didn't want to wake you up, but I, um, was going to go to the Art Museum today, about eleven-thirty or so, and was going to see if maybe you wanted to meet me. Maybe we could grab lunch there or something and I could give you the item I've been keeping for you. If not, then hey, maybe some other time."

I pushed the pound key to finish recording and then dialed his number and pushed the pound key again to send the message to him.

I got to the museum a half hour early and killed the time until eleven-thirty by flipping through books in the gift shop. When it was time, I went into the café and got a sandwich. I didn't know if he'd come or not, and I didn't want to seem too eager, but as I went to find a table I was relieved to see him sitting by the window, reading a book and drinking coffee. I went over and sat down.

"What are you reading?" I asked.

"Hey!" He smiled, and looked briefly at the cover of the book before handing it to me.

"Sewing Methods of the Inuit Indians. I've been meaning to get around to this one."

I flipped casually through the pages and then gave it back to him. His hair was still black and he was wearing an outfit similar to the one he'd had on the other night: heavy black sweater, blue denim jeans, and some heavy-soled black shoes, the tongues of which were a furry black-and-white leopard print. He picked up the book again and put it into a small black leather backpack, much like the duffel bag I had in my trunk.

"That book was hard to find," he said, his voice rough and gravelly, and I noticed, as he spoke, that his tongue was pierced too, but that it did not seem to interfere with his speaking.

"Do you sew?" I asked.

"Yeah, actually I do a lot of sewing." He smiled and sounded genuine, but something, his arched brow maybe, made me unsure if he was being sarcastic or not. We then talked airily about the weather and the museum and Hole, which reminded me of his comment about Ray's artwork.

"So Hole tells me you're an artist," I said, looking down at my sandwich and thus avoiding his eyes. "What kind of work do you do?"

"You know, it's hard to pinpoint," he said. "I do what I guess people would consider shock art."

Not surprising, I thought, and wondered what other body parts he had punctured.

"But I don't like being lumped in that category. I have a better sense of humor."

I nodded.

"So . . . what?" I asked, somewhat derisively. "You paint with your own blood? Make sculptures out of feces?" I took a bite of my sandwich.

"Nah." He laughed. "Nothing like that, but I do think it's cool there are people out there doing that—and that you've heard of it. I do mostly installation pieces, some painting, some photography. How 'bout you? You spend a lot of time here—do you paint or anything?"

I stopped chewing and thought a minute. I thought about lying, about making up, right then and there, a fictional talent, something to make myself seem much more interesting and dynamic than I was, but I didn't. With another person, someone I doubted I'd see again, I surely would have lied, but with him I didn't.

"No," I said. "I don't really have any skill." (That cursed word!) "Any talent, I mean. I studied art history," I said, as if that should explain all my shortcomings, and I felt sure he'd concur.

He nodded, took a sip of his coffee, and said, "That's cool."

"Cool that I don't have any talent, or cool that I studied art history?" I asked.

"Cool that you studied art history. I think most artists need to know more about what came before, especially when it comes to technique, but history can weigh you down, too. I think there's a lot to be said for just doing your own thing, not worrying about what anyone's done in the past."

I nodded, reflecting on this.

"So what kind of art do you like?" he asked.

I thought for a minute. Again I thought about lying, about making up something that he might like to hear, or about reciting Paul's opinions, which I was far more familiar with than my own, but again I did not, and spouted a mishmash of esoteric things that came to mind.

"I used to love classical architecture," I said, "but I'm not so interested in that anymore. I like a lot of the Japanese arts and crafts, anything by the Pre-Raphaelites. I like Neoclassical, too: David, Ingres—"

"What about twentieth-century stuff?" he asked.

"Hmm, I guess I like Mondrian the most. In architecture I like the Bauhaus movement."

I stopped and took another bite of my sandwich, but he was staring at me intently, which made it difficult to eat, so I pushed the rest of the sandwich aside and looked up at him. His eyes were serious and seemed to be analyzing something.

"You like order, don't you?" he said, somewhat smugly, I thought.

"What makes you say that?" I was offended by his tone, but curious nonetheless. He laughed a knowing little laugh.

"Come on," he said. "You're not stupid. All those artists and movements and styles you named are tight and controlled. They're all prescribed orders, and perspective and balance."

"I think you're simplifying things a bit," I said defensively, but also feeling a little thrill at the turn the discussion was taking. "But so what if you're right, isn't that what art is: taking random materials and giving them some order, some meaning?"

"It is and it isn't," he said, leaning forward. "You can take wood and bricks and order them into a house, but is that art? But that's not what I was getting at. What I wonder is why you like everything so neat and orderly."

I was getting a little angry—at myself, mostly—and wished I had given Paul's opinions, since I wasn't really sure how to defend my own— or even what my own even were.

"I don't know; that's what I like," I said, and regretted almost immediately how stupid it sounded. "Why do you care?" I asked. "Are you suddenly my analyst? Okay, Mr. Shock Art, let's hear your definition—what do you like? Oh, but wait, wait, wait, I think I can guess. You like Mapplethorpe!" I said, emphatically. "Which pretty much says it all. He is your dark angel. The trendy bad boy of the art world, attacking the establishment. Stick a whip up your ass while you're sucking some gigantic dick and call it art. Take a picture of a crucifix in a bucket of pee and call it art."

"That's not Mapplethorpe," he said calmly.

"Whatever," I said, waving my hand dismissively. "Same difference. The point is, anything that's naughty or taboo is right up your alley, isn't it?"

The funny thing about arguments that start this way, with a perceived insult, is how logic seems to take a backseat to competition. I was on the defensive, but instead of defending my own ideas, I criticized his. I went on and on, arguing points I didn't agree with, trying to assert a superior knowledge, discounting his opinion, until suddenly I realized that this was precisely the condescending way Paul had always argued with me, and I stopped. This was not hard to do, since my vitriolic flow was obviously not having the desired effect on him. He continued regarding me calmly, the same bemused smile on his face.

"What?" I asked, feeling even more embarrassed.

"I think there's a senator in North Carolina who'd be glad to hire you as an intern."

I had to laugh.

"I'm sorry," I said.

"What for?"

"For sounding like such a jerk."

He shrugged his shoulders, sipped his coffee, and for several moments we sat, saying nothing. The silence made me uneasy, and I felt like I wanted a drink or a cigarette or something to do with my hands. My eyes darted around, landing on the sandwich, which I wanted, but I still did not want to eat in front of him.

"You wanna get out of here?" he said, breaking the silence, and I was unsure if he was asking a question or making a statement. "Maybe walk around outside?"

I nodded, although the idea was ridiculous because it was raining steadily and I didn't have an umbrella. I had thought we'd spend the afternoon walking around the museum, but now the prospect of looking at art seemed stifling and faintly pretentious.

With no destination in mind we walked through the Civic Center and down the Sixteenth Street mall. The mall is really a walking street, usually clogged at the noon hour with office workers on their lunch breaks, but that day, because of the rain, it was nearly deserted.

Our conversation started slowly, but soon we were both talking freely, about buildings mostly, as we pointed out and commented on the different styles along our route. I felt much more at ease talking to him while we walked. Walking was the cigarette or the drink I'd wanted earlier—the something to occupy my body. It gave my eyes something to look at other than his eyes, and that made me much less self-conscious and much more talkative.

"I'm glad you got my message," I said, feeling genuinely happy, and somewhat decadent, like I was ditching school with a friend.

"I'm glad you sent it," he said. "I thought maybe you were kind of mad about the other morning at Burl's."

"Oh, I was." And I thought back, with embarrassment, to my indignant fit. It all seemed so silly and sophomoric in retrospect. "I guess I wasn't really ready to see what I was doing then, you know? And I certainly wasn't ready to hear it from someone else."

He laughed knowingly. "Yeah, I remember how strange I felt the first time someone tagged me with it. I was probably, like, fifteen or sixteen or something. It pissed me off."

"You've been doing it since you were fifteen?" I asked, surprised.

"Well, off and on, yeah."

"What made you get into it?" I asked, trying not to sound too curious.

"Drugs," he said, and laughed. "I was pretty hooked then, and that kind of gets in the way of having a steady job."

A steady job. The words echoed in my head.

"But you're off of it now . . . ?" I inquired carefully. "Heroin, I mean." He looked at me quizzically and I remembered that he'd not said it was heroin. He must have realized that Hole and I had been discussing him.

"I've been clean for almost two years now."

"So why do you still do it?"

"Do what?" he asked. I stopped and looked at the ground, trying to think of a delicate way of putting it. Then he realized what I meant.

"Oh, why do I still turn tricks?"

"Yes," I said, and resumed walking.

"The money. Plain and simple. That and the time. It gives me time to work on my art," he said.

We walked in silence again. I had so much I wanted to ask, and so far he wasn't reticent about answering, but while one side of me was pulling toward the topic, the other was pushing me away.

"Does it ever bother you?" I asked timidly.

"Sometimes," he said. "Some days. But like I said, it can be good money and gives me a lot of time."

Again I paused, trying to choose my words carefully. Then I gave up. *Screw it,* I thought, and decided to just jump in and stop all the tiptoeing.

"I guess that's why I'm considering it more," I said, boldly. "And that's part of the reason I called you."

"I know," he said. I looked up, surprised.

"My motivation is not nearly as noble as yours," I said. "I mean, I'm no artist, but I have managed to sort of paint myself into a corner." I laughed at my little joke. "I'm in a little financial trouble and, well, I won't bother you with the details. Suffice to say, I need money."

"I know," he said again.

"How do you know?" I asked.

"From Burl, mostly. He told me about your boyfriend dying and all. The rest I just put together."

I nodded, but didn't look at him.

"I was hoping," I said, warming to the topic, "that maybe you could give me some pointers on how to . . . go about this, I guess."

"I could," he said, "but I don't know that I will."

"Why not?" I asked, thinking maybe he didn't want the competition.

"Because I think you've got stars in your eyes. You've turned a few tricks and gotten some quick cash and now you've got the idea in your head that it's easy money. Sometimes it is," he said, "but a lot of times it's not. A lot of times it's gross and degrading and you come away feeling about this high." And he lowered his hand to a point just below his knee.

"Believe me," I said, thinking back to the authorizations job, "I've done degrading work, but I think I know what you mean and I do appreciate the concern."

"Isn't there anything else you can do?" he asked. I didn't answer, but for the next several blocks I considered it. *Is there anything else I could do?* I wondered and I thought about all the temp work and the coffee shop, the fiasco of waiting tables, my blank page of a resume. Then I thought of my sister starting medical school next year, and my brother in his little law office, and wished I could crawl under a rock. I'd been so absorbed in my thoughts that I hadn't even noticed when we crossed the light-rail tracks where Paul had been struck.

We reached lower downtown and I paused in front of a gallery window displaying some old posters of Soviet propaganda: large, colorful cartoons of Lenin and tractors and factories. The one directly in front of us depicted a group of smiling peasant women clustered behind a broad-shouldered, square-jawed man in overalls. In one hand he held a large hammer, while with the other he pointed the way to a bright future.

"You're an artist," I said, resurrecting our previous, comparatively light conversation. "What does your art say? Why do you do it?"

I focused on his reflection on the rain-speckled window. He was thinking, his brow furrowed, and when he spoke, it was with a confidence I found enviable.

"The way I see it," he said, turning and starting to walk, "society has spent thousands of years building up some pretty senseless taboos and sacraments—men having sex with men, interracial relationships, questioning religious doctrine, shame of bodily functions. Stupid ideas which, over the years, people start believing as fact. With my art, I like to subvert some of those ideas, or at least make people reconsider them."

"And how do you do that?" I asked, and pictured him running through a temple smashing idols. His brow became even more furrowed and his tone became serious.

"What I'm working on now," he said, gesturing with his hands, "is taking two things, things not usually associated with each other, at least one of which people have very strong feelings about, and combining them. In that way people are forced to look at them differently than they've been programmed by society to look at them." He gave a satisfied nod, evidently proud of his concise explanation.

"I don't get it." He laughed and then pulled me over to a soggy bench and sat me down.

"Take something as simple as colors, for example, and all the preconceived ideas people have about them. We'll use apples and oranges. Imagine if you had an orange apple, or a red orange. You'd definitely take a second look. You'd reconsider your ideas about both the forms and the colors. I like that. That's why I admire a lot of shock art; it

causes you to look at something—God, society, ideals, etc.—in a different perspective."

I considered this and remembered the "Piss Christ."

"Interesting," I said, "and I see your point, but a lot of shock art is so
offensive I think the message gets lost. Don't you think when you offend
people you just alienate them more and then they just cling even more
tightly to their own beliefs?"

He thought for a moment.

"Maybe, yeah, but that's why I try and keep it funny. If you can
make people laugh, they'll remember, and if they remember, they're
more likely to give it some real consideration later. But I'll admit, in
some pieces I do deliberately try to piss people off. Obviously you're not
over the moon about Robert Mapplethorpe, but you have to admit his
work, because some of it is so offensive and controversial, has been seen
by minds that never would have seen it otherwise. It's subversive. It
plants a seed in the mind."

The rain came down harder.

"Do you want to go back to my place?" he asked, teeth chattering.
"It's not far if we take the shuttle back. We could dry off."

I was cold, so I nodded and we made our way up the street.

"Did you ever work in a gallery?" Ray asked later, as we sat on the
shuttle. I thought of lying again, but didn't, and just shook my head.

"I mean with your degree and all, seems like you would have."

I remembered the postcard on Andre's fridge: Maggie the Cat and
her frustrated glare. I remembered all the fights with Paul, and how he'd
implored me to go after a career using my degree, and how that had always confused me. *Get real!* I'd thought. I knew I wasn't entirely stupid,
but I always thought there were lines of smarter, more capable, more organized people ahead of me. I felt the same about my looks—I knew I was
good-looking but was never satisfied with my body, never felt really confident. No matter how much I worked out, no matter how big and strong
I got, inside I was still the awkward little boy who struck out at T-ball.

Ray went on, oblivious to my thoughts. I pushed them aside and
gave him my attention.

"I'd like to have my own gallery someday," he said, "just for con-
temporary stuff. Different from anything that's out there. Less stuffy,
more accessible."

"I agree with you there," I said. "Most galleries are about as lively and inviting as the dentist's office, and they always seem to be run by such uptight people. I know they're going after rich clients, but that's no reason to be so boring."

"Totally," Ray said. "I know it's a business, but you'd think for that reason they'd want to get people in there and expose them to things they haven't seen or thought of before."

"Exactly," I said.

"Cool. We're on the same page. We'll open a gallery and run it together—how's that sound?"

"Sounds great," I said.

Get real, I thought.

The section of the city in which Ray lived was about to be transformed. In fact, I doubt the house we returned to that day is still standing today. It was a triangular area comprised of several blocks, hemmed in by Broadway, Speer Boulevard, and Thirteenth Avenue, and was once a residential area. At the time it was mostly parking lots with a few neglected houses dotting the asphalt landscape. The large city jail dominates one edge of the triangle, and consequently most of the houses that remained had been turned into bail-bond businesses and were painted in bright primary colors or bizarre patterns in order to catch the eye of those in need of their services. Ray's was one of the very few that hadn't been altered, and he was one of a handful of people, other than prisoners, who actually lived in the area. Recently, because of its proximity to downtown and the views it affords of the Art Museum, the new library, and the capitol building, the land value has skyrocketed and it is now known, named by some optimistic developer, no doubt, as the Golden Triangle. The old houses and small apartments that had been falling down anyway were helped along to their demise by eager builders anxious to replace them with swank new condos and lofts to accommodate the city's swelling moneyed population.

As we approached his house that afternoon (a dark green, two-story pile of loose bricks and rotted shingles that looked as though it had just been pulled from the bottom of a lake), the first thing I noticed—indeed how I realized it was his house—was the red station wagon parked out front. The same one I'd seen parked out in front of Burl's last weekend. However, viewed in profile, it became obvious that it was not a station wagon at all, but a hearse.

"Nice car."

"Yeah," he said. "Sobering, isn't it? I got it from a friend of mine."
He opened the front door and I followed him into a dark foyer.

"Give me your coat," he said, peeling it off my wet shoulders. He
switched on a light and hung my coat from one of the many hooks that
lined the wall. They were not metal hooks, nor even wood, but were all
the amputated front legs of unfortunate animals, turned upside down
and bent at the joint. I helped him off with his coat, hung it on a dainty
white hoof, and followed him into the house.

"We'd better take off our shoes," he said, kicking his off and stamp-
ing up the dark, narrow staircase, while I remained below trying to
untie wet laces with fingers made less than nimble from the cold.

The door to my right was open a crack. I nudged it open a little farther with my shoulder and peered in, but the room was too dark to see
anything. I stopped myself suddenly with the thought that maybe he had
roommates, or maybe the ground floor was rented by someone else.

I took off my socks, which were sopping and had stained my feet
brown, and followed Ray's wet footprints up the dark wooden stairs.
When I reached the top and pushed open the door it was all brightness.
The walls of the large room were white and almost free of decoration.
The ceiling followed the roof lines and was therefore very high in the
middle, but along the sides scarcely a foot of wall space separated it
from the pine floor. Four skylights gave views of the gray sky above.
Against one wall a large mattress and box spring rested on the floor,
covered by a heavy white comforter and several white pillows. Books
littered the floor by the bed, and there was a full ashtray on the bedside
table. On the far wall was a brick fireplace, also painted white, and in
front of that was a small, tan canvas sofa, which partially blocked my
view of Ray, who was squatted down by the fireplace adjusting the gas
flame. The only other furniture in the room was a large TV on the floor
opposite the bed and next to that an equally large stereo. In the two opposing corners stood two identical speakers, at least five feet tall.

"Hang on, we'll have some heat here in a minute," he said, rising and
pulling off his wet shirt, again revealing the piercings on his chest. He
removed the rest of his clothing, and again I had a view of the rest of his
body, lean and smooth and wet from the rain which dripped from his
hair. My pulse quickened and I noticed that my palms were sweaty.

"Give me your clothes," he said, standing naked before the fireplace,
clearly intending to stand facing me while I undressed. "I'll take them
down and put them in the dryer."

I'd been naked thousands of times at the gym in front of several men, and sometimes even took pride in strutting around, towelless, admiring myself in the mirrors. I had no reason to be ashamed of my body or my penis (even though I was afraid it would appear smaller than it normally was because of the cold), but for some reason I felt shy then. I hesitated a moment, standing stupidly, listening to the drips from my wet clothes hitting the floor. I did not hesitate for long, however, as I realized with alarm that soon I would not have to worry about my penis appearing small. On the contrary. I could feel it straining against the wet fabric of my underwear. I took a deep breath and started unbuttoning my shirt, all the while trying to imagine as many repulsive things as I could, anything to halt the progress of my erection. I thought of guillotined heads, my naked grandmother, a basket of dead kittens, my authorizations job. . . .

I quickly finished undressing, tossed my clothes over to him and then watched as he took them back out the door and down the stairs. I went over to the bed, grabbed a sheet from under the comforter, and wrapped it around me like a toga. Feeling relieved, I took a seat on the floor next to the fire and had just gotten comfortable when it started up again. It was the sheet that had triggered it this time, infused as it was with his smell, much the way old track uniforms issued at the beginning of the season in high school were permeated with the faint scents of the previous wearers.

Bloody car crashes, farm machinery accidents, lung cancer . . . I thought desperately as I heard him bounding up the stairs. He laughed when he saw me in my improvised Greek attire.

"I do have some clothes you can borrow," he said.

"No!" I said, my cock now rigid and pressed up against my stomach. "Uh, I'm fine like this."

"Okay," he said, walking over to the bed. He whipped off the other sheet and tied it similarly around himself.

"Looks comfortable enough. Do you smoke?" he asked, and I knew somehow that he didn't mean cigarettes.

"Not often," I said, remembering the last time I had smoked. It had been at the drive-in with some friends, and I had been so overcome by giggles that I was banished to the playground next to the concession stand, where I was quite content to swing all night singing an endless version of Prince's "Purple Rain."

He pulled a small pouch out of his backpack and from it he took rolling papers and a film canister and set to work rolling a joint. When he'd finished, he lit it, inhaled deeply, and handed it to me. Weak, pathetic victim of peer pressure that I have always been, I took it and inhaled the acrid smoke just as Carey had taught me, being careful not to wet the end. It was strong and I coughed, revealing my rookie status. I took one more drag and handed it back to him.

"This is a nice place," I said. "Is it all yours, or is the downstairs rented out?"

"Oh, I rent the whole thing," he said. "It's falling apart, so the rent's cheap. I live up here pretty much, and the downstairs is where I do all my work."

"Ohh," I said knowingly, imagining cellars full of whips and chains, or mirrored rooms with large beds canopied in red velvet.

"My *art*work," he said, successfully interpreting my "Ohh," and correcting me. "The work you're thinking of I try to do at their place, but if they don't have one—and a lot of them don't—we'll usually get a room somewhere. I try not to bring people back here. This is my space."

I wondered if I should feel flattered that he had brought me here. I puzzled over it a minute but then concluded only that I felt hot, and, as my "condition" had improved enough that I could stand without tenting my toga, I got up and moved back to the small couch.

"We can pull that closer if you want," he said, nodding at the couch and getting up to help me. I swayed a bit, feeling the first wave of the pot, but together we pulled the couch closer to the fire. Then it started. Suddenly I thought there was nothing so absurd as me pulling the couch—*Imagine! The whole couch!*—nearer to the fire! And I fell down on it in a fit of giggles. Ray was laughing now too, albeit somewhat unsure of the reason, and sat down beside me. He got up again and grabbed a pack of cigarettes off the mantel, lit two, and gave me one. I was halfway finished with it before my giggles subsided, and we sat quietly, slouched down, mesmerized by the fire.

"Do you think I could do it?" I asked.

"Do what?"

"You know, the thing that you don't do here."

He laughed. "You mean hustle? Sure you could. I mean I don't really know you, but you're young, you're good-looking, you've got the body. It's just a matter of whether your head's in the right place. It's not just about sex."

"What do you mean?" I asked, and tried to sit up.

"A lot of times you have to do more. You have to be a counselor to guys who are married or just coming out, or a baby-sitter for the ones who just want someone to go out with. You have to act interested in the sex, of course, but that isn't half as hard as acting interested in what they're saying sometimes. You have to make sure they're having a good time. I'd say half the time it's great. Fun. But the other half can be as exciting as a math problem."

"Sounds like living with Paul," I mumbled.

"Huh?"

"Nothing."

"If you're really interested I can introduce you to some guys, but don't say I didn't warn you. You might hate it."

He got up and went into another room and came back with a box of Rice Krispies Treats. We ate and talked, and, emboldened by the pot, I thought of asking him about his mottled hands. I looked at them as he ate, and then I noticed something that made me shiver and feel instantly lucid. As he tore open the wrapper of another treat I saw, on each wrist, a vertical scar almost identical to Hole's. I grabbed one of his wrists in mine and looked at it. His shoulders tensed.

"Why did you do that?" I asked.

He looked down at his wrist.

"That? Oh, I cut myself shaving," he said, and flashed a sardonic grin.

"No, really."

He looked thoughtfully at both wrists. "I . . . don't know," he said. "You're the only one who's ever asked me that. Everyone else just thought it was the drugs, but they were just a symptom of the problem, not the problem itself. The truth is, I was sober when I did it." He paused, and chewed slowly.

"I guess I felt trapped. I wasn't happy with the way things were but I didn't see any way of changing them."

I nodded, understanding. I swallowed hard, feeling like I might cry, although more for myself than for him.

"What . . . changed your mind?" I asked, still clinging to his wrist, eager to hear his answer. Eager to hear what he'd grabbed onto to pull himself out.

He laughed, took back his hand, and took a large bite of his treat, mumbling something that sounded like "Taxes hurt me" or "Take me Thursday."

"What?" I asked. He chewed slowly and swallowed.

"Taxidermy," he said, grinning broadly. "I know it sounds stupid but that's it. That's also how my hands got stained—I know you were wondering about that. Everybody does. I was a little careless at first with the chemicals."

He held up his hands and gave me a good view of the dark stains on both sides.

"See, when I was doing methadone treatment I was in this resident clinic and shared a room with an old guy from Montana. He used to lead hunting trips before he got hooked. He wanted to talk and I needed something to do with my hands, so we made a good team. He taught me and talked me through most of it, and I totally got into it. It's a great thing to know, and it's going to be very important in the future." I gave him a confused, questioning look. He sat up on the edge of the sofa and faced me.

"It's like this," he said. "As time goes by the world's getting smaller and the population's getting bigger. We're all fighting for a limited amount of space, and the animals are the ones who suffer for it. Man is the dominant species, and we're taking over all of the animals' habitats. At the rate we're going extinction for many species is inevitable. In fact, there have been five massive extinctions in the Earth's history, and scientists are speculating that right now we're smack-dab in the middle of the sixth, so preserving animals may be the only record we have. I'm willing to bet that in a thousand years good taxidermy work will be prized and inspire as much awe and wonder as the Egyptian mummies do today. My work will be a valuable historical record. If I can learn some more, that is. There's this school in Paris I'd like to go to. There's one in upstate New York, too, but the one in Paris is supposedly better. . . ."

Wow, I thought, and shook my head, *this stuff's stronger than I thought*. I was finding it increasingly difficult to stay awake, and I leaned over drowsily on the couch and rested my head on Ray's lap. He talked on and on, and I listened, but I wasn't hearing. The last thing I remembered before I fell into sleep was gazing drowsily at the flames and feeling his fingers run gently through my hair.

I don't know how long I was asleep, but it was dark outside when I awoke and I was alarmed for a minute as I struggled to orient myself and remember where I was. I had been moved from the couch and was now sitting up on the bed, my toga still firmly tied at the shoulder and Ray's sheet covering me. The fire was still going, but had been turned down. I felt like Kim Novak in *Vertigo,* when she wakes up naked in Jimmy Stewart's apartment. I got up and went over to the small kitchen, where I drank three large glasses of water in quick succession. Ray was not there. Nor was he in the bathroom. The door leading downstairs was open and I could hear music playing. Spanish guitar. I felt for a light switch but, feeling only smooth wall, I inched my way down the dark stairwell. At the bottom I hesitated. I was still curious about the room to the right and I now knew it was not someone else's, so I nudged open the door. Again I felt for a switch, found one, and turned it on.

It was a small room, maybe twelve by twelve, and was clearly the room where he did all his painting. There was an easel and several canvases, some painted and some blank; there were paint tubes, large coffee cans full of brushes, and some sort of small paint sprayer attached to a long air hose. The inside of the fireplace, evidently no longer used, had been painted to resemble fire, and on closer inspection there were little painted devils peeking out from the flames. Several canvases hung on the walls, abstracts mostly, and more were stacked against one wall. I looked through one pile of small drawings. Most were of faces, male and female, while others were of cars, a package of cigarettes, various dogs. All had been executed quickly, some on napkins or notebook paper, all with pencil or pen. I heard a noise coming from the other side of the foyer, so I quickly set the drawings back down, turned out the light, and left the room. I crossed the dark foyer and pushed open the door to the other side of the house.

The room I entered was large, probably intended as a dining room, as it had a large chandelier hanging from the middle of the ceiling, but now it looked like a cross between a sweatshop and an auto-body shop. In one corner there was a large, square table on which sat an old sewing machine. In an open cupboard above it there were spools of thread, clear mostly, like fishing line, and a case full of sewing needles, some large and oddly curved, others so small you could barely see the eyelet. On the floor was another cabinet, this one devoted to adhesives: glues in small tubes and large bottles, different sizes of glue guns and caulk dispensers, and roll after roll of duct tape. On the other side of the room there was a large workbench over which hung a collection of hammers and wrenches, arranged according to size. There were large rolls of chicken wire, bolts of burlap, and unopened boxes of clay (the same brand my mother had used during her stint as a potter). In one corner he had been welding something, as there was an acetylene torch, various pieces of metal, and a large spool of solder.

In the middle of all this was evidently the piece on which all these tools were being used. It was a rather large diorama, much like those at the Natural History Museum, but this one was composed entirely of stuffed dogs. Some were complete and sat, unstirring, off to the side. Others were still in the process of being sewn together over their plaster frames, as evidenced by the body of some unfortunate cocker spaniel, the head of which gazed longingly down from the workbench at its corpse sitting obediently on the floor. Hanging from the ceiling, by an almost invisible thread, was a small white French poodle, forever frozen in the act of leaping forward. Attached to its back, and looking as if they'd grown there quite naturally, was a pair of soft white wings taken from either a duck or a goose. I batted the winged poodle gently and watched, awestruck and amused, as it swung to and fro.

This will muddy the waters in the next millennium, I thought.

A swinging door opened, from the kitchen I guessed, and Ray appeared.

"You're up," he said brightly. "I was just coming to wake you. Your clothes are dry now."

He was dressed in a nicely tailored blue two-piece suit, the kind with small, high-cut lapels. In each hand he carried a mug of coffee. He handed one to me and we stood, side by side, examining the canine display.

"It's not finished yet," he said.

"So I gathered," I said, pointing to the spaniel.

"This is going to be Mary," he said, picking up the floppy-eared head and gazing at it reverently. "Poor girl got hit by a car. Her body was pretty trashed but she has the perfect face, don't you think? Serene. So I found another spaniel body and I'm going to sew her head on its body. Kind of like Frankenstein, eh?"

I nodded and wondered if maybe I wasn't quite awake yet.

"Is this, by chance, going to be a nativity scene?" I asked, trying, and failing, to keep a straight face.

"Yeah, it is," he said proudly. "I'm having a hell of a time finding a Christ child, though. Puppies aren't easy to find, and of course it can't be just *any* puppy."

"Oh, of course not. Jesus and all . . ."

"I was hoping to have it done by Christmas, but obviously I didn't make it. By next year it'll be all set, and I'll have a lot of other pieces to go along with it."

"Do the others have a Christmas theme?" I asked.

"Yeah." He nodded eagerly. "It's a perfect example of what I was telling you before when you asked about what kind of art I do."

"How so?" I asked. I was interested and tried to remember our conversation from earlier that day.

"Well, it's like this," he said, his face becoming serious and intent. "There's so much hypocrisy surrounding Christmas. Here we've got one of the two most sacred holidays in the Christian faith and yet it's been mass-marketed and exploited in ways that are more offensive than any I could ever hope to dream up, so I'm working on a group of pieces illustrating that hypocrisy."

I looked at him blankly.

"Hang on a minute; I'll show you."

He set his coffee down on the sewing table and ran excitedly to the kitchen, returning a moment later with a large wooden wine crate that he rested on a chair in front of the workbench. With his back to me, his body shielding my view, he pulled several objects from the box and appeared to be arranging them. Then he stood back, assessed it, made a few alterations, and then moved farther back and lit a cigarette.

What he'd composed was a colorful arrangement of dolls. There was a small toy sleigh, filled with tiny, painstakingly wrapped presents, in which sat a twelve-inch doll, which, I concluded from his Bedouin robes and small halo, was intended to be Jesus. In his hands, Jesus held little reins that were harnessed to twelve identical Ken dolls. Identical that is, except for the white names that had been boldly and painstakingly embroidered across their identical red sweaters. There were Peter and Andrew, John and James, Matthew and Bartholomew, and on and on down through the list of apostles, with Judas in the forefront, taking the place of Rudolph, his lips painted a bright red.

"I'm actually working on several nativity scenes, most of which will be in Christmas-card form, and will of course be for sale at the show in boxes of twenty-five. One is of Mr. and Mrs. Claus in a stable with a little baby Santa in the manger, another with Barbie and Ken as Mary and Joseph, precious stuff like that. But this," he said, gesturing grandly to the loose arrangement of dogs on the floor, "will be the bomb."

I looked at it, all of it, the strange room with its odd tools, the blasphemous displays, the maniacal expression on Ray's face as he gently stroked the spaniel's head, like Salome with John the Baptist.

I should feel afraid, I thought, *or at least alarmed.* But I did not. I was amused. Amused and, to be honest, impressed by the effort he'd expended, the cleverness, the absurdity of it all. He looked at his watch and quickly snapped out of his reverie.

"Shit!" he said. "I'm late again. I'm taking some old guy to the symphony tonight. Get dressed and I can give you a ride back to your car." He set down the head and I followed him into the kitchen, which was a large but crowded room, a huge butcher-block table at its center. Shelves on the walls were lined with bottles of chemicals, each boldly labeled— ARSENIC, BORAX, LYE—and each marked with a skull and crossbones and lists of warnings. On a Peg-Board wall hung large knives and scissors and an assortment of odd-looking tools, the likes of which I'd never seen and could scarcely imagine a use for. He tossed me my clothes from the dryer and stood, calmly sipping his coffee and smoking while I dressed.

"I wrote down the number of someone for you to call," he said. I looked up inquisitively.

"He makes amateur movies, just for his own kicks, and pays you a hundred and fifty bucks a pop. It's easy stuff. Strictly solo the first time, and if he likes you he'll call you back and hook you up with a partner. He never participates himself."

He handed me the piece of paper. I glanced at it and then folded it up and put it in my pocket, my stomach doing flip-flops.

"Tell him you got his number from me."

"Thanks," I said, thinking one hundred and fifty dollars would surely be enough to appease the people at Discover for another month. "I really appreciate this."

"Don't thank me yet. You may be cursing me by the time it's over with."

I finished dressing and together we left the house. Outside, the rain had turned to snow, but as I sat in the cold hearse, listening to him scrape the ice from the windshield, I shivered—but more from excitement than from the cold. He finished scraping and drove me to the snowy parking lot where my car sat alone under a street lamp. I got out, opened my trunk, and removed the duffel bag containing the hyena pup. His face lit up when he saw it.

"What will you do with it?" I asked.

"Study it," he said. "Then I'll probably put it back."

He thanked me again, said a hasty good-bye, and then sped off. I started my car and watched him drive away as I scraped my own windows, the huge red vehicle speeding up Fourteenth Avenue, fishtailing as it struggled to make it up the hill.

As I got back in my car I thought back on the almost surreal afternoon. Ray was much more intelligent and complex than I'd assumed earlier that day in the cafeteria, and I was sorry I'd been so quick to judge him. Again I felt myself becoming aroused as I remembered the rain and the bed and the smell of the sheets.

I guess I should feel relieved that nothing happened, I thought to myself. *Something like that could really complicate things.*

I should have felt relieved, but I didn't.

SCHOOL FOR SCANDAL

After much internal debate I called the number Ray had given me and described myself to the man on the other end of the phone.

"That sounds fine," he said, sounding very matter-of-fact. "Can you come by tomorrow about eleven?"

I said I could, and he gave me the address, which was alarmingly close to my parents' house. At the appointed time I arrived at the door of a sprawling one-story stucco house. I rang the bell and was greeted shortly by a small, weasely man, about fifty years old, wearing a boyish shorts-and-T-shirt outfit. He ushered me inside to a dark living room, the large windows almost entirely hidden by mustard-colored velvet curtains. The room was done in a Mexican style—rough stucco walls and tile floors, and filled with dark, heavy furniture, on which several cats were reclining. He offered me a drink and then, after some small talk, explained what Ray had told me the day before: he makes these movies for his own enjoyment, he never shows them to anyone else, and that in the event he should die suddenly he has a trustworthy friend who would destroy them immediately. To my surprise, I found I wasn't really concerned about that. He then produced a rather large video camera and gave me my directions.

"I'll have you go back outside and ring the doorbell, see; then I'll answer, filming all the while, and you just act natural and answer the questions I ask, okay?"

I nodded and he led me back outside and closed the door. I looked past the house across the street and could see in the distance the turret of my parents' house and the sloping roofline of my mother's recently completed teahouse. I wished I'd parked my car somewhere else, but shrugged it off and rang the doorbell. He opened the door, camera in hand, an annoyingly bright light attached to it.

"Why, hello, Jack," he said, panning the camera slowly up and down my body. "What a nice surprise! Come in."

Oh, God, I thought. *This is going to be corny. You need the money. Remember that. You need the money.*

"Thank you," I said, and reentered the dark house, camera rolling.

"Sit down," he said.

I did so, shooing away one of the cats. The light was nearly blinding me now.

"And how old are you?" he asked, his voice booming.

"Twenty-two," I lied.

"Talk a little louder," he whispered. "This mike isn't the greatest."

"Twenty-two," I said, louder this time.

"Twenty-two," he repeated. "Ooowee!"

I gave a sheepish shrug of the shoulders.

"Any more at home as cute as you?" he asked.

If you talk any louder, I thought, *my mother can answer that question for you.*

"No, I'm the only one." I smiled. "Made me and broke the mold! Ha ha ha."

He laughed, the camera bobbing up and down. I remember thinking that if this tape ever did come to light I'd surely be more embarrassed by this "small-talk" beginning than by any lewd acts that would follow, but I remembered Ray's words: *You have to make sure they're having fun.* And on I went.

"It sure is hot out there today," he said, panning to the window and the wan crack of January sunlight it admitted.

"It sure is," I said, "a real scorcher," and wondered if this was his cue for me to remove my shirt.

"Whaddaya say we go downstairs and turn up the heat a little more . . ." he said suggestively, with a demented little laugh.

"Sure!" I said, and, warming to my role, I gave a little wink to the camera. I rose and walked down the steps, feeling more like I was at the beginning of a horror movie than a porno, descending into the dark basement to meet an uncertain fate, a freak with a camera right on my heels, but the basement proved brighter and more inviting than the living room. He turned off the camera a moment and went ahead of me into a large room. On one side there was a raised landing—a sort of stage, I guess, about six inches higher than the floor, and on this was an over-stuffed brown sofa (badly stained from the countless previous perfor-mances) and a large TV with a built-in VCR. He turned on the set, pushed the tape in, and a graphic porno movie began. I remember distinctly that the actors were speaking French and that I was somewhat distracted as I struggled to hear what I knew must be really naughty French words. He picked up the camera again and switched on the annoying light.

"Okay, now just watch the movie and act natural, okay? Do what-ever you want to do, okay? You want any lube or dildoes?"

"Um, no, thank you."

I watched the movie, took off my clothes, and did what came natu-rally. Of course I enhanced the performance by caressing and probing my body, moaning and changing positions many more times than I ever would have if I'd been alone, and I have to admit it was fun. I felt so naughty, and he was so excited (even stumbling backwards off the stage at one point) that I, in turn, got excited and had to slow down to keep myself from coming too quickly. I was not attracted to him, but to the camera and to the money and to the vain fact that I was responsible for exciting someone so much.

When it was over, I showered off, got dressed, and we met again in the dark living room, where he discreetly pressed a neatly folded pack of twenties into my hand.

"That Ray sure knows what I like," he said, sitting down opposite me, sweat beading on his brow and upper lip. "You be sure and thank him for me."

"I will," I said.

"Say, any chance you two would like to do a duo together?"

"Uh, maybe that's not such a good idea," I said rapidly, and then wondered why. Ray wasn't unattractive—on the contrary—but there was something about this, the camera, the silly theatrics, maybe, that I didn't really want him to see.

"What about someone else, then?" Dave asked.

"Sure, I'd like that."

"Great!" he said. "Now, would you rather be on bottom or top, or does it matter?"

"Top," I said quickly, figuring that would be the easier and less em-barrassing of the two, at least the first time.

"Okay, then," he said brightly. "I'll see what I can set up and give you a call."

I left, having been there less than an hour. As soon as I'd driven a discreet distance I pulled over and counted the money. One hundred and sixty dollars. The easiest hundred and sixty dollars I'd ever made.

I immediately deposited it in the bank and fired off a check to Discover.

A little over a week later, Dave called back and arranged a duo. It was with a clean-cut, good-looking twenty-year-old student named Sean. It was great fun, and again I couldn't believe someone was paying me to do it. Afterward I put Sean's bike on the bike rack on my car and gave him a ride back to the DU campus. He was a political science major and said he went to Dave about once a month to supplement his student loan money. I myself returned to Dave's about once every two months after that, mostly as a steady that he could call when he had someone doing a duo for the first time.

As winter raged on, I got more work. I still saw Burl and Hole on occasion, and was still paid for it, but now there were others, too. After I'd cleared the Dave hurdle, Ray referred me to a few more of his regulars, some of whom lived in town and some of whom came into town on business. Most of these men were married and had families but obviously wanted something that their wives could not supply. I found I liked these married men best, as opposed to men who were openly gay, as they were usually so nervous and excited that the sex never took long at all. I spent more time trying to prevent their orgasms than to bring them about. Later we'd usually just lie around talking for the rest of the hour in their hotel room or in my room, since, unlike Ray, I didn't have a problem bringing someone back to my apartment, and I usually got more money when they found they wouldn't have to spring for a hotel. I had quite a "lunch crowd," and most weekdays I was booked solid from eleven to two, mostly with businessmen who worked downtown, and who were grateful to have a clean, safe place to go.

One day, between lunchtime tricks, as I was changing the sheets for the third time, I got a page from Ray on my newly acquired pager. It was his cell phone number.

"What have you got going this afternoon?" he asked when I called him back.

"Nothing much," I said, looking at my watch. "I've got one more lunch special, which shouldn't take more than half an hour. It's that accountant you sent my way. He's usually in a hurry. Then I don't have anything until seven tonight. Why?"

"Well, something sort of came up. Look, I don't have a lot of time to explain it. It'd be great money for you, but we'd have to travel a ways, and, um, he wants both of us."

I was silent, thinking of the duos at Dave's and how I'd avoided doing one with Ray.

"Oh" was all I came up with.

"He's pretty old," Ray continued, "so I guess he can't really participate. What he wants to do is watch the two of us together. I don't know how far we have to go or if you're even into it, but you'd really be doing me a favor. . . ." He trailed off, waiting for my response.

I bit my lip and scrunched up my face, trying to think of some way out of it, but curious all the same and eager not to sound too Pollyanna-ish.

"I don't know," I said, considering the consequences. "I mean, I guess I could. Yeah, sure, I'll do it."

"Good," he said. "Do you think you could drive, too? We kind of need to be discreet about this, and my car . . . well, you know."

"Sure."

"Great. You're a stud! Come over as soon as you're done and I'll fill you in on the rest of it. If I'm not there just go on in, make yourself at home."

I made it to Ray's by one-thirty. I didn't see his car so I let myself in. Curious to see how his project was progressing I went into the living room—as inappropriate as that name was, given its contents—and waited.

Mary's spaniel head was now attached quite seamlessly to her body and she sat in a blue robe next to Joseph, a large terrier of some sort dressed in a brown robe and brown turban, one paw somehow made to clutch a staff. He was, as yet, eyeless, a collection of glass possibilities staring up from an open tackle box on the floor next to him. The winged poodle still hung from the ceiling but was now in possession of a halo and a small toy trumpet. It hovered over a shepherd of German origin. The wise men were a trio of schnauzers partially dressed in gold brocade robes, their empty paws positioned stiffly in front of them to carry yet unseen offerings. All were present and accounted for except for the baby Jesus, whose empty manger was now the focus of every gaze. (Except for Joseph's, of course.) As interesting as all that was, it was not enough to distract my mind from what was going to happen.

Why am I so nervous? I thought. *I've probably had sex with thirty different guys in the past two months. Why should I feel nervous?*

I heard Ray's car pull up and watched through the window as he unloaded some camera equipment and placed it in the backseat of my car. I went outside.

"What's all that for?" I asked.

"Oh, hey!" he said, smiling broadly. "You ready?"

"Yes, I guess so."

"I'll explain on the way then. We're kind of late—come on."

He explained that he wanted to take some pictures of me and the man together.

"Nothing obscene," he said. "Some art pictures."

My nervousness was replaced by a slight annoyance, but I said nothing. He had been extremely helpful, so I figured I owed him something in return. We drove for about twenty minutes out into the east suburbs as he gave me directions from a crumpled piece of paper and loaded a large thirty-five millimeter camera with film. It had snowed heavily the night before and was starting to snow again.

"Look," he said, trying to appease me, "I know I'm asking a lot but I'll give you my take of the money, and I think you'll actually like it. Oh, hey, turn left here; there it is."

I pulled in and parked next to the building, which appeared to be some sort of hospital or hospice, as there were groups of overweight nurses standing outside smoking, their smoky breath made all the smokier by the cold.

"What is this?" I asked, feeling sure we must be at the wrong address.

"Sit tight a minute," he said, and scanned the group of nurses. "We're supposed to just wait here for a guy named"—he uncrumpled the paper and looked at it once more—"Hector."

"If this is some drug deal," I said, remembering similar meetings I'd driven to with Carey when we were in high school, my voice tinged with irritation, "I don't want any part of it."

"It's not a drug deal," he said, "at least not between us. Oh, hey, I think that's him."

I followed his gaze to a lanky Latino man, probably about my age, with long hair and a faint mustache, who was shoveling the sidewalk in front of the building. He was looking at Ray and Ray was looking at him, and then they both nodded slightly to each other. He approached Ray's side of the car and Ray lowered the window.

"You lookin' for Hector?" he asked, tapping the shovel on the ground and looking around shiftily.

Ray nodded.

"Go to room two-oh-nine," he whispered. "Anyone talks to you, tell 'em you're visiting Mr. Johansen."

"And the money," Ray said firmly.

The man nodded and pulled a small envelope from his jacket. He dropped it through the window into Ray's lap and went quickly back toward the building. Ray handed me the envelope, which I stuffed in the glove compartment, not wanting to touch it if it was drug money, but curious all the same how much we were getting. My heart was racing and I was sweating, but I said nothing.

"Looks like we're in business," Ray said, getting out of the car and taking his camera bag. Reluctantly I followed and we entered a dimly lit lobby, the edges of which were lined with elderly men and women, some dozing in wheelchairs, others sitting on easy chairs, their walkers or canes in front of them. An algae-choked aquarium gurgled in one corner under a large bulletin board advertising a bus trip to a shopping mall. Some raised their white heads with a vague curiosity when we entered, but most just continued dozing or staring vacantly off into the distance. The smell of urine and disinfectant was nearly overpowering.

Ray strode purposefully across the lobby to the reception desk. I hung back.

"Hi, we're here to see my uncle, Mr. Johansen. Up those stairs there? Thanks." Ray motioned for me to follow. We went down a dark hallway, very wide, and lined on both sides with a handrail, until we reached the stairs. He went up a few steps till he was out of view of the desk and then turned to me.

"How ya doin?" he asked, and gave me a pat on the shoulder.

I shook my head and gave him a look of worry and annoyance, but continued up the stairs. On the second floor, we entered a hallway identical to the one below. Several TVs were blaring loudly, and someone was moaning, "I'm so thirsty; please can't I have just a little water?"

We stood looking around. It was dark and I couldn't make out the room numbers on the doors. Then I spied the man from the parking lot standing at the far end of the hall beckoning to us.

"There," I said, pulling on Ray's sleeve. "Let's go."

He ushered us into one of the rooms and closed the door behind him. The view into the room was blocked by one of those track curtains used as a room divider. Hector grabbed this and pulled it back, revealing a small, very old man in a red cardigan sweater. He was sitting up on a hospital bed, his extended legs covered by a green afghan, grinning broadly at us and squinting through his glasses.

"This what you wanted?" Hector asked him, "this" being Ray and myself.

"Splendid!" he said, clasping his hands together. Hector leaned closer to him and whispered, "You got the stuff?"

The man nodded and then reached in his sweater and removed a large plastic bag full of pills and handed it to Hector, who took it over to the window and examined it briefly before placing it inside the front of his shirt, just above his waistline, making him look like he had acquired a small paunch. He adjusted it until it looked natural and then turned back to us.

"It's two-thirty now," he said gravely, looking at his watch. "He won't get medicine till three-twenty, so you should be safe until a little after three. I'll be watching the door outside, okay? And I'll knock twice if anyone's coming."

He adjusted his parcel again and left, quietly closing the door behind him.

I looked at the little man on the bed and then looked to Ray, hoping for some indication as to how we should start or what we should do, but his back was to us as he fiddled with the camera. I looked back at the man, who was still beaming, and smiled weakly, the ends of my mouth twitching slightly.

"What's your name?" I asked, figuring I was in it now, so I might as well make the best of it.

"Walter," he said, wringing his hands together excitedly.

"Walter, I'm Jack and this," I said, reaching over and pinching Ray hard on the ass, "is Ray."

"Ow! Fuck!" he cried, but did not turn around. "Hey, Walt, I'll be right with you."

I pulled off my sweater and approached the bed. Obviously I wasn't going to get much help initiating things from either party so I decided to start things moving myself. I smiled at Walter.

"What do you like to do?" I purred suggestively. His eyes widened and his wrinkled hands reached out to me eagerly. He ran them slowly up and down my torso, over the ridges of my abdominals and up between my pectorals. They were large hands, traversed by large ropes of veins, and looked pale, nearly transparent, next to my skin, and felt somewhat rough and scratchy. I heard the click of the camera but it seemed muffled, or as if it were coming from very far away. I removed the rest of my clothes and got up onto the narrow bed, straddling his narrow, afghan-draped legs. He reached around me and ran his hands up and down my spine. I was surprised to feel that I was becoming aroused, and we both stared at the oddity of his hand as it encircled my hard shaft, his other now gently squeezing my ass cheeks. *Click, click, click* went the camera, but the sound was subtle, almost soft, like the uneven ticking of a large clock. I leaned down, removed his glasses, and kissed him gently on the mouth. His lips felt chapped and rough, and his scent was of an ancient shaving product that reminded me of a summer vacation years ago. Fishing. I'd been cold and my grandfather had given me his flannel shirt.

My hair fell forward and he brushed it back from my face with both hands. With my hands, I eased his sweater and pajama top back from his thin shoulders and massaged them and his neck. His skin was dry, almost leathery, but his body went almost limp under my touch, and he emitted a soft, plaintive cry. It was evident that he had not been touched like that in years. Then I noticed other hands on me, moving slowly up my abdominals to my chest, and felt arms encircling me from behind. I was pulled back gently and felt Ray's torso meet my back, his hardness firm against my spine, his goatee gently brushing my neck. I turned my head sideways to kiss him and it was then that I saw her standing in the open doorway—the stout, bug-eyed nurse, her chest heaving in its tight polyester casing, as she struggled to both take in and shut out what she was seeing.

I gave a startled yell and squirmed from Ray's arms. The nurse bolted from the doorway and we could hear her running down the hallway yelling, "Security! Security!" Ray vaulted off the bed and slammed the door. I looked back down at the poor man I was straddling. He looked concerned and a little disappointed, but was still smiling. His white hair looked windblown and his face was flushed. In that instant I had a glimpse of him as he must have looked as a young man. I gave him a kiss and then jumped down off of the bed, frantically collecting my clothes, hearing fabric rip as I struggled to put them on. Hector came in quickly and shut the door, his face white with fear.

"I tried to stop her. Oh, shit!" he hissed, peering back out in to the hallway and waving his hands frantically. "The window, the window!"

Ray and I paused, looking at each other and then over at the window. I was in my boxers at this point and had one leg in my pants. I stumbled over to the window and looked down. It was only one story, but it was a sheer drop to the parking lot below, and it was snowing hard. I turned the crank and a frigid breeze entered the room. I looked back at Ray, who was busy again with the fucking camera bag!

"Come on!" I hissed, pulling my other leg into my pants and buttoning the top button.

"Okay! You go first and I'll toss the rest down to you," he said, indicating the camera bag. I then watched as he absently grabbed my T-shirt, mistaking it for his boxers, and stepped into it, one leg in each arm hole, his cock and balls totally exposed. I tossed a wad of clothing into the snowy parking lot and climbed up through the narrow window frame. I paused, trying to determine a suitable landing spot to aim for, when I felt a hand shove me from behind and I landed, doggie-style, on the hood of a car.

"God damn it!" I said, pain creeping into my knees and wrists as I crawled off, leaving a sizable depression. I looked up and saw Ray's face, mildly concerned, but smiling, his hand gently swinging the camera bag.

"Catch," he said, and I did. He quickly followed, landing feet-first on the pavement, but then he slipped and landed hard on his ass. Our shoes and socks followed, courtesy of Hector, and I left Ray to gather them up while I ran and got the car, fishing in my pockets for the keys.

A small crowd was gathering at the smoking lounge, so I gunned the engine and put it in reverse. I couldn't get much traction because of the snow, but eventually I backed out of the space and spun forward to where Ray, in his ridiculous outfit, hopped from one foot to the other, shivering. I slowed the car as I approached him, flung open the passenger door, and in he jumped. I pushed the gas pedal to the floor and we slid sideways, the open door smacking a light pole and slamming violently shut.

"Jesus!" he cried, and nearly jumped into my lap. I drove fast and wordlessly out of the lot and toward the highway, thinking of the dent on the door and that I was glad I'd mailed my insurance payment on time.

When we were at what I perceived to be a safe distance, I slowed down and looked over at the shivering Ray. He looked at me and started laughing.

"It's not funny," I said sternly, but was beginning to laugh myself. He leaned over, put his arm around my neck, and pulled my head close to his. He bit my earlobe gently and whispered, "That was beautiful!"

Then he returned to his seat and started sorting and putting on his clothes.

While driving I thought of myself on the bed and how surprised I'd been when I felt Ray's hands on my chest, his chest on my back. How disappointed I'd been that the whole thing was interrupted. Then I remembered the feel of his teeth on my ear just then. . . .

"Hey, what's that?" Ray said, grinning and pointing to the rod that was poking out of my unzipped pants. I smiled and blushed.

"Sometimes it takes a while to go down," I said, and pushed it back inside. "And give me my shirt!"

LIES AND SECRETS

My family and Andre were all growing curious about what I was doing for money, and my vague responses succeeded only in making them suspicious. So for lack of any better idea I decided I'd stick to the same line I was using in the microbusiness classes: that I was doing fitness training full-time but now had many more clients. This flew with my parents, who were both relieved that I finally seemed to be fending for myself. My father even got me a pager and a cell phone, which helped immensely, since it freed me from having to sit at home and wait for calls, and from constantly checking voice mail. It was also deductible as a business expense, as Tina informed me in class one day as my pager went off. The other students looked at me enviously, and by the following week there was a chorus of bells and whistles in the classroom.

Over dinner one night, my first dinner at home with the family since my banishment, my dad mentioned that he'd be glad to send a few clients my way.

"Some of the guys in the office could stand to lose a few pounds; maybe you could give us a corporate rate."

"Maybe in the future," I said, and laughed inwardly as I pictured the "services" I could provide to my father's associates, "but I'm too busy now as it is, and I'm concerned about managing the growth of the business, since statistically forty percent of small businesses fail in the beginning because they don't have the infrastructure to support a rapid increase in volume."

His jaw dropped. "Why, yes, that's true, but how—"

"And furthermore, I think it's vital to maintain the level of customer satisfaction I've established so far, since word of mouth can often be the most effective form of advertising."

"Hey, you're really learning something in those classes of yours."

"Yes, sir, I am." I said proudly, basking in my father's awe.

Unfortunately, all my entrepreneurial zeal set the wheels spinning in my mother's head. The teahouse finished, her interest in the Japanese garden was on the wane. Mr. Matsumoto came by once a week to rake the leaves and trim the bonsai, so all she really had to do was feed the koi. Similarly, Bobby and Ethel, the pair of mastiffs that she had acquired, had been well trained over the winter months and sat quietly and obediently at her feet, no longer challenging enough to keep her occupied. For that reason, the focus of her curiosity lighted on me and the class I was taking. Only Andre knew about my food stamp folly, and I was not eager to share the information with anyone else, especially my conservative, welfare-bashing father, whose nascent respect I did not want to destroy by having him find out I was now leeching from the government instead of from him. This secret, I saw, was in danger of being exposed by my mother's prying, so I tried, in vain, to change the subject.

"That sounds so interesting, honey," she said, regarding me intently from across the table. "Now where did you say you signed up for this class?"

"Uh, I didn't. It's through the state. I don't think they do it anymore."

"Well maybe your teacher knows—could you ask her for me? Maybe I could sit in on one of your classes."

"No! I mean, I don't think you'd like it."

"Oh, I know I would. Will you at least ask her?"

"Sure, yeah, I'll ask her, Mom."

"A small business! Imagine! It sounds so exciting! I bet I could do that."

I eventually put her off the scent by giving her a course catalog from the Free University, highlighting a business course and telling her it was the same one I was taking.

"Is it exactly the same?" she asked skeptically, skimming over the course description. "Because yours sounds so detailed."

"Exactly," I lied.

"I thought you said yours was through the state."

"Uh, yeah, it was, but they, uh, lost the funding. You know, spending cuts and all, so they had to turn it over to the private sector."

"Oh."

"Yes."

"That's probably better, isn't it? The private sector. It is a business class, after all."

"Exactly."

And thus she was off on her next campaign, through which my father and Mr. Matsumoto suffered terribly. She decided to sell something for which there was clearly a high demand and came to the conclusion that the market was crying out for mastiff puppies. A fact she was well aware of, having paid almost one thousand dollars each for hers.

Although my parents were more or less satisfied with my facade, Andre and my sister were less gullible.

"Girl, I know you're up to something tricky," Andre said one day as I picked up the check from lunch. "But as long as you're paying . . ."

And paying I was! The microbusiness class was teaching me all about personal finance, and I made up a budget and payment plan to get myself out of debt. I made huge monthly payments to credit card companies, slowly punching down the balances, and one day I even released my cards from their icy prisons, only to execute them, once and forever, with scissors, although I did spare one, my very first Visa, to which I had a sentimental attachment, but for emergency use only, of course.

MY OWN PRIVATE
MADISON AVENUE

After I'd been working steadily for about two months, business began to drop off. Although most of the clients Ray had sent my way were very happy with my services, they also wanted variety, and after two months I was no longer a novelty. They would visit me three or four times, sample what I had to offer, but then, like travelers on a ten-day tour of Europe, were eager to see the next city. Not all clients were so fickle, thank God. These more conservative and loyal men had reached a level of comfort with me and saw no reason to look elsewhere. It's not that they didn't like variety, but that they liked the intimacy that developed between us over time, and in that intimacy there was a different type of variety. After a few visits, I knew what they liked and how they liked it, and they came to appreciate my memory and my techniques. There were probably ten or so of these loyal clients, who came at least once every two weeks, and though I was grateful for their patronage, they were not enough to pay my bills.

Three-ways with Ray were another good source of income, and we did them as often as possible now that I was less inhibited, but they too were becoming fewer and farther between. What we needed was a steady stream of new business to augment the regulars. What we came up with, Ray and I, was an elaborate plan to start marketing ourselves.

Contrary to what I had told my father at dinner, word of mouth was not an effective means of advertising sex for sale. Somehow it seemed implausible that Suburban Joe, pausing in his weekend lawn mowing, would lean over the fence and tell Suburban Bob about the great cock he'd sucked the other day.

"I'm tellin' ya, it was just perfect, not too long but ample, ya know, satisfying, and the price was really reasonable."

And thank God these conversations didn't take place, because if Suburban Joe ever realizes that Suburban Bob is after the same thing, then they'll probably just service each other, and that certainly wouldn't be good for business. No, our marketing would have to be less oral.

Since moving to Denver two years ago, Ray had advertised only twice, each time placing small, pictureless ads in one of the local gay papers offering escort services. From these, he had established a relatively loyal clientele, but he too saw the need for an aggressive marketing plan, as his taxidermy was eating up more money, and the good turn he'd done me by sending several of his clients my way was not doing much for his wallet.

In the microbusiness class we had spent several weeks discussing and developing different advertising and marketing strategies, so I knew all about the importance of finding my target market and researching the competition.

"Don't be shy about calling up your competitors and pretending you're a client," Tina said one day in class. "If you become successful, I guarantee they'll be calling you. And be sure and call more than one and compare their prices; that way you can do a better job deciding what you're going to charge."

Until then, I had thought that picking Ray's brain on the subject of pricing was all the research I needed to do, but as our services became more specialized and unique, even he would sometimes shrug his shoulders and admit that he really wasn't sure how much we should charge. With that in mind, we decided to follow Tina's advice and do some research, which was not as easy as it sounds. Since pricing in our line of business is by nature vague and fluid, I couldn't really call up other hustlers and ask them outright how much they charged for a blow job or an hour of sex. If they were anything like me they charged more to people they didn't particularly like or who wanted them to do things they were not really keen to do. On the other hand, if they had a sentimental streak, they probably charged less to the really cute ones, or the ones they felt sorry for. With this in mind, I decided not to call other hustlers but to study their ads closely, and to interview my clients about their experiences with them.

Scanning the classifieds in the gay papers I noticed that ads for prostitution fell under three categories: massage, model, and escort. Some of the massage ads were clearly legitimate, picturing the face of the masseuse and using specific technical terms like Reiki, or shiatsu, or deep-tissue reflexology, none of which sounded very sexual to me. Other ads, those with headless pictures, or no pictures at all, offered massage in the nude, and listed the physical dimensions of the masseuse. These ads were obviously offering prostitution, and the fact that there were pages and pages of them indicated that they were an effective way to generate business. But I knew nothing about massage, except that I liked getting one and hated giving one, so that didn't seem the way to go.

The ads for models and escorts were less veiled. Again, the pictures were nearly always headless photos of well-defined, well-oiled torsos in skimpy underwear, or no underwear at all but with a large piece of black tape censoring the groin area. Some ads actually included the head of their subject, but these were rare, and when they did appear, the guy was usually pictured looking down or wearing sunglasses and a ball cap to conceal his identity. The ads that were the most explicit—those that showed the entire face, unadorned and promising impossibly large penises—were usually for escort agencies. These were easy to spot, as their graphics and lettering were always a little more sophisticated, and they often featured a recognizable porn star as their model. I asked some of my clients about their experiences with these agencies and was told they were notoriously disappointing, never delivering anything close to what they advertised (which explained why so many of the independent hustlers often included the urgent statement "This is me!" under their photos). The boys from the agencies (and they were almost always very young boys) were not very good-looking, were often drug addicted, and usually did not enjoy, or even pretend to enjoy, what they were doing. Their price was never less than a hundred dollars, and that amount was paid in full to the agency beforehand, leaving the client uncertain how much money the boy was actually getting. I later learned that they sometimes got forty percent, but more often than not it was thirty, or even twenty. Better than flipping burgers, but only just.

"They almost always try to gouge more out of you," one seasoned client told me wearily. "You've already paid the agency, but still the kid'll try and nickel and dime you to death. 'If you want to do this it will cost extra.' 'If you want to do that it will cost extra.' Hell, it's easier to troll the park or go to one of the bars on Broadway and pick up a street hustler. At least it cuts out the middleman."

Which brings up yet another class of prostitute, although one that caters to clients in a lower income bracket than mine. The street hustler is a guy who does no advertising, other than posing on a park bench or a bar stool, and has often turned to prostitution out of desperation. Not that I didn't, too, but there are levels of desperation, and theirs is the lowest. They are always young, usually dirty, and very often not even gay. These are the Dickensian characters I'd expected to find at the food stamp office. The boys who run away from home, enter a life of crime in the big city, and have been the subject of countless TV docudramas. You see them hitchhiking on the edge of the road, making hopeful eye contact with the cruising driver, or hanging around public rest rooms, never getting more than ten or twenty dollars for their services. Often they do it in trade for a meal and a place to stay, or, as Ray had done in the beginning, for drugs.

The next category, my category, was the independent hustler: the guy who runs a small business with himself as the product/service. Within this category are several subcategories, catering to the many sexual whims and yens of the human male.

One of the largest of these (judging by the number of ads) is for men who want older, larger, hairier men. The top men. The daddies. The bears. Rugged masculinity personified. The men you'd imagine hunting for big game in Africa or chopping down trees in the Pacific Northwest. Men who will take charge and tell you, the client, what to do, instead of vice versa. In their ads they wear ripped flannel shirts and denim jeans, or black leather chaps and body harnesses. Often they're dressed in uniforms—as cops or firemen or construction workers—and their photos are usually no-nonsense frontal shots, emphasizing their size or body hair. The text underneath invariably promises to deliver all the masculinity and dominance that go along with their uniforms, and invariably they have the one-syllable names—Dirk or Jake or Hank—usually reserved for gas station attendants.

Although my name was one syllable, I still had the peachy complexion and hairlessness of youth, which is what the men that called me wanted. I was the young, clean-cut, boy-next-door type. The college student. The young athlete. The Abercrombie & Fitch advertisement. With that in mind, I put the focus of my study on the ads featuring guys like me, of which there was, unfortunately, no shortage. I thumbed through page after page after page of provocative ads, all featuring young, hairless, well-oiled abdominals, each almost indistinguishable from the next. These pictures were each placed over a small box of text listing (somewhat redundantly, I thought) the physical dimensions of the boy pictured, his first name (usually Jimmy or Michael or Christopher), and a phone or pager number. I studied these ads closely and tried to think of ways to improve on them. It wasn't hard.

For the most part, the ads were straightforward—what you see is what you get, no surprises—which is, to a certain extent, what the majority of clients want. And yet, all of these "boy ads" seemed to be lacking something—a mystique, a fantasy, a gimmick, I guess—and for that reason they all blended together like a naughty collage. The daddies were not so monochromatic. They had gimmicks. They used props and costumes and words to great effect, but my competition seemed to think that youth and beauty, plain set, was enough of an enticement. I did not agree.

When I'd finished studying the ads, I turned the focus on myself and made an assessment of what I had to offer. I looked in the mirror and was not disappointed to see a blond version of Robbie from *My Three Sons* looking back at me. I was young, square-jawed, wholesome, well built, educated, and athletic. What I needed was a way to convey all that information in one picture and a few words.

Ray and I discussed all of this extensively, and, after doing some additional research into advertising rates for the local papers, decided to compose three of our own picture ads. He would do one, I would do one, and we would do one featuring the two of us.

In preparation for our photo shoot, I led Ray, kicking and screaming all the way, to the gym for a few workouts. His body was fine—lean and taut—but I figured it wouldn't hurt to firm it up a bit and give his muscles some definition. It was hardly worth it. One would think that someone who had, more than once, been under the tatooist's needle, and who had also somehow endured the pain of having a bolt put through his tongue, would be able to take the pain of a little muscle strain, but for that week and the week following, he moved as slowly and whined as loudly as poor arthritic Hole ever had.

Our first ads were relatively conservative and required little as far as props or costumes. In mine, my upper body appeared sweaty and speckled with mud, and was photographed in a twisting profile, captured in the act of catching a pass. I wore an impossibly tight pair of shorts (emblazoned with the insignia of an East Coast prep school), which accentuated both the bulge of my cock and the firmness of my ass, while at the same time exposing my abdominals, my pecs, and my biceps. In my right hand I clutched a weathered football. Under this picture, in block capitals, were the words COLLEGE JOCK, my first name, my cell phone number, and my pager number.

Ray's ad was more difficult to come up with. He wasn't really rough trade, but wasn't exactly the type you'd take home to meet Mother, either, so we decided to imitate one of the construction worker ads we'd seen in a magazine from L.A. First we dressed him in a pair of old cutoffs, leaving the top button suggestively undone. We covered his naked chest and arms in baby oil, to mimic sweat, and photographed him in the action of swinging a sledgehammer. His head was visible but his face was not, shielded by a bright yellow hard hat. It wasn't completely original, but it looked okay.

For the duo ad, we sat down and composed a list of all the famous male duos we could think of: Lewis and Clark, Laurel and Hardy, Batman and Robin, the Lone Ranger and Tonto, Butch Cassidy and the Sundance Kid, Siegfried and Roy . . . but the duo we finally decided on, because they seemed the most emblematic of the "naughty boyishness" we felt we were trying to push, was Tom Sawyer and Huckleberry Finn.

The costumes for this were quite simple—ripped cutoffs, ratty straw hats, corncob pipes clenched tightly in our teeth—and we posed in front of a quickly painted backdrop of the Mississippi. We faced forward, each with an arm affectionately around the other. In my free hand I held a wooden bucket of whitewash, while in his, Ray held a crude bamboo fishing pole.

When we'd finished photographing these first three scenarios, Ray quickly took the film into his closet/darkroom for development. When he emerged sometime later, we excitedly spread out the finished products on his sewing table and assessed them critically. Alone, they looked fine. The messages they sent were clear and sufficiently titillating. Then

Ray grabbed one of the papers and we set our ads in among all the others. The one featuring Tom and Huck was like nothing else on the page and caught the eye immediately, but our individual ads blended in seamlessly with all of the others, which was not good.

"This sucks," Ray said, looking down at the papers. "It's like we put two new zebras in a herd of zebras."

And it was true. We were two sets of oiled abdominals in a sea of oiled abdominals. I lit a cigarette and Ray filled his corncob pipe with pot and we sat down and thought long and hard about what would convey the image of youthful masculinity in a striking, memorable way. Military uniforms came to mind—sailor suits, camouflage pants, flight coveralls—but we abandoned that idea when we perused the classifieds again and found representatives from all four branches of the armed forces already well represented. Similarly, the sports world had been mined for all it was worth with football, basketball, baseball, and hockey players all pictured in their appropriate costumes, clutching the appropriate props. We scratched our heads, feeling somewhat discouraged, and decided to sleep on it, which was a good idea because the next day it came to me.

I was sitting in my apartment, killing time before the arrival of my one o'clock, idly thumbing through some of my old art books from college, wondering again if my degree was ever going to be of the slightest use to me. I opened one on Greek art and flipped through the pages until I got to the sculpture section. My eyes wandered across the pages and were drawn repeatedly to a statue of a discus thrower, all naked muscle and twisting motion. I felt myself becoming aroused. I turned the page and saw that there were several titillating statues—wrestlers and runners and gods in action—and each one jumping off the page crying for attention.

Yes, I thought, *maybe the answer to our dilemma can be found in the past.*

Excited, I quickly grabbed one of the gay papers and scanned the ads again. No, nothing at all like that discus thrower! I ran to the kitchen, got some scissors from the drawer, and cut the picture out of the book. Then I positioned it in among the ads and I gasped. Even in grainy black-and-white, it stood out boldly. I immediately called Ray and arranged to meet him at a coffee shop later that afternoon. When the time came, I arrived with a big stack of art books under my arm. I showed him the discus thrower and again placed it in the ads and he too gave a little gasp.

For the next two hours we stayed seated, excitedly flipping through the books and marking the pages of any and all possibilities with yellow Post-it notes. We then weeded through these choices and narrowed down the selections as best we could.

The very next day we rescheduled or canceled several appointments and set out to acquire any costumes or props we'd need, most of which we were able to rent from a costume shop, and what we couldn't rent we bought, figuring we'd use it eventually for fantasy purposes, especially if the ads were successful.

The next morning we rescheduled or canceled appointments again, and got started. I dragged Ray to the gym one last time and made him do several reps to pump up his chest and biceps. After that, we ate a quick breakfast, returned to his house, and dug into our cache of Egyptian costumes, since we'd determined that the Ptolemaic era was the first really sexy period in history, and since we were, after all, working chronologically.

We dressed as pharaohs and slaves, our faces made largely unrecognizable by large gold headdresses and the dark kohl we spread around our eyes, and posed in front of a backdrop of pyramids with a Blue Nile running through them. Our poses were appropriately rigid, which was good because it made it easier to flex our muscles.

When we'd finished with Egypt, Ray removed his headdress and took the first roll of film into the darkroom, while I stood before the bathroom mirror and began the arduous and painful process of removing the kohl from around my eyes. When he emerged, there was a smile on his face as he rushed the dripping images over to the table where the gay paper lay open to the classifieds. He placed them in among the others and they immediately jumped out.

"Perfect!" he cried, giving me a high five.

"Let's do the Greeks next," I said, rummaging excitedly in the next bag of costumes.

Ray, being slender and dark-skinned, looked better than I as an Egyptian. He also looked better as Mercury when we moved onto the gods, his naked body painted gold, a winged hat, winged shoes, and a gold lightning bolt his only accessories. He was a natural for Dionysus, vine leaves in his hair, a stream of liquid flowing into his mouth from a wineskin held overhead, and we successfully transformed him into a lusty satyr by fusing a picture of the upper half of his body with an elk torso he borrowed from one of his friends in the taxidermy trade.

I myself did much better as a Greek, posing as Atlas, a large inflatable globe resting on my outstretched shoulders, and as Prometheus, struggling in vain to unchain myself from the rock.

We traveled up through the ages, mimicking the poses of several Roman and then Renaissance statues. We both looked best as Roman soldiers, so we did several poses together in these costumes, always engaged in suggestive swordplay, and decided to use one of these photos for the duo ad. On my own, I tried posing as Michelangelo's *David,* and the bound slave, while Ray became an anguished Saint Sebastian, tied to the stake, arrows piercing his flesh.

It was all great fun, and as you can tell we got more than a little carried away with it. In the end we had spent over a week of evenings on the project, and gone through thirty-seven rolls of film and much more money than we'd intended, but in time it proved worthwhile, as the monetary return on our investment exceeded all expectations. More than that, although I didn't know it at the time, it was an event I would add to my album of nostalgia. One I'd look back on as fondly as I look back on the trip to Italy with Paul.

When it came to actually placing the ads, we decided that since we had made so many and hated to eliminate any of them, we would put them on a rotation, changing them every month or so, and tracking which were the most effective. We also placed them in several different publications and tracked the number of responses we got from each one, pulling our ads from the papers that gave us little business.

And the business took off! Skyrocketed, as they say. The first day my Prometheus appeared in print I got over forty calls. Granted at least half of these were cranks—people calling and hanging up or people trying to engage me in phone sex—but the other half were legitimate, and I struggled to schedule them all in. After the first hour of calls I left the phone off the hook and drove down to an office supply store, where I bought a large, sleek, aluminum Day-Timer and transferred all the new appointments, which I'd written on scrap bits of paper, to its neatly columned pages.

For the next two weeks I was booked solid. From ten A.M. to three P.M.

and from five P.M. usually on through the night, I seemed to do nothing but entertain clients, but surprisingly I felt alive and energized by all the entertaining and running around. I was making around eight hundred dollars a day, and often more, but it was hectic trying to juggle all the time for clients and the work I needed to do for the business class, and still budget time to work out.

As with any job, a routine developed, and for a short while I managed my time and clients well. For a very short while. Then we ran multiple ads in multiple papers and it all started getting out of hand. I had too much business and seemed to do nothing but entertain clients, answer the phone, schedule appointments, and, of course, change sheets.

Ray was just as busy, and the only time we saw each other was when we were doing three-ways. This was, on average, once a day, but although these sessions were intimate (in that we were both naked together), there was never really any chance to talk privately during them, and as soon as they were over, we both hurried off to other appointments. We did develop a sort of Sunday-night ritual, however, in which we'd meet up at his house at around seven or eight, and would sit and talk shop for ten minutes while our crab shampoo did its work. (Crabs were an occupational hazard, and one we safeguarded against twice a week just to be sure. Oh, there were other, graver hazards, this being the nineties, but more about those later.) For these ten minutes each week we sat naked together, Day-Timers open on our knees, and talked about scheduling and how much money we'd made, expenses we'd had, etc. . . . After that we'd shut the Day-Timers, turn off our pagers, and wash all business seriousness down the drain with the crab shampoo and order Chinese food. We'd loll around, reading or playing cards, or just listen to music and talk in Ray's big white bed. Eventually, and usually quite early, we'd fall into exhausted sleep.

I can't tell you how much I looked forward to these Sunday nights, and was glad that Ray maintained his apartment as a sanctuary from the working world, especially since my own apartment, with its piles of dirty laundry and endless parade of clients, had become such a place of business that I felt as at home there as most people would feel in their office cubicle. I found myself wanting to spend more and more of my leisure hours with Ray, and less and less with my friends and family. Part of this was due to the fact that prostitution, like all illegal activities, does have a somewhat desocializing effect, making you feel odd and cagey around people who don't know what you're up to. The other reason was that in the relatively brief time Ray and I had known each other we'd developed an odd closeness. We were intimate in a sexual way that most friends are not, and yet this intimacy was almost neutralized by the fact that there was always a third person between us. We could be naked and gyrating and moaning in bed together but the presence of someone else always made it safe. We were working. Perhaps that's why, on our Sunday nights together, we were both more . . . careful, I guess. There was a definite line over which we did not cross. We slept together, yes, but we never crossed the line. We were physically intimate, yes, but in a high school athletic sort of way: headlocks, shadowboxing, sporting smacks on the butt. Aw, shucks. I'd lie there in bed next to him, hard-on raging, wanting him, but at the same time knowing that if we crossed the line, it just might muck up the friendship, and I definitely didn't want to do that. Everything was going great, so I figured why rock the boat.

On one such Sunday, as he sat on the toilet lid and I sat on the edge of the bathtub, our crotches covered in Rid, I was talking on and on about how I was now more than a third of the way out of debt and if it kept up I'd be back to zero in a few months.

"Can you believe it? And I was thinking I was going to have to file bankruptcy. I think we need to start charging more for the three-ways, though. I mean we don't do as much work but they are getting twice as much. I think we should up it to two hundred dollars, maybe even two hundred and fifty. What do you think?" I asked.

He lit a cigarette and exhaled deeply, saying nothing, his head drooping between his shoulders.

"How many did we do this past week? Seven? Let's see, seven times . . . that's more than fifteen hundred dollars we could have made instead of . . ." His head was bobbing. "Ray? You all right?"

"Wha?" he said, coming out of his doze.

"Did you hear anything I said?"

"Did you say something?" he asked.

"Oh, Christ!" I looked at my watch and tried to remember what time we'd applied the shampoo. I could feel it burning so I figured it had, if anything, been on too long.

"Let's get tired little guy showered and to bed," I said, turning on the water.

He showered first and I followed. I always went second because I needed my shower to be as cold as possible before I got into bed. When I got out and dried off, he was already in bed, sitting up, smoking absently. I put on a pair of clean boxers and crawled in next to him. He seemed to be deep in thought, and I figured it would be best to wait for him to speak instead of asking what he was thinking.

"How long do you think you want to do this?" he asked, breaking the silence.

"Do what?" I asked, my pulse quickening. I wondered if he meant the hustling or our sleeping together, and I did not particularly want to discuss either one. I was happy with both and didn't want anything to change.

"The sex-for-money business."

"Oh," I said. "I don't know. Definitely until I get out of debt. After that, I'll have to see. Why, are you . . . thinking . . . of stopping?" I asked gingerly, not wanting to hear his response. I realized then that I was scared of going on alone. Oh, I was sure I could do it, but somehow I didn't want to think about doing it without him. He was Beatrice to my Dante, Pocahontas to my John Smith, Huck to my Tom.

"Ahh, I don't know," he said wistfully. "I guess I'm just feeling overwhelmed. I haven't even touched any of my artwork in almost a month."

I said nothing. He went on.

"You're doing it for the money, I know, and that's cool, that's fine, but I'm doing it for the time, and lately I'm feeling pretty shortchanged."

I nodded, not knowing what to say. I was doing it for the money, undeniably, but I was also doing it because it was fun. I liked that men found me so attractive they were willing to pay for my body. I liked that men found me interesting enough to pay just to talk to me (although this was probably more from loneliness than because I was interesting). I liked the fact that I was privy to sides of people they showed to no one else—the married man, the priest, the respectable businessman—who all let me see behind the facade of their everyday lives. But it did always come back to the money. More money than I'd ever made in my life. Granted, it was money made from literally selling myself, but this literal selling seemed better to me than the figurative selling that went along with so many other jobs. Selling your time and your mental faculties to answer a phone, or drive a truck, or underwrite mortgages, or sell insurance seemed much worse to me, much more mind-numbing and de-grading. What I was doing hardly felt degrading. To me it was elevating. I felt more in control and more self-confident than I ever had, and it was all so exciting.

But as I looked over at Ray that night, his shoulders drooping deject-edly, he looked anything but excited. I put my arm around him and noo-gied his head, playfully. Aw, shucks.

"The money's great now," he said, pulling his head away, "better than it's ever been, and I have enough that I could just quit for a while. . . ." He trailed off.

"But?" I asked, afraid of where this was leading. Afraid he was going to say that he was quitting. My heart was really going now. Could Tom go on without Huck? I didn't even want to consider the possibility.

He hesitated, thinking, and took a final drag on his cigarette before crushing it out in the choked ashtray.

"Don't you have a dream?" he asked, turning to face me.

I lit my own cigarette. *A dream,* I thought to myself, *a dream. I had one once, but I woke up. Ha ha ha.* I tried to think up something funny and light to respond with, something to push all this seriousness back down the drain where it belonged, but I couldn't. I could feel its pres-ence in the room and felt it nudging the steering wheel of the conversa-tion dangerously close to the cliff of self-examination.

"Remember that day in the rain?" Ray asked, trying to catch my eye. I nodded, but looked away.

"Well, I wasn't joking about that gallery idea."

I said nothing, but examined my palm intently, as if it held all the an-swers. Ray got out from under the covers and sat on the bed facing me. His drowsiness was replaced by excitement.

"Listen, I know we haven't known each other all that long," he said, "but I think you and I make a pretty good team. We're both smart, we both work hard, we both love art, and I, well, I think together we could do it. I'm not so sure I could on my own—and I'm not so sure I'd want to, because I really love my artwork and I could see a business like that sucking up all my creative time."

He was wide awake now, and his cheeks were flushed. He went on and on about how we could save up some money and scope out a place to rent or buy. He grabbed paper and pencil from the drawer of the bed-side table and drew pictures and added figures and on and on and on.

I sat listening and thinking, mostly about possible ways to change the subject, but also about why I was so afraid of this topic. And afraid I was! I could feel my stomach churning and my hands growing cold, but I couldn't find the reason for it. When he finished talking, he looked up at me expectantly. I smiled weakly and said, with strained enthusiasm, that it was definitely worth some thought, and I would think about it seriously, but now we were both tired; we should sleep on it, and could talk about it in the morning, when we were both clearheaded (knowing full well that we would not, since we were both booked solid all the next day).

"You're probably right." He sighed, and rubbed his eyes. He set his papers on the bedside table, turned out the light, and crawled into bed, giving my head a little pat.

"Good night," he said.

"Good night," I said.

And yet, long after he'd fallen asleep, his face so close to my shoulder that I could feel his breath, I lay awake, staring at the ceiling. All my life I felt like I'd been playing childish games; I'd played house with Paul, and I'd played at various jobs, never taking any of it very seriously because I never really had a stake in any of it. Paul's house was always Paul's house, and our partnership was hardly equal. But with Ray, and the life that he was proposing, I felt for the first time like I was on the threshold of the adult world. Unfortunately, I was not quite confident enough to enter and could feel myself backing away.

The next morning I got up quietly at eight o'clock, and sneaked out without waking Ray. I stopped for a bagel and ate it while I drove to the gym. While I worked out (legs and shoulders) I thought again about the night before, and my head felt cloudy, the way it does when I'm hungover. I was confused about Ray, yes, but also about what I was doing and why. Was it really the money? And if so, was it worth it? And how long would it last? And what about all that gallery bullshit? It was ridiculous. A pipe dream, but Ray had seemed serious about it. Didn't he see how farfetched it was? It's not like you just go out and open a gallery. It would take planning and money and brains and connections. There were all sorts of hoops to jump through, I felt sure. Bars to clear. Hoops other people were surely more adept at jumping through, bars . . . other . . . people . . . I dropped the dumbbells to my sides and stared at my reflection in the mirror. The tiny specter of Sister Melanie had somehow floated in and perched smugly on my shoulder, and I almost had one of those rare moments of insight that make you see your folly and change your course. Almost.

Buzzz, buzzz, buzzz.

The feel of my pager vibrating made her vanish. I reracked the weights, got a quick drink of water, and spent the next ten minutes on the phone in the locker room. When I was finished, I showered, dressed, and headed to my first appointment, all those annoying insights washed right back down the drain.

FROM THE PAGES OF THE LITTLE SILVER BOOK

To give you an indication of just how busy we were then, let me take you on a trip through an average day via my Day-Timer, which was only recently returned to me by the police, who had been keeping it as Exhibit A in the criminal trial against me. It would have been of no legal or historical importance whatsoever if I had not, when it became apparent that we were going to be caught, erased the computer hard drive containing all of the detailed client records. But erase them I did, and so the little silver book took center stage.

It was dubbed "the little silver book" by a columnist for the *Denver Post* (it's really aluminum, but it looks silver and "little silver book" sounds so much more original than "little black book"), and was much sought after by members of the news media, who hoped it would be chock-full of the names and perverse proclivities of Denver's elite. It wasn't. But that didn't stop the press from dissecting its contents, making wild speculations as to the identities of the names I had listed. It was easy for them to speculate wildly because I wrote all of my entries in my own version of shorthand, which the press dubbed "the silver code," and spent weeks trying to decipher. They saw an entry like *Bob @ Cap 210, dildo 150* and immediately jumped to the conclusion that Bob was none other than Bob the prominent sports figure, or Bob the community leader, or Bob the senator, and that @ *Cap 210* clearly meant that we had had sex in room 210 of the state capitol building. Never mind that there are probably ten thousand Bobs in the state, or that room 210 of the capitol building is nonexistent.

The truth was, as the truth usually is in tabloid cases such as this, much less exciting: most of my clients were plain-vanilla suburban husbands who, more than likely, used an alias with me, making speculation by the press as to identities doubly inaccurate, and creating a lot of potential business for some clever libel lawyers.

Even more perplexing than the silver code were the witty little "silver epigrams" Ray and I had first seen at the Art Museum and which we were constantly volleying back and forth, in a sort of endless contest. I took to penciling them in the margins of the little silver book as I thought them up, so I wouldn't forget them and could share them with Ray on Sunday evenings. As I said, it was an endless game, so the pages of my Day-Timer were peppered with filthy sentences like "Sperm Inside Larry Vacated Evan's Ramrod" or "Sixteen Incoherent Lesbians Violate Edward's Rectum." You would scarcely believe the conclusions people can draw from something like that.

I bought the little silver book not because I wanted to keep track of famous clients, and not for blackmail purposes, and not because I wanted to have a trump card in case I got arrested, because God knows it didn't work if those were the goals. No, I got the book, as I said before, because when the business took off I realized I would have to get organized if I was going to keep things under control. I wanted to avoid double bookings and to make sure I didn't miss appointments. There was no secret code or scheming intrigue. The most extensive plotting I ever did was as I sat each night at the kitchen table, usually at about three A.M., and wearily penciled in my schedule for the following day. By so doing, I could flip open the book first thing in the morning, look to the appropriate time, and see where I was supposed to be, who I was supposed to meet, and what accessories I needed to have with me. No different from any traveling salesman, although I guess my appointments were a little more tawdry than those of, say, someone selling encyclopedias.

I was also a touch more meticulous than I needed to be and wrote everything down in exhaustive detail: when I'd wake up, what I'd eat for breakfast, who I needed to call and how long I was allowed to speak to them. It was neurotic, I guess, but it was the first time in my life I'd ever kept a book like that, and they don't come with instruction manuals. I just assumed that was the way everyone did it.

So let's see, let me take you to a day about a month after Ray and I started advertising. April 22, 1996. A typical and an atypical day. A day that was, in retrospect, the day when things began coming apart just a little bit faster than I could manage to put them together.

I got up at seven A.M., which I had taken care to pencil in the night before, in case I forgot. At seven-fifteen, I see, I ate a bagel, and had a teaspoon of muscle-building Creatine and eight ounces of grape juice, all of which I saw fit to document as well. Then I drove to the gym, where from seven-thirty to eight-fifteen I worked out. It was shoulders and back that day.

In the nine o'clock slot, the following "code" is written: *Steve @ Adam's 832. U-wear. Ginza manana, 7:30. $150.*

And what that translates to is this: At nine A.M. I met my first client of the day at the Adam's Mark Hotel. There, in room 832, I modeled several different undergarments for "Steve," a middle-aged businessman from Detroit, who took pleasure in slowly pulling down the waistband of each pair and watching my cock spring out like a jack-in-the-box. When we'd finished, he treated me to a huge room-service breakfast while we talked about which restaurants he should sample while in Denver. We arranged to meet the following evening for dinner at Ginza, a Japanese restaurant in Cherry Creek. As I was getting dressed he stuffed one hundred and fifty dollars in my pocket and kissed me good-bye. Everything accounted for.

As you can see I also kept track of all of my money in the Day-Timer, which proved highly incriminating later on. All I can say is thank God I never used last names, and thank God I paid my taxes.

Next entry: *10:30 A.M. Talker Todd @ home, B.O., 160., Mom's chairs?*

Translation: At ten-fifteen I drove back to my apartment and met Todd, one of my semiregulars. Todd is a prominent psychiatrist who liked to get me excited by telling me what he was going to do to me (although he never actually did any of it) while we sat opposite each other in my club chairs and masturbated (B.O. = beat off).

"First I'm going to kiss your mouth," he'd say, unzipping his pants, "and you're going to reach down and feel my cock getting hard."

"Yeah?" I'd respond in a breathy voice.

"Oh, yeah. Feels good, doesn't it?"

"Mmmmm."

"You want this big dick, don't you?"

"Oh, yeah, please. I want your cock."

Some days this involved more acting on my part than others, but I was usually intrigued, if not actually excited, by listening to someone so conservative (with his horn-rimmed glasses and graying temples) talk such filth, his pants down around his ankles. He'd never say anything really derogatory, so I didn't find it offensive, and the more I got into it, moaning and writhing in my chair, the quicker he came, and that, after all, was the goal. It was understood between us, although how I've never been sure, that if I came he would pay extra, and it looks like on Tuesday, March 22, I did, because he paid me a hundred and sixty dollars instead of the usual hundred and twenty. The rest of the "code" is to remind me to ask my mom where she got the club chairs in which we'd been seated because Todd thought he might like a pair for his office.

12:30 P.M. Naughty Warren @ home, water-wiggle 60. 2 wks.

Translation: Warren was a gay client of mine—a cop. He was ridiculously muscular, even by my standards, and handsome—Nordic-looking, with a blond crew cut, prominent cheekbones, and snow white teeth. He had been with the same lover for several years, and they were then, and I believe still are, committed to each other. And yet Warren enjoyed doing several things his lover evidently did not, and that is why he came to me once every two weeks. He enjoyed being on the receiving end of spankings, verbal humiliation, being tied in compromising positions, and, last but most often, having anal sex toys used on him (his favorite being a series of balls on a string, which I would gently push, ball by ball, up into his ass and then slowly pull back out as he came).

On this particular day he brought something new, which he carried in a black plastic bag.

"I brought this," he said, thrusting the bag toward me. I opened it and removed a four-foot-long piece of rubber tubing, two inches wide at one end and narrow and cock-shaped at the other. I wasn't very experienced with toys then so I looked at it, perplexed.

"It's an enema." He blushed. I looked at it again and smiled deviously.

"Well, then, get in there and get those clothes off!" I ordered gruffly, pushing him into the bathroom.

I watched as he stripped down, but left my own clothes on. I sat on the edge of the tub, rolled up my sleeves, and fiddled with the bath knobs, trying to get the water temperature just right. Warren took his place in the tub and stood, legs spread, facing the wall.

I borrowed some dialogue from Todd.

"You want this bad, don't you," I said, and gave his ass a spank. "You've been carrying this dirty little secret around all week waiting for this, just getting hard thinking about it."

And he, responding with my earlier dialogue, would sigh, "Oh, yeah!"

I attached one end of the hose to the bath spigot and watched, not without amusement, as water sprayed in all directions from small holes in the other end, like a miniature fountain or a Water Wiggle.

"Spread those cheeks and show me that ass!" He complied, and slowly, gently, I inserted the tube and listened to him moan as he filled with water. A moment later I reached back to turn off the tap but accidentally turned it the wrong way.

"Aooowwhh!" he cried, and I quickly removed the tube.

"Sorry."

"Make me hold it," he cried, scrunching up his face and flexing his ass cheeks. "Make me hold it!"

"Yeah, you'll hold it, all right," I said, and gave his cheek another playful smack, the sound echoing off the tiled walls of the tiny bathroom. "You'll hold it till I say let go. Till I'm good and ready. I'm gonna make you squirm!"

After about thirty seconds of this banter I stood up, reached around his waist, and grabbed his cock, which was rock hard, pointing straight in front of him. I had barely touched it when he cried out and shot in both directions. When he was empty, he sat, exhausted, on the edge of the tub.

"That was great!" He sighed, flashing his perfect grin. I sighed myself, wondering how anyone could be so beautiful, rubbed his crew cut affectionately, and then left him to recompose himself. He emerged a few minutes later, dressed once again in his uniform, and shyly handed me the black plastic bag.

"Can I keep it here?" he asked.

"Sure," I said, and placed it alongside his balls on a string, fraternity initiation paddle, ball gag, and triple-ripple butt plug, in the "Warren drawer" of my dresser.

Cops evidently don't make a whole lot of money and he never stays very long, so he hands me three twenties and we make an appointment for two weeks later.

* * *

Let's take a break here from the Day-Timer and let me go into an aside on the subject of Warren, since I feel that entry really doesn't do him justice. I thought Warren strange at first, having a lover he seemed incompatible with, and I felt sure they must be clinging to the wreckage of a now loveless relationship, a mortgage or a dog they had bought together the only things keeping them together. That all changed one night when I was out on a dinner date with a client and spied Warren sitting with his boyfriend in a booth by the wall. They were with another couple, seated opposite them, and all through dinner Warren and his boyfriend were laughing and smiling and hanging all over each other like newlyweds. Warren kept resting his head on his boyfriend's shoulder, giving him admiring looks and little kisses, and something about it all reminded me of Paul and of Siena, and I knew then that they were genuinely happy with each other.

In fact most of my married clients were happy with their wives. Wives who could be everything to their husbands but one thing—a boy, a fantasy, a perversion, an aching curiosity. Warren's lover may have been perfect in every way, may have fulfilled all of his needs but one, and for that one thing there were people like me.

To men, sex and love are like the yolk and the white of an egg. They can exist together but they can also be separated, and most men are, ironically, very skilled when it comes to separating the two. Women, on the other hand, tend to scramble them together. Obviously I'm not a woman, so I don't know this for sure, but from what I've seen I would venture that most women think love and sex are necessarily synonymous. I can't agree. If they were I'd have fallen in love with my clients, and they'd have showered me with bouquets and love notes and boxes of chocolates—and that didn't happen. Oh, occasionally I'd have a man become infatuated and entertain ideas of saving me (from what exactly, I was never quite sure), but the only notes I ever received were printed on paper that was legal tender. The sex was a business transaction between us. A commodity. Love is not nearly so simple.

Maybe you can condemn Warren and the other married men for not having the discipline to shelve their desire (as I'm sure Sister Melanie would), or can accuse them of failing to communicate fully with their mates out of fear of the consequences. Ninety people out of a hundred would probably agree with you, but I don't think it's that simple. In fact, I'll be so bold as to say that it's not like that at all. My take on the matter is that the men who visit prostitutes and hustlers are often wiser and more in control for having indulged themselves. In my mind sexual desire is not unlike diabetes: definitely manageable, but if ignored and untreated, it will wreak havoc on your daily life. It will overwhelm your being and your thoughts, making you physically and mentally unable to function. But if you do treat it—with insulin, or with an occasional blow job—your head and body will be less riotous and life can go on harmoniously.

As an example let me tell you my "sexorcism" story. It's good, and one that I often recited to all the guilt-ridden souls who crossed my threshold.

There is a Catholic priest, Father Toby, who came to see me about once a month. He is a good priest, attentive to the needs of his numerous parishioners, honest and hardworking, with fingers in all sorts of charitable pies. He works with single mothers, and runs a homeless shelter and a program to keep inner-city youth out of trouble by building houses for the poor. He does so much for other people, but once a month he would come to my apartment to get some attention of his own. Invariably he'd arrive late at night, distressed and upset, overwhelmed by feelings of guilt for what we were about to do. I'd open a bottle of wine to try to relax him but this usually led to drunken tears, and then, as if that weren't bad enough, he'd lower himself to begging for my forgiveness. Tears and pleading are difficult to take from anyone, but when they come from a six-foot-five, barrel-chested priest like Father Toby, they're particularly difficult.

"Look," I said, giving vent to my annoyance one night as he sat blubbering at my kitchen table, having knocked back a few too many glasses of the blood of Christ. "Maybe it is wrong for you to be doing these things, and maybe you should have more self-control, but don't you find you feel better when it's over?" I asked. He looked up at me, confused.

"Think about it," I said, snatching away his wineglass and emptying it in the sink. "Isn't your head clearer and less obsessed with sex once you've finally had it?"

He seemed to ponder this for a moment, but then his head collapsed in a blubbering heap on his arms. I looked at my watch, feeling frustrated and annoyed. I heaved him up out of the chair and led him into the bedroom. There I quickly removed my clothes, forcibly removed his, and pushed him down on the bed. Force was the only way to shut him up and get him in and out in less than an hour. I did, after all, have a schedule to adhere to. Once it was over, he was fine. In fact he was more than fine; he was at peace. He sighed contentedly and whistled while he dressed, telling me about the bake sale the church was having next Thursday. His demon, if not actually exorcised, was at least appeased for another month.

1:30 P.M. Nick, new, discus, @ home, band fags, 150.

Translation: Nick was a new client who had responded to the ad with me poised to throw the discus. He became a regular, but Tuesday, March 22, was his first visit. He was nervous and married, which I suspected by his ring and confirmed later when he was in the shower and I took the liberty of looking at the pictures in his wallet (elegant-looking wife, daughter who plays softball). He was not bad-looking, forties, a little soft around the middle, and expensively dressed in a suit and tie, which was why I decided not to bring up the subject of money beforehand. If they look like they can afford it, they probably can. Even if they don't, and they can't, they usually pay close to what you ask, and discussing money first is rarely a good idea. It puts your relationship on too much of a business level, which is fine in postorgasmic sobriety, but can be lethal in the beginning, when magic and illusion are so important.

"I'm Jack," I said, giving his hand a firm shake.

"Nick," he said, barely meeting my eyes.

"So, Nick, am I what you expected?" He nodded and smiled and looked around my apartment curiously.

"Can I get you something to drink?"

"Uh, no, thanks."

"Okay, well, come in, sit down." He perched on the edge of the couch and I took a seat at the other end, giving him some space until he felt more comfortable.

"I'm a little nervous," he said, giving me a quick sideways glance, unsure of what to do with his hands. "I've never done this before."

"That's okay," I said reassuringly. "Have you ever been with another guy?" He shook his head no, but then added as an afterthought, "Well, not really. Just one. But not since high school."

If I'd put a notch on the bedpost (if my bed had posts) for every time I heard that, the bed would soon have been whittled down to toothpicks. So many married men have had that single chance encounter—messing around in the locker room, sleeping in the same tent with a buddy on a fishing trip, a drunken tumble with their college roommate—and have carried the memory of it with them, over decades sometimes, telling no one, alternately thrilled and ashamed, until the desire to try to recapture it becomes so strong that they call someone like me.

"Tell me about it," I said, and was truly interested. All of these stories were similar, formulaic almost, but the characters and the settings were always different, and the way it was told—comically or sadly—it was always with a tone of dreamy nostalgia.

He looked around nervously to see if anyone might be listening, to see that the shades were drawn, to make sure no one would discover his secret but me.

"It was on a band trip," he said rapidly. "I just messed around with another guy."

I swing at his volley and hit the ball back.

"Tell me about it. I get really turned on hearing stories like that."

"Really?"

"Oh, yeah," I said, moving a little closer to him on the couch.

"Let's see," he said, pretending to search through the mental files, as if it wasn't the foremost thought in his mind. "Band trip. Oh, yes. We were going to the Sun Bowl to be in the halftime show, sort of a battle-of-the-bands thing."

"What instrument did you play?" I asked, trying to picture him as an adolescent, walking to school with his case.

"The trumpet."

"Cool."

"Yeah. So anyway," he continued, warming to the story, his nervousness nearly evaporated, "we all had to double up in rooms, you know, class trips, and each room was supposed to have two twin beds in it. One for each guy. Well, some of them didn't, some had just one double bed, and I got one of those rooms and I had to share it with Tommy Morrison."

"And what instrument did he play?"

"Bass drum. So anyhow, we got to drinking with the other kids and partying in the hallway and we were both really drunk."

Drinking always plays a role in these little dramas.

"I don't remember going to bed—I guess I kind of passed out, 'cause when I woke up, it was all quiet, must have been early in the morning, like five or something, because there was a little bit of light, but it was mostly still dark. Kind of a blue light, you know? And Tommy was in bed next to me, lying on his back, asleep. I looked at him and I could see he had a big hard-on under the blanket. Well, I got up to pee and when I came back his eyes were open and he watched me walk all the way back to the bed but didn't say anything. I tried not to, but I couldn't help looking at that hard-on! Well, he saw me looking so I got in the bed real quick and lay down on my side, facing away from him. I tried to go to sleep, but I couldn't, and then a couple minutes later I felt the bed moving and I could hear him breathing, heavy-like."

"And you knew he was beating something other than the drum," I said. He laughed.

"Exactly?"

"So then what happened?" I asked, moving closer still.

"Well, I got scared. I figured he'd just finish up and that would be that, so I just lay there, but he didn't. He kept going, and he was making more and more noise. You know, moaning and stuff."

"So what did you do?" I asked, rubbing my own crotch, an action he observed peripherally. He swallowed hard and continued, haltingly.

"Uh, well, I uh, I sort of turned over on my back and looked at him. He'd pulled the blanket all the way down by then so I could see everything, and he had this giant dick, or at least it looked that way then, and he was stroking it and looking over at me and then back at it. Well, I didn't know what to do so I just watched for a minute and then I pulled off my underwear and started doing the same to mine and we sort of did it together and kept looking at each other. Then he reached out and grabbed mine and . . . I . . . uh . . . I, ohhh!"

He stopped in the telling then because I had stood, lowered my shorts to the floor, and taken over the role of Tommy Morrison, bass drummer. We moved to my bedroom, where there was also a double bed, and for the next forty-five minutes he shed his business suit and was sixteen again.

A hundred and fifty dollars.

2:45 P.M. Seth @ home. Bike shorts, PC 250.

Translation: Seth, the boy-genius computer wizard, arrived next. At twenty-two, he was one of my youngest clients and one of the wealthiest (by age seventeen he was pulling in fifty thousand dollars a year and his finances had only improved since then). Seth proved enormously helpful in getting our computer system up and running when I expanded the business, and I don't know what I would have done without him and

Sharise from the microbusiness class, who helped us create our Web site. Unfortunately, their systems, which made running the business so much easier, also proved the most incriminating when the trouble started.

It might seem surprising that someone as young as Seth would be paying for sex, but then Seth was not what you'd call an ideal twenty-two-year-old. He stood no taller than five-foot-five, which would have been fine had he not weighed close to three hundred pounds. His hair was clean, but never combed, and he was completely indifferent when it came to clothing, consistently appearing at my doorway in the same white button-down shirt tucked tightly into tan pants, with no belt. The pants were too short and revealed an expanse of baggy white socks that ended in a loud pair of running shoes. Although he didn't care about his own dress, he was nevertheless highly particular about mine, and always called ahead of time to tell me what I should be wearing when he arrived—usually a tight pair of black spandex bike shorts.

Life is difficult for Seth because he is a person both lauded and rejected by society. Lauded because of his genius and his value to employers, but rejected because of his ugliness and lack of social skills. Oddly enough, that was our connection: we were the same in our oppositeness. I had beauty and social skills, but no knowledge or expertise that anyone could profit from. The sex with Seth usually took no more than fifteen or twenty minutes, after which we would lie in bed together talking while he ran his fingers slowly up and down my back. During these times of postcoital sobriety, we would each take turns telling tales and recounting experiences from our respective ends of the social spectrum.

I had many clients like Seth, those who didn't fit into conventional society, the overweight, the ugly, the aged, or as I called them, the untouchables. As much as they were rejected by the conventional straight world, this rejection was tenfold from the beauty-, youth-, and money-obsessed "gay society," which can be, ironically enough, as tyrannical in its exclusion and discrimination as any caste system, class system, or country club.

Until Paul's death, all of my friends had either money or good looks (usually both) in abundance, and I almost never strayed from this genteel circle. Then Paul died, and my status changed rapidly. Since I still possessed my beauty I was tolerated, but my lack of money could not be ignored. I was invited to a few dinner parties, but since I had no way of reciprocating (having no dining room, for a start) I was soon dropped from everyone's mental list of dynamic invitees. Nor could I participate in the sport of shopping, always so popular with moneyed fags, and indeed it was even feared by some that soon I might actually be seen on the other side of one of the retail registers, which was another reason for them to avoid me. Nor could I tag along on the leisurely trips to Aruba, or Amsterdam, or even Aspen, and so was no longer asked—was actively avoided so that the awkward prospect would not even be presented to me. I actually felt myself fading from everyone's memory. I was stashed away like an old photo in their mental album, pulled out and dusted off only when I came up in conversation or they chanced to see me on the street.

I became one of the untouchables, and as such took my place on the other side of the fence, which was maybe not all that bad, for it was in my exile with the Seths of this world that I learned the value of my looks and grace, but also I learned the silly uselessness of ostentation and the ugliness of snobbery. All of which made me a different person when, later, my fame became my passport back over to the other side. My time as an untouchable added a texture to my life that was not there before. It's hard to explain what I mean, but I think the pictures Ray took on our disastrous trip to the nursing home best illustrate what I'm trying to say. In them, my flesh looks taut and smooth and simple. More often than not it falls into the background and goes unnoticed—I am little more than a backdrop. The fascinating subject matter, what really jumps out and captures your attention, are the wrinkled, thickly veined hands, the age-spotted arms, the deeply lined forehead, which are all like an atlas of wisdom and experience.

4:00 P.M. Tom, new, football, @ home. All Fucked Up.

Translation: The next client was new. A new client and a new experience. Memorable, but hardly pleasant. He had called in response to my football-player ad, which I had run despite the fact that it seemed so boring in comparison to the others. I didn't know his age or status or what he was into, so I put on the shorts I'd worn in the photo, figuring they'd be a safe bet. When he arrived, I saw that he was very good-looking—tall and solidly built, with thick black hair. He was dressed casually in jeans and a houndstooth-check shirt, and he smelled, not unpleasantly, of cologne and cigarette smoke. He removed his dark sunglasses and assessed me from the doorway. His eyes were green and had a sort of spooky intensity—that pop-eyed look of surprise seen most notably in Barbara Bush and Boston terriers. He crossed the threshold and looked me over, grabbing my shoulder and turning me around, examining all sides of the merchandise.

Obviously he's done this before, I thought.

"You'll do fine!" he said, and smacked my ass. He walked past me into the room, dropping his sunglasses and keys (which hung on a ridiculously large Porsche key ring) ostentatiously on the end table.

"You got anything to drink?" he asked.

"Sure, what would you like?"

"Scotch?"

I nodded.

"Is it shit?"

Oh, Christ, I thought, feeling tired. *I'll bet this is a size issue; let me make up for what I'm lacking downstairs by being a haughty little snot.*

"It's Dewar's," I said, trying my damnedest to sound polite.

"Okay, it's shit," he said, and took a seat on the sofa, spreading both arms over the back. I went into the kitchen and removed one of the many airline bottles (courtesy of Andre) from the door of the refrigerator, and some ice from the freezer. I poured his drink, and then seriously considered spitting in it. Instead I took a deep breath and reminded myself that this was the last client until nine o'clock, and the sooner I got it over with the sooner I could take a break. I went back in and handed him the drink, saying nothing. His feet were up on the coffee table, exposing a pricey pair of Italian boots I had long coveted. He held the glass in one hand and started stroking his crotch with the other, swallowing the drink in three quick gulps. He set the empty glass on the end table and pointed to his crotch with his index finger.

"Suck it," he said, looking up at me and then down at his crotch.

What a jerk! I thought. I don't have a problem being submissive—in fact, sometimes I prefer it—but this guy had obviously seen far too many prison movies. I got down, spread his legs apart, and unbuckled his belt. His cock was not small. In fact, it was a size to match his ego, and as it got hard it became impossible to fit in my mouth. I pulled back and started using my hand on it.

"Take it!" he yelled, and pushed my head back down forcefully. I did the best I could but ended up sort of licking it around the head. He reached over me, grabbed the fabric of my shorts in both hands, and ripped them at the seam, exposing my ass.

"Yeah! This big dick's gonna feel good up that tight, white ass! You fuckin' slut."

His hand came down hard on my lower back. I rose and glared at him.

"Don't," I said, and then slowly resumed my task.

Smack! He did it again, harder this time. I jumped back this time, overturning the coffee table as I did so, but just as quickly he was up too, grabbing my hair in one of his hands and pulling me back down toward his crotch. I tried to push him away with my arms but he was surprisingly strong and managed to grab both my hands by the fingers with one of his hands and hold them in a vise grip, twisting them and laughing demonically.

"You're gonna take this cock!" he boomed. "Get it lubed up and I'm gonna fuck the shit out of you!"

I was scared and angry now.

"Let go!" I cried, struggling as he tightened the grip on my hair and pushed my head down. I struggled to pull back but it was useless and only made him pull harder on my hair. In desperation and anger, I pushed forward and rammed my head as hard as I could into his crotch. He yanked me back violently and threw me backward, over the coffee table. I landed hard, on my back, my head bouncing against the floorboards.

"Fuckin' bitch!" he yelled, eyes flashing. "You like it rough, huh?" And before I knew it, he had me by the hair again, pulled me up, and then threw me facedown onto the couch, my arms locked behind me, my face buried in the cushion. I tried to kick but he was sitting on my legs. I heard him rip off the remainder of my shorts and then felt the searing pain as he forced a dry finger up into my asshole. I panicked. I couldn't move and I couldn't breathe. I tried to scream, but I couldn't get any air in my lungs. I convulsed my body violently, but all of his body weight was on me and I barely moved. I managed to free one of my arms, and for a moment he let go of the other one in order to try to grab them both again, but I flailed them around wildly and then pulled them down in front of me so they were up against my chest. Then, with all the strength I could summon, I pushed my torso up off the couch and twisted around, just like the discus thrower, and landed one solid punch on his ear. He grabbed my hair again, which enraged me this time as it was arching my back severely, and with another surge of adrenaline I twisted around, hearing my spine crack and my hair rip away from my head as I did so. I punched the side of his head, harder this time, again and again, as fast as I could. Then, on the third or fourth strike, I opened my fist and I grabbed the skin of his neck in my hand, digging my fingers in and pushing my thumb as hard as I could into the concave area just below his Adam's apple. He immediately released my hair and jumped up, clutching his throat and coughing. I scrambled to get off the couch, but before I could I felt his hand smack into my face. The impact pushed me far enough away that I was out of his reach. I stood up quickly, grabbed a floor lamp, ripping the cord from the wall, and held it threateningly, like a baseball bat. My heart was racing and I could feel and hear my pulse as it throbbed in my head. He looked at me with those psychotic, bulging eyes and then started to laugh between his coughs, shaking the strands of my hair loose from his fingers.

"Get out!" I said, my voice shaky and low, but my body rigid and ready to strike. He looked at me, almost offended, but then smiled and said, "We were just getting started."

He then took his wallet from his back pocket and flipped through a thick pile of cash, pulling out a hundred and dropping it on the floor. He watched it fall and then looked up at me expectantly.

"Get the fuck out before I call the police!" I said, shaking the lamp. He looked back down at the money.

"There's lots more where that came from," he said, fanning three more bills out of his wallet, his eyebrow raised.

I could not quite believe this, and as usual in incredible situations, my wit abandoned me.

"Just get the fuck out!" I yelled. Neither of us made a move. Then he clicked his tongue, shook his head disappointedly, picked up the hundred from the floor, and put it back in his wallet.

"You coulda made a lot of money," he said, shaking his head, his tone that of a stockbroker admonishing me for failing to heed his advice on an investment that had proven profitable. Again I could not quite believe it. He walked over to the end table, calmly retrieved his sunglasses and his keys, and walked out the front door.

"Fuckin' stupid prick!" he yelled, slamming it after him.

Still clutching the lamp, I walked over to the door, turned the dead bolt, and latched the chain. I'd been in fights before, but never any that had taken me so completely by surprise. I dropped the lamp and fell into one of the chairs, feeling an uneasy relief, like I'd just survived the climax of a Hitchcock movie. When I was breathing normally again I picked up the phone and called Ray. There was no answer. I tried his cell phone, but still no answer. I was starting to shake, which I found strange because I knew I was safe; the danger had obviously passed. I got up, checked that the door was locked again, and went to the kitchen, where I quickly took another one of the airline bottles from the fridge, twisted it open, and took a sip. It burned going down, and I coughed. I lifted it again and emptied it. The liquor steadied me a little, but my whole body had begun trembling and my wrists and scalp and asshole burned just like the liquor. I could feel my face swelling where he'd hit me. I went into the bedroom and dressed quickly, pulling on a pair of jeans, a sweatshirt, and a ball cap. I put on a pair of shoes and tried to tie the laces but my hands were shaking too hard, so I abandoned them and stepped into some sandals. I went to the front door and peered through the peephole into the hallway, seeing no one. Slowly I unlocked the dead bolt and unlatched the chain. I pushed open the door a crack and peered down the hallway. Empty. I pulled the ball cap low over my forehead and walked quickly out the back door of the building to my car and drove straight to Ray's house. When I arrived, his car wasn't in the driveway, so I parked there, went into the house, and locked the door behind me. I took off my shoes, ran straight upstairs, and crawled under the heavy white comforter, shivering.

When Ray finally did arrive I was asleep and it was almost dark. He sat next to me on the edge of the bed, causing me to wake with a start, whipping back the sheets and jumping up in a disoriented panic. He quickly turned on the light next to the bed and regarded me curiously. It was then that he saw my cheek, which in the time I had been sleeping had become swollen and bruised. His expression changed, and he crawled across the bed tentatively, catlike, and approached me.

"What happened?" he asked, and moving his hand up, he touched the bruise. I pulled away and tried to orient myself. His eyes were wide with concern and darted back and forth from the bruise to my eyes questioningly. I rubbed my head, feeling the sore spot where my scalp had been pulled, and the bump where my head had bounced on the floor, and it all came back to me. We sat next to each other on the edge of the bed and I recounted, in a confused, drowsy voice, what had happened. He listened attentively, his arm reassuringly around my shoulder, but as I spoke I could feel his body tense.

"I'm calling the cops," he said suddenly, and picked up the phone by the bed.

"And what will you tell them?" I asked, knowing the impossibility of making such a call. The same knowledge soon came to him.

"Shit," he said, and slammed down the phone. "Shit, shit, shit! You're sure you don't know who he was?"

I shook my head.

"Well, we gotta find out." He was all compressed energy, and I watched him uneasily as he swaggered around the room like a boxer, punching his palm with his fist in frustration. When he reached the end of the room he stopped and rocked up and down on the balls of his feet. Then, without warning, he drew back his fist and landed a punch squarely on the wall in front of him, sending paint chips and plaster falling to the floor. I watched this from the edge of the bed, too startled to move at first. He stood, similarly dazed, but then dropped to the floor clutching his bleeding fist. I rose and went over to where he was sitting by the fireplace and examined his hand. He had split the skin over his stained knuckles and was bleeding. I got up and went quickly to the kitchen, where I grabbed two dish towels from the bar over the sink and moistened one with some water from the tap. It's good that I had some nursing to do because I don't know how I'd have reacted to his outburst otherwise. I went back and he was still sitting on the floor, rocking back and forth, staring into the empty fireplace, the blood pooling beneath him. I knelt down, took his hand gently in mine, and noticed that he was trembling. I dabbed at the knuckles with the wet towel and then wound the dry towel tightly around his hand to stop the bleeding. He looked up at me, his eyes full of embarrassment and tenderness, and he took my head in his hands.

"I'm sorry," he said, and his body shook violently as he tried unsuccessfully to stifle a sob. "I was so scared," he cried. "You're okay, aren't you? Please tell me you're okay." His expression was almost pleading, as if he'd been the one who hit me. I took him in my arms and held his shaking body as tightly as I could.

"I'm all right," I said. "It's okay. Everything's okay now." But I did not believe it. I knew then that Ray felt strongly for me, was in love with me, and even as I held him tightly, reassuringly, I felt myself pulling away, more frightened than I'd been at any time that day.

LABOR RELATIONS

At the beginning of each microbusiness class Tina went around the room, and for fifteen minutes we the students were given time to relate how our businesses were doing. Fifteen minutes to celebrate and share our triumphs and successes or, as was more often the case, fifteen minutes to whine and moan about our failures and problems. On this particular morning, I was the last to arrive, having come straight from a bed at the Westin Hotel, still dressed in my smoky evening clothes from the night before, and all eyes followed me as I quickly took my seat, all bleary eyed and bedheaded, quietly eating my usual breakfast (a chocolate doughnut with rainbow sprinkles and a large 7-Eleven coffee), vaguely conscious of the fact that I looked more like Richard Gere in *American Gigolo* than the Richard Simmons I was supposed to be.

"Okay," Tina said, moving in front of the desk and deftly crossing her legs at the ankles. She looked at her watch and did a five-second countdown.

"The bitch session starts . . . now!"

Eager hands shot up. She looked up and around and then pointed to Antonio and Victor. As usual, Antonio did all the talking while Victor sat nodding, sometimes prodding Antonio and whispering in his ear.

"We're having a bad week," Antonio said. "Kinda good and kinda bad, ya know? Like, we got tons of business, and we just pumped a lot of the . . . what you call it, capital? into some new tools that we needed and a newspaper ad, so that's good, eh? But the bad is that now we got axed from our biggest contractor 'cause we don't got insurance.

"'I'll get some,' I says to him, but then I find out, damn, that shit's expensive, we ain't got the money for it."

They both shrugged their shoulders helplessly and looked to Tina.

Tina nodded. "That's a tough one," she said, drumming her long red nails rapidly on the desk. "But at least you paid for your ad and you got some tools, right?" They nodded.

"Contractors are nice 'cause they give you steady work, but you gotta have insurance. . . . Well, okay, then you can't work for them until you get some more capital built up to get the insurance, right?" They nodded again.

"So who can tell them what they need to do?" she asked, scanning the room and eventually calling on Sharise, who was not paying attention. Sharise looked startled, and mulled over the problem for a moment; then she turned and looked back at Antonio and Victor.

"It seems to me you gotta go back to some smaller jobs maybe, see what you can get from your newspaper ad, and try to build up some capital again." They nodded, but didn't look happy.

"I know it's a drag," Tina said, "but sometimes you gotta take one step back for every two forward, okay?"

She looked around the room again at the upraised arms.

"Salvatore," she called out, pointing at the little bug of a man, dressed, as ever, in his black suit.

"Yes, ma'am," he said, folding his hands neatly on the table, his manner still that of the gentle mortician.

"I too am having problems," he said, clearing his throat. "I too have invested all of my capital in new equipment: video cameras, light meters, tripods, and the like, but these things are now in danger of being repossessed because I haven't any customers. I'm certain there will be more weddings in the summer, but now the market is not doing well and I'm afraid I'm going to be forced to take a small job I've been offered at a cemetery."

"Okay," Tina said, as consolingly as one can say *okay,* "that doesn't sound good, does it, class? But it can be. You're learning, Salvatore, just like Antonio and Victor. One step back for every two forward. What should he do, class?"

Antonio and Victor both raised a hand.

"Take the graveyard job, bro," said Victor.

"Take any job, but keep your equipment," said Antonio, "and while you're diggin' graves or planting flowers or whatever, think about how you can get some more customers."

"Excellent," said Tina. "If you're just focusing on weddings, maybe your market is too small. Take your downtime to reassess what you're doing; think of other things you could do."

Salvatore nodded thoughtfully and scribbled some notes on his legal pad.

"Millie," Tina said, pointing at the woman to whom I had recently started paying twenty-five dollars every three days to do my laundry. She stood up.

"I think I have a different problem," she said. "I've got lots of work, almost too much! I'm doing some washing and ironing, and I did go around to those vintage stores, like you all said, and handed out my cards for alterations and repairs, and I've had lots of responses for that, but I think that's my problem—I'm so busy I don't have any time to do my own sewing."

"Millie, girl, I hear you," Sharise said, nodding eagerly. "I've got no time! And Lord, I'm getting scared. I'm working so much and I still have to take care of my daughter and try and keep track of all the money coming in and going out and my taxes and, ohhh . . ." She buried her face in her hands at the thought of it all.

"Take a deep breath, ladies." Tina chuckled, although none of the rest of us found it very funny and threw her hostile glances. "Everybody take a deep breath."

"I'm good at what I do," Sharise continued, "but I'm getting too much, and that's dangerous because I have to stay on top of the technology, and I can't do that when I'm bustin' ass on all the busywork."

"Yes!" said Millie, identifying with the term. "Busywork!"

I thought of what Ray had said the Sunday before about his neglected artwork.

"Okay, hang on to those thoughts—we'll deal with them today, I promise—but let's get through everyone's troubles first." She pointed to me. "Jack."

I looked up and quickly swallowed my mouthful of doughnut.

"Oh, I'm doing good," I said. "I'm busy, but I don't mind because I'm really getting my debt down, which as all of you know is nothing less than a miracle. If anything I wish I had more time to fit more people in. I feel like I could make more money if there was another me, and if I had someone to take care of the bookkeeping and taxes and the scheduling. Especially the scheduling."

Again everyone nodded. "Okay, sounds like the same things Sharise and Millie are dealing with. Good, I think that's everyone."

She turned her back to us and rummaged around in one of her boxes, eventually pulling out several half-inch-thick packets. She counted them and then teetered her way around the tables, dropping one at each of our places.

"Now, I know some of you will think this is useless information, okay, but I guarantee as time goes by you'll need it. Others—Millie, Jack, Sharise—this could be the answer to some of your problems."

I looked down at the packet. "State and Federal Regulations Governing the Hiring and Firing of Employees."

We all looked up, perplexed.

"Whoa!" said Sharise. "I don't know about this."

"Employees!" cried Millie, and looked up at Tina as if she had suggested the hiring of trained hamsters.

"Be patient," Tina said, and flipped open her booklet to page one.

I thought again about Ray. He was clearly as overwhelmed as Millie and Sharise, and as for me, I did honestly wish there was another me so that I could bring in more money. I opened the booklet eagerly.

For the next hour and a half we talked about budgets and cash-flow projections and how much of a wage we could pay and still maintain a profit. We did some figuring, and Millie actually began to look hopeful, like maybe this employee thing wasn't so farfetched. Then Tina pulled the bottom out and told us about how much more money we would need to have to cover state taxes, and federal taxes, and Social Security, and worker's compensation. We did some more figuring, silently, and then one by one looked up at Tina resentfully, as a child might look at a teasing parent waving a piece of candy at an impossible height.

"Man, this sucks," said Sharise. "If I did the math right, I'm coming out way in the hole. Now you're telling me that if I want to pay someone six bucks an hour, I'm really going to have to pay twelve or thirteen because half of it goes to the government!"

Tina nodded, smiling. "Welcome to the legal world of business."

"Fuck that," Antonio said, crumpling up his sheet full of figures, and tossing it on the floor. "I'll just pay 'em under the table."

Again Tina smiled calmly, evidently prepared for this response.

"Okay, suppose you do that, pay your workers under the table. What do you do when it comes time to pay your taxes—or worse, what if you get audited? How are you gonna account for that missing money? Are you gonna let your employees take the money while you pay the taxes on it?"

He puzzled a minute.

"I just wouldn't tell the IRS I made that much money." Antonio smiled. "I just tell 'em I made less than I actually did. I done it before and they never caught me."

"Well, yes, you could do that," Tina said wearily, "but we're teaching you how to run a legal business and keep out of trouble, and besides, you're wanting to work for big contractors, right?"

He and Victor looked at each other and nodded.

"Okay, well, those big contractors have big accountants, who are going to report every penny they pay you to the IRS. The same pennies you use to pay your workers. How are you suddenly gonna say you made less than what the accountant says you made?"

Antonio said nothing. Victor nudged him. "She's right, homie."

She let us stew in our misery for a minute longer. Millie wept quietly.

"Does anyone see a solution here?" Tina asked. "It's hidden in what we were just talking about."

None of us said anything, unable—and at this point unwilling—to play her stupid games, feeling betrayed and wondering why she'd spent the last half hour inflating our hopes, only to gleefully stab them with a sharp pin.

"Yes, Salvatore," she said, pointing to where he was seated at the back of the room.

"Ma'am," he said softly, "it would seem to me that the answer lies in the word 'contractor.'"

We all looked back, confused.

"Exactly!" Tina said, clapping her hands together. "And why the contractor?"

"Well," Salvatore continued nervously, all eyes on him now, "as I see it, and I may very well be incorrect, he, the contractor, has managed to place the burden of paying taxes onto the employees."

"Oh, Salvatore, excellent! I was wondering if you were with us this morning; you're always so quiet there in the back. Excellent. Okay, now do the rest of you see that? The contractor hires subcontractors to do the work for him and has them take care of their own taxes. Also, if you subcontract you don't have to pay worker's compensation."

We all gave a sigh of relief.

"Well, why doesn't everyone do that, then?" asked Sharise skeptically.

"Okay, good question!" She turned her back again and removed more papers from her box, giving us each a two-sided list of the subtle differences between an employee and a subcontractor, which we went through line by line.

"Okay, now it is very important to follow these requirements if you decide to subcontract work because the people down at Workman's Comp don't like this loophole one little bit, and if they catch you crossing the line, if they can prove you really have an employee instead of a subcontractor, they'll hit you with everything they've got: every penalty, every charge, all the interest, and you'll be out of business so fast it will make your head spin."

We trudged on through the list for the remainder of the class time, but once we'd finished I still had questions. Subcontracting people seemed the natural solution to my problems and Ray's. It would give me more time to run the business and bring in more money, and give Ray the free time he wanted, but how would I go about finding subcontractors? How would I front the business? What facade could I use? And then how would I do the books? All valid questions to which I needed answers, but questions I was wary of voicing in class, afraid I would slip up and reveal the truth that I was not, as they all thought, a personal trainer, but a personal hooker. I needed to talk to someone who had a good business sense but who also knew what I was doing.

Naturally, I thought of Hole.

After class, I stepped outside, lowered my sunglasses, and looked at my watch: ten-thirty. I didn't have an appointment until noon, so I walked down to Sixteenth Street, caught the shuttle, and headed to lower downtown. I thought maybe I ought to have called first, but he'd either be home or he wouldn't, and if he wasn't, maybe Andre would be home and we could go for coffee.

When I got there, I buzzed Hole's apartment and was let into the building without any questions as to my identity. I walked to the apartment door, knocked, and was admitted by a large, barrel-shaped man, whom I immediately recognized, despite the addition of a handlebar mustache, as my old partner in misery, Marvin.

"Marvin?" I asked, and he looked at me for a moment, puzzled. "It's me, Jack, from Cardmember Authorizations. . . ." His face lit up with recognition and he grabbed me in a crushing hug. Then he pulled back and clasped his hands together in a feminine gesture of surprise.

"Oh, Jack! What are you doing here?" he asked.

"I'm a friend of Ho—Frank's. I just stopped by to see him. I didn't call, so he's not expecting me. Is he here?"

"Yes, I think he's napping tho—"

Hole's shrill voice called out from the bedroom: "Who the fuck can sleep with all that goddamned noise!"

Marvin and I smiled at each other. He ushered me in, closed the front door, and then tiptoed his large frame over to the bedroom door and pulled it shut with a thud.

"But what are you doing here?" I asked him.

"I'm the nurse's aide," he said cheerfully. "The regular nurse quit yesterday. I guess Mr. Crabby in there had a little tantrum and threw an oxygen bottle at him, so they sent me until they can find a new one."

We talked for a while, and he told me how he'd been fired from the authorizations job for showing up late and had been doing "this and that" since then—"You know, cleaning some houses, walking some dogs, things like that."

"Who the hell are you talking to!" Hole cried from behind the door, and I saw the knob twist slowly back and forth, never with enough force to actually disengage it. Marvin rolled his eyes. I smiled and went over to the bedroom, giving Marvin a little pat on the shoulder and a look that said *We'll talk later.*

I knocked on the door and opened it. Hole looked up and smiled.

"Oh, it's you! I'm glad you're okay," he said, eyeing the fading bruise on my cheek. "Ray told me about your trouble the other night. Come in, come in. And shut that door!"

He shuffled over and sat down at his desk, which was covered with neat piles of papers and receipts. I looked around the spartan room for something to sit on.

"There's a stool in the closet," he said. I went and retrieved it and seated myself next to him.

"I'm trying to do some paperwork," he whined, "but big sissy out there won't let me close the door—in case I fall, or some stupid crap— so I have to listen to all his fuckin' soap operas, and game shows on that fuckin' TV, which is a helluva lot better than havin' it off, because then

I have to listen to him mince around singin' some goddamned show tune. Why do they keep sending me guys like that! This is his first and his last day, that's for sure!"

Poor Marvin, I thought. But that was not why I was here, and I twiddled my thumbs as I thought how best to approach the subject.

"I like your Ray," he said teasingly. "That boy's a real catch!" He looked up to catch my response. I smiled weakly.

"You're not playing matchmaker in your old age, are you?" I asked, patting him on the shoulder. He raised what was left of one eyebrow and grinned slyly. I thought of Ray and his reaction the other day after the attack, and felt confused. I was thrilled to discover the depth of his feelings for me, but scared for the same reason. I knew I felt strongly for him, but what exactly that meant, I didn't know. I shook my head, willing it away, for the moment at least.

"Actually, I did come for some of your help," I said, leaning forward, "but not in matters of the heart." And I related to him the topic of that day's class, and my desire to legally subcontract people, and to learn more about bookkeeping, and taxes, and how to do payroll.

"I know you've done all that for your own businesses," I said, "so I was hoping maybe you'd help me out with some of it. I really want to do it right."

He listened intently, but when I'd finished he switched off the oxygen and lit a cigarette.

"You do realize," he said, exhaling a gray stream of smoke, "that what you're doing, no matter how you paint it, is prostitution?"

I nodded.

"And of course you know it's illegal?"

"Well, yes, but—" I was silenced by his upheld hand.

"Now I know you're not stupid, Jack, but do you mind telling me why you want to set up a legal structure for an illegal business? That's like robbin' a bank and then sending in taxes on the money you stole."

"So you won't help me," I whined, in the piteous voice I'd always used when I was in trouble with Paul.

"Good Christ," he said with faint disgust, evidently surprised that such a pathetic tone could come from my mouth. "I didn't say that! I just want to know why. I mean, if you wanna set up some dummy front so you have something to report to the IRS, I can definitely help with that, but there's no need to go overboard and pay everything you owe."

I sat there silently, watching his smoke as it rose into the afternoon light, and considered my classmates: a roomful of welfare losers and me one of them—or at least so I'd thought at first. I considered how the class we'd all agreed to take because it would exempt us from having to do the Job Search program had invested a belief in us, had given us all a goal, something important to fight for, and how for the first time in our lives we were all trying to succeed. Were all trying to play by the rules. I thought of my father then too, and how I still wanted to prove something to him, and then again, I thought of Ray. I saw him sitting on the bed, excitedly explaining his dreams and ideas, and the faith he had in me to be a part of them. I wanted to do things right for once. Or at least see if I could.

All of these realizations came into my mind at once, and I tried to think how I could explain my reasoning to Hole in a way that would make any sense to him.

"Look," I said finally, "I know it seems silly, but it's important to me. I'm not going to be in this line of work forever, but I'm in it now, so I might as well learn from it. I'd like to learn to run a business the right way. The legal way. And you seem to know how to do that better than anyone I know."

He shook his head, exhaled noisily, and stubbed out his cigarette in the ashtray in a disgusted way that seemed to say, *Kids! Will they never learn?* But my flattery had worked, and what he actually said was something quite different.

"Be here every Wednesday and Friday at ten-thirty. Bring whatever records you have and a calculator. Plan to be here for at least an hour, probably two."

"You mean it?" I asked, excited, almost giving in to the urge to clasp my hands together as Marvin had done earlier.

"You heard what I said!" he snapped, and turned back to his desk.

"Yes, yes, I'll be here. This really means—"

"But there's one more thing," he interrupted, looking up at me.

"What's that?"

He raised his eyebrow again and the corners of his thin lips crept upward.

"I want you and Ray to take me out together on Sunday nights. Someplace nice. To that Pinocchio's place."

"Deal," I said, and planted a kiss on his bald head.

"Now get out of here," he barked, pushing me away. "I've got my own work to do. And shut that door when you leave and tell the Nelly Green Giant to turn down the fucking TV!"

On the way out, I exchanged numbers with the soon-to-be-unemployed Marvin, promised to call, and then hurried back to my apartment with just enough time to shower, change, and answer the door for my nooner.

CRAZY AL AND THE
THAI STICK

Ray called a few days later and played me a message that had been left on his home phone—the one we used to take calls for our mutual ad. It was a young, foreign voice saying he'd seen the ad and was wondering if we were hiring. He left his name, Johnny, and a number to call back, asking us to be discreet because of his roommate.

We both laughed at that.

"Hiring!" I said. "Can you imagine?" I knew his likely response but toyed with him anyway.

"Yes," he said, his voice grave. "I can completely imagine it; I'm fucking exhausted. Roommate or not, call him!"

And so it started. Our first employee. Or rather, our first subcontractor, an engineering student from Thailand studying at the Colorado School of Mines. He was small and slender and smooth, almost feminine, with skin the color of milky tea. He smiled easily and often, and had a cute, boyish face even though he was twenty-seven. Best of all, he had experience! He had grown up in a small town in northern Thailand and had gone to Bangkok to study. There he had turned to sex-for-hire because he needed extra money to cover his expenses, and because he liked to send a little extra back to his family. He still wanted the extra money to send home, and had a student work permit, but since he was an engineering student his free hours were limited, and he didn't want to waste them making six dollars an hour working nights at a convenience store. He was hoping, he said, that we could set him up with some work in exchange for a portion of his take. Ray and I interviewed him together and, after a brief conference, decided we'd offer him the job—er, decided to offer to subcontract him. I told him, in a loud, clear voice, that we could give him as much or as little work as he wanted, that we would take forty percent of what we charged for his services and the cost of running his ad, and that he would be responsible for paying his own taxes, which I could show him how to do, if he wasn't sure.

"DOES THAT SOUND FAIR?"

"Would you stop yelling?" Ray said. "He's not deaf and he's on a full-ride scholarship. I think he can understand English."

"I guess you're right." I smiled at Johnny.

He nodded and smiled back, but I could tell something was bothering him.

"You look confused," I said.

"Sorry." He shook his head. "I guess I have one question."

"What's that?" I asked.

He hesitated, trying to be as diplomatic as possible, but then asked, quite bluntly, "Why the tax?"

"The taxes, well, yes," I stammered. "I just feel like it's safer."

He nodded his agreement, but I could still see the confused look in his eye. He leaned in closer and whispered. "But it's . . . illegal, yes?"

"Uh, yes, it is," I said, and groaned as I thought about trying to explain myself again.

"Did you ever hear of Al Capone?" I asked, deciding to offer an explanation in a roundabout way.

"The gangster?" he asked.

"Yes," I said, and mimed shooting a gun.

He nodded.

"Okay, well, then, you probably know he finally got caught and went to jail."

Again he nodded.

"But what you probably don't know," I said in my best Mr. Rogers voice, "is what Al Capone finally went to jail for." He shook his head, agreeing that no, he did not know.

"Well," I said, leaning forward in my chair and lowering my voice to a conspiratorial whisper, "it wasn't murder, and it wasn't racketeering, and it wasn't bootlegging. It wasn't even prostitution. No, what finally sent Al Capone to the big house was . . . tax evasion!"

I leaned back in my chair and paused dramatically to let the power of my words sink in. He and Ray both stared at me, unimpressed. I continued. "Even though all the money he made was illegal, they said he still should have paid taxes on it, and because he hadn't they shipped him off to jail. And you know what, I don't want to go to jail, because jail is what ruined Al Capone. He went crazy locked up in Alcatraz!"

And here I paused and mimed *crazy,* rolling my eyes in their sockets and pointing a twirling index finger at my head. (I selectively deleted from my tale the fact that an untreated case of syphilis was what had really driven Al crazy.)

"He was such a mess," I continued, "shitting his pants all the time and drooling everywhere, that they finally just let him out of jail early, figuring he was no longer a threat to society. But it was too late for Al," I said, shaking my head sadly. "Prison had ruined him. Not paying his taxes had ruined him. And he spent the rest of his days on his Florida estate, fishing in his swimming pool and talking to the little voices in his head. So yes, it's illegal," I said in my own deadpan voice, "and yes, we could probably get away without paying taxes, but we won't, okay?"

He nodded, but both he and Ray were regarding me wide-eyed, as if I were the one hearing little voices.

"Don't worry about it," I said, trying to sound reassuring. "Really. Just tell the IRS that you are a weight trainer." And here I mimed the act of weight lifting, doing curls with both arms and straining the muscles in my face. He looked down at his slight body, all one hundred pounds of it; then he looked back up at me and then over at Ray, who rolled his eyes and shrugged his shoulders.

"Well, I want the work," Johnny said, "so okay, I guess. I'll pay the taxes."

We shook hands amiably, and then Ray and I took him into the other room to take a picture for his ad.

We discussed possibilities for a few minutes, dug around in our prop box, and then proceeded to dress him up. Although he was Thai, we ignored the relatively peaceful history of his native land and outfitted him in a ragtag guerrilla outfit consisting of a ripped white shirt, a large pistol tucked into his belt, and a red bandanna tied around his head. He posed in front of a large rubber plant, in which Ray positioned some stuffed birds and a stuffed monkey. The overall effect was supposed to be that of a sexy young member of the Viet Cong or the Khmer Rouge, but I have to admit it was more campy and frightening than erotic.

Nevertheless it did the trick and garnered him lots of business with the veteran community. Above the photo we placed the naughty heading *Thai Stick,* and underneath it we listed his age as twenty-two (the age we put in almost every ad, regardless of what it actually was), and gave his dimensions and my phone number, since I would handle all of the scheduling.

As soon as we'd finished and Johnny had gone, Ray started right in on me.

"What is the deal with these taxes?" he said. "Why are you so set on it? And don't give me any more of that Al Capone shit."

I thought of what I'd told Hole and I tried to explain it to Ray. He looked at me much the same way Johnny had. Finally I stopped trying.

"Look," I said, lighting a cigarette, "I'm taking care of the money and the scheduling now so you can have more time, right? Well, then, humor me. Or better yet, think of it as another expression of your artistic philosophy: I'm smashing senseless taboos. I've taken two opposite things or two things that aren't usually associated with each other— taxes and dirty money—and put them together. How about that?"

That was weak, I knew, and saw it was not going to do. He was still looking at me skeptically. If I'd had a mirror, I'd have looked at me skeptically, too.

"Besides," I went on, "I have Hole helping me with the books now and I really want to learn to do everything legally, completely on the level, so that wh—" Something caught in my throat. "So that when we have the gallery I'll know how to run it."

His head bobbed up from the camera he was rewinding, as I knew it would, at the mention of the G word.

"What did you say?"

"Something about a stupid gallery, I think." And I avoided his eyes by examining the filter of my cigarette.

He said nothing, or at least nothing intelligible, but dropped the camera and charged at me from across the room, bowling me over like some cartoon dog greeting his master, hooting and howling. We rolled around laughing and yelling, and somehow my mouth came across his and sort of stayed there, which triggered a frenzied removal of clothes and a frantic rubbing of parts, and . . . well, you know. It was still sex, the fundamentals of which are always essentially the same, but I remember thinking that with Ray, maybe because we'd waited so long, it seemed better than usual, somehow *un*usual.

When it was over I remember feeling disappointed that it was over so quickly, so I pulled him back down and we did it again, and when that was over, as we lay there kissing and running our hands over each other's bodies, I still felt somewhat shortchanged. Like I was owed something for having held back for so long. As we started the third time I remember glancing at my watch and realizing that I was ridiculously late for my next appointment—and not really caring all that much.

EXPANSION AND DIVERSIFICATION

After Johnny had been with us a while and it was clear that we were making money on him and he was happy with the arrangement, I started to consider other people as subcontractors. Just as Tina had predicted, I knew I was successful when the competition started coming to me. They had seen our ads (how could they miss them?) and wanted to be a part of it. Most of them were law students looking for help with the bills, so we took three of them on and got them set up on their symbiotic relationship with Harden Up. I also began to look for others when I was on my nightly outings with clients. Most often these evenings consisted of entertaining businessmen in from out of town who had hired me more as a guide to the gay life of Denver than as a sex partner. They usually wanted to go to "the" spot for that particular night, so I'd select the newest flash-in-the-pan restaurant, sure to be crowded with fags, and then take them to whichever bar was likely to be most crowded.

I had gradually abandoned my fear of being seen by old friends and acquaintances, but when I was seen and approached I lied nonetheless, introducing them to my cousin/uncle from out of town. This worked remarkably well with everyone except Andre, who saw me out on many of these evenings. He would wave and smile from across the restaurant but never approached my table and never mentioned it in our subsequent phone conversations or coffee outings. Consequently our relationship moved into even shallower waters than it had been in previously and was in danger of evaporating completely. A fact that saddened me.

In the dance clubs I frequented on these nights there were usually professional dancers: well-built guys paid to dance on the bar in clubs and teasingly remove their clothing until they were down to a G-string and a pair of boots. The patrons would then slip cash in the waistband, or the crotch string, or wherever they could stuff it. These dancers either worked for the bar or for a company that supplied strippers, and many of them purported to be straight. (Although how I'd enjoy taking my clothes off in a roomful of gay men if I were not gay, I can only surmise. To me it seems sort of like picking a scab in shark-infested waters.)

It was in such a club that I first came across James. My client for that evening was off at the bar getting another round of drinks, which would probably be sloshed empty by the time he made it back through the crowd, and I was standing against the wall watching, with considerable amusement, the worst dancer I have ever seen. Oh, he was certainly cute enough—short, well built, with shoulder-length brown hair, his body glistening with sweat from his vain struggle to find the beat of the music. He grew more and more flustered and confused as he went on, and consequently was oblivious to the men waving tips at him. Eventually they gave up trying to catch his eye and either left the money on the bar (where, more often than not, it was inadvertently kicked to the floor) or walked away, shrugging their shoulders.

It is common practice among "dick dancers" (as they are affectionately called) to wear a condom half-full of birdseed on the end of the penis. This prosthetic fills out the pouch of the G-string nicely, giving it a larger, more pendulous appearance. As James thrashed and gyrated and convulsed like an epileptic, it became grossly apparent that he had employed this birdseed technique, and that it was failing miserably, as small seeds began spilling from the corner of his crotch every time he did a high kick—which was much more often than necessary. Worst of all, these tiny orbs made his dance surface even more treacherous, and he surely would have slipped and fallen to the floor had not fate intervened, in the form of a new song, and thus a new dancer who took James's place on the bar. James descended, to amused applause, and wandered around dazedly collecting the tips, given mostly out of pity. He then wove his way through the crowd over to where an older gentleman, whom I had entertained on previous occasions, was waiting. The two spoke briefly. James gave him a kiss, and then ran off to change.

Maybe I was stupid—I've often thought so in retrospect. If not stupid, then at least stupidly sentimental, but after he'd gone that night, I kept thinking of him up there, so clumsy and awkward, and remembered myself at Palladio's and how I'd been just as clumsy. I went back to the bar the next night, alone, and when he finished his set I caught up with him and bought him a drink. We talked briefly, and I mentioned that I'd seen him leave with the older gentleman the night before. He went pale. I assured him that I knew his friend well and that I ran a company called Harden Up. He said he'd heard of it and liked the ads.

"Would you like me to get some work for you?" I asked, not having time to beat around the bush since I was due at the Oxford in fifteen minutes.

"You mean, like, doing *that?*" he asked, clearly shocked. I thought maybe I'd made a mistake, but went on.

"Yes, as an escort. A hustler. If you're not interested, I'm sorry. I didn't mean to offend you."

"No, no, no," he protested. "I thought maybe you wanted me to answer phones or something."

We laughed and then made arrangements to work out together the next day, during which we could talk and hammer out the details. It went well and he started that very night, his first client being none other than Burl, who had been designated the official test driver for all new employees.

And the stable was, how shall I say, filling up nicely. At our peak, we had eight subcontractors working, and that variety helped retain clients and encouraged repeat business. We also tried to establish some fairly concrete price guidelines, although this was hard to do since sex is so malleable. You could go in with something specific in mind and it could so quickly escalate into more. We even printed up a "frequent friend" card—after six sessions your seventh was free. In addition, I set up an incentive program for the subcontractors, giving them fifty dollars for every new client they brought in, which not only brought in new clients but also helped discourage the subs from moonlighting.

My apartment at this point was anything but an apartment. It was an office with a bed. I had adopted the rectangular kitchen table as my desk, and had one side of it reserved for scheduling while the other was devoted to bookkeeping and finances. Everything was well organized except the phone, the incessant sound of which was unbelievably irritating.

Instead of having a separate phone for each person, I gave each one a different pager number, which appeared in their respective ad, but which rang on my pager. When it did, I would then call the client back, get the information, and then page the emp—er, subcontractor on his real pager number—the one that actually rang on his pager instead of mine. When he called me back on my cell phone I would give him the who, what, where, when, and how much, and with any luck they'd be on their merry way. Confused? Me too. Imagine having to go through that no less than forty times a day—and having to weed out all the cranks, of which there were many, and having to entertain my own clients, keep books, and make sure everyone got paid. I felt like some weird Pavlovian experiment, constantly responding to beeps and vibrations.

I tried to implement a system where I'd check pages only once an hour. Then, wherever I was, whoever I was with, I'd sneak away to an isolated corner with my Day-Timer and my cell phone, and answer page after page as quickly as I could, do the scheduling, and then call everyone to make sure they each knew where they were going. It was unnerving, to say the least, and I realized that I was going to have to do something when one Saturday evening I kept a trick waiting in the car while I sat in a convenience-store bathroom for thirty minutes on the phone.

So here's what I did: I spoke to Ray and to all the guys who were working then and asked if they would feel comfortable if we rented a place, maybe one with multiple rooms, and started working out of there. Of course we'd still do outcalls, but if tricks wanted or needed to come to us, then they could do so. I'd have to take another five percent of their gross, I told them, but we were so in demand then that I figured we could probably raise prices to compensate for the amount and they probably wouldn't even feel the pinch. A place of our own would be safer and it would make it much easier to keep track of everything. Everyone agreed, and we all decided something centrally located in Capitol Hill would be best. I started looking immediately, but was quickly discouraged because all of the live-in rentals I looked at were always short on rooms and usually had an on-site landlord. I banged my head against this wall for a week until Roger, one of the poli-sci students, who was doing an internship at the state capitol, mentioned that he'd seen some office space for rent on Thirteenth Avenue, within spitting distance of the capitol building itself.

"Office space!" I said doubtfully. "That won't work. People coming and going all day. Too suspicious."

"Dude, it's not like that," he said. "This is crappy office space. It's been for rent forever. Check it out." And he gave me the number of the leasing agent.

I called it right away, figuring it was worth a shot, and arranged to meet the landlord that very afternoon. I showed up on time, but he kept me waiting for nearly forty minutes, which infuriated me because I'd already had to reschedule one client and now it looked like I'd have to reschedule another. I was just about to leave when a man pulled up in a wheezing Plymouth from the seventies. He got out, and the first thing I noticed was that his suit had evidently last been cleaned sometime in that same decade, covered as it was with a menu of dried food. He apologized and explained that he was coming from Golden, a dismal city that can use the name only satirically, and it had taken him a while to get the car started. I nodded impatiently and asked some general questions about the building.

"This place was built back in the thirties," he said, smoothing his greasy locks and opening the door. I looked at the building and had to agree; everything about it screamed Depression. From the outside it wasn't terrible—a simple, rectangular, two-tone blond-brick made gray from auto pollution, with large metal windows, but inside it was dark and miserable: a central hallway lit by wan fluorescent tubes, off of which were dark rooms of various sizes. I smelled bathrooms, but saw none. The offices he showed me were on the second floor, which was completely vacant. The lower level, a series of storefronts accessible only from the sidewalk, was partially rented out to a hip-hop clothing store and an Indian restaurant.

I walked around from room to dismal room, and somehow I saw potential. The whole place was in desperate need of paint, and the carpet was beyond cleaning, but these units were not going to rent anytime soon and they were cheap!

It would be possible, I thought. *Definitely possible.*

I ended up renting four of the six rooms on the top floor, two of which were equipped with small bathrooms, each containing a sink and a toilet. I told him we would be setting up private exercise rooms, and was there any way we could run plumbing for two small showers.

"I don't have anything against you doing improvements on the place," he said, "but it's Mother's property, really, and I don't know if she'd pay for any of it. We're sort of hoping for someone to buy the place up."

Not likely, I thought, looking up at the water-stained ceiling tiles.

"Well, what about a break on the rent, then?" I asked. "If we paint and recarpet . . ."

He hesitated, thinking.

"I guess I could do that. You save the receipts and I'll pay for one-third of the materials," he said.

"Half," I countered.

"I don't know if Mother—"

"Look," I said, not liking this "Mother" woman, "I'm renting almost the whole top floor; give me a break. The improvements will surely help the resale value."

"Well, I guess that seems okay," he said finally, and I wrote him a check for the deposit and first month's rent and drew up a contract stating that he would pay for half the cost of materials and had him sign it.

And that's how we started our office complex of ill fame.

I immediately hired Antonio and Victor to come in and plumb two showers and recarpet and paint. They were very professional about the whole thing: covering the windows with makeshift curtains and working at night so that the building-code enforcer wouldn't discover that they hadn't pulled permits, and buying twice the amount of supplies necessary so that my receipts would add up to the full amount, later returning what was not used for cash. In a little over two weeks, it was ready for us to move in. I didn't have much capital left after I paid them, but I took what I had and bought four refurbished, full-size mattresses and box springs from Goodwill for a cost of only three hundred and ten dollars, and as many cheap sets of sheets as I could afford from Kmart. Then I bought four small "used" TV-VCR combos from, uh, "associates" of Antonio and Victor for thirty-five dollars apiece, all of which I was able to deduct from my taxes, along with the cost of the building improvements as business expenses since, under Hole's tutelage, I had recently filed articles of incorporation and was now officially operating under the name Harden Up Inc.

I took the largest of the four rooms and made that into the office/waiting room, and moved my kitchen table, to which I had now grown attached as a desk, to this office. I had a phone hooked up with three lines, and Seth donated a computer system and got us set up with some excellent bookkeeping and accounting software. He also set up a spread sheet from which we could print everyone's daily schedule complete with room assignments.

Millie's girl Josie, for Millie had become a contractor too, came by twice daily for laundry pickups and drop-offs, and always did just the nicest job, everything pressed and boxed up like little presents, and no questions asked. Most of the guys took to giving her their own laundry to do as well, the cost of which I deducted automatically from their pay.

Print ads were giving us a lot of business, but with all of the new expenses I found we still needed more. I took a gamble on Sharise and it proved a profitable one. I approached her one day after class and asked if she would be interested in setting up a Web page for us, intimating that I wasn't exactly running the type of business I'd indicated in class.

"Honey," she said, giving me a world-weary look, "this is the Net we're talking about. The World Wide Web! Believe me, I've seen it all. I'm telling you there is piss little that shocks me anymore."

And, true to her word, she worked quickly and efficiently, apparently oblivious to the content. We gave her all of our print ads, and she scanned them and made us an incredible site, that at its peak was getting up to two hundred hits a day.

As if there weren't enough on our plate, Ray and I decided to extend a branch of the business into filmmaking. The topic arose one night when we were lying in bed discussing what we found erotic, and agreed that most gay pornography would not make the cut.

"Everyone is so young and shaved and clean-cut," I said, "which would be fine if there were some variety, but it's all so one-dimensional and boring."

"And all the limp dicks!" Ray added. "How exciting is that?"

And it was true. The majority of gay film stars may very well be as straight as they say they are, since they never seem very aroused by their male counterparts.

"You know what would be my ideal porno movie?" Ray said thoughtfully. "Mormon missionaries."

I laughed.

"No, really," he said. "It'd be perfect. You have two fresh young guys sent out into the world in suits and on ten-speeds to spread the word of Brigham Young. Then, on some lonely night, in a barn, or maybe some hot afternoon when they stop for a swim . . . things happen. Later on they can get seduced by—or seduce—guys in the outside world, going from house to friendly house, getting help with a flat tire from a horny gas station attendant . . . It'd be great! It's taboo, it's sacrilegious, and it would be funny!"

I wasn't laughing; I was thinking. Thinking that it didn't sound at all like a bad idea. All of us working for Harden Up Inc. had, at one time or another, made movies in Dave's basement or elsewhere, so we were all relatively comfortable in front of the camera, and most of us had slept together in duos at least once. My mind whizzed as I thought of the potential money to be made. Production costs would be cheap, copying videos could not be that expensive, packaging and distribution I could learn about from Hole, and I'm sure we could sell them in his stores. Hell, we could sell them on the Web site, maybe put an ad in *Advocate Men;* it was perfect!

I snapped out of my reverie. Ray was off on another plot. . . .

". . . and so they could all be camping in the woods, you know, to get their last Eagle Scout badge or something, and then the Scoutmast—"

"How soon do you think we could do this?" I interrupted.

"You serious?"

"Completely serious."

He thought for a moment. "Well, let's see, I know this friend, the one who helped me get my car, actually. I'm pretty sure Sally's got all the equipment—and knows how to use it."

I said nothing but got up to retrieve my cell phone. Ray looked up the number, called, and arranged for "Sally" to meet us at the office the next day. Well, imagine my surprise when Sally walked through the door and I saw that "she" was none other than slow-eyed Salvatore from the microbusiness class.

"Here's the friend I was telling you about," Ray said, leading him into the office and sitting down on the couch. Salvatore and I stared at each other, both terribly embarrassed, but said nothing about our connection. I filled Ray in on the details later.

"I pitched the idea to him," Ray said, "and he's definitely interested, aren't ya, Sal?"

"Why, uh, yes," he stammered. "It sounds most satisfactory."

"Uh, great," I said, and together we sat down very professionally and worked out the details in a contract, agreeing that in exchange for his filming services, we would pay off the balance he owed on his equipment, thus enabling him to get it out of hock.

Later that night, after I'd informed Ray of my previous acquaintance with Salvatore, he told me the story of how they had met: Ray had been taking pictures around the mortuary one day and Salvatore, curious about cameras, had approached him. They talked, and Ray persuaded him to let him take some pictures inside the mortuary, and a morbid friendship was born, one result of which was Ray's acquisition of his unique mode of transportation.

"Sal's a good guy," Ray said reassuringly. "And he needs money. He's had a hard time since he got fired, but I guess you know that."

I nodded. "Why did he get fired?"

Ray laughed.

"Oh, big scandal! He got caught stealing the fillings from the stiffs when they came out of the oven. He had a nice little scam going with this crooked jeweler on Larimer Street."

And thus we began our movie careers, with Salvatore, the former filling-stealer, as our cameraman. Ray and I wrote the script (which filled almost an entire page), and of course we cast ourselves in the lead roles, and our few free evenings were soon occupied with scouting sites and preparing the costumes and props, which was as much, if not more fun than making our advertisements had been.

Costuming wasn't much of a problem, requiring only two identical dark blue suits and a couple of skinny ties, all of which we got from a vintage shop on Colfax. For props, we dug up a pair of bikes, a pair of small backpacks, and of course, two Bibles.

We did several outside shots of us riding our bikes together and walking together, Bibles always clutched tightly in our hands, and one scene where we sat on some porch steps and pretended to convert Millie's girl Josie, who was confused and a little frightened, but played along anyway. The initial sex scene, the one in which Ray and I finally satisfy our long-repressed adolescent longing for each other, took place in a wheat field and was, to say the least, rough. The wheat stalks, although beautiful, were sharp and itchy, and the bugs and the traffic helicopter circling overhead were constant pests. But, being consummate professionals, we acted through the adversity and finished the show, only to discover later that the action, while highly arousing, was not visible much of the time, since Salvatore hadn't thought it necessary to zoom in and get tight shots, or to really change the camera angles very much at all. A problem that was soon remedied after we sent him home with a stack of Falcon tapes to study. When we resumed filming a few days later, all went smoothly. All except the scene in which Ray and I are seduced by Burl, who, like a child at his own birthday party, smiled and waved at the camera.

That and the fact that I did something that almost brought the whole business down like a house of cards.

GAY MARVIN

I've often wondered about the thought processes, or lack thereof, that are behind really bad ideas. I don't mean bad ideas like the Edsel, or the movie *Waterworld,* that started out well, but failed because they didn't appeal to the market or because they were so over budget that they could never hope to make a profit. No, I'm talking about the ideas that were clearly destined for failure from the start, like meat-flavored ice cream or plus sizes of spandex shorts. What is it that clouds sound business judgment and hinders informed decision making, leading you to believe that you are doing the right thing, and only later, after the dust has settled following the explosion, are you able to see clearly how terribly stupid the idea was from the beginning?

Hiring Marvin as the Harden Up Inc. receptionist was just such an idea.

In my case, my judgment was obscured by a mix of things: overwork, fatigue, desperation, tenderhearted pity for those less fortunate than myself . . . but if I'm truly honest with myself (self-delusion being self-pollution), it was all vanity. Oh, I was definitely overworked, fatigued, and desperate, as the business had increased exponentially in the past six weeks and the administrative work—the scheduling, the bookkeeping, the taxes, etc.—was killing me. But what really drove me to my bad idea was the vain decision to cast myself in the starring role of *Missionary Positions.* Filming would pull me away from the office for days, and I realized that I could not just abandon ship without having someone there to steer it in my absence. Why I thought Marvin would be capable of the task, I'm not sure. I knew he had some office experience (although I also knew he'd been fired for incompetence or tardiness from every job he'd ever had), and knew he wouldn't be shocked about the product we were selling. Most of all, I knew he needed a job, and I liked the image of myself as his savior, giving him the chance, the opportunity, the brass ring he so desperately wanted and needed. I could help him change his life for the better. Could help him get back on track. Saint Jack. It was stupid, especially when you consider that I, of all people, should have known better, remembering Paul's failed attempts at saving me. But, believing it was a good idea and would be a simple solution to my scheduling problem, I called him up and offered him the job.

I worked with him for an entire afternoon and evening, showing him how to handle calls and schedule appointments, how to keep track of the money, and then the next day at nine A.M., I confidently left the entire operation in his hands while I went off to have sex in a wheat field.

"You'll be all right?" I asked as I headed out the door. "Any questions?"

"Oh, no, no, I'll be fine," he said, nibbling his fingernails and staring apprehensively at the computer screen. "You go on; don't worry about a thing."

I did so.

Before noon the entire operation of Harden Up Inc. had essentially come to a standstill. Marvin had, quite inadvertently, sabotaged the whole business with a rapidity and thoroughness any Arab terrorist, computer virus, or Monkey Wrencher would have found admirable. He had hopelessly jammed the computer, had double-booked rooms and triple-booked subcontractors, had lost the keys to the building on one of his numerous cigarette breaks, and somehow managed to screw up every phone message he took, either writing down the name but not the number of the caller, or vice versa.

When I finally returned to the office, sunburned and itchy, in response to more enraged phone calls and pages than I cared to count, I found the room full of screaming people—clients, subcontractors, a locksmith, Millie's girl, Josie, and of course Marvin, the large target of everyone's ire. He was seated, as I'd left him, behind the desk, eyes staring blankly at the computer screen, but instead of his nails, he nibbled calmly on the remnants of a banana Moon Pie, which, I ascertained from the pile of wrappers on the desk, was not the first he had consumed that day. As soon as I entered (in my missionary garb, still clutching my Bible) and my entrance was detected, all the frustrated, angry, griping, whiny ones shifted their attention from Marvin to me, demanding I take action and do something, which I did, by calmly wheeling the saboteur and his Moon Pie to one side, pulling up a chair, and starting the slow process of extinguishing all the temper flare-ups, and restoring order.

Later, many hours later, when everyone had been placed or compensated accordingly, the computer was back up and running, and things had generally calmed down, I looked up, ready to deal with the next difficulty, and saw, to my relief, that Ray and I were alone in the office. He smiled, rose wordlessly from the sofa, and began turning out the lights. He walked behind my chair, and started massaging my shoulders with his gloved hands. I leaned back and closed my eyes.

"How 'bout we pick up some food and go back to my place?" he said, nuzzling his goatee into my neck suggestively. It felt wonderful, and the thought of "rehearsing" for tomorrow's filming was a pleasant idea, but one that was soon usurped by the thought of the large cause of all the trouble.

"Where's Marvin?" I asked. Ray pulled back, swung me around in the chair, and kissed me.

"I don't know," he said, and took a seat on my lap. He put his arm around my neck, pulled my head toward his, and kissed me again. "And I don't give a shit right now." Another kiss, longer and deeper this time. I tried to speak in between them.

"I should . . . probably find him . . . and . . . apologize."

"Apologize!" Ray pulled his head back, slightly annoyed, but his voice was still breathy and rough. "I'm trying to get you naked and you keep bringing up Marvin, which isn't the image I want in my head when I'm all . . . aroused like this." He kissed me again and placed my hand on his arousal. "Besides," he said, casually picking some wheat chaff from my hair, "he's the one who should apologize. Nothing like cleaning up after a three-hundred-pound tornado."

"Ah, I know," I said, "but it's probably my fault, too. I shouldn't have left him alone so soon. I knew he needed more training. Poor guy, he looked so pathetic sitting there eating, like some big kid."

Ray got up and pulled on his suit coat. "Come on. Let's get out of here."

I exhaled noisily, switched off the computer, and got up and put on my own coat.

"Do you think he's good-looking?" I asked as we stepped into the hallway.

"Who?" Ray asked, lighting a cigarette. "Marvin? If he lost some weight, maybe, and got some wrist splints."

I laughed, but then tried to picture a thinner, less effeminate Marvin. Yes, I could see it—a good cardiovascular program, some diet changes, a shorter haircut. *All he needs is guidance,* I thought. *Training.* An idea was fermenting.

"What if he was more masculine?" I asked, continuing the conversation as I locked the door and followed Ray across the parking lot to his car.

"But he's not," he said tersely.

"It would bring in a whole different clientele . . ." I said suggestively. He stopped and looked at me over the roof of the hearse.

"You're not thinking . . ." he said, shaking his head. "But he's not masculine, and I don't think all the testosterone in the world could change him." We got in and he started the engine.

"I like the guy, too," he said, "but get real. Some leopards just can't change their spots."

"Maybe you're right." I sighed, and surrendered all thoughts on the matter to my growling stomach and the discussion of where to eat. We decided on spring rolls and drove to a Vietnamese restaurant on Federal Boulevard. There was a huge line, and after we put in our order we sat outside on the sidewalk to wait. It was June and the night air was warm and perfumed with the strong smell of curry. While we waited, Ray and I smoked and he read one of the weekly papers, *Tally-Ho,* while I sat up on the step behind him and read over his shoulder. When he got to the entertainment section, I scanned the movie schedule longingly, wishing I had the time to see movies, or even the energy to stay awake through an entire video on the rare occasions when we rented movies. I got to the schedule for one of the revival movie houses, and remembered fondly the days I'd spent there with my mother during my period of unemployment, and I felt guilty for having gone so long without returning her calls. It was Audrey Hepburn week. *She'd love that,* I thought and scanned the list of the movies that were going to be shown: *Roman Holiday, Breakfast at Tiffany's, My Fair Lady, Charade, Sabrina*—all the classics. And again I thought of Marvin, and remembered his dismal cubicle at Cardmember Authorizations, every inch of which he had plastered with the photos of old movie stars. I was still staring blankly at the schedule, thinking, when they called Ray's name. He folded up the paper, got up, and went inside to pay. *There must be something poor Marvin can do,* I thought.

"Ready?" Ray said when he returned with the bag.

"Uh, yeah." And I picked up the paper and put it under my arm.

It was a stupid idea, looking back on it, but sometimes the most outlandish ideas, the ideas you think will never work, are the best ever. I felt sure that if it was a bad idea it was at least the Edsel and not the meat-flavored ice cream.

"Do you mind if we make another stop?" I asked as innocently as I could.

"The food's cold anyway." He shrugged. "Where to?"

"I know this sounds dumb, but I just want to find out if Marvin is okay."

"Sure," he said, and there was a surprising softness in his voice. "I'm a little worried myself. He's just the type to OD on Tylenol over something like this."

I looked up Marvin's address in my Day-Timer and we headed back up Colfax to Washington Street.

Marvin's address was not a coveted one. The building was one in a series of brick buildings that had been constructed after World War II, all named after women. This one in particular was called the Susie Lynn, and it was obvious from her peeling paint and rotting window frames that she had let herself go. We parked on the street and walked up the cracked steps into the small security lobby. I looked over the mailboxes, found Marvin's apartment number, and pressed the buzzer. Nothing. We waited for a minute and I buzzed again. Nothing. I was beginning to worry when Ray nudged me and pointed to a bundle of wires coming out from behind the mailboxes, their frayed ends dangling uselessly a foot from the floor. We tried the door, which wasn't locked, so we entered, went up two steps, and followed a dank passageway to apartment number four. Inside, I heard the tinny sound of a small TV struggling to do justice to a dramatically soaring violin soundtrack. We were most definitely at the right apartment. I knocked. The TV went silent. I knocked again.

"Marvin, it's Jack." No response, but I heard the sound of crinkling plastic.

"I know you're in there," I said, "unless there's someone else in this building watching AMC."

He shuffled over slowly toward the door and threw it open, his enormous frame blocking the view inside. He had obviously been crying.

"What?" he asked defensively.

"We just want to talk to you, okay? I wanted to make sure you're okay. Can we come in?" I asked. He didn't move.

"Look," he said, and tears started welling in his eyes, "I'm sorry about today. I know I fucked everything up, but—"

"It's okay," I said. "It was my fault. I didn't give you enough training. Forget about it. We have something else you might be interested in," I said.

"We do?" Ray said, surprised.

"Yes, we do. Now, can we come in?" I asked again.

He shrugged, turned, and walked back into the apartment. Inside it was dark, save for the blue glow from the TV, and there was the unmistakable stench of a litter box in need of emptying. He led us to the sofa and turned on a Tiffanyesque lamp on the end table. The floor in front of him was littered with plastic wrappers, and several boxes of Little Debbies sat open on the coffee table next to a can of diet soda. On the screen a young Fred Astaire was effortlessly tossing Ginger Rogers up and around. Ray helped himself to a Nutty Bar, opening the wrapper and sniffing the contents cautiously.

"Look," I said, "I'm sorry I yelled at you today."

He shrugged again, and continued staring at the screen.

"It's just that I've worked really hard to get things running smoothly, and I guess I assumed someone else could just slide in and understand my system."

"Well, I couldn't!" he said petulantly. "Call me stupid."

I sighed and examined him again with professional eyes. He was good looking. His jawline and facial structure were strong, and the five-o'clock shadow was very becoming. I hesitated a moment and spied a framed picture of him and his lover sitting behind a piano, playing and singing. It was obviously a posed shot, but they looked so happy and content sitting there. I decided to continue.

"I've been thinking," I said, staring back at the TV screen, "that maybe you could come back to work for Harden Up, not as a receptionist, but, you know, as one of the guys."

Ray choked on his Nutty Bar. Marvin looked at me and emitted a dubious hiss.

"I'm serious," I said, pushing aside the boxes of snack cakes and taking a seat on the coffee table facing them both. I spoke more to Ray than to Marvin.

"We don't have any guys like Marvin, and I think with a little work—okay, maybe with a lot of work—we could open up a whole new market."

Blank stares.

"What do you think?" I asked.

"I think you're insane," said Marvin. Ray heartily nodded his agreement.

"I'm not," I protested. "There is a market for guys like you."

"Look at me!" Marvin cried, and made a sweeping gesture down his body. "I'm fat! Nobody wants a fat girl."

I chuckled in spite of myself and could hear Ray doing the same. I looked down at the floor and struggled to regain my composure.

"You are . . . large," I said. "Granted. But there's a huge market for bigger, macho top guys like yourself, and I think with you we could really tap into that."

"Oh, you do?" Marvin said, his voice oozing sarcasm.

"Hey," Ray whispered to me. "Could I talk to you outside for a minute?"

"Yes, I do!" I said, ignoring Ray and focusing all my attention on Marvin.

"Well, there are two little problems with that. First," he said, pointing to Fred and Ginger, "I'm not macho. And second!" he boomed. "I'm not a top!"

I nodded and rocked back and forth pensively for a moment.

"Like I said, it will take a little work."

"Oh, Christ!" said Ray and Marvin, both certain I'd gone mad. I was beginning to wonder myself. I thought of giving up, but then thought of something and quickly took out the copy of *Tally-Ho* that I had folded under my Day-Timer.

"Hang on a minute," I said, and I flipped through the pages until I found the movie schedules. "Haven't you ever seen this movie?" I asked, thrusting the paper at him and pointing at the ad for the art house. He looked at it a moment and his expression softened.

"Ohh," he said wistfully, his chubby hand caressing his stubbly neck as if it were Audrey's long, elegant one. "That poor George Peppard! How can you start out with such promise and end up opposite Mr. T?"

"Not that one," I said, leaning toward him and pointing at *My Fair Lady.*

"Yes, of course," he said, and started humming "I Could Have Danced All Night." I felt a swift kick in the shin from Ray's foot. I winced, but didn't look at him.

"Have you seen that one?" I asked. He rolled his eyes and clicked his tongue as if I'd just asked the most ridiculous of questions. I went on.

"Well, then, you know the story, right, about the Cockney flower seller that Rex Harrison transforms into the elegant lady?"

"Girl, duh!" he said, dropping the paper to his lap and shooting me a condescending glare. "Of course you know Julie Andrews should have had the lead. She had it on Broadway, so the movie was rightfully hers. Audrey doesn't even sing. She lip-synchs through the whole movie," he said, nodding his head knowingly. He then closed his eyes and began humming "The Rain In Spain."

"What are you doing?" Ray hissed, grabbing my arm firmly. I pulled away and continued.

"Well, my point exactly!" I said to Marvin, suddenly seeing an opportunity. "She was acting. She couldn't sing but she pulled it off! And in the movie her character was acting, too, right? She wasn't really a lady, at least not in the beginning; she was just some dirty, foul-mouthed daisy seller."

"Violets," Marvin corrected.

"Whatever. The point is," I said, "she transforms into something else, right?"

He nodded.

"She was still the same person, but Rex Harrison taught her how to act differently, how to play a role. Get it? It's all acting. What I do, what Ray does, what all the guys do is acting. Top or bottom, you just need to learn how to play the part. But in your case, we'll need to do the opposite: make you into less of a lady and more of a lower-class thug. More of a young Brando."

"Oh . . . yes?" Marvin said, leaning forward on the sofa, cautiously interested.

"Oh, God!" Ray groaned, and fell back into the cushions.

*   *   *

And that is how we came to add our eighth subcontractor. Our seventh was a young boy, Josh, fresh off the bus from Cheyenne, who had come in hoping for a hustling position, but at the age of seventeen was a risk I didn't want to take. He was a quick learner, but nevertheless I spent a full week teaching him everything he'd need to know to be a receptionist. Then I pulled my ads out of the paper and focused on making movies during the day and watching movies at night with Marvin.

As the first step in Marvin's transformation we went to the library, which has an excellent collection of classic videotapes, and checked out every early Brando film we could get hold of: *The Wild One, Streetcar Named Desire, On the Waterfront, One-Eyed Jacks*—and studied them closely. We studied his movements and gestures, the way he sat and the way he walked, but most of all what he did with his hands, since these were the appendages that gave Marvin the most trouble. Brando's voice, being somewhat whiny and nasally, would not work, so we went to one of Hole's boutiques and bought some Jeff Stryker videos, since his speech (both its form and its content) would be best suited to our purpose. We took them back to Marvin's apartment and listened to them with the picture blacked out so that we wouldn't be distracted. Before I left, I made a sweep of the apartment and confiscated all of his Broadway musical videos (they filled two garbage bags) and placed him on a strict television diet of police shows and ESPN.

Next I got him started on a cardiovascular and weight-training program at the gym, with me as his personal trainer. The first two weeks were difficult, but once he got over the initial shyness and soreness, he became almost fanatical about it and started going on his own.

His appearance presented other problems. I envisioned making money off of him as a leather top, but we were both alarmed when we saw the prices of the equipment, so I abandoned that idea and together we hit the thrift stores, where we bought several pairs of used Levi's, several tight undershirts, and several flannel shirts, some weathered workboots, and a well-worn Carhartt jacket (all of which I deducted as a uniform expense). We had a barber cut his hair very short, and I instructed him to shave only in the evening before he went to bed so that he'd wake up ready to go with a five-o'clock shadow. When we were finished, I stood back and assessed him. He looked like some sort of blue-collar something, an image we were both satisfied with.

Then, gradually, almost as gradually as the seasons change, Marvin began to change. He began warming to this new character. No, more than warming—he started becoming him. Ray had done an ad for him and we posted it on the Web under the name Chet, figuring we couldn't go wrong with one syllable. He studied the ad, unable to believe that it was himself, but soon he began to adopt the persona, and gradually his Pygmalionation was complete.

The whole process was a huge investment, but from a financial standpoint the risk proved well worth it. Within hours of posting his ad, we had twenty-seven hits, and we started making back the money. He developed a strong client base of repeat customers and had far more young, good-looking guys than any of the rest of us. Guys who wanted to believe they were getting a manly man. And, after a while, he had them, and himself, convinced.

TOIL AND TROUBLE

Ray and Salvatore and I were sitting in the office one morning before our day of filming began. They were discussing camera angles and were readying the equipment, and I was seated at the desk typing up the last few schedules for the day, and calling the guys to make sure they knew where they were supposed to be and when. We were all busy and scarcely noticed when Johnny came in. I saw him out of the corner of my eye and gave a silent nod hello, as I was on the phone. I looked again and saw that his eye was black and his upper lip had been split.

"I'll call you back," I said, and hung up. "What the hell happened to you!" I quickly came around the desk, led him over toward the window, and tilted his chin up to the light. The skin around his eye was dark purple and there were fingerprint bruises on his throat.

"That new guy last night, the one I met here," he said. "He got kind of rough."

"Christ!" said Ray, who had now joined us by the window.

"I thought I better come in and tell you, because he punched a hole in the wall of room three," he said, swallowing hard.

"Screw the wall!" Ray said. "Are you okay?" We led him over to the sofa, and Salvatore, always calm in tense situations, went and got him a glass of water.

"I think I'm okay," he said softly, "but I'm scared. He didn't use a condom."

Ray and I glanced up at each other.

"Who was he?" Ray asked me. I got up and went back over to the computer and pulled up the spread sheet from the day before. I had only the name "Tom first-timer" listed.

"I don't know," I said. "He was new and he called the number for Johnny's ad, so I just set it up."

"Here's the money," Johnny said, fishing in his pocket.

"No, no, forget it," I said. "Just tell us what happened."

Johnny described the scene slowly. The man had arrived before he did and was waiting in his car when Johnny arrived. They went inside, got started, and everything was fine at first.

"Then he started getting rough and pulling hair," he said.

"He . . . pulled . . . your hair," I stammered, and looked again at Ray. His eyes went dark.

Sal returned with the water and Johnny drank with difficulty, avoiding the side of his mouth that had been split.

"What exactly did he look like?" Ray asked.

Johnny set down the glass. "He was tall. Taller than you, Jack, and he had black hair."

"What kind of car did he drive?" I asked. "Did you see that?"

"It was blue, a sports car, I think a Porsche or BMW, I don't know for sure, but I did see the license plate. It was some word, but I didn't see what it said."

"Oh, God," I said, and a chill went through me as I remembered the size of his cock. I took Johnny by the shoulders and looked at him squarely.

"You're not okay, are you?" I said.

He started crying and shook his head. I put my arm around him and he rested his head on my chest. I could feel him crying. I looked to Ray and Sal for some sort of help.

"Are you bleeding?" I asked, and felt his head nod slightly.

"We have to get him to a doctor." Ray and Salvatore seemed suddenly nervous. I knew what they were thinking: if we took him to a hospital there would be questions, possibly police.

"No!" Johnny said, sitting up and wiping away his tears. "No trouble! I don't want any trouble. It's okay. I'll be okay. After I knew I couldn't stop him, I didn't fight."

"He needs a doctor," I said sternly.

Ray and Salvatore looked at each other and then both nodded.

"We'll take care of it," Ray said.

"Yes." Sal nodded, and began quietly repacking the camera equipment.

Ray helped the bewildered and somewhat reluctant Johnny up and led him to the door.

"But where will you take him?" I asked.

"We know a doctor," Ray said. "He'll check him out and tell us if it's bad. No questions. You stay here and try to track the guy down."

I nodded reluctantly, more because I was suddenly afraid of being alone, but I trusted Ray and Sal, and as they gently led Johnny down the stairs and helped him into the front seat of the hearse, I felt a warm admiration for them and this "other world" they knew so much about. The world of crooked jewelers and unscrupulous doctors who asked no questions. I'd lived in Denver all my life and had never run into such people, had never even known such people existed. I felt so sheltered and naive.

When they'd gone, I went back up to the office and locked the door. I paced around a bit and then went and looked out the window at the traffic whizzing by on Thirteenth. I remembered my attack and how closely it paralleled Johnny's. I was sure it was the same guy, but I knew next to nothing about him, and what if I did? I couldn't very well go to the police and say, "This guy attacked me and raped one of my guys when we were working as prostitutes. Go get him!" I drummed my fingers on the windowsill, thinking. Then I smiled as I realized I had my own doctor! I had my own crooked jeweler! But in my case it was a cop who liked sex toys. I went over to the desk, pulled up Warren's number on the computer screen, and called him at work. I got through the receptionist, waited on hold for a while, but eventually he answered and I asked if it was safe to talk. He said it was, so, as concisely as I could, I told him the situation. I gave him all the information I had about the guy and his car and the license plate, and Warren said he'd be glad to run a check on it, and would call back if he found anything. I thanked him and hung up, feeling very self-satisfied, but the feeling was short-lived, and soon I was up again pacing the room nervously. I had planned to be filming all day, so I hadn't scheduled myself anything until that night. It was only nine-thirty and none of the guys, not even the receptionist, was scheduled to come in until eleven. I tried to do some paper-work but couldn't concentrate and ended up staring absently at the flying windows on the computer screen. I thought of Johnny and all the rest of the guys now under my aegis. Clearly I needed to formulate some better way to protect them, and I made a mental note to call my dad and ask about paging options. Maybe we could have a special pager number or something to indicate trouble.

I also needed to get everyone checked for STDs, which we could do at the central hospital's free STD clinic. Ray and I were in the habit of going every six weeks, and it couldn't hurt to have all the guys do the same. I pulled up all the schedules and typed in a time for the following week. It would be good moral support for Johnny if we all went together.

Ray returned late that afternoon, by which time other crises had arisen, and I was busy behind the desk taking calls and helping Josh with the scheduling for that evening. We stopped everything when he came in and both waited expectantly.

"He'll be okay," Ray said. "I took him back to his dorm. The doctor had seen that kind of thing all the time in prison. He cleaned him up, gave him some antibiotics and a shot of Demerol, and, well, let's just say he won't be studying much tonight."

The phone rang and it was Warren.

"I ran that check on the car, a blue Porsche, license plate BUCKS . . ." he said, trailing off.

"And . . . what?" I asked. "You didn't find him?"

"Oh, no, I found him all right. He's a Carlyle."

"You mean one of *the* Carlyles?"

"None other."

Saying Carlyle in Colorado is like saying Kennedy in Massachusetts, or Windsor in Britain. The Carlyles are a wealthy Colorado family whose initial nest egg came from silver mining. Oswald Carlyle had been one of the few to strike it rich in the 1800s, and his family had not only held on to, but increased their money in the years following. They now had interests in uranium, land development, ski resorts, trucking, broadcasting, etc. . . . But, as so often happens with wealthy families, great empires, and certain ancient breeds of dogs, subsequent generations tend to mutate and decline. A sort of social and moral decay sets in, and to this the Carlyles were not immune. They were now more notorious for their messy divorces, troubled children, and poor driving records than for any of their business or philanthropic ventures.

"So which one owns the car?" I asked eagerly.

"The car is registered to a Johnathan Oswald Carlyle the third, and he's got a rap sheet almost as long as his name. Let's see here, we've got one arrest for cocaine possession, one for aggravated assault, and . . . hmmm, I'm assuming you didn't see him driving, because I'm showing here that his license is suspended until next month for his second drunk-driving conviction."

"What a loser!"

"You said it. Listen, if he does anything like that again, or if he even comes around, you let me know," Warren said. "Maybe we can nail him on something else."

"Thanks," I said. "I will," and hung up.

Later that evening, back at Ray's house, where I was then spending all of my evenings that weren't spent staring at the ceilings of strange hotel rooms, we talked about the day. I sat on a bar stool in the kitchen drinking a beer while Ray made dinner. We were both angry, but only I was angry and frustrated. Frustrated because I felt helpless to protest against something that was so clearly unjust. I felt like someone had "gotten" me, like someone had pulled one over on me, much the way I'd felt after Paul's sister tossed me out, although the circumstances were hardly similar. Having lived outside of the law for most of his life, and having endured more of life's slings and arrows than I, Ray was not nearly so credulous. He had survived the neglect and indifference of parents and teachers, had experienced unjust drug deals, and tricks who refused to pay, and so he was rarely surprised when he faced injustice. In fact, he almost expected it.

"Don't let it get to you," he said, sensing my frustration. "The police were helpful in finding out who he was, but we don't need them to deal with this. We can take care of it ourselves."

I wondered how.

Later, as we lay in the dark, looking up at the stars through the skylights, each lost in our own heads, I thought about the business, the paper castle I'd constructed, and how any number of events—a tax audit, trouble with the police, or even my parents finding out—would be just enough to crumple it all up. I thought again about getting out of it, just stopping and moving on to something else. I couldn't expect this to go on forever, and I was feeling more confident that I could do something else, something legal and legitimate. I knew I wouldn't feel much remorse about walking away from hustling, since lately it had become much like any other job: a lot of hard work. Oh, I'd feel some remorse about leaving the subs high and dry, but they each had their own ad and would need only to change the phone number to continue doing business. I knew that Ray was still awake, so I decided to broach the subject of the gallery again.

"I think after my graduation from the business class, I want to get out of this," I said. "Move on to something else." Ray said nothing but shifted his weight slightly.

"I'm out of debt now and I've, uh, been thinking about the gallery more. I think we should seriously work on a business plan and maybe start scoping out a space." Still no response, but I knew he was listening, so I continued.

"I've been thinking about some marketing strategies, and I think that if we do it we should open with a big bang. Something really funny and controversial, and then think up some new way to publicize the hell out of it."

Still nothing.

"Are you listening?" I asked.

"Yeah."

"Well, why aren't you saying anything?"

He sat up in the darkness and gave a frustrated sigh.

"I guess . . ." he started, and then stopped to try to better formulate his words. "I guess I'm just wondering how serious you are." He paused again, and again I knew he was considering the best way to say what he had to say.

"Now don't take this the wrong way, Jack, but I kind of feel like you've been leading me on with the whole gallery idea, and I feel sort of stupid for having gone along. Not stupid really, but I . . . Jack, I . . . Shit!" He smacked his head with his fists. He was clearly frustrated, which was rare for him, and I sensed that he knew what he wanted to say but really didn't want to say it. He fell back on the bed and exhaled loudly.

"Look," he said. "I have really strong feelings for you, and I don't know how or what you feel about me. I think it's fucking great that you're interested in the gallery, but I don't even know if you're serious about it, and if you are, I don't . . . I don't know if I could work with you, feeling the way I do. I mean, if you don't feel anything. If it's just sex. If it's just friendship."

Now it was my turn to say nothing. I felt something akin to resentment boiling inside me. So now our plans were contingent upon my loving Ray. This was just the way it had been with Paul. Or was it? I knew

I liked Ray, whereas I had never really liked Paul. I'd been impressed with him, and been attracted to his money, and his notoriety, and his education, but I really hadn't liked him. Yes, I liked Ray, of that I was certain, and there was no one I would rather spend time with, but he was trying to tell me that he was in love with me, and I didn't know how to respond. When I was with Paul this would have been one of the times I mechanically said "I love you, too" and then I would have had sex with him, exaggerating my enthusiasm in order to get my way (which is, if one considers it, the really criminal type of prostitution). I thought of doing that then, of appeasing his worries with a few false words and a sexual Band-Aid, but I knew I shouldn't. I liked Ray, yes, but more than that I respected him, and I decided not to lie. Instead I was as honest as I could be. I pulled him toward me and ran my fingers through his hair.

"That," I said thoughtfully, "is something I really hadn't considered."

POETIC JUSTICE

About a week later I was sitting at the desk typing up some things for class when he called. Tom, a.k.a. Johnathan Oswald Carlyle the third. I recognized the voice but didn't make the connection at first. He was calling the number for James's ad, and said he was a first-time caller, and that he wanted James to meet him at a motel on Sixth Avenue. I hesitated a moment. We usually didn't send guys out to unknown clients because so many of them turned out to be cranks, and since Johnny's attack, we were certainly not going to do it. Rather than explain all that, I said that James didn't have a car and so they would have to meet at the office. He reluctantly agreed and I asked his name.

"Tom," he said, and it was then that I made the connection. Something in his voice made me certain it was Carlyle, and I could feel myself getting flustered.

"Uh, I'm going to put you on hold for just a minute," I said, and placed the phone back in its cradle, eyeing it with revulsion. I opened another line, picked up the receiver again, and paged Ray, leaving the new emergency code we'd established. I took another deep breath and reconnected with "Tom."

"Okay," I said, "I just had to check James's schedule. Is nine-thirty tonight okay?"

"Fine."

"Then it's all set. I've got you down for nine-thirty in room two," I said, and quickly hung up.

Ray called a minute later, and I told him what had happened and what I'd done.

"You didn't let on that you knew it was him?" he asked.

"No."

"And you're sure it was him?"

"Positive. Should I call Warren?" I asked.

"No! No, don't do that. Cancel all my stuff for today; I'll be there in about half an hour."

When he showed up, he had Salvatore and a lot of camera equipment with him. Ray told me to cancel all in-house appointments after seven-thirty that night and to call Vince and Craig, two of the larger college students, and Marvin, and tell them to come in at nine. That done, I was instructed to go out and buy three pairs of nylons, any size, twenty feet of nylon rope, and three videotapes. I kept asking what he was doing, but all I got was, "I'm not sure; I'm making it up as I go along. Go get the stuff; I'll tell you later."

I had my microbusiness class to go to and a few tricks that afternoon, which Ray said I should attend to. I did so, and was soon so busy I nearly forgot about Carlyle.

The class was getting frantic now, as we were all finalizing our business plans for submission to the loan committee. It was stressful, tedious work charting the course you expected your business to take and then coming up with the numbers to match. We worked in pairs that day, and I tried to get with Salvatore so I could find out if he knew anything about what Ray was planning, but I got assigned Millie, and before long we were lost in a sea of cash-flow projections and payment schedules. By the time we finished up, all the others, Sal included, had left.

"Start thinking of who you want to speak at graduation, class," Tina called out as Millie and I were leaving. "Because we really need to send out invitations no later than next week."

After class I drove down to Hole's for the biweekly help with financials, which took a long time because he was brutally tough, insisting I do all the work on paper with no help from the computer.

"If you can't figure this shit out on your own, at least the first time, you're never going to figure it out."

It was nearly twelve-thirty when we finished, and I rushed back to my apartment, arriving just in time to entertain the first of my four lunchtime clients. I then worked out with Marvin, and after that he accompanied me to Kmart, where we shopped for the items on Ray's cryptic list. We stopped for dinner at one of those salad cafeterias and then headed back to the office, arriving a little before nine.

When we arrived, Vince and Craig were seated on the couch watching TV and each playing with a pair of handcuffs. They gave little waves and said that Ray was in the back room finalizing things with Sal. I headed in that direction but met Ray on the way. He smiled at me and then took my hand and led me back into the office and shut off the TV. I almost didn't recognize him because he had removed all of his piercings, had his hair combed, and was dressed in his rarely used workout clothes. He had us all sit down, lit a cigarette and briefed us on the plan.

"Okay, I've told Vince and Craig a little of what's going on, but I want to finalize everything before Carlyle gets here, okay?"

We nodded.

"All right, he'll come in and I'll take him into room two. Hopefully I can pass as James, since his ad doesn't show his head."

It doesn't show any tattoos, either, I thought, but kept that comment to myself.

"We've got the room rigged with a camera," Ray continued, "so we can film all of what goes on. Hopefully he'll do the same stuff he did before. I'll keep him busy for a while, and hopefully we'll get some nasty shit on tape."

We nodded and he led us into room three. Sal was sitting in a swivel chair, adjusting the view of room two that now appeared on the TV screen. He had used the existing hole that Carlyle had conveniently knocked out the week before and had inserted the camera into it. Then he had carved another, more elegant hole in the wall of room two, poked the lens through that, and placed a two-way mirror over it.

"When I give the signal to Sal," Ray said, "I want you all to come in from room three with the stockings over your heads, get his hands and feet cuffed, and then take the rope and tie his chest and his legs to the bed so he can't thrash around. Wrap it around him and the entire mattress twice, like so," he said, pulling the rope from under the bed, "and then one guy on either side pull it tight. After that, well, I guess we'll just wing it. Now everybody back in room three and Sal will tell you when I give the signal."

I handed the bag of stockings and rope to Vince, and when everyone else had left I shut the door and went over to Ray.

"We'll just *wing it?*" I said somewhat angrily. "We're going to take someone hostage and we're just going to *wing it?*"

"Yeah!" he said, grinning and nodding excitedly.

"And what are we going to do with him once we've got him tied up?"

"Nothing too bad," he said reassuringly. "We'll just give him a good scare and then send him on his way."

I shook my head doubtfully, but had to admit I was excited.

"You'd better be careful!" I said. "He's not some nelly little businessman. He's big and mean and he moves fast, so don't take any stupid chances."

He nodded impatiently, pushed me into room three, and closed the door.

The two pairs of handcuffs from the fantasy closet, both lined with fake leopard fur, were laid out neatly on the bed. Marvin unwrapped the stockings, cut off the control-top panties, and gave us each a leg, which we pulled over our heads. Vince unwrapped the rope, and he and Craig mugged and posed in their stockings.

At nine-thirty-five we heard voices in the hall, and Marvin turned off the lights. We stood silently and watched the screen. In a moment they entered the room. The picture was somewhat grainy, but it was definitely the same guy who had attacked me: tall, dark-haired, and broad-shouldered. Ray closed the door. As it had with me, and as it had with Johnny, the encounter began innocently enough: he and Ray touched, kissed, and had some verbal exchanges, but then Carlyle pulled away and took something from his pants pocket. He held a small vial up to the light and tapped the edge of it with his finger before offering some to Ray. Ray shook his head.

"What's he got?" I whispered. "Poppers?"

"No," Craig said excitedly. "I think it's coke!"

And sure enough we watched amazed as Carlyle calmly tapped some of the powder onto a magazine cover and shaped it into a thin line. Salvatore zoomed in on him. He then rolled up a twenty-dollar bill and deftly snorted the powder up his nose. Again he offered some to a beaming Ray, who politely declined. They kissed again and Carlyle patted Ray on the ass. Then, without any warning, the whole scene changed. He grabbed Ray's head, kissed him hard, and then threw him down on the bed. He removed his own clothes quickly and, standing naked now, he grabbed Ray by the neck and forced him down toward his ridiculously large cock. About a minute later, Carlyle pulled Ray back, kicked him to the floor, and dragged him over to the bed by his ankles. He pulled him up by the hair, kissed him hard, and then pushed him across the room causing him to hit the wall concealing the camera. We heard Ray's head hit and all gasped nervously as the mirror rattled but did not fall.

"This is bad," Marvin whispered, placing his hand on my shoulder. And it was bad. It was like a horribly one-sided All-Star Wrestling match, and I was horrified as I watched it.

Ray was now struggling to get away, but Carlyle had him again, this time by one arm, which he twisted sharply behind Ray's back. He tripped him, and Ray fell face-first onto the floor.

"Let's go!" I hissed.

"No!" Sal said, blocking the doorway with his outstretched arm, his eyes never leaving the screen. "No! He hasn't given the signal and I need more tape."

I looked over at Vince and Craig. Despite their muted features I could tell they were worried too. I looked back at the screen.

Carlyle had Ray back up and I saw that his nose was bleeding. He turned his head toward the camera consciously and Sal zoomed in, giving a close-up view.

"See, he's okay; he's still working with me."

I looked back at Marvin, who was attempting to bite his nails through his stocking.

Ray was now begging him to stop, repeating again and again, "I said no! Please stop!"

"Let's go now!" I said, and Craig moved toward the door. Sal jumped up this time and blocked the door with his body.

"No! Don't you see what he's doing? We need this! This is what makes it rape! Just wait! He'll give the signal!"

We held back. Craig fiddled nervously with the rope, and we all leaned in closer to the screen. Ray was on his back now and Carlyle was sitting on his chest. He'd pulled Ray's legs up in the air, exposing his ass. I looked down, not wanting to watch, but that only made the voices, one pleading, the other rough and degrading, all the more audible. Then Ray's tone changed and I heard him cry out Sal's name. I looked up. Carlyle was just about to enter him.

"Now!" Sal yelled.

Vince threw open the door and we all burst into the room, adrenaline rushing. From behind me came a deep, guttural scream, and I was pushed aside like a rag doll as Marvin—the Nelly Green Giant, the big sissy—charged past me into the room and pounced on Carlyle's back. He grabbed him firmly by the shoulders, threw him on the floor, and plopped down on his chest. We were all momentarily stunned.

"Come on!" Marvin barked up at us. "Get him tied up!"

We snapped out of our shock and I quickly cuffed Carlyle's ankles together, while Vince and Craig each took one of his arms, brought them together behind his back, and did the same. Once cuffed, Marvin pulled him up by the hair and led him stumbling over to the bed, where Vince and Craig were now ready with the rope. Until then Carlyle had been too surprised to speak, but now he'd found his voice and he was yelling.

"You better fucking untie me now, goddamnit! I'm gonna kill you fags when I get out of this!"

Smack! Marvin's huge paw came down on Carlyle's cheek, à la Stanley Kowalski.

"Shut the fuck up!" he boomed, as all the resentment for the years of schoolyard bullying and merciless teasing bubbled to the surface. Marvin looked around and picked up Ray's underwear from the floor. He wadded them up and stuffed them in Carlyle's mouth.

"That'll shut you up!"

I looked around for Ray but he had left the room. We all taunted Carlyle, Vince and Craig pulling the ropes tighter and tighter.

"We're all gonna fuck that virgin hole!" Vince said.

"Yeah, we are!" Craig chimed in. "And without condoms!"

"Or lube!"

Carlyle's eyes flashed wildly, whether from anger or fear I couldn't tell.

"Your ass is gonna be wider than the Grand Canyon by the time we're through with you!"

Ray appeared a moment later, his face still bloody. He had evidently been to the fantasy closet, because he held in his hands what we jokingly referred to as "the floor model." It was an impossibly large dildo, resembling a traffic cone more than a penis, and was something Marvin's/ Chet's clients liked to be threatened with, but until then it had never been used. Ray tossed it over to a grinning Marvin, who tried to catch it but missed. (Some things you just can't change.) Then Ray beckoned me into room two and shut the door behind me.

"Wasn't that great?" he said, jumping up and down excitedly. I smiled but was still so distressed by what I'd seen on the monitor that I could hardly share his gleeful enthusiasm.

"Are you all right?" I asked gravely, looking at the blood he'd splattered around. "That scared the crap out of me!" I took him in my arms and held him tightly, oblivious to the blood and the noises from the next room. Not wanting to let go of him and not quite sure why.

"Yeah, I'm all right," he said, and I felt his arms encircle me. "I was pretty scared toward the end there, but I'm okay." He held me tighter and ran his hand up and down my back, and I thought it odd that he seemed to be reassuring me—and that I needed reassuring.

"I'd better get cleaned up," he said, pulling back and grinning at me. "I got blood all over your shirt."

I led him to the bathroom, sat him on the toilet, and dabbed at his nose with a wet washcloth. It was still bleeding and looked like it might even be broken, and his right eye was beginning to swell. He winced when I touched it, and we both noticed that I was shaking. He took my hand in both of his and held it tightly.

"You all right?" he asked, smiling.

"Fine. I just got scared, that's all. Watching it and not being able to stop it was almost worse. You sure you're okay?"

"Never been better!" And he lifted up my chin and kissed me. We heard a crash in the next room.

"*I'm* fine," Ray said, "but I don't think our friend is. Maybe we'd better go and call off the beast. Jesus, Marvin scared me more than Carlyle!"

Back in room two, Carlyle was hog-tied on the floor. Vince and Craig each held an end of the rope while Marvin knelt on the floor in front of Carlyle's face, vainly trying to stuff the floor model into his mouth.

Ray flashed the lights on and off.

"Fun's over!" he said, and Marvin looked up at him with an expression of true disappointment.

"Let's get him out of here."

Reluctantly Marvin replaced Carlyle's underwear gag, and Vince and Craig loosened the rope and removed the handcuffs. They stood him up and Marvin twisted Carlyle's arm behind his back and escorted him down the hallway and then down the stairs. I went ahead of them and opened the door. Carlyle was struggling, but when he did so Marvin twisted his arm even harder.

At the bottom of the stairs Marvin stopped, removed the underwear gag, and planted a dainty kiss on Carlyle's lips and then stuffed the underwear back in his mouth. He then pushed him, still naked, out into the parking lot and stood blocking the door with his arms across his chest. Carlyle got up, pulled Ray's underwear out of his mouth, and put them on, glaring and cursing. Craig came down the stairs with a pile of clothes and tossed them out to him. We all stood and high-fived as he dressed and then got in his car. As he was pulling away, screaming at us through the windshield, Marvin blew a kiss and gave a feminine little wave.

The next day the rest of the plan was implemented. Ray and Sal were busy editing the tape so that it showed nothing but Carlyle doing lines and raping Ray, and I was busy getting James ready for his role as a UPS delivery man. The uniform was too big for him, and I was busy trying to pin up the legs so they wouldn't drag on the ground when he walked. That plain brown uniform was by far the most in demand for fantasies. It had also been the most difficult to come by, and, as I readied it for its use in a blackmail scheme, I realized why.

Warren had given me the home address of Johnathan Oswald Carlyle the third, so we decided to deliver the tape there. It would have been better, I thought, to deliver it to his place of business, but alas, not surprisingly, he was not currently employed. We wrapped the tape in an old paper grocery sack and made it look official with an address and some smeared rubber stamps. I wanted to write a note, and I thought we should ask for money. After all, he was a Carlyle, and who ever heard of blackmail without money, but I was dissuaded from this by Ray and Sal, who said that was the way to really get into some trouble. This way we had nothing linking us to the tape and, after all, it was just supposed to scare him.

I completed James's outfit with a brown baseball hat and clipboard, on which I attached a pad of the official-looking graph paper Hole made me use to chart my monthly financials. Then we got in my car and I drove him to the address. It was in lower downtown, near the baseball stadium, and not all that far from the building where Andre and Hole lived. James went to the door, was buzzed in quickly, and then disappeared. I was scared as I waited, since I hadn't even considered what to do if he didn't come out again. Should I go in after him? Call the police? But as I sat there worrying I didn't even notice James skipping from the building toward the car. He opened the door, jumped in, and I drove off as quickly as I could.

"Oh, my God, that was fun!" He panted, removing the cap and shaking out his long mane.

"Was he there?" I asked anxiously. "Did you see him?"

"He was there, all right, and he'll probably be there for a while. At least until his face heals. His jaw's all swollen and he's got a big scrape on his forehead."

"That must be from the parking lot," I said, thinking back to the night before. "And he didn't suspect anything?"

"Not a thing. Look," he said, proudly showing me the clipboard. "Got a signature and everything."

It did not take long for Carlyle to respond. We had not even returned to the office when my cell phone rang. I answered it and out came a barrage of threats and profanity. He was so angry he was not even making sense, and all I got was some shrieking that sounded like "Fuckin' kill prick bastards!" and "Lawyers, police, nail you to wall!"

I held the phone away from my ear and looked wearily at James.

"I think he watched the tape," I said.

"Johnathan!" I yelled, but he went on. "Johnathan Oswald Carlyle the third," I singsonged. "Please stop cursing, or I'll have to hang up."

He went on:

"You're all gonna fuckin' fry when the police get hold of you, you fuckin' assholes! Blackmail me! You're gonna pay like you never paid before!"

I grew annoyed by this spoiled-brat tantrum and swerved sharply into an alley, skidding the car to a stop.

"Now you listen to me!" I yelled, startling James. "If you want all that publicity then you go to the police! Go right ahead! I understand they know you pretty well. I'm sure they'd love to watch a tape of you soliciting prostitution, snorting coke, and committing rape. I'm sure Daddy and Grandpa would love it even more, and imagine the press you'd get! Just imagine! 'Carlyle heir caught in another, yes, yet another messy scandal!' Reporters dream of a person like you fucking up! And you have, my friend. You have fucked up royally! If I ever even catch wind of you roughing anyone up again, you can bet the police, your family, and the press will all receive their own personal copies of your film debut."

I hung up, and couldn't help thinking how terribly unsatisfying it is to hang up on someone with a cell phone. There's no cradle on which to slam down the receiver. Just the push of a button and bye-bye. I took a deep breath and looked over at an astonished James.

"Dude, that was awesome!"

I was nervous for a while after that, but Ray assured me nothing would come of it, and when a week passed and nothing did, I relaxed a bit and went on with the daily routine. In addition to turning tricks, we finished editing *Missionary Positions,* and were waiting for the packaged tapes to come back from the manufacturer. I was also working closely with Hole on my quarterly taxes and the final draft of my business plan for submission to the microbusiness review board.

As planned we all went down to the free clinic to get tested for STDs. Johnny was worried about his results, but all the guys rallied around to support him, telling stories of their scary experiences with the HIV test that had come out okay in the end. We all got HIV tests, of course, but while we were there I thought it would be a good idea if we also got tested for the big three: syphilis, gonorrhea, and chlamydia. The tests for all three can now be administered by simply drawing blood, but this is a recent innovation and was not available when we got tested. Then it was still done by taking cultures from the inside of the penis, which are obtained by inserting a tiny metal Q-tip up into the urethra and scraping the sides. It is as excruciatingly painful as it sounds, and even now I cringe just thinking about it. On that day I'm afraid I did more than cringe. The nurse drew my blood for the HIV test with no problem. Then I stood up, dropped my drawers, and she went to work with her sharp swabs. The first one was bad; I gritted my teeth and my eyes teared up. The second was worse, and I felt sweat break out on my upper lip and forehead. Of the third I remember only the sharp pain as she jabbed it in with as much gentle tenderness as a jackhammer operator. The next thing I knew someone was shining a light first in one eye, then the other. My head hurt terribly.

"Jaaack."

I squinted my eyes open. There was a very bright light overhead and I could see some fuzzy figures shuffling around me.

"Where am I?" I asked groggily.

A soft, lilting voice responded, "Why, you're in heaven." A voice that despite its sweetness sounded very familiar.

I sat up quickly and looked around. My sister Carey stood beside me, laughing hysterically.

"I'm sorry," she said to the aged doctor on my other side, who was regarding her with an annoyed expression. "I've always wanted to say that, and he is my brother."

"You're in the emergency room," the doctor said soberly, placing a reassuring hand on my shoulder. "You passed out in the clinic and hit your head on the filing cabinet, so they brought you over here to have it checked out."

He shone the penlight in my eyes again.

"It doesn't look like you have a concussion, but why don't you rest here awhile and I'll check back on you in a few minutes."

He left, and Carey and I were alone.

"You bitch," I said, smiling and rubbing the bump on my head.

"I'm sorry." She laughed. "I couldn't help myself."

I lay back down.

"You have quite the attractive fan club in the waiting room," she said. "Two of them, a big guy dressed like Paul Bunyan and a skinny guy in gloves, got so pushy we had to call security. They're waiting outside."

I groaned, but laughed slightly as I pictured Ray and Marvin.

"What's going on, Jack? Who are all these guys?" she asked.

I rubbed my head. "Subcontractors," I mumbled.

"What?"

"Just some of my friends. We all came down together to get HIV tests."

"You don't think you have it, do you?" she asked, genuinely concerned.

I shook my head. "No, but it never hurts to get tested, eh?"

She looked at me, trying to read my face, and for a while we said nothing. The doctor returned, looked at my eyes again, and said that when I felt like it I was free to go. I got up and tried my legs. Carey helped me to the door and to the waiting room, where all the guys crowded around me asking if I was all right. I nodded and introduced Carey.

"Guys, this is my twin sister, Carey." They all went silent and glanced nervously back and forth at one another. Carey looked questioningly at me. I shrugged.

"Did everyone get their tests?" I asked. They nodded.

"Good," I said. "Then I guess we can head back." I kissed Carey on the cheek and knew she'd be grilling me about all this again, probably before the day was over.

"Call me," she said sternly, squeezing my biceps. "Tonight!"

I nodded and followed the guys toward the exit.

Looking back, that was the real beginning of my paranoia. After that day in the emergency room my sister became determined to discover the secret she felt sure I was hiding from her, and I became equally determined to keep it hidden. She took to dropping by my apartment at odd hours, often when I was working, and referred a steady stream of clients to me for fitness training, which was annoying because the more I put them off, saying my schedule was full and I couldn't possibly take on any more clients, the more determined most of them became to actually obtain my training services, figuring that if I was so booked up I must really have something good to sell.

"I know you're up to something," Carey said one day on the phone. "Do you have a new boyfriend?"

I rolled my eyes, but then decided that this might be a good explanation to throw her off the scent.

"Yeah," I said sheepishly. "I've kind of been spending a lot of time with this new guy."

"I knew it!" she said. "It must be pretty serious if you're getting all your blood work done. That is why you were at the hospital, isn't it?" she said, satisfied with her effective detective work.

"Exactly," I said. "He's kind of a special guy, and it's the first guy I've really dated since Paul."

"Well, I want to meet him. Maybe we can go out to dinner some night, just the three of us. I'll prescreen him before you show him to Mom and Dad."

"That sounds great," I said, but weeks passed and I kept putting her off and putting her off and again she became suspicious.

Andre was also suspicious, and he had obviously been in contact with Carey, which made it worse. He had invited me out to lunch and to dinner and to cocktail parties but I had politely declined all invitations, saying, not untruthfully, that I was far too busy with work and with my new boyfriend, whom I named Dirk. I was busy, yes, but I also felt uncomfortable with the amount of lying I was doing and knew that I'd be forced to weave ever more elaborate lies if I were to socialize with either of them. Not that lying would have hidden much at that point. I was, as they say, getting a reputation in the gay community for my ever-widening network of business, and I was sure these rumors had been picked up by Andre's acute radar. These suspicions were confirmed when I began receiving "anonymous" packages in the mail. CDs and videotapes mostly. Some, like Donna Summer's *Bad Girls* disc, and a copy of the video *Butterfield 8,* were easy to decipher. Others, like the Ella Fitzgerald disc, took more time and thought, but then I'd listen to it and get to the song "Love for Sale" and I'd know that it was the one I was intended to hear. I probably should have said something, responded somehow, because the packages clearly indicated that Andre had a sense of humor about it and was probably more intrigued than scandalized, but I guess I was a little ashamed, so I said nothing and tried to ignore the packages. Tried and failed. Over time my paranoia, fueled by uneasiness over the Carlyle blackmail, my sister's intrusiveness, and Andre's packages, got worse. I felt like they were all knocking at the door of my microbusiness facade, trying to expose what was really behind it. I felt that everyone was suspicious of me, and I in turn became suspicious of everyone. I began to suspect the guys of moonlighting, or of hiding money from me, even though the money was coming in faster than I could count it and everyone was happy. I also began to fear that the phone was tapped and felt certain that I was being followed. Consequently I started using my cell phone for almost all calls, and took elaborate, circuitous routes to reach my destinations whenever I was driving or walking. I was certain a police raid was about to occur and took to phoning Warren almost every day to ask if he knew anything. He calmly reminded me that vice raids were extremely rare on businesses like mine, but assured me time and again that he would still tip me off if he caught wind of anything.

As if that wasn't enough to worry about, one of the two vacant units on our floor was also rented at about this time. This was bad because up until then we'd had stomping rights—no need to worry about tricks coming and going, or the odd noises coming from the rooms, or the guys roaming, scantily clad, to and from the showers. Suddenly, with the arrival of this new tenant, all that had to change, and we had to be much more cautious.

The new tenant was a heavyset, red-haired man, about thirty-five, with a beard and mustache and tiny eyeglasses. Invariably he was dressed in khaki pants, a striped dress shirt with the sleeves rolled up, and a paisley bow tie. I introduced myself the first time I saw him in the hall, mistaking him for a lost client.

"The name's MacNamara," he said cheerfully. "Rob MacNamara. I've rented the office right next to yours."

"Oh . . . have you?" I said, trying to conceal my surprise. "Great. Welcome. I'm Jack Thompson," I said, vigorously shaking his hand. "We run, uh, a sort of fitness training company. Mostly one on one. Weight training, aerobics, that sort of thing. What do you do?"

"I'm a writer," he said. "A journalist. I write for *Tally-Ho,* but I'm writing a novel now, and that's why I've rented this space. It gives me a place away from the office and away from the wife and kids where I can work."

Tally-Ho was one of the weekly papers that did long, mildly interesting exposés on corrupt city officials, or local pollution scandals, but was known mainly for its many pages of comics and its extensive section of personal ads.

"A writer," I said, trying to sound impressed. "Wouldn't it be quieter on the ground floor?" I asked, hoping that maybe he hadn't considered that.

"I suppose it might," he said, giving me a creepy smile. "But I'm all moved in; I might as well stay awhile."

"Yes," I said, my mouth twitching, "might as well."

I was suspicious of him from the beginning, but I grew more so when I repeatedly found him wandering the hallway at all hours of the day and night, and when he kept coming in to our office to use the phone, since his "hadn't been hooked up yet." At these times he almost never got hold of the person he was trying to reach and would just stand there, holding the receiver to his ear, scanning the room, examining the papers on the desk or the gay magazines fanned out on the waiting room table.

Who doesn't have voice mail? I thought to myself one day as he stood there holding the phone, the cord stretched to its limit as he tried to peer into room one, the door of which was open a crack. *He never leaves a message.*

Then one night my paranoia got the best of me. I was heading down the hall to the bathroom and saw that he was locking up and leaving. I said good night and waved and then waited in the bathroom until I heard the downstairs door slam shut. When I was sure he was gone, I sauntered, ever so nonchalantly, back down the hallway to his door. The door and handle were cheap and old, and it took me less than three minutes' work with a credit card (the first time I'd used one in months!) to jimmy it open. Once inside, I saw the gold dome of the capitol lit up outside his window. There were no window coverings, so I probably shouldn't have turned on the light, but curiosity got the best of me and I flipped the switch. The room was bare except for a folding chair and a card table on which rested an old electric typewriter, which, I noticed on closer inspection, was not plugged in and had no ribbon. It was all very strange. He spent so many hours here each day and yet the place was so uninviting and uncomfortable. I mentioned it to Ray later that night (who was surprisingly unfazed to hear I was jimmying my way into strange offices), and he said that yes, it seemed strange, but then Mac-Namara probably thought the same about our office and its obvious lack of anything resembling exercise equipment.

"Maybe he just wants a place to get away from the wife for a while," Ray said.

I nodded, but wasn't convinced. *What a pathetic retreat,* I thought, remembering the card table and folding chair.

And maybe it was karma. Maybe paranoia begets paranoia, but after I broke into Rob's office I became convinced that someone was repeatedly breaking into mine. I'd arrive some mornings and feel certain that the papers on the desk had been shuffled. Or, during the course of the day, I'd notice one or two of the files out of order and would panic and look around, expecting Allen Funt to jump out. I thought of installing an alarm system, but instead Ray brought in his large stuffed shepherd. He placed this sentry in front of the desk and connected it to a motion detector that made a barking noise whenever anyone touched the door handle. This became very tiresome and succeeded only in putting my nerves more on edge.

When I was away from the office the paranoia got worse. I grew more certain I was being followed and started lengthening my routes even more, doubling around and back before finally reaching my destination. Driving was worse, as I would park a minimum of five blocks away from where I was going, and would then walk up and over, up and over, over and back, etc., in order to be sure no one had followed me.

On one such day, I arrived fifteen minutes late to my microbusiness class because I'd taken such a labyrinthine route from the car that I'd actually gotten lost! When I walked in, everyone was cheering and jumping up and down, but it was not, as I initially thought, because of my arrival. I stood there for a moment, confused, but then went over to my seat.

"Can you believe it?" Sharise said.

"What?" I asked. "I missed it."

"We got the governor and Sister Melanie to speak at our graduation!"

"What!" I cried, and felt all the blood rush from my face.

"I know, isn't it great!" she said, and put her hand up for a high five. I raised mine weakly to hit it and missed. We had tossed out ideas for possible candidates some weeks before and had decided to send our fantasy requests to the governor, the mayor, Ben and Jerry, Donald Trump, Hillary Clinton, Bill Gates, and Sister Melanie. I thought the list so ridiculous that I had completely forgotten about it. And yet, as I sat there regarding my cheering classmates I realized that of course the governor would come, of course Sister Melanie would come. This was right up their alley: a program designed to get people off welfare through entrepreneurship. And who could ask for a more diverse group: an African-American who was also a single mother, three Latinos, an elderly woman—it was a politician's dream! Until you add me to the pot. Me, an upper-middle-class white fag hustler. I moaned and put my head down on the desk as I realized that now we would be getting media attention.

As if reading my thoughts, Tina handed back our graded business plans. I'd been unanimously approved for the five-hundred-dollar loan. Then she announced that we would each be getting calls from the *Denver Business Daily* newspaper because they wanted to do a profile of the program and focus on the individual participants and their businesses.

"It's a great opportunity for you to get some free publicity," Tina said. "They want to follow each of you around for a day and see what you've learned, how your businesses operate."

I felt the rumblings of nervous diarrhea and quickly left the room.

Ray and I had also started working on a business plan for the gallery, fueled largely by my sudden desire for legitimacy. We found a large space on Broadway that we liked, near enough to downtown to ensure that it would get a lot of foot traffic. It was in an economically depressed area that had been declared an "enterprise zone" by the city and, as such, would exempt us from several taxes if we opened a business there. We had been looking to rent, but the owner wanted to sell, and the price seemed very reasonable, so we had Antonio and Victor look at it. They checked out the structural soundness, the electrical and plumbing, and listened carefully to our descriptions of what we wanted done. Since it was an old building that had been neglected over the years, their bid for the renovation was high and would necessitate Ray's and my getting a loan. I shuddered at the thought of debt, and shuddered even more at the thought of once again resurrecting the issue of my relationship with Ray, since we would have to purchase the building jointly if we were going to buy it at all. We had never resolved the issue of how I felt. Or rather, we had left it hanging, unanswered since that confused night in bed, but Ray seemed less concerned with it, or was at least keeping his thoughts on the matter to himself, so I followed his lead and did the same thing: I kept my internal struggle just that—internal.

And yet when I thought about it I felt a new kind of anxiety. I felt something had changed in me, most notably when I'd stood watching the TV screen as Ray was being attacked. I felt an ache that I'd never felt before. A desire to switch places, to protect him. Watching the attack was the first time I'd felt anything like that, but since then I had noticed it creeping into my day-to-day dealings with him. I found myself wanting to help him, wanting to do things to please him, with no ulterior motive, and that confused me more than anything. I had always looked out for myself, had always done things with an eye on the payoff for me, but suddenly I was factoring someone else's feelings into the equation. Was this love? I wasn't sure. It was disconcerting to discover, at the age of twenty-six, that I didn't know how to recognize when I was in love because I'd never been there before. I spent every free night with Ray, we had sex, we laughed, we argued, and we never seemed to run out of things to talk about, but was that love?

Parental Consent

Hole will always be remembered in my mind for his bluntness, and thank God he was so blunt because had he not been, the gallery idea would probably have remained just that: another idea, heaped on the pile of unrealized ideas. I was sitting with him at his little desk one afternoon, going over the business plan Ray and I had been working on to get his input before I submitted it to the bank, but it was obvious my interest in it was only halfhearted. I gave vague answers to his questions and was doodling on the pad of paper I held in my lap.

"Why the hell are we doing this?" he asked, slamming his pencil down on the desk. "You're wasting my time and yours and I've got much less to waste than you, my friend."

I sat looking down at my doodlings, embarrassed, and then for some reason I started to cry.

"Oh, Christ," he said, in a voice that was somehow soft and shrill at the same time. "Don't do that. I didn't mean it in that way. I meant . . . well, hell, I mean it seems like you're just going through the motions here."

He reached for a cigarette. I switched off the oxygen tank, opened the window, and came back and lit it for him.

"You wanna tell me what's the matter?" he asked. "You can't have that thin of skin that you can't take a little criticism. Criminy."

I shook my head and then in a sobbing gush I told him all about the troubles with the microbusiness class and Sister Melanie and the reporter from the *Denver Business Daily* and my nosy sister and Andre's little packages. I told him of my fear that I was being followed and that my phone was tapped and how I was sick of always looking over my shoulder. I told him of my desire to get this gallery off the ground and get out of hustling, but also of my fear of doing so because of my confusion about my feelings for Ray, of how I thought I was in love with him but I didn't know for sure and why should it matter since we work well together and we like to be with each other, yadda yadda yadda. . . .

He listened attentively until I got to the part about me and Ray and then he started laughing, and the laughing turned into a violent fit of coughing, which led to his gasping for breath. I quickly crushed out his cigarette and started the oxygen flowing and in a few minutes he was breathing easily again.

"Oh, you're killin' me!" He chuckled, his eyes teary. "Fuckin' killin' me. I don't know about the other troubles—sounds like you may be screwed, frankly—but what is this shit about you and Ray?" he asked, laughing and slapping the table.

"Now maybe I'm not the best judge, but I'm not blind, and if you two aren't in love then the Pope's not Catholic. Fuck, I could tell there was something going on that first night I saw you together in Monroe's, remember? When I was sitting up on the bench with that key-pounder. You think I stayed up there for the pleasure of it? Hell, no! Or on Sundays, when we go to Patricio's, or whatever the fuck it's called, and you two sit and coo over each other."

"We don't . . . coo!"

"The hell you don't!" He coughed. "Or when you argue, oh, that's the fuckin' cutest. You're like two college roommates with all this unresolved sexual tension. Christ, sometimes I just want to push you together and scream 'Mate, goddamnit! Mate!' "

I laughed in spite of myself and he handed me a tissue.

"You love him, Jack. Fuck, trust me if you don't trust yourself. And he loves you. And that's . . . well, that's something."

I nodded and looked over at him and his eyes were misty. I handed him a tissue, which he slapped away, annoyed.

"Now let's look at those figures," he said, turning back to the desk, "and see if we can't get this picture show open. You've wasted enough of my goddamned time."

A week later Hole and Ray and I all piled into the lemon yellow Coupe de Ville and drove up Seventeenth Street to Colorado National

Bank, where Hole cosigned on a loan with us. Two days after that, we drove to the realty office in Cherry Creek and closed on the property. We then owned the building and had enough money to complete the necessary renovations.

After we'd finished, we celebrated over lunch, and then took Hole back to his loft, as it was time for his daily bath, which he was looking forward to because he had a new, very attractive nurse. On our way back to our respective vehicles (I had a long walk to mine), Ray and I discussed our plans for the rest of the day.

"Will I see you tonight?" he asked as we stood on a corner, surrounded by the noontime crowds.

I opened my Day-Timer and looked at my schedule.

"Let's see," I said, going through the day, "I have two clients back-to-back starting in twenty minutes, then I have class at three, and then I'll meet the guys at the new place and give them the key. After that I'm meeting my parents for dinner, which should last about two hours, but it looks like I'm free after that. Oh, no, wait. Damn. After dinner I have an appointment at this new gallery with the sexiest man in Denver, so hey, maybe some other time."

He smiled and gave me a playful sock in the arm. I closed my Day-Timer and we stood grinning at each other, not wanting to part. Slowly we sauntered up Sixteenth Street.

"Why don't you . . ." I began. "Naw, never mind."

"What?" he asked.

"Nothing."

"No, come on, what?"

"I was just thinking, maybe you'd want to go, too. To dinner, I mean."

"With your parents?"

"Well, yeah. You'll like them, I think. We can tell them all about the gallery now that it looks like it's actually going to happen."

He thought about it silently for a moment. I could tell it made him nervous, and it was rare to see him that way.

"Well, yeah, I guess," he said, and swallowed hard. "Why not?"

"Great! I'll meet you at the office a little after seven and we can go from there."

The rest of the afternoon flew by. I performed my tricks, and then sped over to the microbusiness class, where we had a group interview with the reporter from the *Denver Business Daily*. The interview was fairly innocuous, until the reporter, a skinny weasel of a man with half glasses, started scheduling times to follow us around.

"I'll be just like your shadow for a few hours," he said, and went around the room, smiling as he penciled us into his Day-Timer. When he got to me, I hesitated. Both he and Tina looked at me expectantly. I knew she was proud of my progress and thought that this would be good press for her program. Little did she know. I slowly flipped through my own Day-Timer, trying—and failing—to think up some excuse not to do it.

"Um ... hmmm ... Well, let's see, what about next Thursday?" I asked, wondering what the hell I was going to show him.

"That sounds great," he said. "Eight A.M. all right?"

I nodded.

"Oh, and I understand you and some of the other students have collaborated on a few projects. I'd love to hear about them," he said, looking around the circle. "Especially this exercise video that you and Mr. Varga have been working on."

I looked across at Salvatore, his eyes widened to the size of golf balls, and he gave a nervous little laugh. Sharise and Millie were also wide-eyed, expressions of dread on their faces. Antonio and Victor slowly lowered their sunglasses.

"I'd love to get a copy of it," the reporter said.

"I think we all would," Tina said proudly.

"Sure," I said, my voice cracking.

When I finally got away, I ran some papers to the realtor and picked up more papers for Ray and Hole to sign, and then quickly drove over to the new building, where Antonio and Victor were waiting patiently. We went inside and I showed them the plans Ray and I had sketched out. I then gave them a check for the deposit, a key, and the alarm code.

"We closed on the place today, so you can start anytime," I said. They nodded, and Victor folded up the check, placed it in his shirt pocket, and then placed the key on a large key ring attached to his belt. As we stood on the sidewalk, having just locked up, Antonio put his arm on my shoulder, lowered his glasses, and regarded me over the tops of the frames.

"Listen, homie," he said, his voice low, "we don't know what kind of business you're really running, but what are you gonna do about that reporter?"

I shrugged my shoulders and gave a bothered grumble. "I have no idea." We turned and headed up the street.

"It sucks, man," Antonio added, spitting in the gutter. Victor nodded his agreement.

"I mean, we ain't been pullin' permits, and we do all this work under the table. The last thing we need is for some building inspector to see a story about us and get curious."

"I hear you," I said. "But it's only going to get worse at graduation. With Sister Melanie and the governor speaking, I don't think it's going to be a small ceremony."

"Shit," he said, and kicked at the pavement.

"Hey, if it's any consolation," I said cheerfully, "I think I'll be in more trouble than either of you."

They both laughed, albeit anxiously. We arrived at their truck, said good-bye, and I watched them drive away. I looked at my watch. Six o'clock. I looked around suspiciously, walked around the block once, and then crossed the street and walked to my car. I desperately wanted to work out to relieve some of the tension, but I was so busy then that I was lucky if I had one or two days a week for even an hour-long work-out.

When I arrived at my apartment there was another small package sitting on top of the mailboxes. It was addressed to me but there was no return address. I picked it up, went into my apartment, and opened it, thinking sadly that it had probably been over a month since I'd even spoken to Andre. The package contained a videotape of the French movie *Belle de Jour*—the one in which Catherine Deneuve is a respectable housewife who spends her days secretly working in a bordello.

I looked at my blank expression in the mirror. I had a choice: I could be offended or I could laugh. I wavered between the two for a moment, reflecting that I'd often chosen the former when I received these packages, but then I smiled.

And I was still smiling until I pulled up to the office and saw a car that looked an awful lot like my father's, parked right next to the red hearse.

It can't be, I thought as I ran up the stairs, taking them three at a time. *Please, God, it can't be.* I reached the office and reached for the handle but then stopped suddenly and pressed my ear to the door. I could hear voices, and my mother's twangy laugh.

Shit! I took a deep breath, calmly smoothed back my hair, straightened my shirt, and cleared my throat. I opened the door, trying to appear calm and relaxed and only pleasantly surprised.

My parents were sitting on the waiting room couch, my mother deep in conversation with a leather-bedecked Marvin on the subject of asters, a huge vase of which rested on the table in front of them and very nearly concealed the issues of *Torso* and *Inches* beneath it. My father was busy talking on his phone, obviously to a business associate, and Ray was sitting on the front of the desk looking handsome but stricken, in a dark green crushed-velvet shirt, his only piercings in his ears and one eyebrow. His expression relaxed somewhat when he saw me.

"Mom, Dad," I said, trying to sound natural, but again hearing my voice creak. "I . . . I . . . I thought we were meeting at the restaurant."

"Well, we were," my mother said, rising and moving forward to give me a hug, "but the asters are so beautiful this year, and they're one of the few things the dogs haven't dug up yet, so I thought I'd bring you some."

"Thanks," I said, admiring the pink and purple blossoms. "They look great."

"And we've never seen your office, sweetie, and Chet here has been so nice."

Marvin smiled and tilted his head coyly to one side.

"Oh, and listen, before I forget," she said, tapping the side of her head. "Your father and I are going out of town for a few days. He's got some business in New York and I'm going to tag along because there's a dog show I want to see, so would you mind maybe going by the house once or twice? Carey said she'd take care of the dogs, but she's so busy, and well, I'd just feel better if you'd be the backup."

"Sure, no problem. When are you leaving?"

"Tomorrow," my father answered, lowering the antenna on his phone and replacing it in the inside pocket of his suit coat.

"Love your security system," he said, rising and patting the stuffed shepherd that sat in front of the desk on which Ray was seated. "Wish your mother's beasts were this well behaved."

There was a thud in room one and then a long, drawn-out moan. We all looked at the door and I watched, horrified, as my father walked over to it and cupped his ear. More moaning.

"What do you do to these poor guys, Ray?" my father asked jokingly.

Ray looked up, terrified, and then looked to me for help.

"Sounds like he's being stretched on the rack in there."

"No," Marvin said lightly. "We keep the rack in room two, next to the Catherine wheel, ah ha ha ha."

"Ha ha ha ha," we all laughed daintily.

"Can we have a little tour?" my mother asked, rising and looking around.

"Yeah, give us the tour, Ray?" my father chimed in, putting his arm amiably around Ray's shoulder.

My father's philosophy regarding shy or nervous people was that if you said their name often enough and brought them into every conversation, you were helping them to feel more at ease. Unfortunately, this tactic had the opposite effect on Ray, who visibly flinched every time my father called out his name or slapped him on the back, which was about once every fifteen seconds.

"Maybe we'd better get going," I said, tapping my watch, wanting more than anything to get them out of the building. "The reservation's for seven-thirty." Ray nodded eagerly.

"Nonsense! Give us the tour, Ray."

"Uh, I think all the rooms are occupied now," Ray said, "and you know how people are. They get kind of embarrassed if we just bust in on them in the middle of their workout."

"Oh, I know!" my mother agreed, nodding her head. "I used to take aerobics at that place over on Colorado Boulevard, the one with the big picture window, and I always hated how people would just stand there gawking like we were fish in some aquarium."

"No one's in room three," Marvin chirped. "I'm using it later but my, uh, client doesn't get here till eight. Why don't you show them room three?"

Marvin, Marvin, Marvin, I thought, as I eyed him through narrow slits. *Meddling Marvin. There's a reason you never hold a job for long, isn't there?*

Reluctantly I led them all down the hall to room three. I tried to open the door but something was blocking it. I looked questioningly to Ray and Marvin, who just shrugged their shoulders. I pushed harder and whatever was in the way slid back some. I reached in, felt for the light switch, and turned it on. The room was full, almost floor to ceiling, of large cardboard boxes.

"What the . . . ?"

We pushed our way in, and without thinking, Ray pried open one of the boxes and looked inside. He quickly shut it again and looked up at me, his face white.

"What is it? What's inside?" my mother asked curiously.

"What! Oh, just some equipment we ordered," Ray said. "Remember the equipment we ordered?"

"Wha—? Oh, yes, yes," I said, following his weak lead. "That equipment."

"But you know, oh, no," Ray said, looking back down at the closed box. "I'll have to take this to the office and tape it shut right now while I'm thinking about it because . . . because it's the wrong color! We'll have to ship it right back! Don't open any of the others!" he cried, and darted out carrying the box.

I smiled calmly, backed out of the room, and then sprinted down the hall after him. When I got to the office and shut the door Ray opened the box and lifted out one of the very colorfully packaged copies of *Missionary Positions,* on which Ray and I were both pictured prominently in a variety of compromising poses.

"Oh, God!" I said, stuffing it back in the box and putting the box under the desk. "Let's get out of here." Ray nodded eagerly and together we walked back out into the hallway. We met my parents and Marvin halfway.

"I didn't know you guys did massages, too," Dad said.

I didn't either, I thought, glaring at Marvin, who was now passing us with a load of boxes. He paused. "They saw the massage table," he said, and then, enunciating every word, "The one with the sheets and the pillow."

"Ahh, yes, yes," I said. "Marv—Chet here is quite the masseuse. Just look at the time! We really had better go." And together Ray and I herded my parents down the stairs and out the door.

When we got to the restaurant, Ray and I quickly ordered and downed two martinis, and were just beginning to relax and look over the menu when my mother said, "Oh, look, honey, over there, someone's waving at you."

I followed her gaze and saw Vince and Burl sitting at a table across the room.

"Look, Ray," I said, draining my glass and returning their wave weakly. "Vince and Burl."

"It's so nice seeing a father and son out together," my mom observed, smiling broadly at the two men. I snorted in spite of myself and peered over the top of my menu at Ray, who was biting his lip.

"Is your family from around here?" she asked, looking at Ray. I set down my menu and looked at him too, feeling both curious and embarrassed. We had known each other nearly a year now and not once had I asked about, or had he mentioned, his family. He gazed down at the table.

"No, I grew up on the West Coast," he said. "California."

"Are your parents still out there?" she asked. Again he hesitated.

"My dad might be. I've never met him. My mom died when I was three."

"Oh, I am sorry," she said, reaching across the table and giving his gloved hand a little pat.

My father and I were both interested now.

"I've been on my own pretty much since I was thirteen," Ray said, "and made it out here about three years ago."

"Incredible!" my dad said, shaking his head. "Well, you seem to be a very fine young man."

I looked at Ray, sitting there, his face crimson from all the attention, and thought that my father was certainly correct—he was a very fine young man, and only then was I beginning to appreciate him.

"I'm glad you think so," I said, seizing the opportunity to jump into the gallery topic, "because Ray and I are going to be business partners."

We then told them all about our idea, and the loan, and the space and our plans for it, and they both listened attentively, my father playing devil's advocate as usual. But Ray and I had done our homework well, and either he or I had a ready response to any of the questions he threw our way.

Later, after dinner, when we took them down to show them the building and had walked them around explaining all of our plans, I saw something like pride in my father's expression. The same expression I'd seen when Carey had announced her acceptance to medical school.

"You guys financed this all by yourself?" he asked, looking around.

"We've got a friend," I said. "The guy who helps me with all my financial paperwork, to cosign with us. That helped us get a lower interest rate, but we could probably have done it ourselves. We put together the business plan ourselves, and that's really what got us the loan." He nodded and looked around. Then he came over, between Ray and I, and put an arm over each of our shoulders.

"Good work," he said.

And for the first time in my life I felt that my father and I were two adults, seeing each other at eye level. Unfortunately, it was not a feeling I would savor for long.

When my parents left, and we returned from walking them out to their car, Ray went into the back room and emerged a few moments later, a bottle of champagne in one hand, and a boom box in the other. He pushed play and the smooth voice of a young Sinatra (Frank, not Nancy) echoed through the room. He popped open the champagne, poured some into two Styrofoam cups, and handed one to me.

"To the first of what will hopefully be many joint ventures," he said, raising his cup.

"It's really the second joint venture," I corrected. "Harden Up was the first, remember?"

"Okay, okay." He nodded and kissed me. "To the first of what will hopefully be many *legitimate* joint ventures."

"I will toast to that," I said. We both took a sip of champagne. He pulled me close to him and we moved slowly to the music. Over his shoulder I surveyed the vast, empty gallery-to-be and thought about how right it all felt. It was legitimate. It was honest. I thought about Ray then, too, as I felt him gently swaying back and forth in my arms, and realized that it felt right. He felt right. The two of us together felt right. I moved my mouth up next to his ear and whispered, "I think . . . I love you." He said nothing but turned his face toward mine, looked into my eyes, and smiled.

We danced and drank and kissed the night away and, well, let's just say that it was one of those times I'll always look back on through the Vaseline-covered lens. I'm glad I enjoyed it, because what happened next nearly destroyed it all.

The "What" That Happened Next

Inevitably, the dreaded Thursday rolled around and I met with Noah Bernstein, the reporter from the *Denver Business Daily*. I did everything possible to keep him away from the office, since the subs and clients would be coming and going all day long and I thought the presence of a reporter might make them all a little nervous. We met there briefly, early in the morning, but then I quickly steered him away and took him to a health-food restaurant for a long breakfast.

"Most important meal of the day," I said, lingering over my bagel and slowly sipping my orange juice, struggling to pass the time with some mundane fitness chatter. Later, we went to the gym and in spite of his protests, I got him suited up and had him join my morning workout with Marvin.

"This is my regular workout partner, Chet," I said to Noah. "Chet, this is Noah. He's going to observe us today and see how we operate." Marvin smiled, heartily shook Noah's hand, and we started on some stretching. We'd scarcely gotten started when my pager went off. I glanced down at it and saw that it was an emergency page from a number I didn't immediately recognize. That didn't alarm me much, since the guys had taken to crying wolf for such "emergencies" as needing an advance on their pay for the weekend, or to tell me they were going to be late for appointments. I figured I'd better answer it anyway.

"Why don't you show Noah the inversion boots," I said to Marvin, and then excused myself to go use the pay phone in the locker room. I dialed the number and James answered on the first ring.

"Jack?" he cried.

"Yeah, what's up?"

"Oh, God, oh, God, you gotta come here quick; I'm scared," he whispered urgently.

"All right, calm down. Are you all right? What happened?"

"Ohhh, I don't know, I don't know. He just started grabbing his chest and—oh, God—then he fell over and I, I think he's dead."

"What! Who's dead?" I asked, my heart racing.

"Just come here quick!"

"All right, all right, just sit tight, I'll be right there. Wait a minute, James, James! Where are you?"

"I'm at my apartment," he said, and quickly spit out the address, telling me again to please hurry.

I hung up and dialed Ray's cell phone number. No answer. I dialed his pager and left my cell phone number followed by a frantic series of 911s. I then grabbed my bag from my locker and headed back out to the weight room.

"I'm afraid something's come up," I said to Noah and Marvin, who were both dangling upside down. "A family emergency."

"I hope it's nothing serious," Noah said, a look of concern on his purple face.

"Oh, my God! Their plane didn't crash!" Marvin asked anxiously, ever one to jump to the most dramatic of conclusions.

"No, no, nothing like that, but I've got to go," I said calmly, moving toward the door.

"Maybe we can finish up later!" he called out.

"Yes!" I said, feigning my enthusiasm. "On the phone or something."

Ray called while I was driving. I told him what I knew, gave him the address, and he said he'd be there as soon as he could, but in the meantime we were not to touch anything. There was not much traffic at that time of the morning, so I arrived at James's apartment in about ten minutes. It was a three-story U-shaped building with all of the units facing onto a central courtyard/parking lot. I pulled in, shut off the engine, and got out, realizing I'd forgotten to get the apartment number.

"Up here!" James called, and beckoned me to the second floor, where he stood peering over the railing anxiously. He was wearing a white terry-cloth bathrobe embroidered with the logo of the Adam's Mark Hotel and his long brown hair stood out in all directions.

I ran up the stairs, and as I reached the top I saw the red hearse pull into the lot and park next to my car. Ray got out and both James and I called to him. We waited for him to come up the stairs and then silently followed James into his apartment. We passed through the living room, sparsely furnished with plastic chairs and chaise longues that had evidently been stolen from the pool area of some motel, and into the bedroom. There, lying on the floor next to the bed, eyes wide open, was a tall, heavyset man who looked to be about forty-five years old. Ray knelt down next to him and checked his pulse.

"He's toast," he said, and gently lowered the man's eyelids with his fingers.

"What happened?" I asked, looking over at James, who stood back in the doorway, reluctant to get too close to the body.

"I don't know," he said, pushing his temples and shaking his head. "I don't know! Everything was going along fine. We were having sex, he was on top, and I could tell he was about to come, and then he just, like, grabbed his chest and just collapsed. I couldn't get him off of me and, and . . . eeeww, gross!" he cried, shaking his hands in the air as if to rid them of some sticky substance. "He was still inside of me! Oh, gross, gross, gross!" he cried, and ran quickly past us into the bathroom, where shortly we heard the sound of the shower.

Ray and I sat on the edge of the bed and stared down at the body. He was big and hairy and was wearing nothing but his wedding ring and a shriveled-up condom.

"At least he died happy," Ray said. I went over to the floor, where the man had neatly folded and stacked his clothes the night before, and took his wallet from the back pocket of his pants. I opened it and removed his driver's license.

David L. Bain, 14672 S. Mountain Lion Dr., D.O.B.: 11-03-1955, Sex: M, Ht.: 6'4", Wt.: 230, Hair: Bro., Eyes: Grn. Organ Donor: No.

Ray leaned in and together we examined the remaining contents of the wallet. ATM receipts, credit cards, an old fortune from a Chinese restaurant, about two hundred dollars in twenty-dollar bills, and a small plastic portfolio of family pictures, which, in retrospect, we should never have looked at. Not because they were private and did not belong to us—I had no qualms about that, especially since he was dead. No, we should never have looked at them because if we hadn't then we might have just called the police and been done with it instead of getting all stupid and sentimental. But look at them we did: there was Junior, probably aged twelve or thirteen—a skinny, awkward adolescent posing with a baseball bat; and Sister, dressed in a bunny outfit and tutu. *A dance recital or Halloween costume,* I thought to myself; then the littlest one, all cowlicks and eyeglasses that were much too big for his tiny head, a disgusted expression on his face (not unlike the one James had made on his way to the shower) as he examined the dead trout he held on the end of his finger. Wifey was there, too. Three pictures of her. One, a faded high school yearbook photo; another of her and the deceased in happier times, sitting on a beach together, chubby and pasty-looking, sipping tropical drinks from coconut shells; then another photo, probably the most recent, the toll of three children evident on her body, but still smiling, apparently happy.

I closed the wallet and we both looked back down at the man. Ray lit a cigarette and we shared it in silence. James emerged a few moments later in a fresh bathrobe (this one from the Oxford), refreshed and much calmer, although he seemed surprised that we had not disposed of the body during his absence and winced when he saw that it was still where he'd left it. We moved into the living room and sat down.

"Who is he?" I asked.

"You should know," James said, snottily. "You scheduled him."

"Then I scheduled him at the office," I replied in a scolding tone. Since Johnny's attack, I'd been adamant about knowing where the clients and subs were meeting and tried to schedule all meetings at the office with at least one other sub on the premises.

"Oh, I know," James whined. "And we did meet there, but his wife's out of town and he wanted to spend the night, so we came back here."

Ray looked at his watch.

"We don't have much time," he said, and got up and grabbed the phone from the kitchen wall. He held it out to James.

"You need to call the police," he said. "Make it sound like an emergency, like you woke up and found him that way." James and I looked at each other and then back at Ray.

"What am I going to tell them?" he asked, rising and moving behind his chair, beyond the reach of the phone's cord.

"The truth," Ray said. "That you picked him up at a bar, came back here, and he had a heart attack."

"That's not the truth," James whined.

"It is now," Ray said, thrusting the phone at him again, more urgently this time.

James looked at me imploringly. I shrugged my shoulders.

"I wish there were something else we could do," James said wistfully. "He was such a nice guy, and now I guess the wife and kids will have to find out."

I remembered the pictures.

"That's not our problem," Ray said, shaking the phone. "That's the risk he took when he went out in search of dick. Now make the call; we need to get out of here."

"But that's not her fault," I said.

"Her who?" asked Ray, confused and impatient.

"The wife."

"Yeah!" James agreed, nodding.

"Just look at him," I said, gesturing to the bedroom, through the door of which the soles of the dead man's large, bare feet were visible. "He's not going to be hurt by any of this. The wife and kids are the ones who'll suffer. It hardly seems fair."

"Yeah!" said James, warming to my argument. "It's not fair!"

"Oh, Christ," Ray said, wagging the phone at James, clearly tired of what he perceived to be nonsense. "Just call the fucking cops."

James hesitated a moment, looking at the phone, but then crossed his arms indignantly on his chest and shook his head. Ray looked over at me, exasperated. I looked back at the feet.

"Fine," he said. "Okay. If that's the way you want to play, that's the way we'll play." And with his index finger he calmly pushed the numbers 911. James gasped in horror, quickly crossed the room, and yanked the cord from the wall.

"Goddamnit!" Ray cried. "You stupid little fag!" And he raised his arms as if he meant to strike James with the receiver. Then, veins bulging in his neck and jaw twitching, he slowly lowered his arm. Gently, ever so exaggeratedly gently, he returned the receiver to its cradle. He took a deep breath, looked up at James, and in a restrained but sarcastic voice asked, "And what would you like to do?"

We all stood silent, James looking embarrassed, Ray looking angry and frustrated, and me . . . well, I'm not sure how I looked—pensive maybe, or gaseous, because a moment later another of my less brilliant ideas bubbled to the surface. The kind of idea that is born of sentiment and emotion, and has no ancestry in rational thought or common sense. The kind of "heart thinking" that Sister Melanie routinely rails against on her radio show and in her newspaper column, because "the heart was never meant to think."

I turned to James.

"You said his wife's out of town, right?" He nodded.

"Yeah, she took the kids to Disney World."

"Disney World," I said in a childlike voice, and gave Ray a little nudge. "Did you hear that? They're going to come back in their little mouse ears, all stuffed with cotton candy and happy memories, only to have all that obliterated by bad news. Isn't it bad enough that Daddy's dead? Do we really have to compound that sadness by letting them know all the seedy details of his death?"

It was Ray's turn to stand with his arms indignantly crossed.

"That's not our problem," he said resolutely, but I was not ready to give up.

"Look here," I said, and again took the man's license from his wallet. "We have his address and his car keys. All we need to do is get him back to his house and drop him off and it will look like it happened there. It's clear that he died of natural causes, so no one will ever know the difference."

An idea occurred to Ray and me simultaneously, and we both looked up and over at James.

"He did die of natural causes?" Ray asked. James looked confused.

"You weren't . . . doing any drugs?" I added apprehensively.

"Oh, God, no! Look around you." He laughed, gesturing to the patio furniture. "You think I can afford drugs? We had a few beers over dinner last night, that's all." Ray and I relaxed again. I continued my argument.

"Then it would be easy," I said. "We'll just put him in his own bed and it will look like nothing out of the ordinary."

"And just how would we get him in the house?" Ray asked. We puzzled for a minute, but then James snapped his fingers.

"He lives in the suburbs," he said. "I bet he's got one of those garage-door openers; in fact I'm pretty sure I saw the little button thingy hooked on the sun visor. I remember it fell off every time I lowered it to look in the mirror. We'll just open the door and haul him in." I nodded eagerly. Ray pursed his lips.

"If he's got one of those openers," said Ray, "then he's probably got an alarm system too."

It was an undeniable possibility, but one for which I saw a weak solution.

"Well, if that's the case," I said brightly, "we'll just leave him in the garage. Make it seem like he'd just locked up the house to go out and died on his way from the house to the car."

James nodded eagerly.

"I don't like it . . ." Ray said, shaking his head, but I detected a slight upturn at the ends of his mouth, a tiny glimmer in his eye, and I suspected that he would not be able to pass up this combination of morbidity and adventure. My suspicions proved correct.

Once committed to our vague plan of action, we faced the more immediate problem of how to get the body out of James's apartment, down the all too visible stairs, and into his minivan. Wrapping him in a sheet seemed too flagrant, and James did not possess any boxes or luggage that could possibly contain his massive body. We thought and thought, and in the end decided to dress him, cover his head with a hat and sunglasses, and then, with one of his arms over Ray's shoulder and the other arm over my shoulder, we would "walk" him down the steps to the parking lot.

His feet were useless, so it was really more of a "drag" than a "walk," but our method worked well and gave the impression of three friends escorting their poor, alcoholic friend back down to his car. Then we reached the stairs and things got messy. His head lolled from side to side, causing the hat to fall backward, and he began drooling (if a dead man can be said to drool). The glasses then slid off his nose, fell through a gap between the steps to the concrete below, and dislodged one of the lenses, which shattered noisily. James hurriedly collected all of these accessories, reapplied them as we "walked," and somehow we managed to get him down to the minivan and installed in the passenger seat, more or less unnoticed by any of the other apartment dwellers.

Who would drive which vehicle was the next hurdle. My car was a stick, so James could not drive it. That left him with either the minivan (which he refused to drive) or the hearse (which Ray was reluctant to let him drive, so shocked was he by the fact of James's ignorance of the rudimentary workings of the manual transmission). We argued about this in the parking lot until the sound of our cargo's head thudding against the side window pulled us away from our petty squabbles and back to the matter at hand. Reluctantly Ray acquiesced and gave James the keys to his car. Ray drove the minivan, I drove my own car, and together the three of us made the procession to the office, where we intended to get a map book and finalize our plan of action.

When we arrived, Marvin was sitting cross-legged on the couch in the office eating a custard-filled chocolate Bismarck, engrossed in an episode of *All My Children* on TV. On seeing that it was me, as opposed to, say, the pizza delivery man, he quickly switched the channel, uncrossed his legs, and spread both arms over the back of the sofa, effectively concealing the Bismarck.

"You have chocolate on your lip," I said, and went straight to the filing cabinet, from which I retrieved one of the map books. Ray read me the address from the driver's license and I looked it up in the index. Our destination lay in a sprawling, densely populated subdivision known as Harmony Ranch, and was located on the ominous-sounding Mountain Lion Drive. I went to the page indicated, but Mountain Lion Drive was surprisingly hard to find, seeing as it was in close proximity to Mountain Lion Way, Mountain Lion Court, Mountain Lion Lane, and Mountain Lion Circle.

"Either the area is infested with mountain lions," I said wearily, following the small red lines on the map with my finger, "or the developer had a criminal lack of imagination."

Eventually, with the aid of a magnifying glass, I did find the street, marked it with a fluorescent pink highlighter, and bent down the corner of the page, so I'd easily be able to find it again.

Next, I set to work with Josh the receptionist, canceling or reassigning all of my and Ray's afternoon clients, something I was doing far too often. I knew the damage it was doing to customer relations, not to mention the income I was missing, which, with a new mortgage hanging over my head, I was suddenly highly conscious of. Nevertheless, I made apologetic calls and Ray made apologetic calls and Josh made apologetic calls, and in little less than an hour we had everything settled. We were just on our way out the door when I turned and casually inquired of Marvin how the workout had gone.

"Fine," he said. "We did some leg and ab work, sat in the steam room a while, and then I brought him back here and gave him a copy of the video."

"What . . . video?" I asked, turning back into the room.

"*Missionary Positions,*" he said absently, his eyes back on *All My Children.* There was a commercial break and he turned to look at me. Something in my expression clearly made him nervous.

"He told me you said you'd give him a copy of your video, the one you and Salvatore worked on, so I brought him back here and gave him one. It's not like there aren't enough of them." And he gestured to the mountain of boxes against the wall. My knees buckled and I nearly fell. When I'd steadied myself I gasped for breath, unable to verbalize my horror.

"What?" Marvin asked, alarmed. He inched his large frame to the far end of the sofa. "What's the big deal?"

My response was low and measured. "I'm . . . going . . . to kill you," I said, and without warning I vaulted at him, swinging the map book wildly at his big, empty head, while Ray and James struggled to pull me off.

"What'd I do? What'd I do?" Marvin cried, his big, hairy forearms blocking his face.

"You stupid fuck! You stupid, stupid fuck!" I cried, as James and Ray succeeded in pulling me back. "That was a reporter! Not a client! A fucking reporter!"

"Ohhh," Marvin groaned, and buried his face in his hands. I felt somewhat ashamed by my outburst, as I realized that it wasn't entirely his fault. He had not known who Bernstein was because, as I thought back on that morning, I had neglected to tell him. Then we were all silent, while the meaning of what had happened and its potential consequences sank in. Suddenly the body in the minivan seemed stupid and merely bothersome, and I wished that we had just left it at James's house and called the police. I went back to the desk and opened my Day-Timer, trying to remember what I'd done with Bernstein's business card. I couldn't find it, so I called information and got the number for the *Denver Business Daily.* Before dialing I hesitated, trying to mentally compose what I would say. All eyes were on me. I dialed. A cheerful, feminine voice answered.

"Denver Business Daily. How may I direct your call?"

"Yes, uh, is Noah, er, could you put me through to Noah Bernstein?"

"Do you have his extension number?"

"Uh, no, I don't."

There was silence while she looked him up and tried his number.

"I'm sorry, but Mr. Bernstein is away from his desk. Can I give you his voice mail?"

"Do you expect him back soon?"

"Sir, I have no idea. I'm not his personal secretary. I just route calls."

"I see. Well, yes, then give me his voice mail."

She transferred me, and I listened absently to his message until I heard the beep.

"Uh, Noah, this is Jack Thompson with Harden Up. I'm terribly sorry about this morning. I hope Marv—er, Chet took good care of you. I understand he gave you a copy of the video, hee hee hee, but as you can probably tell, he gave you the wrong one, hee hee hee. Uh, if you could give me a call as soon as you get this message, I'd appreciate it. . . ." I recited my cell phone number and hung up.

"Oh, Jack," Marvin said, spreading his hand over his chest remorsefully. "I am so sorry. But I really didn't know. You didn't tell me."

I shut my Day-Timer slowly and walked around the desk toward Marvin. He winced, and the other three retreated to the wall of cardboard boxes, but they needn't have been afraid. My temper was under control. I picked up the map book, calmly straightened the pages, and then stacked it neatly beneath my Day-Timer.

"All right," I said, and stared directly at Marvin, my voice excessively calm. "You're right. I didn't tell you. Let's not point the finger of blame; let's just fix it, okay? Josh," I said, turning to the shaking receptionist, "I want you to cancel all of today's appointments for both Marvin and James." He nodded and immediately took his seat behind the computer to pull up their schedules.

"You two," I said, pointing to the two grains of sand in the Vaseline. "Your mission is to pool your resources, as shallow as that pool may be, and do whatever you have to do—beg, steal, lie, cheat, whatever—to get that tape back." They nodded somberly. I looked at Marvin.

"Can you drive a stick?" He nodded. I took that as a good omen and tossed him my car keys, which he did manage to catch. I took that as a better omen.

"Good. Then you two can take my car. When—and only when—you have the tape back in your hands, I want you to call me on my cell phone, or page me right away. Is that clear?" Again they nodded and I turned and exited the office, Ray trailing a safe distance behind me.

It was nearly two-thirty when we finally pulled away. We had driven for at least half an hour, Ray navigating from the backseat, before it hit me.

"Shit!" I cried, and smacked the steering wheel with my fist.

"What?" Ray cried, wary of another tantrum. I eyed him in the rearview mirror.

"How are we supposed to get back once we drop him off?" I asked. He smacked his forehead with his palm and fell back into the seat. I pulled over to the side of the road, our passenger bobbing and drooling next to me.

"Okay," Ray said, exhaling nervously. He'd been chain-smoking since we got in the van. "Okay, okay, okay, here's what we'll do. We'll just backtrack a little, back to the office, and we'll take my car."

"Good idea!" I said sarcastically. "That won't draw any attention to us. You've never been to Harmony Ranch, have you, city boy? What we're driving now is pretty much standard issue. We can't drive a fucking red hearse in the suburbs!"

"Your car," he offered.

"No dice. The idiot twins have it."

We thought for a minute in silence, and Ray took out his pouch and started rolling a joint.

"What if we get pulled over?" I said, annoyed that he would choose that moment to get stoned.

"We are pulled over," he said, and ran his tongue along the edge of the paper. He lit it, and the acrid smell filled the van. We sat thinking, hazard lights flashing while the traffic whizzed past. I hated to drive all the way back downtown to borrow Hole's or Andre's car, but they were both options, and at that point I didn't see any others. Ray could drive Hole's car and I'd drive the van. I'd pull into the garage, get the body out, get him upstairs to bed, and then be out the door, and Ray could swing by and pick me up.

No, that would never work, I thought, looking over at the body slumped in the seat next to me and remembering how difficult it had been to get him down the stairs. I'd never be able to get him up stairs. I was strong, but I was not that strong. No, Ray would have to park Hole's car up the street, get in the van, help me unload him, and then we could just walk back up to the car once we'd finished.

"What . . . about . . . your parents," Ray sputtered.

"What about my parents!" I barked. "You want to bring them along?"

"No," he said, releasing the plume of smoke he'd been holding captive in his lungs. "What about their car—aren't they out of town?"

Yes, yes, yes! I reached back, pulled his head forward, and kissed him. I then slammed the car into drive and pulled back onto the road. They were indeed out of town, and we were minutes from their house. I was sure that my mother's humongous Buick was just waiting in the garage. It might take some time to find the keys, but much less time than it would take to drive all the way downtown, and there would be no explaining to do. I made a U-turn at the next light, and five minutes later we pulled into the familiar driveway. I got out and punched in the code on the security box mounted to the trim of the garage door. It went up slowly and as the expansive chrome bumper of the Roadmaster came into view, I was nearly overcome by feelings of relief and gratitude. I got back in the van and pulled it in next to the Buick. I then shut off the engine, got out, and quickly closed the garage door.

"I'll have to find the keys," I said, and went to the side door leading to the house. Ray followed slowly. The lights were on in the kitchen, which I found odd, but then remembered that Carey was taking care of the dogs and had undoubtedly left them on when she'd come by that morning.

"Wow!" Ray said, as he made his way over to the mud-smeared sliding glass door. Outside there was a pack of very large, black-masked puppies, with Bobby and Ethel standing protectively in the background, their baritone barks shaking the glass.

"Are they dogs or cattle?" Ray asked, sizing them up.

"*Don't* let them in!" I said, imagining the ensuing chaos. Then, remembering that he still had not found a baby Jesus for his diorama, I added, "They're my mother's. She'd be just devastated if anything happened to them, so don't get any ideas."

I rummaged through the kitchen drawers and cabinets and, finding nothing even resembling keys, I decided to look upstairs.

"This might take me a while," I called as I headed down the hallway. "There's probably soda or something in the fridge. Help yourself."

I went to my parents' bedroom and stood on the threshold looking in, trying to think where they'd have put a spare key. I looked in dresser drawers and jewelry boxes, in the purses hanging in the closet, and even in the medicine cabinet. Finding nothing in this last place, I sat down dejectedly on the toilet seat to think. I was dismayed to see a copy of the *Denver Business Daily* in the magazine rack under the toilet-paper dispenser. I wondered if Noah had called. I felt my phone in my jacket pocket, removed it to make sure it was still turned on, and then I got up, went back into the hallway, and took the narrow staircase up to my father's study on the third floor. The door was unlocked and stood partly open, so I went in and looked through all the desk drawers that weren't locked. Envelopes, paper clips, a stapler, rubber bands, but the only keys I found were tiny luggage keys. Discouraged, I walked over to the window and looked out over the rooftops. I could see Dave's house quite clearly on the next street over and wondered if he was filming that day. I looked down. Across the street a woman in a large straw hat was kneeling and digging at her petunias. A flock of pigeons soared by. A blue station wagon inched its way along the street as if looking for an address. The car stopped about half a block away and a large man in a baseball cap got out and stretched casually. He then reached back in the car and removed some sort of rectangular case with a shoulder strap. He walked a few steps forward, but then made a lateral move and disappeared into the thick evergreen hedge that divided two of the residences. I watched and waited, and felt my paranoia creeping back.

My phone rang and startled me. I pulled it out of my pocket, turned away from the window, and answered as casually as I could.

"Hello. This is Jack."

"Jack, it's Marvin."

"Did you get the tape?" I asked, hoping that his assignment was going more smoothly than mine.

"Well, not exactly. We're downtown now, at the newspaper office, but what . . . was the guy's name again? The one we're supposed to be looking for . . . ? We asked for Noah Webster but they said no one by that name works here."

"Oh, Christ." I rubbed my eyes again. "It's Bernstein. Noah Bernstein!"

"Ohhhh," he said, and it was clear he was writing it down. "Bern . . . stein. Bernstein. Now where did I come up with Webster?"

I hung up and turned back to the window. The man and the car were gone now. *Strange,* I thought, but then I reflected that it was no stranger than a man making amateur pornography in his basement or me driving a dead body around. I shrugged my shoulders and left the office, taking the back staircase down to the kitchen, and by the time I emerged my mind was back on finding the key.

Ray was not to be seen. I called out his name and thought that maybe he'd gone out, against my warning, to see the dogs, but they were still whining and staring in just as I'd left them. Then I heard the sound of an engine turning over. I ran to the door to the garage and whipped it open. The light was on and I saw Ray's legs dangling out of the driver's-side door of the Buick. The engine stopped and he sat up. I went over and knelt down.

"It's not the best system," he said humbly, wiping his hands on his shirt. "But it should get us there and back."

I pushed him back down on the front seat and jumped on top of him.

"You never cease to amaze me," I said, nuzzling my face in his neck. "My little criminal." He giggled and we kissed.

"Maybe we should wait until dark to do this," he said, turning his head to the side.

"You're probably right." I sighed and pushed myself up and off of him. "It is a little morbid with a dead body in the car next to us."

"No, not that." He laughed. "I mean maybe we should wait until dark to take the body."

"You think?" He nodded and twisted my wrist so he could see my watch.

"It's almost rush hour and everyone'll be coming and going from work. I just think it would be safer at night." I agreed, and we went back inside to wait.

While Ray made us some sandwiches, I started out to feed the dogs.

"I'd better call my sister," I said, remembering as I filled the giant bowls with kibble that Carey was the designated dog-sitter, "and tell her not to come tonight."

I dialed the number for the hospital, but they said she wasn't scheduled until tomorrow, so I tried her apartment. No luck. I then dialed her cell phone number and it rang. Then a half a second later I heard a muffled echo of the ring. Both Ray and I looked up, confused. It rang again. Another muffled echo, but this time we heard it more clearly and followed it over to the coat closet in the hallway. Some sort of struggle was going on inside, and we heard something drop to the floor with a thud. Ray grasped the knob and slowly opened the door. There was Carey, squashed in among the coats, digging furiously in her giant bag trying to get at her phone to shut it off. She looked up guiltily, her round glasses askew on her face. I grabbed her arm and yanked her out.

"Ow!" she cried, and pushed me away with her free hand. "I was about to suffocate in there."

"What were you doing in there in the first place?" I asked sternly. She straightened her glasses and pushed her hair back from her sweaty face.

"I could ask you the same thing. I'm supposed to be here."

"Where's your car?" I asked.

"It's in the shop. I'm driving Mom's. Why do you think I agreed to dog-sit?"

"What are you doing hiding in the closet?" I asked, more insistently this time. She looked around searchingly, as if an answer might fall out of the air. Clearly she had been spying on me.

"I . . . I . . . I, well, I was afraid," she said, none too convincingly. "I saw this strange car pull into the garage and I got scared, so I hid."

We are twins. We both stutter when we lie. She should have known better.

"Liar. I know you heard my voice." She shook her head, all wide-eyed and innocent. Denial. Since childhood it had been her last resort when backed into a corner. She hadn't changed.

"I *was* scared," she protested. "Whose minivan is that, and who's this guy?" she said, pointing an accusing finger at Ray. "What's going on, Jack?"

"Look," I said, leading her toward the garage door. "I'll tell you about it later, but right now we need you to leave for just a little while."

She pulled away from me, crossing her arms indignantly, and shook her head. At that point I had had just about all the indignant arm-crossing I could take for one day.

"Carey, *now!*" I yelled.

"Unh-uh." And she sat down on the floor—a tactic she'd undoubtedly learned during some university protest or other. Chanting slogans was sure to follow.

"I'm not going anywhere till I get some answers!" she said. "Something's up with you, Jack, I know it. I know you're up to something or in some trouble. We all know it. Andre knows. Mom knows. We don't know what it is, but I'm going to find out."

She hadn't changed, I thought. She's still the same as when we were kids and I wouldn't let her be in my club or wouldn't tell her the combination of my bike lock, or wouldn't let her have the prize in the cereal box. She always found a way to get what she was after. Well, not this time! I pinched her earlobe tightly between my thumb and index finger and pulled her up.

"Oooww!" she howled, and swung her purse. It hit me squarely in the stomach, knocking the wind out of me. I released her and doubled over, gasping for breath.

"You'd better tell her," Ray said, chuckling at the spectacle of us both. "She can't leave. We need the car, remember?"

I continued to gasp for breath, but more out of exasperation than from the purse blow. I felt myself starting to panic as I realized that telling her about the body would entail telling her about everything, and the thought of that almost made me hyperventilate. Then I remembered that if we didn't get that stupid videotape back, or get this damn body stowed someplace soon, it was all going to come out anyway. All she'd done was to pull on the thread of the already rapidly unraveling sleeve.

"Oh, Christ!" I yelled, pounding my head with my fists and lurching toward the living room. "Shit fuck goddamnit! God fucking damnit all to hell!" And I collapsed in a heap on the sofa, covering my head with a pillow. When I emerged, she was standing and looking down at me, as expectantly as the dogs now waiting for their dinner. Ray stood behind her, a slight smile on his face.

"I'm going to need a drink for this." I groaned, rubbing my temples.

"I'll get some ice," Carey said, skipping off excitedly to the kitchen.

Introductions were made while I indiscriminately grabbed bottles of random liquor and mixed us a pitcher of suicides.

"Carey, this is Ray," I said, facing neither of them, intent on my mixing. "We, uh, work together. Ray, meet my nosey, conniving brat of a sister, Carey."

"You're the guy from the hospital," she said, recognizing him at last. "I'm the one who called security, remember?"

"Oh, yeah." He laughed. "I remember."

"So are you two, like, dating?" she asked. " 'Cause I could tell there was something going on that day by the way you pitched a fit. That was so cute."

I turned around in time to see Ray blush. I then turned back and strained the vile concoction into three highballs, and handed one to each of them, although it was clear that neither one really wanted it. I took a burning gulp of mine, winced, and shook out my jowls.

"Sorry about the security thing," Carey continued, lighting a cigarette, "but I didn't know you two were boyfriends, or whatever. I was kind of worried about little Jack, too. I mean imagine them wheeling your brother into the emergency room like that."

She hadn't been all that worried, I thought to myself, remembering my near-death experience.

"Well," I said, breaking into their tête-à-tête, oddly jealous of her talking to Ray. "Are you ready for the awful truth?"

She nodded, dragging hard on her cigarette. I took another gulp, coughed, set down my glass, and gave her a whirlwind synopsis. The kind they give you at the beginning of the season on *Melrose Place,* where they show you clips of events from last season's episodes and somehow, if you didn't see them, you're supposed to be able to piece them all together. I told her about my credit card troubles and about Burl and Dave and Hole, and then paused to appropriate Ray's drink. I told her about the food stamps and the business class, about the hustling, and how that was the real business of Harden Up Inc., and the reason I turned away all of the business she sent my way. I told her about the advertisements, and the Web pages, and the movie, my tongue loosening as I rolled along. I then told her about Ray and how I felt about him. About how I loved him and wanted to start a new life with him, which was strange, because telling her was basically the first time I'd told him. The first time I told myself, really, and as I reached for Carey's highball I hoped I'd remember it later. I told her about our new building, and our loan, and our plans for the gallery, and eventually I wove the thread of my story back to the events of that morning—the reporter, and the body in the minivan—and it was only then that her eyes widened in disbelief and she ran out to the garage to see for herself.

"Well, tha's over," I said, moving to set the empty highball back onto the tray, and missing completely. It made a thud on the floor and rolled in a graceful arc. Ray picked it up, collected the spilled ice, and set it in the bar sink. He returned, sat on the arm of my chair, and took my hand in his, grinning.

"You gonna be okay, Otis?" he asked.

"Ssure," I said. "Dead body. Videotape. Jes' told my sis'er I'm a prostitu—I be ffine."

"Oh, my God!" Carey said, bursting into the room, flushed with excitement. "What are we going to do?"

It took me a minute to focus on her. I didn't like that "we." I shook my head.

" 'We?' " I said, attempting, and failing, to rise from my chair. " 'We?' " I said, trying again and managing to stand this time.

"*We* aren't gonna do anything. *We* aren't going to say anysing about this to anybodys. Unnerstan'? Ray and I are going to take the body back to 'is 'ouse, tuck it in 'is bed, and you, li'l sister, are gonna stay right here and sssmoke you marijuana cigarettes till you forget you heard any of this."

She shook her head obstinately, but the suggestion of pot clearly appealed to her, and she removed her little leather pouch from her purse.

"Carey, please don' argue."

"No, now listen, I can help you," she said, shaking some pot from a film canister into her small wooden bong. "I know a thing or two about dead bodies."

"No!" I shouted. "Jes' go home!"

"Relax," Ray said, coming from behind and rubbing my shoulders.

"Oh, he's always been uptight like this," she said. "We knew he was going to be gay way back in kindergarten when he made my parents change their clothes before they went to parent-teacher conferences." Ray laughed.

"He also had a poster of Shaun Cassidy on the ceiling above his bed, and he slept with a G.I. Joe doll"—they were both laughing now— "until he was thirteen!" Carey added between puffs.

I waited until the hilarity had subsided somewhat.

"Maybe she could help us," Ray said, still chuckling, the smell of pot drawing him closer to his new best friend. I was mad, and I was drunk, and I was sick of the whole business.

"Fine!" I screamed, throwing my hands up in the air. "You two smarties handle it!" And I swerved off through the kitchen and out into the backyard. I tried to slam the sliding door shut behind me, but even it seemed to be mocking me, as it slid slowly and airily on its track, clicking elegantly when it had finally reached its destination. I turned, stepped off the porch, and was immediately pushed to the ground by ten sets of giant paws. I struggled to push them away but couldn't, and was thus forced to endure several minutes of frenzied face licking. Eventually I was able to wiggle myself free, and I ran as quickly as I could to the safety of the teahouse. Once inside, I slammed the bamboo door, leaned my back against it, and emitted what must have been a highly flammable sigh. It was dark and fairly cool in the teahouse, as the shutters had been closed all day. The relatively new tatami mats gave off a sweet, fresh smell, and, although drunk, I remembered to remove my shoes before walking across them to open one of the windows.

Outside, the mastiffs were running around the yard like big gargoyles come to life, bent on destruction. Some were digging at the roots of the maple tree, another was gnawing on the wooden steps of the teahouse, and yet another was lifting its leg on the base of the stone lantern. The koi pond had become a cloudy soup of algae, in which the fish could only rarely be glimpsed, and was surrounded by a sturdy wire fence to keep the dogs from falling in. The grass around it, once so green and dense—like a putting green—was rutted and worn.

Poor Mr. Matsumoto, I thought, closing the shutter. *I know just how he feels.*

I lay down on the fragrant mats, head spinning, and I must have fallen asleep because the next thing I remember was my sister kneeling by my side and nudging me awake.

"Jack. It's time to go."

I sat up quickly, disoriented and groggy. It was very dark.

"What time is it?" I asked, trying to see the numbers on my watch.

"It's about eight," she said. "Ray's putting the body back in the van."

"What?" I asked, confused, my head aching. "Why did you take it out?"

"Your little mortuary friend thought it would be a good idea to wash him off a bit," she said, "in case they do a really thorough autopsy. You guys left the condom on him, so it's good we checked."

"Salvatore is here?" I asked.

"No," she said. "But Ray called him. I sure like that Ray," she said enthusiastically.

Of course you do, I thought, cynically, again feeling jealous. *Are there any potheads who don't like each other?*

"And he sure thinks you hung the moon," she said, shaking her head in disbelief. "I tried to set him straight on that point, but he wouldn't listen. He's got it bad. I can't believe you are going out with someone who's not a geek or a geriatric—or both! But come on, let's go; everything should be ready by now."

"I wish you wouldn't come with us," I said, standing up and rubbing my eyes.

"Well, I wish I had bigger tits and a boyfriend like yours. Now come on. It'll be easier this way. You and Ray drive the minivan and I'll follow in the Buick and wait outside till you're done. Then I'll just swing by and pick you up and we'll be done with it."

Too groggy to argue effectively, I followed her shadow out of the tea-house. The moon, which I was believed by some to have hung, was nearly full, and illuminated the yard with a grayish light. The dogs, now curiously still, sat watching behind their black masks as we followed the gravel path across the lawn to the garage.

Inside, the light was on, and Ray was doing some last-minute arranging of the passenger. The backseat had been folded down and he was now dressed and laid out neatly. We all stared at him a moment. It looked as though his hair had been washed and combed. Ray lowered the door. He handed me a small flashlight, and together, he, Carey, and I reviewed the plan, and the directions, and what to do in case we got separated. We then got in the minivan, opened the garage door, and backed out, Carey following closely in the Buick.

We drove in silence from Rampart Hills, my parents' subdivision, to Harmony Ranch, and I felt as frightened as one of Heathcliff's victims, being taken from the happy safety of Thrushcross Grange to the unknown darkness of Wuthering Heights. We drove through the illuminated stone entry markers, and I noticed that inside Harmony Ranch was very much like outside of Harmony Ranch: wide, deserted streets, row after row of boxy houses, each emanating the blue glow from big-screen TVs. On and on we drove through the circuitous streets and, after a few wrong turns, we found the Band-Aid-colored split-level we were looking for despite the fact that it was almost indistinguishable from all of the other Band-Aid-colored split-levels that surrounded it. I pushed the button on the "little button thingy" that was, as James had said, hooked to the sun visor, and felt my spirits rise in unison with the large door. Ray pulled up the driveway and into the lighted garage. I pushed the button again and the door closed slowly behind us. Ray shut off the motor and we sat motionless for a moment, half expecting the wife to come out and greet us. Thankfully that did not happen, so we got out and set to work.

There was not much space between the back of the van and the garage door, so we had some difficulty removing the body, as it had stiffened considerably since that morning. Eventually we got him out by rolling him on his side and bending him at the waist. This made a terrible crackling noise, and I winced when I heard it. When he was out we straightened him again, which made a less audible crackling noise, and each got a shoulder under his arms. We then dragged him across the garage and up the small set of stairs. There were no warning stickers or blinking boxes indicating the presence of an alarm system, so Ray tried several of the keys on the ring until he found the one needed to unlock the door. He then slipped the keys back into the homeowner's front pants pocket and we dragged him up the rest of the way.

Inside, it was dark and quiet, the soft, electrical hum of the refrigerator in the kitchen the only sound. We set down the body. Ray clicked on his flashlight and went upstairs to scope out the bedroom. I stayed downstairs and looked around with my own flashlight.

The house was a typical suburban family home: a kitchen decorated with wicker baskets and pastel stencils of geese, a living room with a large sectional sofa facing an oak entertainment center containing an enormous TV, a wallpaper border depicting mallards in flight separating the off-white walls from the off-white popcorn ceiling.

Ray lumbered back down the steps and motioned me back over to the body. I took the feet this time and Ray held him under his shoulders as we lifted him and carried him up the thickly carpeted steps. We walked past the kids' rooms, littered with toys and pieces of sports equipment, to the master bedroom at the end of the hall. Ray was wearing his gloves, but my hands were bare, so I tried to remember not to touch anything.

In the bedroom, the blinds had been lowered and a small lamp had been turned on next to the bed. He was already dressed, and was too stiff to undress again, so, on Carey's advice, we decided to lay him out facedown on the floor, as if he'd been stricken while returning from the bathroom. Her rationale was that most "exertion deaths," like his, happened during sex or while pooping. With that in mind, we arranged him accordingly, even going so far as to place a copy of *Field & Stream,* which we'd found next to the toilet, in his hand as a sort of prop. (Of course he should have been posed sitting on the toilet, since exertion deaths happen while an action is taking place—not usually after the fact—but that seemed a little too degrading, and it would have been difficult given his stiffness and the absence of any shit in the toilet bowl.) His other arm we bent under him, with considerable difficulty, to make it look as though he had been clutching his chest. When we were satisfied with the arrangement, we both stood back and regarded him in silence for a moment.

All that work, I thought, *and if we've done it well, no one will ever appreciate it.*

Ray then switched off the lamp, reopened the blinds, and together we tiptoed back down the dark staircase. He went over to the front window, pulled back the curtain, and flashed his flashlight twice. A moment later, the Buick, its lights off, rolled silently into view. Quietly we opened the front door and went out onto the porch. I turned to close it gently and smiled as I noticed a small, metal NO SOLICITING sign firmly affixed to it. We walked casually down the moonlit sidewalk, opened the rear door of the car, and both climbed into the backseat. Carey slowly moved away from the curb and then suddenly hit the gas, slamming Ray and me into the seat.

"Slow down!" I yelled. "The last thing we need is to get pulled over."

Her eyes were wide and frightened in the rearview mirror.

"Someone's following us!" she hissed.

"What?" I cried, and Ray and I immediately turned and looked out the back window. There was one set of headlights.

"I noticed him just after we left our house," she said. "At first I thought I was just imagining it, but he was behind me all the way and only passed me when I parked up the street to wait for you guys. Then, after you went in, he drove by again!"

"What kind of car?" Ray asked.

"I don't know. It's a Volvo, I think."

"What kind of Volvo?" I asked.

"Old," she said. "A station wagon."

I shivered, remembering the strange man with the case in the bushes.

"I saw the same car in front of the house earlier today," I said.

"But why?" Carey asked. "Who?"

I didn't have an answer. For the next few minutes we drove in silence, all watching the headlights behind us, never able to get a good view of the driver. It was clear he wanted it that way, because every time we stopped at a stop sign or a stoplight he would stay back just far enough to prevent us from seeing in his car.

"What about that reporter?" Ray said. "The one you were with this morning."

I thought about him, about his nerdy suit and his dull questions, and somehow I knew that it couldn't be him, even if he had seen the video by now, which I was assuming he must have, since I hadn't heard anything else from James and Marvin.

We turned a corner onto a bigger street, the one leading out of the subdivision, and we all watched, terrified, as the round headlights turned behind us.

"What should I do?" Carey asked, looking at us in the rearview mirror, her voice trembling. Ray and I looked at each other grimly. I shrugged.

"Go back to your parents' house," he told her. "Just drive nice and slow; don't let him know we suspect anything." Carey nodded eagerly, reduced the speed of the car, and gripped the steering wheel firmly, her hands at the ten- and two-o'clock position. She then flipped the turn signal (for perhaps the first time since driver's ed) and made a slow turn to the right. In minutes we were back on my parents' street.

"Pull into the garage but don't shut the door," Ray said. "And don't get out of the car for a minute."

She did so and we all sat silently. A moment later, a dark Volvo station wagon drove past.

"Did you see him?" I asked.

"Naw," Ray said. "Too dark. He'll be back, though. Shut the door and go inside."

We got out of the car and Carey hit the button, lowering the door. At the last moment, Ray sneaked under it and left the two of us standing alone, staring at the closed door.

"What's he doing?" she whispered.

"I don't fucking know," I said, and threw my hands up in the air.

We went inside, turned off all the lights, and ran to the living room windows, which look out onto the front lawn. We both knelt on the sofa and peered over the back of it, saying nothing, barely breathing. We did not see the car again, could not see any sign of Ray, and after about fifteen minutes, we naturally got a little bored and fidgety. I drummed my fingers on the windowsill, and Carey rummaged in her purse for her cigarettes. She lit two, handed me one, and we went back to staring at the empty street.

"Do you think it's the police?" she whispered.

I shook my head. Vice raids on male hustlers were rare, I knew, and this hardly seemed like a sting operation. I suppose that someone could have seen us moving the body and called the police, but that didn't seem likely either. What police department, outside of Scandinavia, would use an old, beat-up Volvo as an undercover vehicle? No, it probably wasn't the police, but I found myself wishing it was because some of the alternatives were far less palatable: it could be a client, obsessed with Ray or with me, or it could be Carlyle, out for revenge, but truly I had no idea who it was. Regardless, I felt an odd sense of satisfaction. All my distant parking and circuitous walks had been justified. I was not crazy. Someone had been following me.

"What if Mom and Dad find out?" Carey asked. "About the . . . you know . . . your work?"

I felt tired thinking about it.

"I don't know," I said.

"Dad would freak!"

At that point, I did not even want to imagine his possible reaction.

As if in response to mentioning my father there was a tremendous crash in the backyard, followed by a chorus of fierce barking. Carey and I clung to each other, afraid. The barking continued. I got up and gingerly walked through the kitchen, Carey a few steps behind me, to the back door. I slid it open and Carey flipped a switch, flooding the yard with light. Over to the right, the dogs were surrounding something, but all we could see was a pile of frantically wagging tails. Above them, there was a large gap in the wooden fence where several of the pickets had evidently snapped in two and fallen down.

Carey and I made our way cautiously to the edge of the porch and peered into the dog pile. I caught sight of Ray and another person, but I couldn't determine who. They were struggling with each other, but were each struggling more with the dogs, whose merciless licking I knew all too well.

"Come on!" I said, and Carey and I leaped off the porch and began grabbing handfuls of loose puppy skin. One by one we pulled the dogs back, and eventually I managed to grab Ray's wrist and pull him out of the fracas. His face and clothes were muddy and his hair was a slobbery mess, but he quickly joined in grabbing the mastiffs—little David and Michael and Kathleen—and pulling them off, until finally we revealed the body of a giggling man, curled up tightly in a ball. Carey and Ray did their best to corral the puppies with their bodies while I held the giants, Bobby and Ethel, firmly by their collars. The man then lowered his hands, revealing a messy head of red hair. He uncurled himself slowly and I was not surprised to see that it was none other than Rob MacNamara, the reporter/novelist from our office building. He stood up, adjusting his broken glasses on his face. His striped shirt and khaki pants were covered in muddy paw prints; his bow tie was crooked, but still in place.

"I hid in the bushes," Ray panted, "and followed him around to the back. He's got a camera somewhere."

Rob said nothing as he brushed the dirt from his clothes, but was smiling a naughty-boy smile, like he'd just been caught dipping his finger in the frosting of the cake.

"You!" I said. "Somehow I knew it. But why?" I asked.

He looked at me, trying unsuccessfully to contain his smile.

"I can explain," he said.

"You'd better be able to," Ray said, and pushed him toward the back door.

We convened in the living room and Carey took great pleasure in playing the role of hostage taker, tying MacNamara's hands and feet to the chair with some bungee cords she'd found in the garage.

"I don't think that will be necessary," he said, smiling down at her. "I'm not going anywhere."

Ignoring him, she continued to wind the cord around his feet and around his body until he was more or less immobilized.

"Why?" Ray asked again, leaning against the counter, a confused look on his face.

"I can explain," he said again.

"Let's hear it," Ray said.

"Start talking!" Carey chimed in, shaking her fist menacingly at her newly tied captive.

"Carey," I scolded, "why don't you go and get our guest some water or something." She started to protest, but my glare stopped her and she turned reluctantly toward the kitchen, giving MacNamara's chair a little kick on her way out. We stared at him, waiting. He cleared his throat.

"You know I'm a reporter?" he said. We nodded.

"Well, what you probably don't know is that I'm researching a story on your business. I've been following you for about two months now, and I'm just about ready to publish."

I'm sure I went pale because I felt all my blood, indeed all my energy, fall down to my feet.

"I know all about Harden Up, and the food stamps, and the microbusiness program. . . ." He was checking off all of his knowledge on his fingers, which he had easily loosened from their bonds.

"I know about your Web page and advertisements, about the movie you've just made, about your relationship, financial and otherwise, with Frank Glory, and I think I know most of your clients, although what's going on with this last one, I haven't quite figured out yet. Which is why I was sneaking around the yard."

Carey came back in and angrily dropped the six-pack of beer she held when she saw that he'd loosened his cord. She pushed his hands back in and was pulling the cords tighter when I told her to stop and set him loose. She looked at me, disappointed, but could see again from the gravity of my expression that she shouldn't argue and slowly unwound him. He thanked her, but remained seated where he was and continued grinning the same self-satisfied grin.

"But why?" Ray asked again. It was a question that had certainly been exercised that day.

"Why!" he said, surprised that we'd even ask such an obvious question. "Because it's a great story! A career-defining story. No one's ever had a story like this in Denver before. It's got everything: sex, money, welfare, police involvement, the Catholic Church; I could go on and on. . . ."

I slumped down into a chair. Ray was now pacing back and forth.

"How did you find out about us?" he asked, pausing and turning to MacNamara.

"I can't really say. It was a friendly tip and I promised not to drag him into it."

"Who was it?" Ray said, his voice deep and low, his eyes locked on MacNamara's.

"I can't say, really I can't."

Carey then grabbed a handful of his hair, pulled his head back, and moved her face right up next to his.

"You'd better talk, asshole!" she said threateningly. I was beginning to regret the boxed set of Van Damme videos I'd given her last Christmas, when it hit me. I sat up.

"It was Carlyle, wasn't it?" I said.

He said nothing. Carey brutally twisted her handful of red hair.

"Ow, yes!" he cried. She released him.

"Shit!" said Ray, pacing the room. "Shit, shit, shit."

Shit, indeed. We each opened a beer, and as we drank them, Mac-Namara told us all about how Carlyle, whose family owns *Tally-Ho*, had approached him with the story of a gay prostitution ring. How he had then investigated it and followed us around and discovered the microbusiness connection. How he had rented the space next to ours and poked around some more. He even confessed to breaking into our office and to accessing our computer files.

"Which are quite neat and concise," he said, nodding over at me.

"Thank you, I guess." But at that point I hardly felt proud of my professionalism.

He knew we paid taxes, he knew how much we'd grossed last quarter, and he knew I'd been receiving help from, and had cosigned a loan with, Hole.

"This is going to be great!" he said, rubbing his hands together. Carey went up and smacked the side of his head.

"You can't write about this!" she said angrily. "Our parents will find out!"

MacNamara chuckled and rubbed his head where it had been smacked. I felt anxious again. I had realized there was a risk of their finding out from the graduation ceremony, and a risk of their finding out from the *Denver Business Daily,* but this was worse than I could ever have imagined.

"Look," I said, leaning forward on my chair, figuring I'd try to resuscitate the "family argument" I'd used on Ray earlier in the day at James's apartment.

"It's true, my father will crucify me and then burn my body on the cross if you write this story, but forget about me for a minute. If you do go ahead with it, a lot of people are going to get hurt. I mean, the clients are mostly just lonely old men, except for the prick you're protecting, of course, but their families will be torn apart by this. And then there are the guys I've got working: most of them use the money to pay for college, one sends money home to his family in Thailand, one supports his dying lover. . . . Don't you see what this is going to do?"

He didn't even flinch.

"I can't help that," he said, very matter-of-fact. "If I don't write the story Carlyle will just tip off someone else who will, or worse, the police, who are already on your tail anyway."

Carey gasped, and we were all silent.

"How do you know about the police?" I asked anxiously.

"Like I said, I've been following you. I'm not the only one."

"And you're sure it's the police?"

He nodded emphatically.

"We're going to jail anyway," Ray said somberly, from where he stood by the fireplace, smoking. Carey looked at me. I swallowed hard and looked at Ray, who was staring down into the empty, black cavern.

I had never thought of jail or getting into any trouble with the police. Oh, I knew somewhere in a rarely visited corner of my mind that it was always a possibility, but I'd had so little trouble from the police in the past year that jail never really occurred to me. Carey booted Mac-Namara's shin.

"At least I will, won't I, MacNamara?" Ray said. "Jack and the other guys will probably get suspended sentences or maybe just community service, since it's their first offense. Johnny will get deported, but it's my third time in court, and I don't think I stand much of a chance, do I, MacNamara?"

"You'll need a good lawyer," he conceded, rubbing his leg. We were all silent, lost in our own scenarios. Until then my only worry had been the reaction of my father, but that seemed small and much less important when I looked at Ray, who was more downcast and despondent than I'd ever seen him before. I looked at MacNamara, who wasn't saying anything, but was still smiling smugly, waiting for one of us to speak up.

Maybe it was because I was feeling so at ease around dead bodies, but the thought of killing him occurred to me then. I knew I'd never be able to do it and that it would only lead to more trouble down the line, but it was, nevertheless, somewhat pleasant to consider. I was so angry and tired and on edge that I could easily imagine strangling him and burying his body in one of the dogs' numerous holes in the backyard. But when I thought about it, it wasn't him that I wanted to bury—it was the whole story of the life I'd been leading for the past year. I wanted to cover it up and make it go away, which was confusing because on the one hand I was so proud of all I'd done and accomplished, but on the other hand I was realizing how much it placed me outside of society's boundaries. In the eyes of the majority I was an outlaw, an outcast; my behavior was outlandish! Not to mention illegal. I'd tried to hide it, tried to disguise it as something other than what it was, but it looked like I couldn't hide it anymore.

As I sat there staring at MacNamara it was suddenly terribly, horribly, ghastly apparent that the story was going to come out and that there wasn't a thing any of us could do to stop it.

Or was there . . . ?

"Hey, you all look like I just passed a death sentence," MacNamara said, standing stiffly and taking center stage. "The article's going to be written whether you help me or not, but if you help me maybe we can work out some deals about concealing some identities. I mean come on! It's not that bad! You're gay! The gay community loves a scandal, worships porn stars! You'll be mythic figures when all this gets out."

"Somehow this is not how I envisioned my fifteen minutes," I said.

"I understand." He chuckled. "But don't you see, this can have any spin you want to put on it. Think of the Mayflower Madam or Heidi Fleiss—they made lemons out of lemonade, but they didn't squeeze their stories for even half of what they were worth. Now, you . . . you guys are smart; you could go far! It's all a matter of marketing, and you're both obviously talented in that area. I can see you on the talk-show circuit, then maybe a lecture series, and of course you'll write a book. I've got connections. I know the right people. I can help you guys."

Yes, I thought to myself, *connections. And that's why you're driving a seventy-five Volvo.*

"The more you help me the more I'll help you."

"When have you decided the article is coming out?" I asked.

"Well, I'd hoped to have it come out just before your graduation. That way I could get the maximum exposure. I can break the story before the police; that's the beauty of it! I'd like to have an exclusive on you but you probably won't do that, will you?"

"Uh, no," I said. "And to tell you the truth, I don't think you'll need one, because this article is never going to make it into print." He and Ray both looked at me questioningly. I now moved to center stage and pushed him back down into his chair.

"You mentioned that the Carlyle family owns *Tally-Ho,* did you not?" MacNamara nodded.

"And it was the younger one who tipped you off to the story?" Another nod.

"How much is he paying you?" I asked. MacNamara said nothing. "That's it, isn't it? He is paying you. He's paying the rent on your office. He's financed a little 'sabbatical' for you so you can write your little 'novel,' hasn't he?"

MacNamara smiled but said nothing. Carey grabbed his hair again and yanked his head back.

"Ooww!" he cried. "Yes! He's paying me. So what! He's my employer!" I walked over next to him and leaned my face down next to his.

"Which brings us to the question of why?" I motioned for Carey to release her grasp. She did so and he again rubbed his head. I continued.

"In the course of all your investigating and poking around did it never occur to you to investigate the reason for his dropping the story in your lap? I mean, it does seem strange, don't you think, for him to suddenly become so interested in one of the family businesses?"

Ray was smiling, albeit nervously. MacNamara looked confused, but was listening very closely.

"The fact is," I said, moving next to Ray by the fireplace, "we are in possession of a very incriminating videotape in which Mr. Carlyle the third has a starring role. A videotape he evidently did not mention to you. A videotape that you obviously did not find in your frequent forays into our office. A videotape that we will be forced to release copies of to Carlyle Senior, and to the media, if you persist in pursuing our story."

MacNamara's brow was arched, but I saw that he suspected I was bluffing.

"Ahh, you don't believe me? Well, why don't we take a little trip back to the office and I'll show you," I said, gesturing to the door. "I think you'd find it most interesting."

And so, minutes later, we had all piled into our respective vehicles and were speeding toward the office.

"Do you think it will work?" Ray asked. I shrugged my shoulders. I really had no idea.

"It's pretty risky," he said. "We're already in a lot of trouble, but this is blackmail." I nodded but said nothing and continued driving. I knew it was a gamble, but I was betting that MacNamara was more financially mixed up with Carlyle than he'd let on.

Half an hour later, we were all seated in a row on the edge of the double bed in room three, intently watching Carlyle snort and batter and rape on the small screen before us. Two-thirds of the way through, MacNamara asked us to stop it. I pushed the pause button.

"This puts a different spin on things, doesn't it?" He was clearly affected and stood up somberly, staring at the images frozen on the screen.

"I think the Carlyles might be reluctant to have this story printed in one of their papers," I said. He said nothing, but his jaw tightened and I could tell he was angry. Then he smiled at the three of us sitting on the bed, bowed his head slightly, and reached for the door handle.

"I wasn't kidding about the police," he said. "They have been poking around. Carlyle tipped off the INS about your kid from Thailand."

"Thanks for the tip," I said, and meant it. He opened the door, but then paused and took his wallet from his back pocket. He pulled out a business card and handed it to me.

"Call me if you change your mind. Maybe we could work something out. I really could help you. If not in *Tally-Ho* then in one of the other papers."

I took the card and gave him a cold smile. He turned and walked dejectedly down the hall. I almost felt sorry for him. Had I not been so preoccupied with his revelation that the police were closing in, I probably would have felt sorry for him. But sympathy was not something I could afford to expend just then, as I was stockpiling it all for myself.

I was exhausted, and as Ray and Carey and I lay talking on the bed I could feel the adrenaline that had fueled the day ebbing away. The conversation slowed and we were all falling asleep. Carey stuck her feet up in the air and swung herself up and off the bed.

"Well, kids, it's been fun, but I've got class first thing tomorrow and I'd better go back and let the beasts in for the night."

Ray and I got up reluctantly and shut off the lights. We grumbled weary good-byes to Carey in the parking lot, and then Ray and I drove the hearse back to his house, where we both agreed that we were too tired to even speculate on our next move. I was, as they say, asleep before my head hit the pillow, and I'm sure I slept almost as soundly as our friend on Mountain Lion Drive.

The next morning I was awakened by the sound of my cell phone ringing. I thought maybe it was James or Marvin so I quickly fished through the pocket of my jacket for the phone and clicked it on.

"Hello."

"Yes, Jack Thompson, please."

"This is Jack."

"Jack, Noah Bernstein here. Hope I'm not calling too early."

"No, no, not at all." I sat up quickly, nudging Ray awake.

"I got your message yesterday, but I didn't really have time to get back to you."

"About the mix-up with the tape—"

"Yeess . . . The mix-up. But I don't think there was any mix-up," he said somewhat arrogantly. "I asked for the tape you and the other students collaborated on and I see from the credits listed at the end of—what's it called? Oh, yes, I see from the credits of *Missionary Positions* that Mr. Varga was, in fact, in charge of all the cinematography and editing. Although I must say that as an exercise video it is unlike anything I've ever seen."

I said nothing, could think of nothing to say, but fell back on the bed and held the phone so that Ray could hear, too.

"I'm intrigued," he continued, "and I wonder about the real nature of your business. A business that has been subsidized by our state tax dollars. Would you care to comment on that?"

"Uh, no. Not at this time."

"Uh-huh. I'm also intrigued by the family connections," he continued. "You are the son of Steen Thompson, of Thompson Communications, are you not?"

I rubbed my eyes, hoping this was a bad dream from which I'd soon wake up.

"I had the pleasure of meeting your father some months ago when we did a profile of his business for the paper, but I didn't make the connection between you two until I saw your name on the movie's list of credits. Now, of course, I'm no authority on the subject, but don't most people who star in movies of this sort use an alias? A stage name?"

"It's n-n-not what you think. . . ."

"Oh, no? I'm certainly eager to hear any explanations you might have to offer."

"Well . . ." I began, but didn't finish, as I could not think of anything even remotely believable to say. There was a long, expectant silence.

"Then let's review what we do know," he said. "We know that you come from a fairly wealthy family, and yet you were receiving public assistance, is that right?"

"That doesn't mean I have money! Look, I can explain. . . ."

"Uh-huh." He chuckled. "That might be worth hearing." I heard some pages flipping on his end and knew he was flipping through his Day-Timer. "Why don't we meet this afternoon, say, two o'clock, my office?"

"Uh, sure," I said timidly.

"Good. I look forward to seeing you. Tell the receptionist who you are and she'll bring you up."

Click.

I pushed the disconnect button, extended my arm over the side of the bed, and dropped the phone to the floor.

We both stared up at the ceiling, our despair filling the room like a poisonous gas.

"There's always Mexico," Ray said, and for the next half hour we stayed in that position and discussed several fantasy solutions—flight, murder, ritual suicide—but what we finally decided on was something quite different. We called MacNamara.

When he arrived at the office an hour later we led him next door to his barren office, so as not to be overheard by Josh, and recounted the phone conversation with Bernstein. His reaction was a mix of elation and agitation.

"I knew someone else would pick up on it!" he said, pacing the room and cracking his knuckles one by one. "But he's only just found out, right?"

We nodded.

"Good," he said. "Good, good, good, then he's got a lot of home-work to do. We're way ahead of him, but we have to work fast. Look," he said, pausing in his pacing and regarding Ray and me gravely. "I can help you. I will help you. But you've got to work with me."

We looked at each other and shrugged. He was preaching to the con-verted. In our discussion at home Ray and I had come to the conclusion that working with MacNamara was really the only possibility if we hoped to have any control whatsoever over our story.

"What do you want us to do?" Ray asked. MacNamara rubbed his freckled hands together and resumed pacing, more rapidly this time.

"First," he said, raising his index finger, "I want an exclusive. I don't want you talking to anybody but me, and of course your attorney, about any of this. Let me be your mouthpiece."

We nodded, but I wanted to kick myself for not having considered going to an attorney.

"Second, I need complete honesty. You have to tell me the truth. All of it. The more I know the more I can help you, and we can anticipate any unpleasant surprises that might arise."

We agreed and talked on into the afternoon, relating stories and hammering out agreements—what we'd agree to say and agree to leave out—and in the end we had resolved several contentious issues. We agreed that Johnny's name would not appear and we would do our legal best to erase any record of him. Also, Ray's role would be minimized as much as possible, and we would all work together to keep him out of trouble. My parents were a thornier issue. I did not want them to be mentioned at all, but MacNamara pointed out the folly of such an omis-sion, since Bernstein had already discovered the connection and would be sure to use it.

"We've got to beat him to the punch," he said. "That way we can put a positive spin on it. Get some better pictures, better quotes. Do you think they'll talk to me?" he asked. I laughed for a good five minutes at that one, and then excused myself. I laughed all the way down the hall and into the bathroom, where I locked myself in a stall, buried my face in my hands, and wept. There was no way that my role in the story could be minimized or sanitized. I *was* the story. I realized then that I was going to be completely exposed, realized that everyone I'd ever known or even been acquainted with in Denver—my friends, my family, aunts, uncles, cousins, grandparents, the neighbors across the street, my elementary school teachers, my dentist, my mechanic—were all going to read the sordid details. I wanted to run away, wanted to flush myself down the toilet, wanted to do something, anything, to stuff all the scandal back into Pandora's box.

I had to talk to my parents before someone else did—that much was transparently clear—although what I would say, let alone how I would say it, I didn't know. I would cancel my afternoon meeting with Bernstein, I thought, give him some excuse and reschedule, then, as soon as my parents' plane hit the ground (in a fiery crash, perhaps), I would go directly and speak to them.

With this rough outline in mind, I left the stall, washed my face, and went back down the hall to MacNamara's office. I stood in the doorway unnoticed by MacNamara and Ray. They were talking animatedly about their scuffle the night before, and both laughed out loud when they got to the part where the section of fence collapsed. One more thing I have to explain, I thought. Ray seemed much more at ease, and I was glad about that, but while he seemed to think the worst was over, I felt certain it was just beginning.

When we parted from MacNamara, agreeing to meet again the next day, after I'd spoken to my parents, Ray and I immediately set to work doing damage control. First we told Josh what was happening, and had him call all of the subcontractors and summon them to a mandatory meeting later that afternoon. While he did that, I copied all of the client information onto a single floppy disk and erased each and every client file from the hard drive, figuring it would be best to destroy as much of that information as I could. Ray got busy boxing up all of the written records from the file cabinet, which he then loaded into the hearse and disposed of in several different Dumpsters around town. While he was gone, Josh and I phoned as many of the regular clients as we could and warned them of the trouble that was about to come, assured them that we'd taken precautions to conceal their identities, and asked them not to speak to anyone.

When all of the subcontractors were assembled in the main office, I thanked them all for coming on such short notice and told them, as briefly and concisely as I could, that the gig was up. There wasn't any trouble yet, but there was going to be, so we were pulling in our shingle and closing down the shop. Most everyone took the news calmly. Such group meetings were rare, and they had all known something was up. Johnny was the most worried, as he still had a year to go before he got his degree, but I assured him as best I could that we'd do our best to keep him out of it all. Most of the college students were nervous about their parents finding out, but I was touched to see that those concerns took a backseat to their fears for Ray and Johnny and me. Only poor Marvin, looking terribly sad and confused, wept quietly in the corner. I knew his fear wasn't arrest or exposure; it was what that he was, yet again, unemployed. What would he do now? I wondered. He caught me looking at him and quickly reapplied his masculinity. He cleared his throat and wiped his eyes and uncrossed his legs. I smiled at him and tossed him a box of tissues—which he very nearly caught.

The following day, the day before my big graduation, of which my parents still knew nothing, I sat down with them in the living room of their house, the same room in which everything had exploded two days before. Standing by the mantel, my gaze locked on the fireplace, I revealed to them what had happened and what was going to happen. I was getting quite good at recounting the details of my naughty life and troubles, but there was no easy way to say it then. Feelings of shame at what I'd done and pride in my accomplishments swirled in my head like oil and water, and I found myself suppressing them both and recounting my tale in the flat voice of a lobotomy patient.

My mother's reaction was predictable: horror, disbelief, shocked tears, feelings of guilt and embarrassment, all of which I knew she'd overcome or forget about in time, but my father's reaction was quite different than I'd expected; he sat, listening carefully in his wing-backed chair, showing no reaction or emotion, as if he'd been hypnotized by the monotonous sound of my voice.

I finished the tale and waited to hear what they had to say. I waited for what seemed like a light-year. My mother wept into the monogrammed hankie she had pulled from her sleeve, but my father just sat there stoically, like a visiting diplomat to the U.N., patiently waiting for the translation to come through his headset. When he did finally look up, his expression was frighteningly vacant. His head wobbled for a few moments, à la Katherine Hepburn, but then fell forward and stayed there.

"Please leave," I heard him say, with an icy calmness and finality. I hesitated only a moment, wanting to apologize, wanting to offer a rational explanation, but the former would have sounded trite and the latter was impossible, so I said nothing, and walked, as steadily and quietly as I could, out of the living room and out the front door.

To this day, almost two years later, those two words remain the last I've heard from my father. I suppose I should feel penitent—either that or resentful—but I feel neither—and both, if that makes any sense. I feel bad that I did something to cause my parents pain, but I feel no remorse about what I did. I did not cheat old people out of their savings, I did not exploit child labor, I did not rape the land or poison the environment. I conducted personal business transactions between two people. Two consenting adults. I harmed no one. Like Hole said, I may have catered to man's baser desires, but "man bought"! No one was coerced into it, no one was seduced. Men desired what I had and searched for it—actively sought me out. If I didn't provide the service, someone else would have. If somehow no one provided it, the demand would not, as some people actually believe, disappear. If somehow Mayor Giuliani were to achieve his goal of completely ridding New York City of all the whores and porn stores and naughty cinemas, the demand for those things would not magically evaporate. If you destroy providers like me, you will not destroy the problem. The desire will still be there, and new people will always spring up to cater to that desire. It's simple supply and demand. Basic economics. Maybe that is what I should have told my father. The message was the same, but at least it would have been conveyed in a language that he understood.

"Give him time," my mother said on her last visit, as I sat on a bench in the Tuileries, watching her paint with watercolors (her newest campaign). "He'll come around."

I nodded halfheartedly. I wanted to believe her, but I didn't. I was remembering the time, during my freshman year of college, when I first told my parents I was gay. The news severely taxed my father's understanding and tolerance. Oh, he did "come around" eventually, and was always polite and friendly to anyone I brought home for him to meet, but it was a long journey for him to reach that point. I have never asked him about it, but I suspect it was so difficult for him to accept because he, like so many people when they first discover someone they know is gay, immediately pictured me naked in bed having sex with someone of the same gender. A mental *cinema verité* started rolling in my father's head, and when that happened (usually when I was talking about someone new I was dating), I could actually see the revulsion and perplexity on his face as he struggled to banish the images from his mind. For that reason, I know his thinking about my "line of work" must raise the curtain on a lurid triple feature, and that must be nearly overwhelming.

After telling my parents that day, I left their house and sought solace from Andre. I should have known better.

"Come in, whore," he said, whipping open the door. "You're just in time. I was just watching the tail end of *Klute.*" He pirouetted and pranced over to the sofa, waving the remote control from side to side like a wand.

"I must say I'm fonda Jane's outfits in this movie," he said, pointing to the screen. "I mean, look at her with that ol' shag haircut and that maxiskirt and go-go boots. We could probably look outside and see ten girls dressed just like her walking down the street right now. *Plus ca change, plus c'est la meme chose,* that's my motto."

He pushed the pause button and looked up at me expectantly from where he was perched on the edge of the sofa.

"I guess you want to hear the details," I said, looking away from the TV and toward the kitchen, wondering what alcohol I could drink to get my tongue loosened.

"Yesterday's news, girl, yesterday's news. Just got off the phone with Sister Carey and my ear is hot, hot, hot! What I want to know is what you're going to *do,* sweetie. When are you going to tell Steen and Barbara?"

"I just did it."

"No!"

"Yes."

"And?"

"It wasn't a Hallmark moment." I plopped down on the sofa and told him as much of the story as I could while he gasped and applauded and had mock fainting fits, taking immense pleasure as I relayed all the drama.

"Look," I said when I'd finished my tale, "this is all going to erupt really fast. Ray and I need a place to hide out for a day or two. Any chance we can crash here?"

"Hmmm," Andre mused, raising his index finger to his lips and looking up at the ceiling. *"Ray* and I? Ray? Ray who? Baby, we've been the best of friends since we were little girls, right?"

I nodded.

"The kind of dear, close friends who don't keep *any* secrets from each other."

Again I nodded, but I knew he was leading up to something, and I was pretty sure, from his sarcastic tone, that it wasn't going to be nice.

"But sugar," he said. "Sweetie. I don't ever, *ever,* remember hearing you mention anyone named Ray. Is he the pimp?"

I groaned and rubbed my temples. He wasn't going to let me off easily. I had avoided him for months, and I suppose he was entitled to give me some grief. I got up and went over to the refrigerator.

"I'm all out of Thunderbird and Boone's Farm," Andre yelled from the couch. "Isn't that what you working girls like? But wrap that bottle of chardonnay in a brown paper bag and you can pretend."

"Oh, quit it!" I yelled. "Spare me! My parents were bad enough, and unfortunately they were just the beginning. I don't need another busload of crap from my friends. I don't have much time. Can we stay here or not?"

"Oh, I don't know . . ." he said, wringing his hands together. "All the publicity and everything. I'd probably be interviewed and photographed extensively, wouldn't I? People all over the country, maybe even all over the world, would see little well-dressed me, and probably the inside of my tastefully, some might say impeccably, decorated *pied-à-terre . . .* Can you stay? Of course, girl. *Of course."*

"Thanks."

"Do you think *E!* will send someone?"

From Andre's I went home to Ray's. There, in the upstairs bedroom, I closed all the blinds, stripped down to my boxers, and got under the covers of the big, white bed, ready and willing to indulge in a gloomy afternoon of dismal self-pity. The weather, however, was not cooperating and the sun shone obstinately down on me through the skylights, which had no blinds I could close. In frustration, I pulled the comforter over my head, wishing I could just push some button and block out the

annoying orb—a magical remote control that I could use to bring everything into alignment with my moods. I could push one button to change
the weather, another to change my outfit, a third to cue up the appropriate music. I could push yet another and give my father a better sense
of humor and thus change his reaction to my revelation. Heck, while I
was at it I might as well push one and erase the entire situation so he'd
have nothing to react to. I'd just push a button and erase my history
from the past year and a half. Sort of reach back through time and undo
everything I'd done. I could go back to being the person I'd been before
all of this lunacy had started. Back to the Jack unsullied by all of my
deeds. Back to the young, beautiful, clean, and innocent Jack, whom
Paul and my parents had so adored. . . .

Then I started laughing.

"Self-delusion is self-pollution!" I said in a voice mimicking Sister
Melanie's, and threw the comforter off. Try as I might, I could not fool
myself. I knew then, as I had always known, that I had not been clean or
innocent before all of this lunacy. I had been a manipulative, spoiled,
lazy, money-grubbing, underachieving parasite, and I looked back at
that person with no feelings of nostalgia. On the contrary, I was truly
ashamed of the former Jack, and I knew that given the chance I would
not resurrect him. Not for the approval of my father, not for the security
of Paul, not for anything.

I have something now, I thought to myself, remembering the gallery,
and Ray, and the feelings of self-confidence I'd worked so hard to obtain. *But more important, I am someone! Someone I can face when I
look in the mirror. Someone who can stand alone on his own two feet.*

I thought of the future as I lay there, and of all the attention I knew
would be coming my way. I knew it was going to greatly embarrass my
family, and I did feel bad about that, but I knew that if I were to be
ashamed about it myself, it would only make matters worse, because
that shame would imply to the outside world that what I'd done was
wrong, that my actions deserved to be judged, and I didn't believe that.
I realized as I lay there that I had two choices: I could either play the
penitent pansy, and rapidly wither under the harsh light of the public's
disapproval and scorn, or I could rise up and defend myself by not taking the situation as seriously as everyone else seemed to be taking it.

Of course I chose the latter, figuring that by trivializing the scandal I
could knock the wind out of the judgmental sails. Yes, admittedly I'd been
naughty. Yes, my past was sordid, but so what. I didn't feel embarrassed

or ashamed. Not really anyway. I suppose I did feel a bit overwhelmed and naked, but that was not my doing. I was a simple businessman just doing what I had to do to keep my head above water. It was the government and the news media that wanted to interfere and publicize the hell out of it. Well, fine. If that was the case I might as well harness the attention and try to profit from the ride. I'd be stupid not to.

That afternoon, I recited my story one more time, this time to my brother Jay, whom I visited in his dingy law office on Colorado Boulevard. I wanted to hire him to represent me in the legal troubles I knew were bound to confront me and hoped he could help me anticipate some of them and plan some strategy beforehand. Although he too was shocked by many of the details, he wasn't so shocked that he couldn't see a brass ring when one presented itself. He had been dying for a case like mine. One that would give him some publicity and exposure, and here it was right in his own family. It wouldn't score him any points with the old man, but we both reasoned that surely Dad would forgive him when things settled down a bit.

Uh, that part remains to be seen.

Before I left him, I told Jay all about Burl, and how I thought he could probably be helpful with the case, considering his prosecutorial past. He agreed, so I wrote down his number and told Jay to call him as soon as possible. I also gave him MacNamara's number, since Jay said he'd need to confer with him on the contents of the impending *Tally-Ho* article (which he had vowed to publish surreptitiously, even though it would cost him his job). Then I left and went shopping and bought a new tie to go with the suit I planned to wear to my graduation.

Unfortunately, no one at the ceremony got to see it.

The graduation two days later was chaotic, to say the least. Rob's story—all eleven pages of it, complete with photos and movie stills— had come out in *Tally-Ho* the night before. The *Denver Business Daily*'s comparatively tame story had come out that morning—next to the reprint of the profile of my father and Thompson Communications. So by eight A.M. the lobby of the building that housed the microbusiness program was swarming with reporters, cameramen, and police, even though the ceremony wasn't scheduled to start until ten. Or so I heard from Andre and Carey, who both arrived early, anticipating the difficulty of finding a good seat. On the advice of Jay and Burl, I did not attend, since earlier that morning the offices of Harden Up Inc. had been raided by the police. There were arrest warrants out for both Ray and me, so we had installed ourselves, as planned, in Andre's apartment, and had been instructed to stay there until Jay and Burl and MacNamara could arrange our peaceful surrender.

The account of the ceremony I heard later went something like this: At precisely ten o'clock, a harried Tina pushed the play button on her cassette recorder and started the all-too-familiar strains of "Pomp and Circumstance." Then Salvatore, Millie, Sharise, and Antonio and Victor, dressed in blue caps and gowns, all filed through the crowds of reporters and cameramen and into the small microbusiness classroom. They took their places to the right of the oak podium in chairs that had been arranged at the front of the class. To their left, on the other side of the podium, sat Tina and the invited speakers. As the music droned on, they all glanced timidly at the huge assemblage of strangers, although none of them was surprised to see it.

"That short one with the Farrah Fawcett hair and the five-inch fuck-me pumps went first," Andre said, narrating the details later that afternoon. Tina took her place behind the podium and explained the program and its origins, its goal of helping people get off welfare by teaching them the skills of being an entrepreneur. She then praised us all as hardworking and intelligent, and said she hoped we each achieved the success for which we had worked so hard.

The governor was next, but his uneasiness was evidenced by the sweat on his brow and his stilted speech. He praised the program as a sign that the welfare state as we knew it was near an end, and pointed to us as the next wave of pioneers. He praised us for having the courage, strength, and intelligence to better ourselves, and said that by doing so, we bettered our community as well.

Then, in a storm of flashbulbs, to which she was largely oblivious, Sister Melanie was introduced and led to the podium. Small and diminutive in her black sweater and dark glasses, but with a booming voice that shook the asbestos from the ceiling tiles, she congratulated each and every one of us for our accomplishments, and for breaking free from the chains of welfare. For regaining dignity, self-respect, and independence. We were shining examples, she said, of how welfare can and should work: as a tool to help people improve, as a stepping stone to get us across the river of adversity.

"You have all taken a handout and made it stand out!"

And with that, Tina pushed play again, and rose to help Sister Melanie hand out the diplomas.

It was only after the ceremony, as she was being carted to her plane at the airport, that Sister Melanie had any comment about me. She said only that I was "misguided," and that it was unfortunate that this "incident" had drawn attention away from such a noble program.

"But I will certainly pray for him," she said, "to get back on the right track."

Scandal Is Legally Very Entertaining, Really

There is a legend that when the first kangaroo was brought to Britain from Australia, there had been so much advance hype about the curious creature that a large crowd had amassed at the dock to witness its disembarkment. As it was led hopping from the boat, leashed and collared, there was such a riotous push forward to catch a glimpse of it that the poor kangaroo was crushed to death.

As we pulled up to police headquarters that evening for the formal surrender that Burl and Jay and MacNamara had orchestrated, I felt a frightening kinship with the unfortunate marsupial. I was not crushed to death, but I was unpleasantly squashed and jostled and could scarcely believe that all those people were there to see me. There were so many reporters that it was difficult even to open the car door, and in truth, I was afraid to. Eventually we were able to emerge and I clung tightly to Jay's hand in front, and Ray's hand in back, and together we moved away from the car and wove our way through the mass of cameras and microphones and shouting people . . .

"Jack! Give us a statement!"

"Jack! What does your father have to say about all this?"

"Jack! Jack! Jack! Over here! Is it true you sold drugs?"

"What about the Asian slaves?"

. . . and into the equally crowded and echoing lobby of the station. We were led behind a wall of hand-holding policemen, through which the cameras and microphones poked like hungry animals, and were promptly handcuffed and read our Miranda rights by a very handsome vice officer. Then we were led away for the hours of tedious processing that lay ahead.

At the arraignment, we were both formally charged with pandering and prostitution. We plead not guilty, and our bail was set at three thousand dollars each, which Hole, having heard about all the trouble on the five-o'clock news, promptly paid, and we were out by midnight. The crowds of reporters were smaller then, since the newspapers already had their pictures for the morning editions, but the four local TV news stations had trucks set up outside, and when the well-coiffed reporters saw us exit the building they quickly ditched their cups of coffee and made straight for us, cameramen in tow.

"Jack! Answer a few questions? What does your father have to say? Is it true he helped finance your business and referred clients to you?"

"Mr. Thompson! Wait! Is it true that Frank Glory is the one who set your bail? What's your relationship with Mr. Glory?"

"Jack! Just one question! Is it true that John Elway was one of your customers?"

Although the temptation to answer that last question in the affirmative was powerful, I thought better of it and quickly ducked into Burl's large Mercedes for the drive to Ray's house. There we were greeted by another mob camped out on the lawn. Burl parked as close as he could to the house, and Ray and I threw open the car door and ran the gauntlet to the porch. We made it inside, but the door didn't lock, so we barricaded it with a table from Ray's studio. Upstairs it was safe, but it was hardly quiet, as a group of persistent—and evidently drunk—reporters who were camped out on the lawn below called up to us throughout the night, like unrequited lovers, "Jaaack, just one little statement. Just one comment. Puleeeaaassse."

The next day we were in all the local papers, but, considering all the lights, cameras, and action, I expected much more. In truth, the headlines were less than screaming:

GAY PROSTITUTION RING OPERATES TWO BLOCKS FROM CAPITOL, STATE REPRESENTATIVES FINGERED AS CLIENTS.

SON OF THOMPSON COMMUNICATIONS CEO CHARGED WITH RUNNING GAY PROSTITUTION RING.

Welfare Money Used to Finance Gay Bordello. Local Business-man's Son Charged.

In spite of all their tenacious hounding, what the reporters chose to tell was surprisingly timid.

Unfortunately, there is no real tabloid press in Denver—or at least none that would consider themselves as such. The two "serious" dailies are more concerned with Broncos coverage, above all else, and that their articles can be easily read and enjoyed by even those readers with severe mental retardation. Well, I am not a Bronco, and, damn it, I did not have any Broncos that I could expose as clients, but I did think my story was interesting and at least worthy of the front page. However, the gay-sex angle was a little too left of center and filthy for Ward and June to digest with their morning coffee, so I was relegated to page three in one paper and to the "Local News" section in the other, and there were hardly any pictures!

Thank God that wasn't the case nationally, or even internationally. We were hot news on either coast, and in Canada and Europe. *Time, Newsweek, Vanity Fair, People, L'Express, George, Paris Match,* the *National Enquirer, Stern, Hello!,* the *Mirror,* and of course all of the gay papers and magazines—all my dearest old friends—were now yowling for interviews with *me!* At that point I was more than willing to talk, but, in a horrible example of poetic justice, by the time they got to me I was under strict orders from Burl and Jay to speak to no one, out of fear of incriminating myself. All inquiries were sadly directed to my attorneys. All comments would have to wait until after the trial. Predictably, things quieted down.

The day after the surrender we immediately set to work on our defense. My brother and Burl hired consultants and paralegals and researchers and did a wonderful job without actually having to resort to lying. Extreme exaggeration, yes, but actual lying, no. They decided to portray me as someone who had been pushed into prostitution by extreme economic hardship. Paul would be resurrected for the trial and lauded as a loving, nurturing partner, only to be brutally smashed by the light-rail again as a sympathy ploy for me, his poor, unskilled widow. His loving partner for whom he had neglected to provide. Alone and horribly in debt, I was pushed out into the world, unprepared.

I did not especially like this pathetic image of myself, but could not deny that it was somewhat accurate.

At the trial, months later, Jay brought out large, colorful bar graphs to illustrate the enormity of my debt, eliciting shocked gasps from the jurors and the courtroom. He then pulled out another graph that showed the astounding statistics on personal bankruptcy filings, and implied that most people in my situation would surely have gone that route.

"But not my brother," he said, as he addressed the jury in his closing arguments. "He's not one to roll over and admit defeat. He's a fighter. If there's one thing our father taught us, it's to pay our debts—and that's just what Jack did. Now, you may not approve of his methods, but you cannot deny the honor due him for repaying his debts. For not taking the easy way out. For being a fighter. And remember, while he was earning money and repaying his personal debt, he was also paying his debt to society in the form of taxes. Although what he was doing may have been illegal, he was reporting all of the income he made from it and paying the taxes he owed. And he required all of his colleagues to do the same. There was no money laundering, as the prosecution has implied. There was no money exchanged under the table. There was, from a financial standpoint, nothing underhanded about it at all!"

He finished by saying that clearly the shame I would have to endure, the scarlet letter I would be forced to wear for the rest of my life, was punishment enough, and he asked for leniency, especially since it was my first time in court for anything other than a speeding ticket.

While the judge was giving final instructions to the jury, Ray, who was seated directly behind me, leaned forward and tapped me on the shoulder. I turned and he handed me a small piece of paper that he'd folded in the shape of a crane. I took it, unfolded it, and read the following:

> *Savvy*
> *Intelligent*
> *Lawyer's*
> *Verbal*
> *Eloquence*
> *Resonates!*

And resonate it did! In the end victory fell on us! Or sort of. I was found guilty of pandering and prostitution—indeed, Jay had admitted as much in the course of the trial—but was found innocent of money laundering and tax evasion. I was given a suspended sentence, fined two thousand dollars, and required to complete one hundred hours of community service—which I did by lecturing on safe sex to several student groups and by tutoring students in the next class of the microbusiness program.

Ray's trial was a bit more complicated. He was portrayed by Jay as a victim of the system—a child who had fallen through the cracks and who never had a role model to teach him right from wrong. He was struggling to make himself legitimate, Jay said, as a man, as an artist, but he was hampered by his pesky drug addiction—evidence of which could be seen in his prior conviction for heroin possession and the evidence of marijuana use found in his most recent urinalysis. He was clearly crying out for help and should not be punished for that!

At this point I passed my own, less artfully folded note up to Ray.

Stoner
Isn't
Legal.
Vice
Earns
Rehab.

And I was right. He was found guilty and was sentenced to a month of rehab at a mountain treatment center called Fresh Beginnings. After that, there was a month of in-house detention, monitored by an ankle bracelet, and one hundred hours of community service, which he completed by teaching art classes to underprivileged children.

Johnny's involvement, as much as we tried, could not be concealed, and he was eventually deported. But there is a silver lining to this cloud. Jay, under Burl's sage guidance, employed several foot-dragging tactics, even going so far as having Johnny fire him at one point, and hire another lawyer to delay things even more, all with the goal of buying him enough time to finish his studies and graduate, which he did, with honors. He wrote me a postcard, some months after his departure, from Singapore, where he had found a job as a structural engineer on a new skyscraper.

"I work very hard now," he wrote, "sometimes fourteen hours a day!

It is making me crazy. Soon I will undoubtedly be fishing in the swimming pool."

As for the other guys, most of them took the plea bargains offered them and got off with first-time slaps on the wrist and small fines. Only Marvin, ever in search of drama with which to decorate his existence, persisted in demanding a jury trial. His hopes for an elaborate courtroom production were cruelly thwarted, however, when the prosecutor, without explanation, suddenly dropped all charges.

The gallery, finished for months, had languished, empty, while we focused on our legal problems. We had managed to keep up the mortgage and loan payments, but could now see the bottom of the cash barrel, and neither Ray nor I had done any paying work for six months. Now that we were out of legal trouble and able to speak freely to the press, MacNamara was feverishly scheduling the talk-show appearances and the guest lectures and the book deals that would occupy so much of our time in the following months. But all that arranging took time, and Ray and I needed to generate money immediately if we wanted to get the gallery up and running, let alone make the mortgage payment and pay our legal bills. At Andre's suggestion, we decided to throw a huge opening party, and to auction off everything that we could think of that had anything to do with Harden Up Inc.

"Girl, just leave everything to me," Andre said, and I felt safe in doing so because he was obviously enthused about it and was unquestionably the most qualified to undertake the endeavor. Without any hesitation I put all of the planning—the guest list, the food, the music—in his hands. I was a little wary when he presented me with a bill for eleven hundred dollars to cover the invitations, most of which were being sent to celebrities on his fantasy guest list, which he had assembled by flipping through the pages of Vanity Fair, W, People, George, and Details, but to my surprise, many of them called or sent cards, and quite a few of them actually came.

At the party there was no buffet, since Andre had foreseen that the gallery would hardly contain all the guests, and that people would be spilling out onto the sidewalk. For that reason he employed a group of large-pectoraled waiters to mill around shirtless carrying glasses of champagne and trays of hors d'oeuvres. There were cocktail weenies and marinated button mushrooms, bananas dipped in chocolate and tiny jam tarts. It was a tremendous success.

Antonio and Victor had done a wonderful job on the renovation, and the former one-room warehouse was divided into three separate exhibition halls. In the smallest of these we displayed enlarged lithographs of the ads we'd created, our logo prominently displayed at the bottom. These were signed by both the photographer and the subject, and sold for seventy-five dollars unframed or two hundred and fifty dollars framed.

In the next gallery, Ray had set up his Christmas displays. The large doggy nativity scene was at the center of the room, with the other pieces scattered around the edges. In one corner he set up a card table displaying all of his Christmas cards, at which Josh was installed to take orders for boxes of twenty (forty-five dollars), but he ended up taking at least as many orders, if not more, for the poodle angels, (five hundred dollars), and to this day, almost two years later, Ray is still selling them (although they are considerably easier to find now that we live in their natural habitat).

In the third and largest gallery, we displayed a collection of paintings we had made especially for the auction. These rather unique works of art, executed during the six months we were awaiting trial, Ray and I had painted using . . . well, I'm not quite sure how to explain this, but we painted them using our penises instead of brushes. We had spent a few days stretching canvases and thinking up subject matter, and then, over the course of about a month, we would execute a painting whenever the muse was, uh, aroused, so to speak. Of course most of them had sexual innuendo as their subject matter, and so there were lots of paintings of architectural columns and obelisks, and several portraits of Freud, always with a giant cigar. We did a large canvas of Moby Dick and another of Free Willy, and several pieces with religious themes—St. Peter at the pearly gates, Mary Magdalene, etc. The jewelry paintings—cocktail rings, pearl necklaces—sold very well, as did the colorful series of candy suckers. All of the paintings were somewhat crudely painted and looked like a child had done them, but every last one sold that night, and in the end they brought in enough money to make four mortgage payments.

But the bawdiness didn't stop there. We also sold signed articles of underclothing, and, of course, T-shirts emblazoned with our logo on the front and the word *Subcontractor* on the back, since the issue of subcontractor versus employee had been a rather contentious one during our trial.

The rest was predictable. You've heard it before with different characters and you'll inevitably hear it again: circus talk-show appearances, tabloid cover stories linking me romantically with several celebrities, an appearance on *Politically Incorrect* . . . I never dreamed it would all get so out of control. What could I have been thinking?

Part Two

♡

La Vie En Rose

As you've probably guessed by now, Ray and I have settled in Paris. The scarlet spotlight had become too glaring in Denver and, even though the publicity slackened after the trial, we were still local celebrities, and everywhere we went there were pointed fingers and snickers behind our backs. We needed to get away for a while—at least until the next local scandal arose to eclipse ours—so we chose Paris, mainly because it is the location of a great taxidermy school at which Ray decided he would like to study, but also because I thought it would be a good place for me to work on this book.

The gallery's finances had stabilized since the auction, and we had exhibits booked for the next two years, so we felt fairly safe leaving it behind. Before we left we convinced Andre to quit his job with the airline and contracted him to be the gallery manager. We have been in contact with him by telephone and fax several times a week, and so far no problems have arisen that we could not overcome. He is an able, diligent manager and enjoys the air of prestige and elegance that goes along with his position. Not to mention the fact that it gives him a place to display himself and all of his latest outfits.

Paris is the perfect place to come if you want to recover from a scandal. Perhaps that is why so many overthrown dictators and ostracized movie stars seem to land here. The French lead the world in the practice of haughty indifference, but more than that they welcome moral, social, and most political outcasts with open arms and a kiss on both cheeks. Although some people here know who we are and what we're famous for, it's really nothing to be ashamed of. When we go to parties and are introduced it is almost never with a reference to our former careers, but to what we're doing now, which I like. To use a tired cliché, it is like opening a new chapter in a book.

As for books, MacNamara proved to be a better negotiator than I'd thought and managed to snag me a book deal with a hefty advance, which enabled us to live fairly comfortably when we first arrived. My days here have not, as you might expect, been whiled away smoking Gitanes in cafés, or aimlessly wandering the cavernous halls of the Louvre. No, those days are gone. Since we arrived I have been hard at work on the very product you are holding now, and it looks as though I'll actually have it finished a few weeks before the deadline. And yet, I'm afraid this book is not going to be what many of you, or the publisher, expected. It is less a seamy exposé of a hustler and more a personal account of my own messy growth process, so for that I apologize. I apologize to all of you have eagerly scanned page after page hoping that the next one would be the start of the naughty bits and are now disappointed to reach the last page, unsatisfied. That "naughty book" was the one I'd intended to write, but somehow the story didn't come out like that. It had its own direction, and there wasn't much I could do to steer it elsewhere. Oh, that's not true. I certainly could have lied, could have made it a work of fiction, but tomorrow I'll have to face myself in the mirror and . . . well, you know how that goes.